LOVE

in

TRANSLATION

12/6/09

To Krupa,

Thanks so much for reading!

Wendy

Also by Wendy Nelson Tokunaga

Midori by Moonlight

LOVE
in
TRANSLATION

Wendy Nelson Tokunaga

St. Martin's Griffin ❧ New York

This is a work of fiction. All of the characters, organizations, and events portrayed in this novel are either products of the author's imagination or are used fictitiously.

LOVE IN TRANSLATION. Copyright © 2009 by Wendy Nelson Tokunaga. All rights reserved.
Printed in the United States of America. For information, address St. Martin's Press, 175 Fifth Avenue, New York, N.Y. 10010.

www.stmartins.com

Library of Congress Cataloging-in-Publication Data

Tokunaga, Wendy
Love in translation / Wendy Nelson Tokunaga.—1st ed.
p. cm.
ISBN 978-0-312-37266-8
1. Americans—Japan—Fiction. 2. Family secrets—Fiction. 3. Self-realization in women—Fiction. I. Title.
PS3620.O3258L68 2009
813'.6—dc22

2009017044

First Edition: December 2009

10 9 8 7 6 5 4 3 2 1

For Manabu

Acknowledgments

I OFFER MY SINCERE THANKS TO AGENT EXTRAORDINAIRE MARLY RUSOFF, and St. Martin's editors Hilary Rubin Teeman and Jennifer Weis for believing in me. I also appreciate the fine help of St. Martin's editorial assistant Anne Bensson, copy editor Sabrina Soares Roberts, and production editor John Morrone.

I am also grateful for the spot-on feedback I received on this book from Tracy Guzeman, Kristen Austin Sandoval, and Malena Watrous. Thanks also to the fine writers in the University of San Francisco MFA in Writing program's Fall 2007 Long Fiction Workshop who helped with an early draft: Jim Cole, Christopher Jenner, Jess Kroll, Jonathan Lukes, Miranda Mellis, Cynthia Posillico, and Harbeer Sandhu. And a heartfelt *arigato* goes to Hiro Akashi and Etsuko Wright for their invaluable input.

And as always I thank my husband, Manabu Tokunaga, and my mother, Nancy A. Nelson, for their love and support.

Gambarimashita!

LOVE
in
TRANSLATION

1

A PROPOSAL

WHEN I FIRST SET EYES ON TAKUYA, MY IMMEDIATE INCLINATION WAS TO take him in my arms and kiss him like he'd never been kissed before.

Such impulsive, reckless behavior, though, was never my style. And, besides, taking such a course of action would have been inappropriate for several reasons: (1) we had yet to be officially introduced; (2) he, at twenty-eight, was five years younger than me, a fact that would be considered rather scandalous in Japan; (3) I had a kind of a boyfriend back home in San Jose; (4) Takuya was my homestay "brother."

It had been his mother, Mrs. Kubota, who first referred to him as my homestay brother. And the fact that I was experiencing more than sisterly feelings toward him was probably against one of the rules stated in the *Kubota Homestay Handbook*, if there'd been such a thing.

Takuya was lean and lanky, but solid, and towered over his parents. He had just returned to his family home in suburban Tokyo from working for two years in Seattle for the Japanese food products company Sunny Shokuhin. He was far better-looking than in the outdated family portrait in the living room where I first saw him, the one where his conservative hairstyle, school uniform, and studious expression gave him the look of one of those dorky people in the Young Professionals Club I remembered from high school, the types who were seventeen going on thirty-five.

But at twenty-eight, Takuya was quite the stunner, the kind of man who, if I'd seen him on the train, I would have had to keep from staring at so as not to be too obvious—unlike the people who gawked at me, albeit for quite different reasons.

I tried to make my gaze as unobtrusive as possible, while still taking in the scenery.

Takuya's hair was a natural black, not dyed cinnamon or tangerine like so many of the young people in Tokyo, and it hung thick and silky below his collar. His smile was friendly, his nearly black eyes warm, his demeanor easy-going. This was made all the more attractive because I knew how exhausted he must have been from his long trip and how overwhelming it had to be to return home after two years overseas. I'd been the sweaty Saint Bernard cooped up much too long in her carrier when I first arrived in Tokyo, after enduring a ten-hour ride in an airborne sardine can. And the heaviness of jet lag weighed down my neck and shoulders like a sack of bricks. Yet Takuya seemed composed, relaxed.

Once he got settled and I sat down with him and his parents at the family's dining-room table—a setting of fancy take-out sushi and a Domino's squid-and-corn deluxe pizza worthy of a state dinner—Mrs. Kubota finally introduced me. "Celeste Duncan-san," she said.

Takuya extended his hand. "Nice to meet you, Celeste."

Shaking hands, I smiled, but felt nervous. It had only been six weeks since I left San Jose for Tokyo and my Japanese was poor, though I had just started taking free lessons from a teacher named Mariko who, with her penchant for English swear words, was unusual to say the least. I'd asked her what I could say in Japanese to welcome Takuya home so I would make a good impression. In my mind I carefully went over the phrase she taught me. I was ready. I took a breath, and in a slow and clear voice said, "Takuya-san, *kekkon shimasen ka.*"

Silence.

Each member of the Kubota family sat frozen, and the uncomfortable quiet lasted much too long.

I turned to see that Mrs. Kubota's expression was not unlike the one she'd exhibited when I walked into her living room wearing toilet slippers—one of abject horror. I waited for her to say one of the few English phrases she had mastered, "Not good, not good," but she didn't utter a word. Still, I seemed to have done it again, committed another cultural faux pas. I yearned to turn into a potato bug—to curl up into a ball and have someone step on me to put me out of my misery.

What on earth did I say? Was my pronunciation so poor that it came out plain wrong? I knew by now how easy it was in Japanese to leave out a syllable and completely change the meaning of a word. Mariko had warned me about that. If you were sick and needed to go to the hospital, but asked to be taken to the *biyōin* instead of the *byōin,* you'd wind up at the beauty parlor. The crunchy yellow pickle slices I liked that Mrs. Kubota served were called *oshinko,* but leave out that *n* and you'd get something close to *oshikko,* which was what kids said when they needed to pee. I was relieved to know that I at least hadn't said penis—*chimpo*—which was one of the first words Mariko had taught me when she explained (without being asked) about the differences in sexual performance techniques she'd noticed between Japanese and American men.

The lugubrious atmosphere at the Kubota dinner table began to dissipate at the sound of Takuya's laughter. His father smiled, but Mrs. Kubota remained repulsed.

"Did I pronounce something wrong?" I asked.

"No, Celeste," Takuya said, his eyes shining. "You said perfectly."

"Said *what?*"

Takuya could not stop laughing. By then Mrs. Kubota had left the room. Mr. Kubota drank the remainder of beer from his glass. Takuya put his hand on his chest, giving me an earnest, adorable look. "You asking me very important question, Celeste," he said in his slightly cracked English. "I will have to think hard about my answering."

"Question? It wasn't supposed to be a question." I found his teasing endearing, even though at the same time I wanted to scream, *What the hell did I say?* I looked straight into his beautiful face. "Takuya-san, what did I say to you?"

He smiled. "You asked me to marry you."

My first reaction was to laugh, then curse Mariko, but neither seemed appropriate. I turned to Mrs. Kubota, who had come back to the dining room with another beer for her husband and still appeared greatly flummoxed. "I'm sorry, Takuya-san. And please tell your mother that I was told by my Japanese teacher that I was saying, 'Welcome home and nice to meet you.' "

Takuya laughed. "What kind of Japanese teacher is *that?*"

"One who seems to want to get me into trouble," I said. "*Sumimasen*," I apologized to Mrs. Kubota, which I knew for sure meant "I'm sorry."

After an explanation from Takuya, Mrs. Kubota seemed to regain some of her composure.

"She say it hard to believe that a Japanese teacher would do that," Takuya said.

"Tell her I feel the same," I grumbled, wondering about the best way I could pay back Mariko.

Although Takuya seemed to have made it clear to his mother the reason for my mistake, I sensed a continuing stiffness from her throughout dinner. When I tried to catch her glance, to give her an apologetic smile, she would turn her head the other way.

With this latest development I knew that the surest way to receive another black mark on the Kubota homestay test would be if my secret was discovered: that I harbored incestuous feelings toward my homestay brother.

But I needed to keep on my toes and hope that I would be allowed to continue to stay with the Kubotas. Because I wasn't in Japan on a lark to study Japanese, or Zen, or the tea ceremony, or even to conduct research on the sexual habits of Japanese males. I was here on an important journey: to search for a long-lost relative, who could possibly tell me the identity of my father, and to fulfill an important family obligation.

And for someone who didn't have any family, this was a unique opportunity.

2

PERSONAL EFFECTS

I WOULD HAVE BEEN THE LAST PERSON TO THINK THAT I WOULD END UP IN Tokyo. Growing up in San Jose, I'd never traveled outside of California, let alone abroad. Dirk and I had always talked about going to the New Age Music Festival in Switzerland, but, like getting married, it was something we never got around to.

This all began when I received a phone message saying that Michiko Taniguchi was dead.

"I'm calling for Celeste Duncan. This is Patricia Brinker, the administrator from the Sheltering Oaks Convalescent Hospital in Carlmont, Iowa. We have your name on our contact list for Michiko Taniguchi. I'm sorry to say that she has passed away and we would like to get your current address so that we may send you her personal effects. . . ."

I had never heard of anyone named Michiko Taniguchi and concluded that this must have been a mistake. Still, something stopped me from simply deleting the message and flopping into bed. With a death involved, even someone you didn't know, it seemed prudent to not just discount it.

I'd been frantic all day at work to meet my deadline for the final edit of the scintillating *Real Guide to IP Layer Network Administration with Linux* computer manual. Then I'd gone straight to Dirk's for a rehearsal, and we had another fight, an increasingly common occurrence. Instead of spending the night at his place as I normally would, I came home. It was nearly eleven thirty, too late to return the administrator's call.

Yet I was certain they had the wrong Celeste Duncan. I thought hard but came up with nothing: I didn't know any Michiko Taniguchi. I even searched the name on the Internet, but only found a research chemistry professor in Philadelphia, a masseuse in Oxnard, California, and an obscure Hollywood bit player from the 1930s.

Dirk would have been my first choice to call to help me figure this out, but I was still mad at him. My next thought was to phone Zoe, but it was too late, though she could have been awake on a late-night feeding for Amelia. But I didn't want to disturb her. Yet after I pondered further, it finally hit me: Michiko Taniguchi had to be Aunt Mitch, or Aunt Mitch the witch, as my mother Barbara had called her.

Her name was actually Michiko Morgenstern. Taniguchi must have been her maiden name—it was no wonder it didn't register. A war bride, Aunt Mitch married my mother's uncle Melvin after they fell in love while he was in the army during the American occupation of Japan in the early 1950s. Aunt Mitch and Uncle Melvin lived in Saratoga, a town about fifteen miles north of San Jose. What a treat it had been to visit their ranch-style house with the lawn, the oak tree, and the yellow rosebushes in the front yard. To me it was a fairy-tale castle in comparison to the cramped one-bedroom apartment surrounded by concrete, where Barbara and I lived in the Alum Rock neighborhood of San Jose.

Once, in Aunt Mitch's house, it was as if I'd been transported into a magical foreign land. First, I had to take off my shoes and leave them at the front door. And when I sat on the little wooden bench in the entryway to put on my slippers—children's slippers she said were bought especially for me—the sweet incense wafting through the air gave off a fragrance that smelled like exotic candy. It was a welcome scent from the permanent odor of marijuana saturating my mother's apartment. In Aunt Mitch's living room elegant dolls sporting elaborate hairdos and wrapped in kimonos gazed down from shelves filled with books, books with incomprehensible writing that could only be deciphered if you knew the secret code.

Aunt Mitch hadn't crossed my mind for ages. It seemed that she'd always been so nice to my mother and me, always accommodating when I was dropped off at the last minute at that Saratoga refuge when one of the babysitters flaked out. So it was puzzling why Barbara sometimes made a face when her name came up and referred to her as a witch.

I now recalled that Aunt Mitch and Uncle Melvin moved to Texas when I was around seven, but I'd heard nothing further after that. I didn't know if my mother had kept in touch with them, but of course I couldn't ask her—she was long gone.

When I phoned the Sheltering Oaks Convalescent Hospital the next day, the administrator told me what little she knew about Michiko Taniguchi. She passed away at the age of eighty-three and her husband had died eleven years ago. They had no children and I was the only living relative they could track down.

I arranged to have the box containing Aunt Mitch's personal effects sent to my office at TextTrans, the technical document company where I'd been working for the past seven years as chief editor.

I received a call from reception when the package arrived. Upon retrieving it, I couldn't help but notice the pale-skinned young woman behind the desk decked out in the inappropriate halter top. Kylie, our new receptionist, looked no older than a high school sophomore, though I'd heard she was actually twenty. Lately it seemed that everyone was looking extremely young to me—the gynecologist at the clinic, the new apartment manager at my complex, the news anchor on Channel 11. My age obsession was most likely because I was currently two years shy of thirty-five; not old enough to be Kylie's mother but easily qualifying as a very elder sister. It was rather mystifying how I'd become this old when I could have sworn I was twenty myself only a few short years ago.

"Present from your boyfriend?" Kylie chirped, pulling at a chunk of her blond-and-black streaked hair, checking for split ends.

"Not exactly." I gave her a twisted smile. Of course she had no way of knowing about my ongoing issues with Dirk. (And for reasons I couldn't quite explain to myself I still hadn't told him about the call regarding Aunt Mitch.) But wasn't it kind of weird for someone you really didn't know to make such a personal comment? Not to mention an underage coworker.

"Looks like you'll need a box cutter," Kylie said, rummaging through a drawer. She followed me into the empty conference room, where I set the box on the table.

Kylie handed me the tool. As I began to drag it along the tight packing tape, I was surprised to see that instead of leaving me alone and getting back to her desk, Kylie had plopped herself in the chair across from me, eager to watch the birthday girl open her gifts.

It wasn't that I necessarily wanted privacy. Zoe would normally have been here in the cubicle next to mine, and I could imagine her in the conference room with me, bringing along her bouncy enthusiasm and all-encompassing optimism. But she was on maternity leave.

So before I realized it, and like some lonely senior citizen foisting herself on potential conversation partners at the bus stop, I found myself explaining to Kylie about the call from the convalescent hospital, and how it had been a long time since I'd thought of Aunt Mitch.

"I can't imagine what they would send," I said, yanking off the last bit of tape.

Kylie's eyes widened. "Did you see *Instant Millionaire* last night? Maybe there's a check for a million dollars."

I shook my head, the corner of my eye blinded by a sparkling glint that I finally deduced was emanating from her crystal nose stud as it reflected from the fluorescent ceiling light.

"This guy found out that he had this half brother he, like, didn't even know he had, who died in a demolition derby. He left him all the money he won from the lottery in Florida or something.' "

"Things like that don't happen to me."

"He was *so* psyched." She paused. "So they didn't even tell you what they were sending?"

"They hardly told me anything. I got the impression they just wanted to get rid of it."

"Well, that's really, like, kind of sad."

"I know." It was. I pulled at the box flaps.

"And you don't have any other relatives who knew her, your aunt?"

"I don't have any relatives period."

"You don't?" Kylie looked surprised.

"Barbara died when I was ten."

"Barbara?"

"My mom." My mother had always insisted I call her Barbara—never Mommy, Mom, or Mother. This fit, since she always seemed more of an exciting coconspirator than responsible maternal figure. "And I never knew who my father was and Barbara didn't seem to know either."

I stopped myself. Didn't I understand the meaning of "too much information"? And wasn't it rather pathetic to be blabbing on about one's personal life history to the new receptionist? The details, or lack of them, on my father were rather sordid. Whenever I asked who he was, Barbara would smile and shrug, saying that she didn't know because she was just really, really popular. I was too young to understand what that meant, but later it clicked: likely endless one-night stands with guys she didn't know—her groupies. The common question I got asked was "Have you searched for your father?" Of course I'd always wanted to, but there wasn't much you could do with no name, no face, no nothing. But I wasn't about to get into this conversation with Kylie.

"My mom was a singer in a rock band—the Barbara Duncan Band," was the next thing I said. "She was always playing somewhere. She actually supported the two of us on the money she made from her gigs."

"Wow."

"She wanted to be the next Stevie Nicks," I said, removing the plastic bubble packing material. Kylie grabbed a sheet and began squeezing the bubbles with her fingers as if she were popping zits.

"Stevie who?" she asked, looking blank. No surprise there.

Barbara had been a pretty good performer, and I figured she would become famous because she always said she was going to make it. There was no doubt in her mind; it was a given. But then she had the bad luck of dying when she was thirty-three. Leave it to my mother to pass away in a rather spectacular manner.

She had played a big outdoor concert in Napa Valley one weekend. Afterward she and her band members had all gotten high on mushrooms and spontaneously decided to get higher by taking a hot air balloon ride. The pilot was apparently high too. When a massive, sudden gust of wind drove the balloon into a power line, the basket was severed and fell hundreds of feet. Barbara, the band, and the pilot were all killed instantly.

With no family to speak of, I became a ward of the court, and then was put into the foster care system in San Jose. Although I'd told the authorities about Aunt Mitch, they said they were unable to track her down, though I had no way of knowing the extent of their search. How ironic that now somehow I'd been found, albeit twenty-three years too late.

Instead, I was sentenced to three foster homes. The first lasted six months with a family whose name I quickly forgot. Then it was the Kruikshanks for two and a half years and, lastly, five years with the Cavanaughs, until I "aged out" of the system at eighteen. I wasn't as unlucky as some of the kids I'd heard about who seemed to switch families every half a year and suffered all kinds of abuse. I experienced a measure of stability with these two families and they did not treat me badly, though I never felt close to either one of them and they never encouraged any intimacy.

I was allowed to call the Kruikshank couple by their first names—Kenneth and Irma. But with the next family, it had to be Mr. and Mrs. Cavanaugh. I wasn't sure why this was their preference, but I had discovered over the years that it was best not to ask any unnecessary questions and to simply follow orders. Although there were many unpleasant things I'd blocked from my memory, I never forgot the heaviness weighing down my shoulders when Mrs. Cavanaugh would say to someone, "These are our daughters, Jennifer and Amanda, and this is our *foster* daughter, Celeste."

My heart thumped as I began to remove the contents from the box sent from the convalescent home; I didn't anticipate feeling so excited. The first thing I found was a photo album embossed with a pattern of yellow daisies and monarch butterflies on its white plastic cover.

"Oh! There's Aunt Mitch. They both look so young," I murmured.

There were pictures of Aunt Mitch and Uncle Melvin in Japan, probably at the time when they first met. Underneath the photos were captions written in Japanese, some with the years indicated. Uncle Melvin, dressed in his army uniform, and Aunt Mitch, with her fashionable permed hair and dark lipstick, elegant in a kimono, posed in front of a train station in one. Another showed Aunt Mitch in a portrait with a Japanese girl who looked around twelve, dated 1949. Both wore kimonos and solemn, dignified expressions, so different from Aunt Mitch's lively demeanor in the pictures with her soon-to-be husband. Their round jawlines and pert noses were similar—could the little girl have been a sister?

"Your aunt was so pretty," Kylie said.

"Oh, yeah. Even when she was in her fifties she was just gorgeous." I paged through photos of their modest wedding and the couple standing in front of their house in Saratoga. A color picture showed my mother alongside Uncle Melvin, and Aunt Mitch standing next to a young Japanese man. I didn't recognize him but wondered if he was a relative of Aunt Mitch's.

"That's Barbara," I said, pointing to my mom who was even younger than Kylie in this photo, taken before I was born. Her straight butter-colored hair was so long that it covered her breasts, and her bright paisley orange-and-green empire-waisted dress reached down to her chunky sandals.

"You really look like her."

I stared at the photo, a chill covering my neck. "Yeah, I guess I do."

Kylie pointed to another picture below it. "Who's that?"

This was a Caucasian girl with blondish-red hair, about six years old, wearing a pink-and-gold kimono. She stood in front of a tree, her hands folded demurely at her waist. Her hair was done up in a bun, an elegant ornament peeking out from behind her ear.

I sat straight up. "That's me."

The catch in my throat only intensified when Kylie responded to the picture with, "Oh . . . my . . . God! How adorable!"

"I don't even remember that," I finally said in a quiet voice. Why had I never seen this photograph before?

Kylie jumped when she heard the phone ring and rushed out of the room. Yes, it was time for her to actually do some work.

I gazed a few moments longer at my six-year-old self, then reached for one of two manila envelopes sitting in the box. Inside the first one I found three pieces of thin, delicate paper, handwritten in Japanese. Each character I could discern looked like its own work of art, and the overall feeling was more of a painting than words. I immediately thought of Zoe. She'd studied Japanese in high school and college. Maybe she could translate them.

The other manila envelope was bulky, its brown color more faded, and the soft, worn fibers of the paper showed its age. I pulled out a reel of film, eight millimeter, I guessed, most likely a home movie. Was it a film of

Aunt Mitch's and Uncle Melvin's wedding? A travelogue of Japan? Someone at work had his childhood home movies transferred from film to DVD so I knew it was possible to actually watch it without having to track down an old projector.

I seemed to be in my own film, moving in slow motion, and only halfway came out of my trance when Kylie returned.

"Find anything else?"

I opened a small black box. "Look. This is the hair ornament I was wearing in that photo."

Kylie peered over my shoulder. "It's beautiful. Old. Like an antique."

I ran my fingertips over the smooth lacquer of the hair comb, noticing the design of a white crane balancing on its long, thin legs next to a lake, a cherry tree in full bloom in the background. What would my life have been like, I wondered, if I could have lived with Aunt Mitch after my mother died?

There were two more items left to open, both wooden boxes. The smaller one, shaped like a rectangle, was painted with a picture of an old-fashioned geisha, her face long, her narrow eyes focusing on a mirror as she sat primping herself, a short-tailed cat curled up at her feet. I opened the lid but found the box empty, though I could smell the fragrance of cedar. Maybe the written documents would explain the significance.

But the other wooden box definitely housed something. This one was about six inches high and four inches wide, and inside was what looked like a ceramic vase. Painted a robin's-egg blue, the small black top was tightly secured. I shook it. It felt heavy but nothing rattled, though I could tell there was something inside. I pried off the top with difficulty but couldn't see much of anything. When I sniffed the inside, there was no odor, but once I tipped it over, out poured a sprinkling of whitish-gray dust.

"Oh, God," I said.

"Ewww!" was Kylie's reaction.

I looked at her. "This must be Aunt Mitch."

3

A FATHER'S KISSES

AT LUNCH I FOUND A PLACE THAT WOULD TRANSFER THE FILM TO A DVD IN a few hours. Then I phoned Zoe and she said to come over after work.

I was feeling guilty that she was the only one I'd told about what I found in Aunt Mitch's belongings. I had yet to call Dirk. Usually after an argument one of us would get in touch soon enough and make up. But this time was a little different. I still had the usual resentment, but it continued to build. And I thought if I mentioned anything about how excited I felt to get "back in touch" with Aunt Mitch, so to speak, he'd end up ruining it somehow with his pointed remarks.

Our fight had been about music; it was most always what we fought about, though I later realized that these disagreements were never *really* about music. They were about control, about Dirk's procrastination, and maybe about his own insecurities. Of course it was hard to have this kind of perspective while being stuck in the muck of it, and I'd been stuck in this muck for going on six years.

I'd met Dirk when his law firm did some work for TextTrans. Although he was an attorney, his passion was music, and when he found out that my mother had been a singer, he encouraged me to sing. This excited me because the only singing I'd done until then was in my high school chorus, and with a hairbrush and CD player in my bedroom. But I liked to sing and thought I had a pretty good voice, which I probably inherited from my mother.

Dirk played piano and I was the vocalist, and he was constantly gathering guitarists, bass players, and drummers for our little group. But no one ever stayed very long and it always came back down to Dirk and me. There were several reasons for this. First, Dirk insisted on performing only his original songs. Playing covers—hit songs by other artists—was not in his vocabulary. He claimed that he couldn't be a true artist if he played other people's material. Another reason was that he was a perfectionist. When the other musicians wanted to start playing in clubs, his reply was that we weren't ready. There was always some obstacle, a song that wasn't going as well as he liked, and he could never put together a set of material that was perfect enough.

In the beginning, this was all fine with me. I was in awe that anyone could even write a song, and I thought Dirk's tunes, which were in a kind of New Age jazzy style, were as good as anything you could hear on the radio. Besides, I was also not the most confident singer, and the idea of playing in front of people unnerved me. But as the years went by and nothing ever progressed, I was growing tired of the inertia and Dirk's lament of never sounding good enough. We really did sound pretty good, at least I thought so.

"You know, if people come to see us, it's not as if they're expecting something like the Beatles," I would say to him. And he would always take this the wrong way, retorting with, "Are you saying that you don't want to strive to be as good as someone of their caliber?" And that would stop me in my tracks. Yet I couldn't help but think how ridiculous it was that we seemed to have only two choices: to become the equal of the dominant world force in popular music for the past fifty years or to continue to only play in his living room.

By now it had been a while since we had even played with other musicians. Dirk thought we could perform as a duo, but the current roadblock was that there was always something wrong with my singing. I was either "a tad off beat" or "off pitch by a hair." It got to the point where I couldn't tell anymore between the tads and the hairs, and I began to lose any confidence I had, not that there was much to lose in the first place. And when your confidence is lost, everything falls apart from there. When we'd go to a concert, he would point to the vocalist and say, "Listen carefully. You should try and sing more like her." I understood that he thought he was helping me to be the best that I could, but it was easy to take it as criticism.

"It's *his* problem," Zoe would say. "You have a beautiful voice." Zoe heard me sing along with the radio once in a while—my only "public" performances—but I knew she was also being nice. Dirk had studied music since he was a child, and I learned songs strictly by ear with no formal training. He was forced to sing his songs to me so that I could learn the melodies. I'd tried to master sight-reading—reading the notes off the page—but it had been a disaster, like failing geometry in the tenth grade. Singing for me seemed natural, something that came freely out of the spirit. It filled me up; it made me feel good. Dirk's take on music was precise, methodical.

Then there was the issue of getting married. When he wanted to, I wasn't ready, and when I was ready, he suddenly wasn't. I wondered sometimes if deep down neither one of us wanted to but were too afraid of hurting the other's feelings. Or maybe we thought that we'd wake up one day completely in synch about the issue. So we kept on seeing each other, kept up the status quo, kept on practicing several times a week. We liked going to the local clubs (though on the way home I would have to listen to his meticulous critiques of the musicians), to the movies, and still had fun together. But there was this paralysis that I couldn't explain, even though we still seemed to love each other. I was grateful to Dirk for his early encouragement of my singing, but that joy was eroding, and I couldn't sustain the energy it took to keep arguing with him.

We were stuck in a groove that was becoming increasingly worn.

Dirk's small law firm wasn't too far from Zoe's apartment in Willow Glen, and I was careful to park several blocks away. I didn't want there to be any chance of him spotting my car, in case he was working late.

"Peter took the baby over to his mom's," Zoe said as we sat on her couch. "We've got the place to ourselves."

I put the bag of Aunt Mitch's things on the coffee table, taking out the handwritten pages, the comb, the urn, the geisha box, and the DVD.

"This is all so exciting," Zoe said. "Like cracking a case!"

I'd never told Zoe many details about my childhood. She knew my mother had been a singer and had died young, that I was in the dark about my father, and that I grew up in foster homes, but that was about it. Now I explained as much as I could, showing her the photo album and the picture of me in a kimono, telling about my visits to the house in Saratoga and how nice Aunt Mitch had been to me. Enthralled, she seemed to be on the edge of her seat. Her enthusiasm made me think again how grateful I was to be sharing this with her now instead of Dirk.

"Let's do it!" she said, picking up the documents, her eyes shining. Yet in the next instant, a worried look overtook her face.

"What's wrong?" I asked.

"You didn't say they were handwritten."

"Does that make a difference?"

"Well, something printed would be much easier. But have no fear! I've got my dictionaries here in case I need them. You know, I'm a little rusty."

"That's okay. Take your time."

As I watched her carefully peruse the delicate pieces of paper, it was hard to believe that she could make sense out of what looked more like a piece of art than written communication.

"Well, I can tell you this," she said. "This seems to be her will. Or her last wishes. Something like that."

"Really?"

"And it says she has a sister. Named Hiromi. Hiromi Taniguchi. Mmm."

"Maybe the one in the picture with her. That young girl."

Zoe's eyes went wide. "I bet it is. But that young girl would be an old lady by now." She concentrated hard as she peered at the document, her lips moving as she read.

"Let me look at that photo album again," she said.

I handed it to her and she quickly turned the pages, then pointed to the photograph of Aunt Mitch with the young girl. "This is Hiromi Taniguchi. Her sister. In 1949. This is what it says."

I gazed at the portrait, staring at Hiromi's face. "I guess she'd be in her seventies by now."

Zoe went on reading. "And is there some kind of decorative comb? For the hair?"

"Right here," I said, pointing to it.

"She says that it was her mother's. And she would like it returned to her sister. Hiromi. In Japan. Seems like, seems like . . . mmm." She cocked her head. "Seems like she has lost touch with her sister. For many years. She may live in a place called, ah, Kuyama? That is where she lived many years ago." She continued to read. "Yes, Kuyama. Where the family is from. They owned a tofu shop there."

I reached for a small notepad in my purse. "Maybe I better write this all down. What is the name of the place exactly?"

"It's the Higashi Arakawa area in Kuyama. That is all it says. No address."

"Does it say anything about this?" I asked, showing her the pretty wooden box with the painted geisha. "There's nothing in it."

Zoe shook her head. "No, no." She picked up the blue vase. "But what's this?"

That the convalescent home had sent the urn still seemed unbelievable. It gave me the creeps and I almost didn't bring it. "Aunt Mitch's ashes," I said softly. "Her name is written on the bottom."

"Her *ashes?*" Zoe quickly placed the vase back on the table. She picked up the DVD. "Aren't you dying of curiosity to watch this?"

"Yeah, but who knows what's on it? Could be scenic shots of Japan." I removed the DVD from its envelope and slid it into the player. "Or just Aunt Mitch and Uncle Melvin waving at the camera."

"Or maybe it's Aunt Mitch herself—giving the instructions of her last will and testament."

I hadn't thought of that.

The film wasn't in black-and-white but appeared washed-out, more like a faded watercolor than a bright oil. There was no sound. Two Japanese women in close-up, looking to be in their forties or so, smiled and waved at the camera.

"That's Aunt Mitch," I said, my heartbeat jumping into my throat. "The one on the left."

"Yeah," Zoe said. "I recognize her."

The scene changed abruptly to what looked like a dining room, and once I spotted the Japanese-style credenza, I knew we were at Aunt Mitch's house in Saratoga. A baby with plump cheeks and a mostly bald head sat in a high chair at the head of the table, and Aunt Mitch and the other Japanese woman were seated there. The camera lingered on a young woman with straight blond hair. At first she covered her face with her hands, laughing with embarrassment as if she did not want to be filmed. But then she underwent an instant transformation, spreading her arms wide, and swaying her hips as if she were performing on stage.

"That's your mom, right?" Zoe said. "She's every inch the rock star."

"That's for sure," I said, thinking how this was so like Barbara.

"And that has to be you in the high chair."

I nodded, my voice now refusing to emerge from my throat. I'd barely had any photographs from my childhood, let alone home movies. Seeing my mother again after all these years and seeing myself as an infant pierced my heart.

Next to Barbara was a man about her age with brown hair almost as long as hers. He kissed my mother on the lips, then gently took me out of the high chair and cradled me in his arms, looking up to smile at the camera, as though he were showing me off. He wasn't at all awkward with holding a baby, wasn't the all-thumbs type who would immediately freeze and hand off the infant to its mother. Instead, he grinned and rocked me as I stared at him, then planted a kiss on my forehead. The adult me shivered, as if I could feel his lips at that very moment. He tilted me toward the camera and moved my arm in a waving motion. Then he gave me a kiss on the cheek.

"Do you know who that is?" Zoe whispered.

"No. I don't recognize him at all." My voice was a croak, my body frozen. I knew Zoe was thinking the same thing I was.

"He could be . . ."

"I know," I said. "My dad. At least it's a possibility." I couldn't believe that this man was just one of my mother's casual boyfriends. Why would he interact with me that way? And why would he be invited to a family gathering recorded for posterity?

The camera now captured the group—Aunt Mitch and the other Japanese woman, my mother holding me—though I sensed with not as much tenderness as the man with the long brown hair. He now had his arm around my mother's shoulders and they all stood in front of Aunt Mitch's house next to the big oak tree. Everyone waved. Then the film ran out.

"That other Japanese woman," I said. "Don't you think it's Aunt Mitch's sister Hiromi?"

Zoe and I scrutinized the picture of Hiromi Taniguchi as a young girl dressed in a kimono with her sister.

"I think you're right," Zoe said. "Play it again."

We watched the DVD about a half-dozen times. It was obvious to both of us that the other woman was Hiromi Taniguchi; there was no question. I could identify everyone in the film except the man cradling me in his arms, the man who kissed me twice.

"Hiromi would probably be able to tell you who that the guy is with your mother."

"I know." My eyes were becoming moist. "Maybe I can finally find out who . . ." I couldn't finish the sentence.

Zoe squeezed my arm. "You have to go there! To find her!"

Her words echoed throughout the room. This was the last thing I had expected, that receiving Aunt Mitch's things would bring with it a reason and opportunity to go to Japan. The idea excited me but also caused a pang of anxiety in the pit of my stomach; the practicality of such an endeavor was dubious.

Breathless, Zoe could not contain her excitement. "Maybe she kept a diary of when she came to visit her sister in the United States. Maybe she has photos of this guy or even more home movies! Maybe she's—"

"Maybe she's dead."

Zoe frowned. "Why be so negative? Once you locate this woman and can find out about your father, maybe you can search for him. And you can get all this family stuff behind you. Move on with your life."

I nodded. As usual, she sounded convincing.

"Not to mention that your aunt Mitch has asked for these things to be returned to her sister. And it would be so important for Hiromi to have her sister's ashes and for Aunt Mitch to be, well, 'back home.'"

I couldn't speak.

Zoe stared into my face. "And isn't this also a good excuse for you to get away from everything for a while?" she said in a gentle voice. "Get some perspective on where your life is going?"

She didn't say, "Dirk," but I knew this was what she was inferring.

We watched the DVD once more, then couldn't stop replaying it, freezing every frame the man was in. Did I have his nose? His forehead? His mouth? Half the time I thought it was certain I did, the other half it seemed there was no resemblance at all. But I found myself feeling happy, hopeful. This was the only clue I'd ever had about my father, and Hiromi Taniguchi was the closest I'd had to a relative for ages.

Could I really go to Japan? I pictured my meeting with Hiromi Taniguchi, who would be so surprised to find there was a relative, even though only through marriage, who had journeyed all the way from America to carry out her sister's wishes and bring her ashes home. I imagined showing her the photo of me in the kimono, telling her that some of the happiest times in my childhood were my visits with Aunt Mitch. I'd explain that I had no family of my own and ask her if it would be all right if I called her Aunt Hiromi. I could stay with her for a while, then invite her to San Jose; show her the old house again in Saratoga, if I could find it.

I looked once more at the handwritten documents, when something suddenly occurred to me—a memory, lying dormant for years.

"Zoe, is this how you write my name in Japanese?" I tore out another piece of paper from my notepad and wrote the characters:

セレスト・ダンカン

Aunt Mitch had taught me how to write my name, and I must have practiced it hundreds of times at her kitchen table. I wrote it now as though a spirit or force was guiding me, almost as if I wasn't in control of my hand.

Zoe nodded slowly, her eyes zeroing in on me. "Celeste," she said. "You better go apply for your passport."

It didn't seem quite normal to have a feeling of dread at the thought of telling your boyfriend that you might be able to finally track down the father you never knew. Yet that was how I felt when I parked my car in front of

Dirk's compact tract house in a quiet Sunnyvale neighborhood off Homestead Avenue. But that wasn't the only thing I needed to tell him.

My eyes fixed on the garage door, picturing the musical equipment inside, the PA, the piano, the site of many musical moments as well as many fights and frustrations.

When he gave me a hug and a kiss and said he was sorry about the last time, I felt even worse. And when I played the home movie on the DVD, he seemed genuinely interested, though I seemed to be holding my breath the whole time.

"That's pretty cool that you got a home movie with you and your mom in it," he said. "And that you got this stuff of your aunt's." He fingered the handwritten documents. "Wonder what this all says."

"Well, actually I got them translated."

"Yeah? By who?"

"Zoe," I said. I told him about Aunt Mitch's wish to have the comb returned to her sister and how important it would be to bring the ashes back to Japan.

"*Zoe?*" He looked skeptical. "She's not a professional translator. But assuming she read it right, I guess that would be the thing to do, if it were something actually doable."

"Doable?"

"Well, it's not like you can take BART to Tokyo." He said this in typical Dirk fashion, as if it was common knowledge, part of a closing argument to a jury. He looked at my face. "You're not really thinking of going there, are you?"

I pulled out a picture from an envelope, a photo I had made of the man holding me in the DVD. It wasn't the best quality, but his face was fairly clear. I explained to Dirk how Hiromi Taniguchi might know who the man is. "I think that maybe he could be my dad." I pointed to the man's nose. "Don't you think my nose looks like his?"

Dirk cocked his head and stared at my nose, then at the man in the photograph. "Could be, I guess. But that's kind of a leap, isn't it? Just from this one scene in a home movie?"

"Why would he be showering me with such attention? It didn't seem like he was a casual acquaintance."

"The only definitive way to know would be for the guy to get a DNA test and for you to get one too, and even those can be inconclusive. But you don't know for sure where your aunt's sister is or if she's even alive. And even if she is, how do you know she'll even remember who this guy is?"

"I just have this feeling," I said. "I have a feeling I can find her, and I have a feeling this man is my father and she'll be able to tell me who he is."

"Is this something Zoe put in your head?"

"No," I said. I cleared my throat, and my heart thumped hard. "I've decided to go there and search for her."

He didn't say anything for a few moments, seeming to take time to process this new information. Then he said, "Well, how long are you going to go for?"

"I don't know. I've arranged . . . I've arranged to work for a subcontractor of TextTrans in Tokyo."

"Whoa. You're going to *transfer* there?"

"Well, at least temporarily. Zoe says her cousin can sublet my apartment." I braced for his anger but, instead, saw a hurt look on his face that I wasn't expecting.

"Where was I in all this planning?" he asked quietly.

"I was afraid," I said. "I was afraid that if I told you about it ahead of time that you'd talk me out of it." I looked into his eyes. "This is really important to me."

"I understand that, but it's based on such flimsy evidence. And there's a good chance you'll be disappointed in the end."

"I don't want to think that way."

"But why move there? Why not just go for a few weeks?"

"I think I need to get away for a while."

"You mean to get away from me?"

I didn't want to say outright that this was true, even though it was. It was too much to think of this as a breakup, but I knew I needed to get some perspective. I would be killing two birds with one stone with this trip in a certain way. But my guilt prevented me from being so candid with him. "Maybe you can come over there," I said. "And help me search for her." I knew he'd never go for this and I was right.

He sighed. "I've got the big Rainsfield case coming up. I can't just take off and leave. And do you know how expensive it is over there? Have you researched this and looked into all your options?"

He could always come up with a million different reasons not to do something. "Kind of."

He rolled his eyes. "Celeste, this is pretty crazy. Maybe we can think about going there next summer for a couple of weeks. Why is this so important now? What's the urgency?"

Technically he was right. On technicalities he was always right. But I was sick of technicalities. Yes, there was no urgency, *technically*. But it was urgent to me. If I waited for him to be ready, we'd never go. There would always be something in the way. And I was convinced that he would never fully understand my situation, being from a big family of three brothers and two sisters in Virginia whom he was trying to avoid half the time.

"I don't think you've ever been able to relate to what it's like to have no family," I said.

He touched my arm. "Maybe not, but you can't change the past. What's done is done. But, in some ways, you can control your future by the decisions you make and move forward with your life, without having to be encumbered by things you can't control about your childhood."

What he said made sense, but my sinking feeling signaled that it might just be that he would never understand me.

"Besides," he went on. "You've got me." He squeezed my hand.

Had he been a bit of a paternal figure all along? I wasn't sure, but when I thought of the years we'd been together, I knew it hadn't been all bad. And I wasn't looking forward to feeling lonely. And who was the one who'd encouraged me to sing in the first place? Would I have even done it without his urging me on?

It took me a while, but finally I said, "Well, ah . . . this is the decision I've made."

"Don't you want to think about it a little more?"

I told him I would think about it, and even though I was sincere when I said it, I later realized that I'd already made up my mind in Zoe's living room. In the end, I said I would keep in touch, that it wasn't a breakup, just taking a break.

He reluctantly said good-bye and wished me good luck.

A few weeks later I was on my journey.

4

THE SHUTDOWN

LIVING IN TOKYO, NOT A DAY WENT BY WHEN I DID NOT RECEIVE CONSTANT stares from my fellow train passengers.

It wasn't my imagination.

For example, the little girl in the blue T-shirt that said, "Enjoy! Your Creamy Balls." She'd kick her seat in a constant rhythm as she gawked, and it took a moment for me to realize that her tiny green shoes were in the shape of frogs. Or the middle-aged salaryman with the too oily hair, speckled with dandruff, wearing the shiny dark blue business suit. Taking a break now and then from his pornographic comic book, he would fix his wide eyes upon me like those of a curious fish. Even the stylish twenty-something woman in the gray swing coat with the oversized buttons, the fashionable slouchy black boots, a person I figured would be too sophisticated—too cool—to participate in this stare fest, would glance up from her cell phone screen, her gaze upon me unwavering.

These weren't unfriendly stares, but they weren't friendly either. And when I would stare back, the guilty parties lowered their heads or turned the other way. It wasn't that my blouse was unbuttoned or that the corners of my mouth were smeared with lipstick—I always checked. And it was laughable to think that I was garnering this extra attention because I was being mistaken for a movie star or model.

"It because you are gaijin," Yukiko, the office lady at Milky Way Text, explained when I finally asked. "Foreigner."

"And what is so special about that?"

She giggled. "Gaijin for Japanese . . . ah." She thought for a moment. "Big. Different. Funny. Strange."

It wasn't as difficult to get settled in Tokyo as I thought it would. And living in new surroundings seven thousand miles from home made it easier to feel a little less guilty about leaving Dirk behind without much warning, and optimistic about my mission, though I wasn't sure exactly how I was going to accomplish it, not knowing a word of Japanese.

Yukiko had gotten me set up temporarily at the Gaijin Banana House, a cheap dormitory hotel for foreigners only. In a room only slightly bigger than a janitor's closet, I shared a bunk bed with a woman in Japan researching Harajuku Lolita Goth girls, which she explained were young, heavily made-up women who made their fashion statement by wearing frilly Victorian blouses, petticoat skirts, Mary Janes, and carrying parasols while parading around Tokyo. Unfortunately, this multitattooed Australian wasn't fond of bathing and whistled in her sleep. Yukiko, though, promised to help me find my own apartment. The rent for a place, no matter how tiny, would be high in the monetary stratosphere, as Dirk had so correctly pointed out. But luckily my job paid decently, and I'd also made sure to purchase a one-way plane ticket to make the $1,500 in my savings account last as long as possible.

The Gaijin Banana House was only a few blocks from the station where I caught the train with the staring passengers to get to work. I had no idea why the Tokyo office was called Milky Way Text, but I liked that name better than TextTrans. And the work was more tolerable: rewriting snappy high-technology magazine articles that my coworkers translated from Japanese to English. The translations were competent enough, though the translators tended to suffer from pronoun phobia and an aversion to verb agreement.

Only six people worked at Milky Way Text, including Yukiko, plus the boss, Mr. Suzuki. His genial round face reminded me of those you'd see on the laughing Buddha statues in the tourist gift shops on Grant Avenue in San Francisco's Chinatown. He wasn't around much, always seeming to have important things to do outside the office.

My coworkers were fluent enough in reading English to translate documents from Japanese, but their speaking ability was limited to inquiries about my well-being, extolling my expert English ability, analyzing the color of my hair (strawberry blond), and commenting on my size: at five feet eight inches, I seemed to tower over everyone. And when I demonstrated to them at one point how I could write my name in Japanese, they stared, mouths agape, as if a monkey had whipped out a haiku.

Only with the always cheerful, helpful, and petite Yukiko could I carry on some semblance of a rudimentary conversation. I was grateful to have her there.

After about a month I was beginning to feel somewhat acclimated, confident that soon I would be able to settle into my own place, and then get down to business with my quest to find Hiromi Taniguchi. But on a Monday at the beginning of March, the day when I was due to receive my first paycheck, everything seemed to fall apart.

As usual, I headed from the train station, walking the five blocks to the office. I hugged my arms across my chest, trying to ward off the cold. My coat was too thin for the biting air, which was chillier than it ever got in San Jose, and I could feel it down to my bones. But the brilliance of the cherry trees along the route made my shivers less noticeable. The trees were beginning to bloom—earlier than usual I'd been told—and observing the bursting pink blossoms reminded me of my childhood addiction to the sticky sweet popcorn balls at the Santa Cruz Beach Boardwalk.

I figured I would only see postcard-perfect cherry blossoms in the Japanese countryside, framing Buddhist temples lined with gravel paths and red arched bridges, like the scene depicted on Aunt Mitch's antique hair ornament. But here they were in Tokyo along with the thirteen million people calling this place home. The bright flowers invigorated me. I was convinced I had made the right decision to come to Tokyo, which seemed an amazing city. You could not even begin to compare it to San Jose, a place I never understood why anyone would specifically ask the way to.

I stopped at the corner, waiting for the light to change, and, as usual, watched the giant mechanical crab on the seafood restaurant, waving his claws in time to a Japanese version of the old disco tune "Macho Man." I turned toward the modest brown building that housed Milky Way Text. There had been nothing but crowds in Tokyo, and I actually kind of liked this as long as I wasn't trapped in the middle of one. But the weird thing was that there was a crowd surrounding my office building, a place where I'd never seen a crowd before. And along with the multitudes of people clamoring at the entrance were five police cars, their lights flashing, blocking traffic. Television news trucks, satellite dishes attached to their roofs, jammed in next to them.

I hurried over, standing at the periphery of the large but well-behaved mob. "What happened?" I asked no one in particular, though right after I said it I realized it was unlikely that anyone would understand me. I craned my neck to see if I could locate Yukiko or any of my other Japanese coworkers, but I recognized no one. Was there a gas leak? A bomb threat?

Bam! Someone banged into my arm with such force that I almost toppled over. I turned to see a young man dressed in an argyle sweater vest and a tie holding a microphone. He was accompanied by a burly guy in jeans, who was clad in a bright green parka and holding a video camera.

"Excuse me!" the man with the microphone said in English with a heavy Japanese accent. "You work Milky Way Text-o?"

I'd been noticing this Japanese fixation with attaching unnecessary endings to certain English words. Even my name—Celeste—became Se-re-su-to when it was Japanized. And when there'd been a problem with my computer I had to tell Yukiko that some of the keys on the "keyboard-o" were stuck before I was understood.

"Yes," I said. "I work for Milky Way Text. Uh, Text-o."

The man shoved his microphone into my face, the camera now pointing right at me, encroaching on my personal space like an unwelcome intruder. I did not want to be on television. I had no desire to be the focus of any attention, but my role as gaijin—and I was the only gaijin in this crowd—seemed not only to command it but somehow warrant it.

"Can we have your comment-o about shutdown of Milky Way Text-o?" the reporter asked.

"Shutdown? It's *shut down?*"

Before he could answer, voices from the crowd began shouting. The cameraman and the reporter turned their attention toward a figure being led out of the building by police officers. Perched on my tiptoes, I could see that the bald man with glasses, handcuffed, his head lowered, was Mr. Suzuki, minus his laughing Buddha expression.

"Celeste-san!" a woman's voice called out.

I turned around to see Yukiko, her face etched with worry.

"Yukiko-san, what's going on?"

"So horrible. So horrible," she said, shaking her head slowly.

"Is Milky Way Text closed down? What happened to Mr. Suzuki?"

"Ah, ah," was all Yukiko could say. She always struggled with her English, but what little she came up with was usually somewhat understandable. Yet at this point she appeared to be as shut down as the company.

Tell me what the hell is going on, I wanted to say but instead kept quiet. I'd been learning here that remaining calm and vague usually produced better results than jumping down someone's throat and getting right to the point. My neck ached. Looking down at Yukiko, I was the Jolly Green Giant standing guard over Thumbelina.

Thumbelina cleared her throat. "Suzuki-san . . . pachinko . . . yakuza . . . money . . . very bad."

Suzuki-san. Pachinko. Yakuza. Money. Very bad. It was like a Japanese version of Clue: Mr. Suzuki in the Ballroom with the Knife.

Yukiko looked even more upset, probably because the puzzled expression on my face confirmed that her English sentence structure was nearly incomprehensible.

I put my hand on her arm. "Have we lost our jobs, Yukiko-san?"

She dragged her index finger across her neck in a slashing motion.

This time I understood her loud and clear.

By noon I found my newly unemployed self back at the Gaijin Banana House with an uncertain future and a promise to meet Yukiko later that evening to drown our sorrows in a couple of beers or perhaps chocolate parfait sundaes with extra whipped cream. The time difference prevented me from calling Zoe or TextTrans (and I wasn't about to call Dirk and tell him what happened), but they would have had little or no information. Milky Way Text was a subcontractor and didn't have much to do with the home office.

The rooms at the hotel were locked during the day so I had no choice but to hang out on the yellow-and-white polka-dot plastic couch in the small lounge, which always reeked of air freshener that smelled like orange juice. A television was bolted against the wall and I asked Joji, the young reception desk clerk, if he minded if I changed from the octopus cartoon to the news. Flipping through the channels, I finally located a news report and, minutes later, footage of what I'd witnessed that morning.

"Can you tell me what they're saying?" Joji's English wasn't the best, just about like everyone else's, but I hoped I could get a little more information out of him.

Joji looked up from his comic book as the scene unfolded of Mr. Suzuki being led away by the police, then a close-up of the reporter, the guy who bumped into me and asked for my comment-o. Then I came into view looking as if I was about to fall to pieces, wailing, "Shutdown? It's *shut down?*"

"Is it *you?*" Joji asked.

"Oh, God, yes."

I assumed such wretched footage would have ended up on the cutting-room floor. Was this how I looked? You couldn't miss the crow's-feet starting around the eyes, the little lines framing the corners of the mouth, both of which seem to be even more noticeable when compared with the legions of dewy-skinned, wrinkle-free Japanese women I'd been encountering. And as I watched myself against the backdrop of a crowd of Japanese people, it was easy to see why I stuck out—compared to them I was the perfect spokesmodel for the Celeste Duncan Department Store for the Tall and Big-Boned Woman.

I'd never been on television in my life, and along with all of the above, I had made my debut with hair as full-bodied as the strings on a kitchen mop. And that lipstick had to go. It was much too orangey, though it sure didn't look that way in the mirror when I put it on that morning. They had no business calling it Sugar-Coated Pink.

"This man is president of company. He steal the money to pay yakuza," Joji said. "Police say he poison wife for getting insurance money. But maybe not true."

His English was rough, but the tone blasé, as if this happened every day. It was hard to believe that it could have been Mr. Suzuki in the

Kitchen with the Poison. I deduced from what Joji said next that my former boss suffered from a malady known as pachinko addiction, which was the start of his troubles.

"Pachinko?" I remembered the word from Yukiko's list of enigmatic clues.

"Pinball machine," he said. "Like in the Stardust. Down there." He pointed toward the front door.

I knew what he was talking about. It was impossible to miss Stardust with its bright green neon sign and the deafening noise of ringing bells, blaring music, and the click-clacking of those little metal balls, the customers chain-smoking, sitting hypnotized in front of the machines.

"Well, this guy who got arrested, he was head of the company I worked for," I said. "And now it's closed down so I'm out of a job."

"Really?"

I didn't know how much Joji understood, especially since he was giving me a cockeyed, friendly smile that was interrupted when his cell phone burst forth with music and he began an animated conversation in his native language. I picked up the TV remote and started to randomly change the channels that carried everything from samurai movies to Spanish lessons. But I stopped my channel flipping when I came upon a music video depicting a serene night scene. The woman singer, standing on a bridge overlooking a placid lake, the moon reflecting on the water, gazed at the stars in the sky as she sang. She wore a kimono, and its color pattern of pink and gold reminded me of the one I was wearing in the picture in Aunt Mitch's photo album.

The singer in the music video could have been one of Aunt Mitch's dolls, her face as smooth and delicate as if it was made of fine china, her hair a thick mass of blue-black ink strands. Her beauty was a perfect match for the song she sang, its haunting melody tinged with melancholy.

I was struck by the singing but also mesmerized by the musical arrangement of the song. At first it seemed traditionally Japanese, but there was no mistaking the touches of blues and even jazz sprinkled in the mix. I imagined myself singing it, though I couldn't fathom how I'd go about it; it seemed an impossibility. But as I listened further, the song became somehow familiar, and I heard Aunt Mitch's voice. *She used to sing to me in Japanese.* This song, with its precise pattern of repetition of the verse and chorus brought to mind the ones she sang. And even though it resembled nothing like the kind of music Barbara performed, my thoughts couldn't help but turn to her for a fleeting moment.

I closed my eyes, the song taking me into a kind of dream that was so warm and so comforting that I never wanted to come out of it. It was at the song's climax that the emotion in the singer's voice moved me in a way no song had ever done before. Even though I couldn't understand a word, somehow I understood everything.

5

THE CHICK-A-DOODLE INCIDENT

TRAPPED. I WAS TRAPPED IN THE VORTEX OF THE WHIRLPOOL OF HUMANITY called Shinjuku Station. It had to be the biggest, most crowded train station in the world. I made a mental note to look that up—if I survived. The Fremont BART station back home was pure Mayberry by comparison.

Yukiko had said to meet in front of the Studio Alta building at the west exit of Shinjuku Station at seven o'clock the evening of the Milky Way shutdown. It had a big television screen on the front—you couldn't miss it. Well, you'd miss it if you found yourself at the east exit by mistake, which is what I apparently had done. It didn't help that any signs in English were few and far between. While there were sightings of English, much of it didn't make sense: Pocari Sweat, Let's English, Hep Gals Dream Liver. Otherwise, I was bombarded with kanji and it was all over the station. If only Zoe had been there to translate:

新宿駅　非常口　小田急　京王百貨店　地下鉄　中央総武線
北口　小田急小田原線　ルミネ　東口　山手線　北口
歌舞伎町　大人のおもちゃ　中央線　湘南—新宿線　丸の内線
埼京線　京王線　都営新宿線

Not to mention the head-spinning caused by the two thousand people in a place the size of a football field—all walking in an orderly fashion but fast, very fast.

As I tried to go in the opposite direction, from east to west, I attempted to shut out the constant ringing in my ears of words and phrases I couldn't discern but wouldn't have understood anyway even if they had been clear and in English. Announcements over loudspeakers, high-pitched women's voices, music, bells, more announcements. People walking. People running. People staring. People staring. Because I was a gaijin or because it looked as though I was about to collapse?

I was sweating, starting to hyperventilate, convinced that perhaps I would never get out. I envisioned the newspaper summary: *OVERWHELMED, UNEMPLOYED GAIJIN TRAMPLED TO DEATH IN TRAIN STATION: PLANNING TO MEET A FRIEND, SHE NEVER MADE IT. LARGE, CRUMPLED BODY WENT UNNOTICED UNTIL STATION CLOSED AT MIDNIGHT.*

But by some miracle I did find my exit, and the cold air that ripped through me as I had walked to the doomed Milky Way Text was now as welcome as a cool drink. I prayed I would see the big television screen and somehow find Yukiko among the throngs outside.

English—thank God, English. The sign on the building read STUDIO ALTA in *English*. I had found it. An animated penguin smacking his beaky lips as he slurped the remnants of his noodle soup danced on the giant television screen. Tokyo seemed to be saturated with an overabundance of cartoon characters. There were mascots galore; a bespectacled dog promoting a bank, a piglet hawking for the telephone company. And, of course, the queen of them all, Hello Kitty, still going strong despite probably being in her forties, though not looking a day over fifteen. I caught my breath as I watched the soup-swilling penguin giggle, then somersault into his bowl. I had made it. I put my hand on my chest, relieved that my heartbeat was finally slowing to an acceptable rate.

In front of Studio Alta it was teeming with people, not for a special event but apparently just out for a Monday night in Tokyo. This was how it was, the opposite of mild-mannered, mundane San Jose. Music blaring, blinding neon, giant TV screens attached to high-rise buildings, and young people milling about seemingly dressed for fashion shoots, all in well-orchestrated and moving-right-along mobs. Chaos, but chaos that never seemed out of control. Any Tokyo night, even a plain old Monday, seemed to be a night at the opening ceremonies of the Olympics and the Disneyland electric light parade rolled into one.

In another triumph, I was able to spot Yukiko, looking more youthful in a black skirt, leggings, and denim jacket than the conservative office lady façade she presented at work. She grinned and waved, putting the cell phone she'd been texting on into her chic Gucci-like purse, her happy expression a big contrast to how she looked earlier during the Milky Way Text debacle.

"Celeste-san, *ogenki desu ka?*"

Yukiko had taught me how to say, "how are you?" and "I am fine."

"*Hai, genki desu,*" I answered back, saying I was well, since I did not know the correct Japanese for "I have just come back from the dead."

"We go now?

"Go where?

"My favorite place?"

Her favorite place turned out to be the Café Greenwich, an underground *kissaten* tucked away in a Shinjuku alleyway away from the hubbub of Studio Alta, where we ended up with strong coffees and slices of lemon cheesecake. The servers wore black turtlenecks and matching berets, and old New York jazz club posters were tacked on faux brick walls. Bebop music played in the background. I couldn't vouch for the place's authenticity—I'd never been to 1950s Greenwich Village—but I had to say that it sure didn't feel like I was in Japan. Tokyo seemed adept at giving this impression; you never quite knew where the hell you were.

I hadn't had much time to think hard about what I was going to do now that I'd lost my job at Milky Way Text, the only place my visa allowed me to work. And it was certainly something I didn't want to think about since the outlook was so bleak. The thought of running home to Dirk with my tail tucked between my legs was not something I wanted to contemplate. I asked Yukiko what she planned to do. After I reworded the question a few times, she finally understood.

"Maybe go with friend. Kaoru-san. To Paris."

Now that was the ticket: lose your job, go to Paris. If only my life were that simple. I concluded from what Yukiko had explained before that she lived with her parents rent-free, with all her income going straight into her bank account for spending on clothes, handbags, shoes, and travel. Apparently this wasn't uncommon here. Office lady jobs were plentiful, as long as you were young, and Milky Way Text apparently had been Yukiko's fifth such endeavor. She and Kaoru had trekked to Australia last December, and at work she had proudly showed me the photos of the two of them making goo-goo eyes at blasé koalas.

"You stay—Gaijin Banana House?" she asked me.

"I don't know. It's cheap, but my money won't last forever. This was all so sudden."

Again I was unsure if Yukiko had understood me, but she looked thoughtful as she sipped her coffee, then picked delicately at her cheesecake with a tiny gold fork. I, on the other hand, had wolfed down my entire slice in a matter of seconds and was considering what to order next.

"Do you like to stay home?" she finally said.

"Stay home?" I didn't know what she meant, but that was nothing new. "I'm sorry, I don't understand."

She looked flustered. "Ah . . ."

"Do you mean do I want to go back home?"

Yukiko shook her head.

I smiled, not knowing what I could say further.

She seemed to be thinking hard as she stirred her coffee. "Ah . . . my mother's friend, she is Kubota-san . . ."

A saxophone honked in the background, a bluesy voice wailing in response.

"Uh-huh?"

"She like foreigner."

"I see." I didn't see, but it was something to say.

"And she make foreigner stay at house. Teach English."

I realized she had meant homestay. "Teach English?"

"Teach English to her and maybe high school daughter, Rika-san. She has son, Takuya-san, but I think he work America."

I nodded.

"Kubota-san, she is the boring housewife so he—*she*—likes for practice English. And you live there." Her forehead wrinkled. "Maybe can help find sister of aunt. Can I ask?"

A *homestay*. Such a brilliant idea was likely to beat the bottom bunk at the Gaijin Banana House. And it sounded like it could be rent-free. But was it possible to feel elation and dread at the same time? Because this was how I felt. Living with a family I didn't know reminded me of being a foster child. And having someone take you in when you were thirty-three seemed rather strange and, frankly, pathetic. Still, I didn't have much choice, and if this friend of Yukiko's mother liked to practice English so much, maybe her English was better than Yukiko's. I figured maybe she could help me find Hiromi Taniguchi and translate for me once I located her.

I smiled, grateful for this turn of events. "Thank you for thinking of me, Yukiko-san. Yes, please ask her."

It only took a few days to get everything arranged, and the next thing I knew I was meeting Takuya's mother, Mrs. Kubota, for the first time the day I was to move into her family home. I put aside any trepidation about the situation, appreciative that she was letting me stay based only on a recommendation from the office lady from my defunct job. It was unimaginable that something like this would happen back in San Jose: when I became a foster child, those families were paid to take me in.

This lucky break seemed to be the result of the magical power English-speaking foreigners apparently held over some Japanese people. It was bizarre that this somehow had a kind of cachet, that a person could receive room and board because of it, but I was beyond grateful.

The house was in Asahidai, a rather upscale suburb about a ten-minute train ride from the Tokyo district of Shibuya. The Kubota home couldn't have looked more different from Aunt Mitch's old house in Saratoga. There were no woodblock prints, no Japanese dolls, no ornate wooden chests. Instead, the living room consisted of decidedly Western furniture: a rust-colored L-shaped sofa, a coffee table facing a flat-screen television housed in a sleek silver entertainment unit, and a brown leatherette chair that looked suspiciously La-Z-Boy. In the adjacent dining room, sets of English china—not Japanese ceramics—were crammed into a credenza.

Mrs. Kubota had to be around fifty but looked younger, like so many people in Japan. Her black hair was cut short, permed in soft waves; red lipstick and face powder her only concessions to makeup. On the day of my arrival she was dressed in a sky-blue golf shirt with Topaz Hills Links embroidered in delicate orange script on the right breast pocket, a beige skirt hitting below her knees, and thick nylon stockings. The ensemble also included a yellow-and-white-checked apron with a duck proclaiming, "Do! Household Life." This matched her yellow-and-white-checked house slippers, also adorned with ducks and obviously a set.

We sat together on the sofa.

"Do you play golf?" I asked, unsure how else to start a conversation since her English had not been forthcoming.

She looked puzzled and I immediately figured that she didn't understand.

"*Gorufu?* Me?" she finally said, pointing to her nose. This was something else I'd noticed about Japanese people. When they referred to themselves, they pointed not to their chest but to their olfactory organ.

"Your shirt. A golf shirt, right?"

She looked down at her chest, seeming to understand.

"Ah, no!" Her face turned red. "No *gorufu*. Not good." She thought for a moment. "Phillip stay here . . . ah, one year before? Homestay. He gave. From Florida."

"Oh, I see. How nice." Despite all her years of study, Mrs. Kubota's English appeared rudimentary at best—not much better than Yukiko's. I wasn't sure how much help she could be in my search for Hiromi Taniguchi.

I heard a sharp whistle, which seemed to be the sound of the teakettle. Mrs. Kubota suddenly looked distracted, jumped up, and disappeared into the kitchen. A few moments later she presented me with a tray topped with a round, fat, pink teapot and two matching cups proclaiming "Happy Afternoon Tea" in white lettering. Elegant silver spoons rested on each saucer and the pink napkin she placed next to my cup also displayed the message "Happy Afternoon Tea." It was all very precious. After pouring the tea, which looked more British black than Japanese green, she pointed to a small pastry and said, "You eat *shu creem-u?*"

Shoe cream? I knew that couldn't be right, but asking for further explanation would only result in more confusion. Besides, I was always more than willing to try anything that resembled a cream puff. One bite and I was in pastry heaven: I had never tasted a more perfect cream puff. Didn't you normally have to go to Paris to experience something so divine? Crunchy and fluffy at the same time, with a luscious cream that wasn't overly sweet?

"Delicious," I said. I combed my brain, trying to remember the Japanese word I learned from Yukiko. "*Oishii.*"

Mrs. Kubota's face brightened. "Yes! *Oishii!* Your Japanese. So nice!"

It was customary for a gaijin to receive compliments on the slightest accomplishment; a burp probably would have elicited praise. But now we sat in silence, the only sound the ticking of a clock on the wall above the probable La-Z-Boy, a clock with the face of a cat, its whiskers acting as the hands, which at the current time of one thirty-five rendered the feline positively Picasso-like.

I tried hard to think of what to say next. I wanted to be able to tell Mrs. Kubota why I was here. Yukiko was supposed to have explained that, though I was never clear how much Yukiko understood. But it would have been all too difficult and overwhelming, especially when we had only just met. At last, though, it seemed that Mrs. Kubota had come up with something to say. She put down her teacup and reached for a photo album lying on the coffee table.

"My homestay guest," she said. Placing the album on her lap, she opened it, showing me pictures of all the gaijin homestayers who had spent time at the Kubota residence. There was the aforementioned Phillip from Florida, Tammy from Minnesota, Heather from Arizona, James from England, Janet from Oregon, Leanne from Australia, and Zach from Iowa. They all appeared apple-cheeked and Caucasian, and a good decade younger than me. This homestay thing was not intended for the over-thirty crowd was the message that kept getting conveyed. Mrs. Kubota must have been sorely disappointed when I walked in the door; TextTrans child-receptionist Kylie would have been the more preferable candidate.

The pictures were sweet, pleasing, showing grinning faces of foreigners posed with Mrs. Kubota, herself the epitome of cheerfulness.

"Looks like very nice people," I offered, though I found such a tribute book a bit odd.

"Yes," Mrs. Kubota replied, slowly turning the pages, as if savoring each memory.

Further pages also displayed pictures of foreigners, but these were not personal photographs. They were clipped from newspapers and magazines and seemed to be gaijin performers.

"Who are they?" I asked.

"Best gaijin *tarento*. Japanese TV."

There was that *o* again. I tossed the word around in my brain and realized Mrs. Kubota was actually saying "talent." I'd heard of foreigners becoming successful models in Japan who would have only gotten as far as the annual Podunk Department Store fashion show back in their hometown. These people in Mrs. Kubota's album seemed to be well known only on Japanese television, so of course I didn't recognize any of them. Their poses were exaggerated, unnatural—looks of surprise or overly toothy grins, arms spread-eagled into a kind of joyful proclamation: "Although I am only a marginally talented gaijin, look at how exciting my life is!"

"Trevor Templeton," Mrs. Kubota said, pointing to a professorial type with wire-rim glasses and red curly hair, pictured sitting with a panel on what looked like a game show. "I like."

She closed the album and I sipped my tea, gazing longingly at the other shoe cream, though I thought it would be too impolite to take another without being offered first. Instead, my attention turned to that old family portrait where Takuya, in his high school days (and long before I proposed marriage to him) resembled a future Rotary Club member. Yukiko had told me that I wouldn't be teaching English to Takuya's younger sister after all because she herself was on a homestay in the United States.

I did notice that Takuya looked more like his mother than his father. I had always made a point of noting family resemblances or the lack of them, probably from all the time I spent during my childhood scanning the faces of men of a certain age, wondering if any of them could have been the one who'd impregnated my mother. I thought again of the man in the home movie: his nose, his mouth. In this picture it was apparent that Takuya had Mrs. Kubota's large eyes and delicate mouth, but his face was angular instead of round, like his father's.

"Nice family photograph," I said to Mrs. Kubota, still delicately nibbling at her first shoe cream, a bird pecking at her seeds. How did she muster the control to not just shove the whole thing into her mouth? I stared at the other pastry, sitting pristine in its white, ruffled paper cup, desperate for another experience.

Mrs. Kubota beamed as she pointed to the people in the photograph. "Masao, my husband. Rika, my daughter. She Kansas City, Missouri, now."

"How exciting for her."

"And my son, Takuya. He in Seattle, Washington."

"Very international family."

"He come home soon."

"Oh, really? When?"

"Next month. Two year before. He go."

"He's been away for two years?"

"His company—Sunny Shokuhin." From the pride ringing in Mrs. Kubota's voice I felt I was supposed to have heard of it.

I smiled, nodding. "You must be very proud of him."

"Takuya—nice boy!"

After more pleasant but fairly stiff conversation and several cups of tea, I needed to use the rest room. I had no idea where it was; Mrs. Kubota had only served me refreshments and had yet to show me the rest of the house or even the room where I'd be staying. "Excuse me," I said. "But where is the bathroom?" My brain ached as I tried to remember the Japanese word I'd heard from my Milky Way Text coworkers. "*Otearai?*"

Mrs. Kubota smiled. "You know much Japanese!" As I followed her down the hall, I saw that all the doorknobs sported pink crocheted covers, as did the tissue box in the rest room and the telephone in the living room.

It was a relief that I'd been able to carry on a conversation with Mrs. Kubota, though I thought her English would be better. But she seemed to be a nice lady, and warmth trumped English-speaking ability any day, as my experience with native speakers Irma Kruikshank and Mrs. Cavanaugh had demonstrated.

I returned to the living room, determined that the other shoe cream would still have my name on it. But something had changed, and the kind expression that graced Mrs. Kubota's face had turned to one of repugnance.

Her eyes were wide, in shock. "Oh! Ah!" She pointed to my feet. "Not good," she said, shaking her head. "Not good."

My back stiffened. "Excuse me?"

"For toilet! Only toilet!"

"What?"

This was the now-famous toilet slipper screwup, but at the time I was baffled as to what the problem was. My anxiety only intensified as Mrs. Kubota's horrified expression seemed to freeze into a terror-stricken theatrical Noh mask.

She knelt down and pulled at my slippers so that I slipped out of them. Instead of the orange cloth slippers with the pair of chickens that said Chick-a-Doodle, which I put on when I entered the house, I saw that I was now wearing the green plastic slippers with yellow daisies I found in the bathroom, neatly sitting in front of the toilet. I hadn't even realized the switch.

Carrying the plastic slippers, Mrs. Kubota scurried to the bathroom and returned with the Chick-a-Doodle ones.

"I'm sorry," I said.

Mrs. Kubota, armed with a cloth, once again knelt on the floor in front of me. Could I disappear right now? Because I wasn't enjoying the feeling of being five years old again. After wiping the soles of the Chick-a-Doodle slippers, she let me put them back on. I vowed to never again make the mistake of wearing the slippers in front of the toilet outside of the bathroom.

Mrs. Kubota's smile returned, and all seemed right with the world once more. I was relieved but caught off guard about her extreme reaction. Wouldn't a little lighthearted laughter have been in order? Certainly since she had hosted so many gaijin, at least one of them must have made the same error. Wasn't that part of the charm of having a foreigner stay at your house? All those amusing cross-cultural mistakes? But it was possible that all of Mrs. Kubota's previous lodgers had been smart enough, unlike me, to have boned up on Japanese customs ahead of time, something Dirk would have been sure to do as well.

I imagined my photograph, a dopey, unknowing smile on my face, as I posed in the living room, snug in my toilet slippers. It would be prominently displayed in a new special section of Mrs. Kubota's homestay tribute album: the Gaijin Hall of Shame.

6

HOMESTAY BROTHER

HELLO KITTY AND HER ASSORTED ANIMAL FRIENDS MINGLED ON THE WOODEN shelves with Japanese animation figurines, while posters of Japanese boy bands, all skinny and long-haired wispy, their sullen expressions directed at the camera, covered the light mauve walls. Hand drawings copied from Japanese comics and cartoons—saucer-eyed girls dressed in sailor suits and handsome boys with square jaws and steely-eyed stares—shared space with them. A lime-green duvet, sprinkled with a print of white flowers, covered the single bed, which was topped with fuzzy, furry pink pillows.

It took some more conversation, a few more cups of tea, and, yes, the other mind-blowing shoe cream, before Mrs. Kubota finally had me bring in my suitcase to the room where I was to stay, her daughter Rika's.

I knew I should unpack, but the room seemed too abundant with scenarios of what might have been. I seemed paralyzed, unable to do anything but sit on the bed, a teenager caught up in a gauzy daydream. Gazing at the walls and hugging one of those pink fur pillows to my chest, I couldn't help but think that I might have had a room like this when I was in high school, if I'd had anything resembling a normal childhood; if my mother didn't take that balloon ride; if Aunt Mitch could have adopted me; if I hadn't been forced to stay in the Kruikshank and Cavanaugh bedrooms with designs taking inspiration from the early Motel 6 period, not to mention having to share them with way too many people.

I appreciated being in a quintessential teenage-girl room, better late than never. It filled me with a kind of quiet joy, giving off a warm feeling, of youth, of pink, of possibility: an optimism allowing me to believe that I would track down Hiromi Taniguchi and find out about my father.

I took out the sketch pad and colored pencils I'd brought with me. Being able to draw often kept me from going insane from the time I was in junior high school, so I'd made sure to pack them. I wasn't too bad, but it was more therapy than anything to do with artistic talent. I was probably a better singer than artist, though I wasn't sure what Dirk would have said about that.

I began to sketch one of the rock star boys on the wall, a member of a group that appeared to be called SMAP. His cheekbones were so high and taut he might as well have been sucking on a lemon. He wasn't easy to draw and I soon gave up on him.

Instead, I turned to a magazine lying on the bed table. It didn't look like the type a teenage girl would read. In English the title was *Mrs. Lady*, and on the cover was an attractive, middle-aged Japanese woman dressed in a beige suit cradling a tiny Yorkshire terrier. The dog was in a blissful state, his eyes bright, his pink tongue dangling. It had to be one of Mrs. Kubota's magazines.

I began paging through it, noticing the ads for lipstick and perfume. They were mostly in Japanese, but English words and brand names occasionally popped out—Kanebo, modern, Shiseido, human life, Fendi, Gucci, youthful clinic! But the kanji was what fascinated me, the characters I'd been seeing all around that were impossible to decipher, the ones adding to my panic attack in Shinjuku Station, the ones Zoe could miraculously read. They were rendered in all different ways, from typeset to artistic, some resembling the characters that made up my name, others looking completely different. I copied a headline of an article I could only guess might have been about skin care, judging from the photographs of the attractive fortyish women—some Caucasian—rubbing cream on their faces.

Once I treated the characters as if they were little pictures instead of a kind of "alphabet," they were easier to draw. I couldn't stop and soon filled an entire page in my sketchbook. They didn't look too awful, but I was unsure how a Japanese person would judge them. It was still hard to fathom that they meant something as well.

When I finally had enough of my kanji practice, I reached in my purse for the photo I had made from the DVD of the man who could be my father. I stared at his eyes, his lips, his nose, at the same time touching my own, wondering where he was and what he was doing at that very moment.

"Shall we have an English lesson now?" I asked brightly. Since this was the service I was to provide in exchange for my homestay, I thought it better to start right away so as not to disappoint Mrs. Kubota.

"Yes! Please."

We were sitting at the dining-room table the morning following my arrival, the sun streaming through the window, both equipped with our respective Japanese-English and English-Japanese dictionaries.

"Let's begin with an interview," I said in a slow, clear voice.

I'd made my living as a writer and editor of English, but only in the technical realm, ensuring that terms like "Ethernet" were always capitalized and that "firewall" was spelled as one word. I'd never had to concern myself with helping a nonnative speaker become fluent, but I thought a question-and-answer format would at least facilitate some conversation and might get us better acquainted.

"Ask me a question and I will answer," I said.

Mrs. Kubota smiled, thinking for a moment. Then she closed her eyes and silently moved her lips. Upon opening her eyes, she said, "You . . . have . . . blood?"

Somehow I was expecting something a little more innocuous, more along the lines of what is your favorite color or where were you born? Her question stumped me. Could it have been that she was inquiring whether I still had menstrual periods? I might have been older than the other gaijin guests who'd stayed with the Kubotas in the past, but I hoped she realized that I was still far from menopausal. Had she strategically placed that copy of *Mrs. Lady* in my room? Perhaps I was overreacting. I put aside the possibility of such an insult and finally assumed this couldn't possibly be what she was asking. I gave her a smile, as if her inquiry was perfectly normal. "Are you asking me if I have blood?"

Her face flushed. "Not good," she muttered. "Just moment." She flipped through the pages of her dictionary. "*Ketsuekigata.* Blood type . . . blood type?" She uttered the phrase with hesitation, as if giving an answer on a quiz show, perhaps the one with her favorite gaijin panelist Trevor Templeton.

"Are you asking what my blood type is?"

"Yes!"

This wasn't as bad as a question about menstruation but almost as odd. "I'm type O."

Mrs. Kubota smiled. "I see."

"What is your blood type?"

"A," she said proudly. "I . . . am . . . A."

"Next question?"

Mrs. Kubota closed her eyes again. "You . . . no marry?"

Again, I would rather have been asked my preferred pizza topping. "No," I said under my breath. "I no marry. I mean, no, I've never been married."

"Have boyfriend-o?"

"No." Now, why did I say that? Didn't I have a boyfriend? I *guessed* that I did but just didn't want to get into it with her.

Mrs. Kubota's eyes popped. It was obviously a shocking confession, and now I wished I'd mentioned Dirk. She bowed her head, as if in sympathy. "I see."

"Next question?"

"How many brothers, sisters?"

"None. Zero. I am an only child."

"You . . . are . . . only . . . a . . . child."

I tried not to laugh—that would certainly have deflated any student's confidence. "No. When someone doesn't have any brothers or sisters, we say they are an only child. An only child."

"An only child." As she mentally formed her next question, her eyebrows furrowed. "Mother, father live California?"

Another overly complicated question. "No, they're both dead" was the easiest thing to say.

Her expression turned sad. "Dead," she said, and this pronouncement seemed to also deaden the conversation, putting an abrupt end to an only partially successful English lesson.

The sound of the phone ringing came to the rescue. Once Mrs. Kubota answered, she seemed so excited by her caller that it was almost as if she'd been contacted by the Japanese equivalent of Publishers Clearing House. All smiles, her eyes were as big as her Happy Afternoon Tea teacup saucers, her nods ebullient.

I considered leaving the room to allow her some privacy, but then it dawned on me that she probably realized that I couldn't understand a thing so that was rather pointless. I was paging through my dictionary when, a few moments later, Mrs. Kubota, her face shining, handed me the phone. Who would be calling me? Neither Dirk nor Zoe had the number. Was it Yukiko? I doubted it, and I couldn't imagine a call from her eliciting such an enthusiastic response. But, if not Yukiko, who else?

"Who is it?" I asked, feeling my face turn warm.

Mrs. Kubota grinned. "Takuya. My son. In Sunny Shokuhin. Seattle, Washington."

Takuya? From the famous Sunny Shokuhin? Why did *he* want to talk to me?

"*Moshi-moshi.*" I knew enough by now that this is what you said when you answered a Japanese telephone.

"Uh, hello? Celeste?"

"Takuya?"

"Is my mother driving you crazy yet?"

I laughed at his jocular candor. It sounded casual, more American than Japanese, and it didn't quite fit with the much-too-serious student in the family portrait in the living room. "No. No, she's very nice. I'm so grateful that she is letting me stay here."

"She is kind of nuts. I want to warn you."

I kind of agreed with him but wouldn't have dared to say that. "I'll take that into consideration."

He laughed. "Do not tell her I say this."

"Don't worry." I looked at Mrs. Kubota, standing frozen like a mannequin, her eyes bulging, a smile plastered across her face. I smiled back.

"I am coming home after two more Saturdays. I try not to get in your way," Takuya said.

"Well, thanks, but since this is your house, I think I'll try not to get in *your* way."

"Whatever. It is nice meeting you."

"Same here." I handed the phone back to Mrs. Kubota, who I could tell was wishing hard that she could have understood what we were talking about. "Such a nice son," I said to her.

She beamed, then spoke further to him in a bright, animated manner. When she finally hung up, her face was rosy from the excitement. "I . . . miss . . . Takuya," she said.

I nodded. "I'm sure you do."

"Gone long time. Not good."

"Well, he'll be home soon."

"Yes! Your homestay brother!"

Once again at the dining-room table I wondered if I should continue the English lesson, though the interview had largely been a failure. I decided in favor of a different idea.

"Let me show you something," I said to Mrs. Kubota. I went to my room and returned with Aunt Mitch's scrapbook. I turned the pages to the photo of me as a six-year-old dressed in a kimono and pointed to it. "Do you know who this is?"

She shook her head.

"It's me."

"*You?*" she exclaimed, as if deeming it impossible. "Wah! So cute! Like Japanese girl. Where . . . you . . . get . . . kimono?"

In the simplest English I could muster, and sprinkling in a few Japanese words courtesy of my dictionary, I explained to Mrs. Kubota about Aunt Mitch and how I was in Japan to try and find Hiromi Taniguchi to return her things and to ask about the man in the home movie. She seemed to understand about half the story.

I pointed to another picture. "This is my aunt Michiko and her sister. Hiromi Taniguchi. The one who lives in Kuyama."

"Ah!" Mrs. Kubota said, peering at the photograph. "So old picture."

"And here they are in around 1976," I went on. I had a photo made from one of the scenes with Hiromi and Michiko from the DVD. "I need to go there. To Kuyama. To find my relative."

"Kuyama?" She hurried to the living room, bringing back an atlas with a daunting, detailed map of Japan, dotted with hundreds of minuscule kanji.

After perusing it for several minutes, she pointed to the northernmost island of the four that made up Japan. "Kuyama. There," she said, smiling. "In Hokkaido. Far away."

My smile was wistful. "Yes. Far away."

"Gaijin! Gaijin!"

The afternoon was cool and cloudy when I was walking down one of Asahidai's main shopping streets and two little girls in matching straw hats, white blouses, and blue jumpers shouted out the obvious. But before I could greet them, they ran down a side street out of view, unable to suppress their giggles. I didn't know if they were laughing because this had been a regular gaijin sighting, or if their amusement was at the vision of me stuffed into a black jacket that barely made it around my hips and with sleeves that only reached past my elbows? All this and a slogan in bright red letters, Pretzel Club—For Active Gents!

Though Mrs. Kubota couldn't express it well in English, I could tell from her worried expression that once she realized I was preparing to go out, her concern was that I would either become lost or have some other calamity befall me. She wanted to come along, but I gently refused.

She pouted, then tugged at the collar of my thin coat. "Not good," she said, shaking her head. There seemed to be a number of "not good" things in her universe. She motioned for me to remove my coat, then carried it out of the room, perhaps to take it to the incinerator. She returned with the wool Pretzel jacket, which seemed to be her husband's, most likely a better fit than anything she could offer from her wardrobe.

Her other gaijin guests might have found her too overprotective, too hovering, but I rather liked her worry, her thoughtfulness. I assured her as best I could that I would return intact—Asahidai was no Shinjuku—and that I wouldn't be gone long, just enough to take a walk and get my bearings, maybe poke around in a few shops.

The town featured a mix of Japanese and Western architecture. A store made of dark-paneled wood, seeming to sell only rice, was a few doors down from a shiny Starbucks, which was across the street from a trendy salon called Cosmos Hair. The beauty parlor stood next to a booth where an old man was grilling yams to sell, giving the air a pleasant, smoky fragrance.

I walked down another block and came this close to bumping into a giant cardboard penguin with a bright yellow beak, standing at the entrance to a book shop. I had seen this penguin before but couldn't figure out why he looked so familiar. A brief flashback to the panic of Shinjuku Station gave me a wallop, and I realized this was the same penguin in the cartoon who had jumped into his bowl of noodle soup on the giant television screen on the Studio Alta building. It was like recognizing an old friend.

I entered the store with the small hope that perhaps they also sold books or magazines in English, but—no surprise—this was not the case. Everything was in Japanese, kanji was everywhere.

In the back corner I located a travel section, or what I figured must have been the travel section because of the plethora of book covers depicting trains, maps, the Golden Gate Bridge, the Taj Mahal, and the Grand Canyon. There had to be a book here that could tell me all the details on how to get to Kuyama, if I could only read it. Takuya's English had been so good during our short phone chat that the logical conclusion was that he would be the perfect person to help me. Yet I could not quite escape my role as foster child, where I didn't want to make trouble or impose on anyone for fear of losing my home base. I feared offending in a place where it seemed easy to be offensive. Besides, Takuya would be busy getting acclimated to living again in Tokyo and might not have the time. I could not rely on anything.

Understanding any of the books or magazines in the bookshop seemed to be a lost cause, but when I was about to leave, a group of words leaped out at me as if written in Shinjuku neon: Free Japanese Class. Ah, English! The small stack of pink flyers on the counter contained not one word of Japanese. There was a photograph of a young blond woman, winking and giving the "okay" sign, her thumb and index finger making a circle, her other three fingers sticking up. She could easily have been one of the gaijin *tarento* in Mrs. Kubota's photo album—she looked that goofy. I picked up one of the sheets and read that the class, taught by a person named Harris-sensei, was to start soon at a place called the Miyamae Cultural Center. From the hand-drawn map I could tell that it wasn't too far from the Kubota house.

It made no sense to have flyers in English for a Japanese class in a bookstore selling only Japanese books, but there was much in Japan that did not make sense. I was convinced, though, that things were turning for me. I could study with a teacher who would steer me in the right direction, who would maybe even be able to help me find Hiromi Taniguchi, or at least get me prepared for my journey.

I was practically skipping on the way home, a schoolgirl anxious to tell Mom about the latest exciting news.

7

STRANGE FOREIGNER

MRS. KUBOTA'S HUSBAND WAS SHORT AND SHY BUT AFFABLE, AND USUALLY didn't come home from work until at least eight o'clock in the evening. He too could barely speak English, but did not seem to possess the same burning passion for learning it as his wife. Mrs. Kubota dutifully served him dinner, which she and I always had earlier—the couple never ate together. Each evening after dinner Mr. Kubota left the house without fail. Did he go out to the bar? Play poker with the boys? Visit a lady "friend"? I only hoped that he wasn't a pachinko addict with designs on poisoning his spouse. But Mr. Kubota's whereabouts remained a mystery because none of these scenarios seemed to fit.

After dinner Mrs. Kubota watched television, and I watched with her, hoping to pick up a few morsels of Japanese until I could study properly at the free Japanese class.

Hen na Gaijin was not only one of the weirdest TV programs I'd ever seen but one of the most personally offensive as well. And it happened to be Mrs. Kubota's favorite. Looking it up in the dictionary, I found that *hen na* meant "strange" so the show's title translated to "Strange Foreigner." The program consisted of Japanese accosting gaijin on the streets of Tokyo, asking them seemingly embarrassing questions and filming them with hidden cameras anywhere from restaurants to public toilets. Gaijin were also invited to perform various stunts for the live studio audience, showing off their Japanese language and social skills. It appeared that at the same time as they were being lauded for acting Japanese and trying to fit into Japanese society, they were just as quickly ridiculed for it. The only thing I could compare it to was if my Milky Way Text coworkers, who had been so polite and admiring, had suddenly turned against me. The show seemed to be a cross between an amateur talent show and a perverted *Candid Camera*.

Young Japanese women made up most of the audience, and they'd react either by bursting into laughter or shouting "*Heyyyyyy?*" a sound or expression that seemed to denote almost painful incredulity. Another feature was the appearance of large dialogue balloons filled with kanji that occasionally popped up above someone's head, rendering the whole thing one big comic strip.

But the most striking aspect about *Hen na Gaijin* was the host. By now I had witnessed a number of perky Japanese women on television; in fact, except for a few serious newscasters and plain-faced comedians, a rabid cuteness seemed to be a prerequisite for allowing Japanese women to appear on TV. They reminded me of bright-eyed chipmunks the way they nodded their heads in assent every three seconds and blinked about as often.

But the host on *Hen na Gaijin* seemed to have no equal. In comparison to these other women she was the high priestess of perkiness. Her eyes would bug out, her mouth opened into a perfect O, and then she would let out with her own "*Heyyyyyy?*"

Sometimes she even uttered, "*Oh . . . my . . . God!*" in English with a not-too-shabby imitation of a Valley Girl accent. But more often she repeated a Japanese catchphrase that seemed to be her signature line. A giant cartoon balloon erupted over her head every time she said it. I was, of course, clueless as to what it meant.

Princess Perky also appeared to crack incessant jokes seemingly at the gaijin's expense but with an innocent look, causing the audience, as well as Mrs. Kubota, to go into hysterics. It was frustrating to understand so little. I didn't know why I cared about such a silly show, but for some reason a defensiveness rose up in me whenever I saw fellow gaijin being humiliated, no matter how imbecilic they appeared. It was painful to not be able to defend them and, in turn, to perhaps not be able to defend myself.

And not knowing what was being said, and the impossibility of receiving any meaningful translations from Mrs. Kubota, only added to my discomfort. But at the same time it fueled my perverse interest.

The host was always dressed in the most stylish outfits, showing off her willowy figure, the perfect blueprint of a young, radiant Japanese woman. But she struck me as supremely insufferable. Mrs. Kubota, though, had the very opposite reaction. "So cute, so nice," she always said. "So funny." And then she would giggle, her hand covering her mouth. I was tempted to say, "Not good, not good," but kept quiet. One time she pointed to the screen and said, "Takuya—he like!" Good Lord, I thought, was it Takuya's favorite program too?

One night after a viewing of *Hen na Gaijin,* where foreigners were forced to participate in an eating contest, chowing down on what Mrs. Kubota had said were hefty portions of fermented soy beans and sea urchin, she was flipping through the channels with the remote control when I heard something familiar.

"Wait!" I said, holding up my hand like a traffic cop.

Appearing on the screen was the same singer singing the same song I saw when I was watching TV in the lounge at the Gaijin Banana House. But this time, instead of a music video, she was performing live on a stage in front of a cherry blossom tree that must have been phony but looked remarkably realistic. I'd never forgotten the haunting melody and the emotion in the woman's voice and it seemed just as dramatic now. Again, she was dressed in a kimono but one with more vibrant colors, a pattern of purples and blues with a silver background. During one part of the song, she held up her fist, as if to demonstrate her sheer will and determination, her face twisted into a grimace. The lyrics displayed at the bottom of the screen, indecipherable to me.

"I really love this song," I said. I tried to hum along but didn't get very far. "My aunt Mitch used to sing songs like this."

"It is singer Maki Kanda. Song is '*Nozomi no Hoshi,*'" Mrs. Kubota said. She went for the dictionary. "'The . . . Wishing . . . Star.'"

"*The Wishing Star.*" I liked the sound of it. I watched, holding my breath, as Maki Kanda managed to deliver her last, big wavering note, the orchestra playing a crashing and dramatic finale. For a brief moment I saw myself on the same stage singing the same song.

"So beautiful," I murmured.

I turned when I heard the front door open and eyed Mr. Kubota, back from his mysterious outing. He greeted us, smiling. As usual he looked normal enough, neither drunk nor otherwise disheveled. Once he walked down the hall toward the bedroom, I got the courage to ask Mrs. Kubota where it was that he always disappeared to.

"Garage," she said, puffing out her cheeks in disapproval. Pointing at the front door, she seemed to be indicating that the garage was not attached to the house but was in a separate building, perhaps down the street. I knew that the Kubotas did not own a car and that the house had no garage, so it was puzzling as to why they were apparently renting or borrowing one.

"Garage?"

"Yes." Her demeanor was quick to change, as did the subject. "Soon!" she said, smiling. "You meet Takuya!"

FREE JAPANESE CLASS. PLEASE HERE.

This was the sign on the door that greeted me when I arrived at the Miyamae Cultural Center promptly at eleven o'clock on Wednesday morning. Walking inside, I found myself in an empty classroom—no teacher, no students.

I was curious about Harris-sensei, the instructor indicated on the flyer. Could this actually be a gaijin, perhaps one of the fluent guests on *Hen na Gaijin*? But I also supposed it could be a Japanese woman married to a foreigner.

As the minutes ticked by, I glanced around the room, which was devoid of any décor other than a faded world map tacked on the wall next to a chalkboard. Looking for the United States, I at first couldn't locate it. Then I realized why: on every map of the world I'd ever seen, the United States was placed in the middle, but here that spot was reserved for Japan.

After waiting almost fifteen minutes, I didn't know how much longer I should stay; perhaps this class was only a figment of someone's imagination. I was just about to look for a person to ask when a Japanese woman came rushing in, out of breath, her high heels clicking at a clipped pace.

"Sorry to be late," she said in good English with only a slight accent. She looked around, bewildered. "It's just *you?*"

"I'm afraid so."

"*Shit.* Are you fucking kidding?"

I was no prude, but somehow I didn't expect a Japanese teacher to have such a natural affinity for English profanity. "Are you Harris-sensei?" I asked.

"Yeah. But if it's going to be just you and me, you might as well call me Mariko."

Mariko looked about ten years younger than Mrs. Kubota. Her long, slightly wavy hair was almost black except for a slight auburn tint. And like most every Tokyo woman I'd observed, she was rail-thin and dressed to perfection, chic and stylish in bright mustard-yellow stiletto heels, tight-fitting black jeans, and a silver T-shirt peeking out from under a black leather jacket.

"I'm Celeste. Celeste Duncan."

"Okay." Mariko looked distracted as she ran her hands through her hair. She removed her jacket, casually tossing it on the chair next to her and said nothing further.

There was a long silence until I said, "So have you lived abroad? Your English is so good."

Now she seemed back in focus. "Yeah, I'm married to Frederick Harris. He's American, and we've been living in Cleveland for five years. Now he's teaching English at one of the universities here. We're back in Japan for now because my sister's been kind of sick."

"I'm sorry."

"*She'll be okay.*" Mariko said the words as if she had the ability to make it so. She became quiet, staring straight ahead, another pause in the proceedings, but then just as quickly snapped back. "But I can't see myself staying in Japan forever. I'm so like 'get me out of this crazy fucking place'!" She cackled. "So what the hell are *you* doing here?" Before I could answer, she scrunched her face as though she could smell the sewer backing up, then spit out, "And why do you want to learn *Japanese?*"

This seemed an odd take for a Japanese teacher, though I had to admit her forthrightness was refreshing and quite different from what I'd been encountering. But I was so taken aback that for a moment I myself questioned such an endeavor. There was also something about Mariko that put me on edge. The first thing to come out of my mouth was, "Ah . . . I'd like to understand the words to this song I've been hearing. It's by this woman, what is her name?" Now she'd think I was even more of a twerp for pursuing Japanese. "The song is called something like, '*Zonomi*' . . . ah, 'The Wishing Star'?"

Mariko pondered for a moment. "Oh! Maki Kanda? '*Nozomi no Hoshi*'?"

"That's it. I love that song," I said, hoping that maybe she did too. "Is there a name for that type of music?"

"Well, it's not my taste, but it's called *enka* and it's basically for the senior set. But I understand that there are younger singers like Maki Kanda who have made it a little more popular with young people than it used to be." She sniffed. "Sorry, but it just about puts me to sleep."

"No need to apologize."

"*Enka's* sort of like country music in the United States. Songs about yearning to go back to your hometown, losing your love, drinking too much sake, that kind of thing. Tearjerker stuff."

"*Nozomi no Hoshi*" and the songs Aunt Mitch had sung didn't resemble country music in the least to me, but I let that pass. "Or maybe you can help me figure out what they're saying on *Hen na Gaijin*."

Mariko's laugh came out like a honk. "Ah! You watch that crap?"

"It's Mrs. Kubota—she's the woman I'm homestaying with—it's her favorite show."

"Oh, that girl, that Sakura Sasaki is *so* annoying."

"What's her name again?" It was obvious that Mariko had watched such crap at least once.

"Sakura Sasaki."

I knew that *sakura* meant cherry blossom, but the name didn't match the *Hen na Gaijin* host, who appeared more Rottweiler than flower petal.

Mariko made a stab at Sakura's wide-eyed, open-mouthed expression. "*Ii kagen ni shite ne!*"

I couldn't help but laugh; it was a spot-on imitation. I clapped my hands. "That's it. That's what she always says. What does it mean?"

"Let me see. I guess, kind of, 'Give me a break, for God's sake.'" Mariko shook her head. "That girl is about the most obnoxious person on Japanese television and there are *plenty* of those."

"I know. I can't stand her either."

"Did you know she's *haafu?*" Mariko said.

"Haafu?"

"Half. Her father is Japanese and her mother is French, I think."

"Really? She looks Japanese to me."

"Yeah, she does, but not quite. Some people who are half look more Western and others look more Japanese. If you're half, you seem glamorous to Japanese people. Exotic. That's one reason she's so popular. There are lots of *tarento* who are half."

"No wonder Mrs. Kubota seems to worship the ground she walks on."

Mariko nodded but was off in her own world once more. I continued on about Mrs. Kubota, even relaying my unfortunate experience with the toilet slippers. It was such a pleasure to talk at a normal pace, with normal English, and have someone understand. I was tempted to kiss her feet.

"This Kubota-san sounds pretty uptight," Mariko said with a shrug.

I was on a roll. I went into my explanation about how I was in Japan to look for Hiromi Taniguchi, but by now Mariko had temporarily spaced out again and didn't seem to be listening.

She nervously glanced around the room, looked at her watch, then at the open door. "Well, it looks like no one else is going to show up."

"Does that mean the class is canceled?" Despite the rather unusual teacher, I hoped this wasn't the case.

"They pay me no matter what," she said. "I'm happy to give you a private lesson, but . . ." She leaned toward me and in a conspiratorial stage whisper said, "To tell you the truth, I'm starved."

I wasn't sure what she was getting at. Was she going to abandon today's lesson and run off on her own, or was she extending a lunch invitation?

Her eyes flashed. "I've been *dying* for some linguine with clams and a good glass of Chianti." She grabbed her coat and purse and looked into my face. "Shall we have lunch in Venice?"

Two train rides and a monorail later, I found myself not in Venice but in a reasonable facsimile. Mariko had brought me to an area of Tokyo that long ago was part of Tokyo Bay but was now landfilled and home to shopping malls, condos, and amusement parks.

We were in Venezia-Lando, an indoor mall depicting an Italian marketplace with a ceiling that looked uncannily like a real blue sky, resplendent with white fluffy clouds, where the "sun" rose and set every hour. Authentic gondoliers imported from Venice were outfitted in black-and-white-striped shirts and jaunty white straw hats with black bands. They rowed gondolas on the mall's canals, singing the Italian hit parade: *"Funiculì, Funiculà," "O sole mio," "Arrivederci Roma."*

At a restaurant called Oh! My Pasta, overlooking the canal, Mariko pointed to the wine list, then spoke to the Italian waiter. "*Castellare Chianti Classico, per favore.*"

"A beautiful wine for two beautiful ladies! *Ciao, bella. Utsukushii!*" the waiter replied.

He returned promptly with the bottle of wine and a basket of bread sticks. Soon I was indulging in pappardalle pasta with pancetta and Parmesan, putting to shame anything that could be had at Mama Corleone's Spaghetti Shack in Cupertino, but which also cost twice as much. I couldn't make this a habit.

"So who is this Kubota-san again who loves *Hen na Gaijin*? How do you know her?"

It was surprising to find Mariko asking about something she seemed to have lost interest in when we were back in the classroom. All she had talked about on the way to Venezia-Lando was her legendary research on the sexual performance differences she'd noticed between Japanese and American men, a mostly one-sided conversation I was unable to contribute much to.

I explained to Mariko about how I'd lost my job at Milky Way Text and found my way into the Kubota household, and again relayed the story about Hiromi Taniguchi and how she might know about the man on the DVD who could be my father. I wasn't fond of repeating myself, but it seemed to be the only way in dealing with Mariko. And with her excellent English I hoped that maybe she'd be willing to help me with my search.

"So you're looking for this woman? Your aunt?" she asked.

"Well, technically she's my great-aunt's younger sister."

"How are you planning to try and find her?"

"Well . . . I know the name of the place where she last lived."

I could hear the sound of rippling water. A gondolier floated by, his boat empty of passengers. He waved and smiled as if he knew us.

Mariko shouted something in Italian, a phrase that seemed to please the gondolier. He answered back, and soon they were engaged in a conversation peppered with bawdy laughter. I sunk back in my chair and stared at the water in the canal. There was something off about it, though I wasn't sure what. My ears filled with Mariko's raucous laughter, the gondolier's singsong voice, the sound of flirtation. I thought of Dirk. I looked again at the water. That's it, that's what's wrong, I thought. It's much too bright, more a toilet-bowl-cleaner blue. Gazing at the clouds moving across the ceiling like puffs of smoke, I wondered if Frederick Harris tolerated this kind of behavior in his wife or if he was kept in the dark. Finally the gondolier gave a big, enthusiastic wave and called out, "*Ciao!*" as he rowed away.

Mariko poured more Chianti into our glasses. "So where's that?" she said.

"Where's *what?*"

"Where's the place this aunt's sister last lived?"

"Oh. Kuyama. In Hokkaido."

"Do you have an address, a phone number?"

"No. I just know that she lived in the Higashi Arakawa district in the city of Kuyama. The family had a tofu shop there apparently."

Mariko cocked her head, a dubious expression on her face.

"I thought I would visit, see if she's still there, see what I can find out," I continued. "And hopefully be able to return Aunt Mitch's ashes." I told her more about the man in the old home movie who could be my father and how I wanted to ask Hiromi about him. "I'm not sure exactly how I'll get there and how I'll go about it, but . . ."

"Oh! I'll take you there!" That's what I hoped Mariko would say, but it didn't happen. Instead her skeptical look made me feel that I was having this conversation with Dirk, that I was nuts to have embarked on such an endeavor, since once you got down to the details, everything seemed so vague.

I took out the envelope with the photographs I carried in my purse. "This is my aunt Mitch and her sister Hiromi in 1949, and here's a picture from around 1976."

"A long time ago," she said. She fished out a clam with her fork, placed it delicately in her mouth, then dropped the shell into the bowl next to her plate, which was already brimming with discarded shells. "And you don't know any Japanese?"

I shook my head. Yes, Mariko, I am clueless about everything. That is why I signed up for your class, which may not even exist.

Mariko squinted. "Hiromi Taniguchi? That's a pretty common name." She sighed. "You don't have too much to go on."

Tell me something I don't know.

Mariko chased down the last bit of wine in her glass and wiped her mouth primly with her napkin. "So you quit your job, rented out your apartment and everything, and came all the way here just for *this?*"

My stomach lurched. Did she have any right to make that kind of remark? "Yes, I did," I said. "It's important to me. I don't have any family and it was kind of nice to all of a sudden find out that maybe I did. And it's possible I could learn about this guy who could be my father. And I felt I needed a break, to get away from San Jose, to get away from my boyfriend there, get a new perspective. . . ." I could hear the defensiveness in my voice.

She turned her gaze toward the canal, saying nothing.

As if on cue, another gondolier started up with "*Arrivederci Roma*" in a lush baritone. Yes, it was *arrivederci* time. It was time to leave. I had said too much and should have shut up much earlier. It would be best to give Mariko my half of the money I owed for lunch and then just get the hell out of this weird fake Italy. Yet there was one small glitch: I had no idea how to get back home. And jumping into a cab and telling the driver, "Asahidai," would likely incur a ride of two hours in crawling traffic, not to mention a fare of more than one hundred and fifty dollars.

Mariko turned back toward me, shaking her head slowly. "I'm afraid trying to find this person will be like looking for a goddamned haystack in a needle."

I took a deep breath, not bothering to correct her English. I was still mad, but deep down I knew she was right.

8

HYSTERIC ECHO

"THIS FOR YOU," MRS. KUBOTA SAID TO ME, BOWING HER HEAD SLIGHTLY. "*Dozo*. Please."

We were sitting at the kitchen table and I was eating the breakfast she always served me: a slice of toast cut thick as an English-Japanese dictionary, a bowl of Kellogg's Corn Flakes, and a cup of Fortnum and Mason English Breakfast Tea with a splash of milk. In my direction she gently pushed a small square package wrapped in light pink paper tied with brown straw ribbon.

Inside I found a CD with a picture of Maki Kanda, the singer of "*Nozomi no Hoshi*." The cover was completely white with a close-up of her face, so pale it almost blended in with the background. Only her dark eyes and red lips were visible. Her hand was outstretched and her mouth puckered as she blew on a dandelion she held between her fingertips.

"It is Maki Kanda songs," Mrs. Kubota said. "Also '*Nozomi no Hoshi*' on television we saw. You like that song."

"*Arigato!*" I replied, thanking her, also bowing my head in return.

She removed the booklet from the CD case where the lyrics were printed. "I write '*Nozomi no Hoshi*' for you. In *romaji*." She grabbed pen and paper and began to write the words in roman letters, pausing now and then to consider the spelling. Handing the paper to me, she said, "Now . . . you . . . can . . . sing!"

"*Sing?*" She had read my mind. I'd never told her that I sang.

"Yes. You learn. Then we go together—karaoke box!"

With the CD player in Rika's room I began to learn "*Nozomi no Hoshi.*" I had never sung a song in anything other than English, and with my minuscule knowledge of Japanese, it seemed daunting. But I did not want to just learn this song phonetically; I wanted to know its meaning. As I listened to Maki Kanda's emotion in her voice, it was clear how moving this song must be. But it was not easy to find all the words in the dictionary from looking at Mrs. Kubota's *romaji* sheet. The most I could get out of it was that a woman was looking at the sky, wishing on a star. I wished I could understand what she was wishing for.

I listened to the song and read along, first with the roman letters Mrs. Kubota transcribed, then with the kanji on the lyric sheet, alternating between the two.

Then I began to sing.

It was plain that I couldn't stop. I couldn't stop singing "*Nozomi no Hoshi.*" I sang it over and over until I was able to sing along while reading the kanji, without relying on the *romaji*. I was not truly reading it since by now I had just about memorized the words, but a few of the connections began to sink in, and sometimes a kanji reminded me of a word, and vice versa.

The more I sang, the more I became transformed, as if someone else were singing the song, someone fluent in Japanese. I didn't bumble with pronunciation like when I tried to speak. Instead, it was smooth, natural. But although I put in a lot of time to learn this song, I wasn't sure if the Japanese I could now sing so well was the kind that would help me find Hiromi Taniguchi.

The area around the Asahidai train station bustled with shoppers. "Sale," Mrs. Kubota explained, and shopkeepers announced bargains by shouting into bright orange bullhorns. Shrill voices sang over canned music, bleating from loudspeakers, adding to the cacophony. After Mrs. Kubota made her purchases, she scurried through the crowds to make her escape. By now my ears were ringing, and it wasn't easy to keep up with her; I had no idea as to our next destination.

After only a few blocks, the difference in atmosphere was striking. Instead of shopping chaos, an oasis of trees and benches lay ahead. Farther on was a big orange gate, which Mrs. Kubota called a *torii.* The shrine I could make out beyond it seemed to beckon to us. Already I was calm, my head cleared.

Our footsteps made a crunching noise as we walked along the gravel path. I took in the scent of sandalwood incense snaking through the air, blending with the sulfur smell emanating from the candles, which glowed golden in the shrine's altar.

Mrs. Kubota gathered four 100-yen coins from her purse and handed two to me. "First, pray for Takuya safe airplane. He come home soon." She walked up three steep steps to the altar and tossed the coins into a large wooden offering box that sat in front of it, the crisscrossing slats leaving room for the money to be deposited. She clapped her hands twice, closed her eyes, and bowed her head. "*Dozo,* please," she said to me.

I imitated what she had done.

Mrs. Kubota then took out a few more coins from her wallet. "Now pray to finding Hiromi Taniguchi-san."

My heart lifted to hear that she had remembered Aunt Mitch's sister's name and the reason why I'd come to Japan. And I knew there was no way *she* would tell me that searching for Hiromi Taniguchi was like looking for a goddamned haystack in a needle.

After the second prayer, we stood in silence, the only sounds the chirping of birds and their flapping wings as they flitted from tree to tree, picking at berries. I thought hard but concluded that these were my only prayers for now. Still, I didn't want to let go of the serenity so I closed my eyes again, taking in the peacefulness. I could have stayed at the shrine forever wrapped in such quiet calm, letting go of my concerns, living only for the moment.

But Mrs. Kubota broke the tranquility with her cheery, excited voice. "Now! Hysteric Echo!"

After walking a few short blocks toward a different shopping area, we reached the Hysteric Echo karaoke box, a bright yellow building topped with an oversized sign of a red parrot holding a microphone, sitting alongside the Joyful family restaurant.

Mrs. Kubota paid the young woman at the reception desk, who then led us down a hallway consisting of small cubicles with doors that could be mistaken for the entry to some cramped rabbit warren of an office space like Milky Way Text. The attempts at singing from behind the closed doors could only be described as the groaning of cows in heat.

The young woman brought us to a room marked "17." The lighting was dim, and the "box" was about the size of the bathroom in my studio apartment back home. The minute I walked in, I was overcome by the smell of old beer and stale cigarette smoke. There were two small couches placed perpendicular to each other, a large TV screen attached to the wall, and what looked like a DVD player in the corner. A forlorn disco ball, some of its tiny mirrors either chipped or missing, hung from the ceiling. Three binders, two remote controls, and three microphones sat on a low black table.

Mrs. Kubota was quick to take off her jacket and placed her purse on one of the sofas. As we sat together on the other couch, I could sense her excitement. Paging through one of the binders—thick with lists of song titles, artists' names, and selection numbers—she pointed to an entry, then took one of the remote controls and pressed a few buttons. Seconds later I jumped when I heard a big booming sound: the opening introduction to "*Nozomi no Hoshi*." A video of a young woman began to play, her expression wistful as she gazed at the sky.

Once Mrs. Kubota handed me the microphone I became aware of my nerves. Just the thought of singing in a foreign language in front of someone who had never heard me before gave me an adrenaline rush. This felt like a performance, despite its being only the two of us in a box, and I suddenly heard Dirk's voice in my head: *Can't you hear that, Celeste? You're off. You're off by a half step.* I tried to shut it out.

Once I began singing, my voice seemed much too loud. I followed the kanji on the screen, as I did during my practice sessions in my room. My nervousness did not waver and I attempted to block out the sight of Mrs. Kubota whom I could see from the corner of my eye. Finally the instrumental interlude came on and I stopped. Mrs. Kubota broke into furious applause and by the end of the song was giving me a standing ovation. Her reaction stunned me.

"So nice!" she said. "So nice! I do not believe."

I had never enjoyed singing a song so much, and it was both overwhelming and a welcome change to receive such encouragement. But I figured Mrs. Kubota's reaction, in addition to the usual praise that was forthcoming, must have been due to the power of the unusual spectacle of a Caucasian strawberry blonde singing in Japanese. It was one of the attributes that constituted a *hen na gaijin,* which must have both bewildered and fascinated at the same time.

Mrs. Kubota's song choices were all in English. First she sang about having only just begun, with white lace and promises, kissing for luck, and being on her way. Then she moved on to tomorrow; she loved tomorrow, and it was only a day away. After her warbly rendition of what I first mistook as "Moon Liver," Mrs. Kubota asked, "What mean 'huckleberry friend-o'?" I told her I had no clue.

She convinced me to sing "Raindrops Keep Falling on My Head" and "My Way," both of which I could fake only so far. I foolishly glanced for the names of the tunes that I'd been practicing with Dirk. Instead, I picked "Walk Like an Egyptian," a song popular when I was in high school, and then I was encouraged to give an encore performance of "*Nozomi no Hoshi.*" I was glad to have another chance to sing it: how freeing it was to perform without any pressure or criticism.

Mrs. Kubota was just as enthusiastic. "Nice feeling," she gushed. "Nice feeling. Your singing Japanese."

"Will *you* sing a Japanese song?"

It seemed odd that such a request would give Mrs. Kubota pause, but it did. She ended up choosing a song even I could partly sing along to since it had a fair amount of English lyrics mixed with Japanese, an insipid disco number called "Cinderella Boogie-Woogie."

Next up was "Yokohama Twilight," or rather, "Yokohama Twilight-o." "This song comes when Takuya is baby," Mrs. Kubota said, smiling. While performing her other songs, she had been sitting down, but now she was suddenly possessed to stand. I watched, fascinated, as she started to make intricate movements with her left hand, then her right, which went along with the rhythm of the song—a Japanese version of "The Hokey Pokey."

I jumped up and, standing next to her, tried to copy her gestures. Soon we were roughly in synch, as though giving a performance—perhaps an act that could have gotten booked at the Miyamae Cultural Center's annual talent show. I couldn't help but snap my fingers and sway my hips. All of these songs had been absolutely infectious, and when the bouncy tune faded, we looked at each other and flopped on the couch, laughing uncontrollably, our shoulders touching. Mrs. Kubota dabbed at her eyes with her handkerchief, as our laughter died down.

"*Kubota-san, wa jozu desu ne,*" I said slowly, remembering a phrase Mariko taught me, which was how to say someone was good at something.

Mrs. Kubota blushed. "Not good, Kubota-san," she said.

I didn't understand. "Not good, Kubota-san?"

She pointed to her nose. "Call me *Okaasan*."

"*Okaasan?*"

Mrs. Kubota smiled. "Mother."

"Oh!"

I didn't want to make a scene but wondered if the catch in my throat, the moistness in my eyes, were noticeable.

"*Okaasan*," I said softly.

We sang and danced for the rest of the afternoon.

9

A FIANCÉE

AT MY NEXT FEW JAPANESE LESSONS WITH MARIKO, I WAS STILL THE ONLY student, and instead of traveling to Venice, we remained in the classroom, where she had been instructing me on a number of phrases: "How do you do?" "I am well, thank you." "The weather is nice today." "I would like to order your best Chianti." "My, that is the biggest penis I have ever seen."

I couldn't believe what I was learning from this woman, and when I protested and asked for something more practical, Mariko clucked that what she was teaching *was* practical and you never knew when such phrases would come in handy. I figured that the folks at the Miyamae Cultural Center would be shocked if they knew of the questionable content of the class and, in typical Japanese uptightness, might even have Mariko fired; I wondered if it was time to start looking for another teacher.

When the lesson was over, Mariko reached for a piece of paper in her purse. "This is for you," she said, handing it to me. "This is how you would get to Kuyama from here and how much a ticket would cost. I looked up the train timetables. You have to ride three trains and it would take about five and a half hours, but it's doable."

Mariko's consideration both touched and surprised me, since she had been so skeptical about my finding Hiromi Taniguchi at our Oh! My Pasta lunch. Now a feeling of guilt crept in for thinking about switching teachers. Yes, maybe someday I'd be lucky enough to find it useful to know that penis phrase. I never knew quite how to take Mariko, but there was something about her I found appealing.

"Thank you so much, Mariko-san. *Domo arigato.*"

"And I wrote down information on places where you could stay. I looked it up in a guidebook."

It was obvious that she had gone to a lot of trouble, and it would have been too much to ask another favor, if she would be willing to travel with me to Kuyama and help with translation. Mariko would have been far from the ideal traveling companion, though the trip would definitely not be dull. But it wasn't as if I had a whole lot of choices. No offer, though, was forthcoming.

"I really appreciate this," I said, placing the paper in my purse. "Oh, I almost forgot. There's something I wanted to ask you. Mrs. Kubota's son is coming home this Saturday after two years in Seattle—"

"Who is this exactly?" she interrupted.

"Takuya Kubota. Mrs. Kubota's son. The woman I'm homestaying with."

"How old is he?"

"Twenty-eight."

Mariko raised her eyebrows. "So he's going to be *living* there?"

"I guess so. It *is* his house."

She put her hand on her chest and looked at me with batting eyes that almost rivaled those of *Hen na Gaijin* host Sakura Sasaki. "Oh!"

I frowned. "What's that supposed to mean?"

"It means whatever the hell you want it to mean."

I still was not sure what she was getting at, and I didn't understand her exaggerated excitement concerning Takuya. "Anyway, can you teach me a phrase that means something like, 'Nice to meet you and welcome home'?"

"Sure."

Mariko pondered for a moment and wrote it down. "This should do it." She advised me on the correct pronunciation, then sent me off. Speaking Japanese was still so different from singing it, and on the way home I repeated the phrase many times to make sure I could say it as naturally as possible, hoping to make a good impression.

I *was* able to say the phrase as naturally as possible, but I did not make a good impression, at least not with Mrs. Kubota. A marriage proposal from me to her only son, no matter how inadvertent, somehow did not agree with her.

Seattle, however, seemed to have agreed with Takuya; he exhibited none of the Japanese mannerisms I'd been noticing—the pointing at the nose to refer to oneself, the constant nodding of the head in agreement when someone else was talking, the general hesitation to express an opinion. Of course I suspected that Mariko had shaken these off too from living in Cleveland for five years, but so far Takuya hadn't demonstrated any of her American crassness, overbearing personality, or ease with swear words. Nor her perverse sense of humor. And somehow I didn't expect that he would.

After dinner was over and Mr. and Mrs. Kubota went to bed (Mr. Kubota did not go to his "garage" on this special welcome-home evening for his son), I sat with Takuya in the living room.

"Aren't you exhausted?" I asked.

"Not yet. But I am sure I will feel the jet sag soon."

"Jet sag? I think you mean jet *lag*."

"My English—so terrible. Even though I am in Seattle two years," he said.

"Don't say that. Your English is very good. So are you excited to be home?"

"No and yes. I liked to being in Seattle, but I missed Japan too."

"What kind of work do you do at Sunny Shokuhin?" I couldn't help but bombard him with questions; I wanted to know everything about him.

He laughed. "How do you know name of my company?"

"Your mother told me."

Rolling his eyes, he said, "My mother? Does she tell you all my secrets?"

"You tell your secrets to your mother?"

"Not really. It is joke."

His poker face was deceiving, but it made me laugh. "Ah. Well, I felt bad because I'd never heard of Sunny Shokuhin, but I didn't say that to your mom. Is it a big company in Japan?"

"Yeah, it is famous company. A secure place for working."

"What's your job?"

"I am *hi-ra-sha-in*." He pronounced each syllable clearly so I could understand. "That mean kind of general employee, at least for now," he continued. "They make me do little bit of everything. In Seattle I was manager of Curry Zone chain restaurant. They just opened."

"Curry? Isn't that an Indian food?"

"Yeah, but Japanese adapted it long time ago and it very popular. You eat with rice—*karee raisu*, they call it. I will have to take you to the Curry Zone here so you can try."

"I'd like that." The idea of eating curry rice with Takuya caused the little hairs on the back of my neck to stand up. I wondered if I was blushing, if I looked like an inexperienced teenager.

"Are you student?" he asked. "Here for to study Japanese?"

I was at first flattered that he thought I looked young enough to be a student, but then who else but a student was usually a homestay guest? I told him no and gave him a brief explanation about Aunt Mitch, Hiromi Taniguchi, Milky Way Text, and Yukiko introducing me to his mother. It was like a release to be able to tell him everything, and my first time to feel truly comfortable with someone since I'd set foot in Japan. It was different from being with Mariko, who usually dominated the conversation and then seemed to space out when I tried to make my point. And it was different from Yukiko and the Milky Way Text crew or Mrs. Kubota, who could barely express their thoughts in English.

"You know, there is one thing I wanted to ask you," I said. "Your mother asked me a strange question."

He raised his eyebrows. "Question?"

I explained how she'd inquired about my blood type.

"She ask that? I guess she was scoping you out."

I wasn't sure what he meant by this, but before I could answer, he went on to explain that some Japanese believed that people's personalities are tied to their blood type. I wasn't about to tell him what I first thought she might be snooping about.

"So what is it?" he asked.

"What?"

"Your blood type."

"O. What's yours?"

"A."

"So what does that mean?"

He laughed. "I do not know."

As he stood up, I gazed at that lanky frame, the long legs.

"Do you want a beer or something?" he asked. He went to the kitchen and returned with two bottles of Kirin and two glasses.

"There are lots of things that are part of the Japanese culture. Kind of—how do you say? Superstitions?" he continued, pouring my beer than his. "Like writing your wish on a piece of paper at the temple and tying it to wishing tree."

"Wishing tree?"

"Yes. And there is also the animal for the year you are born—I was born in Year of Monkey," he said.

To my relief he seemed too polite to ask about my birth year.

He sipped his beer, closing his eyes for a moment, taking in the flavor. "So you are here for searching your aunt's sister?"

I nodded, taking a sip.

"Where is she?"

"Kuyama. In Hokkaido. At least that is where she was."

He paused as if he was thinking hard. "Mmm. I have never heard of Kuyama, but part of my territory before I left was in Hokkaido."

"Territory?"

"Yeah. I had to sell the curry powder to grocery stores all over Japan."

"That sounds interesting."

"It is not interesting."

"I mean, at least you got to travel."

His look was dubious. "Maybe. Have you planned your trip?"

I told him how Mariko had done some research and given me details on how to travel to Kuyama and where to stay. "But I think I need to wait and get a little better at Japanese before I go."

"You need a translator."

"Maybe so." Would you be willing? I wanted to say but stopped myself. It was too much to ask him when he hadn't even been home for a day.

"I do not want to think what time it is in Seattle now." Takuya looked at the clock with the cat's face and yawned. "I am hungry, but I also feel suddenly to be wanting to sleep." He smiled wearily. "I am sorry to be rude, Celeste, but I think I am going to bed now."

"Well, thanks for talking. I'm sorry if I babbled on and kept you up too long—it just feels really good to speak English with someone so fluent."

He looked pleased but embarrassed at my compliment, a sweetness that became him. "Thank you. It has been my pleasure." He gave me a serious look. "It important that my fiancée and I can speak the same language."

His fiancée? What was he saying?

He gave a slight pout in response to my puzzled expression. "Did you forget already that you ask me to marry you?" he asked.

The back of my head turned prickly, my face flushing. "I guess I didn't realize that you had accepted my proposal."

His eyes grew large, his smile playful. Then his laughter filled the room.

10

JAPANESE BREAKFAST

I AWAKENED THE NEXT MORNING STILL BOTHERED BY MRS. KUBOTA'S FROSTY reaction to my unintentional proposal of marriage to her only son. Should I feel offended? Embarrassed? Hurt? I guessed that I felt a bit of each. But I also woke with the remnants of a memory that at first I thought was left over from a dream but realized had actually happened. I hadn't thought about it for years.

I had just turned thirteen and was living with Irma and Kenneth Kruikshank when a foster child named Jason Fullerton came to live in the household. He was fourteen and had been taken away from his mother whose cocaine addiction made it impossible for her to care for him. Jason's downward-turned eyes were a deep brown, his hair dark, long, and smooth. Looking at his profile made me think of Matt Dillon, my major movie star crush at the time. There were three other foster girls in the house along with the Kruikshank's pudgy fourteen-year-old daughter Melody, but it seemed that Celeste Duncan had captured Jason's attention.

Irma Kruikshank was always scolding us for our tickle fights and for running around the house laughing and making too much noise. Kenneth Kruikshank worked nights as a machinist in a factory in Alviso so he slept during the day; his wife was always trying to keep the house quiet. One day after a tickling session on the couch in the family room downstairs, I was catching my breath and getting over my giggles when Jason began to kiss me. He'd never done this before. And these were not regular smacking kisses like those I'd shared with Hector Veracruz in the fifth grade; these were the kind where a tongue was being stuck in your mouth.

At first I was grossed out, then a little scared, but soon enough I started to enjoy the feeling and liked it even more when I moved my tongue along with Jason's. Pretending to be kissing Matt Dillon made it even more exciting. The next thing I knew Jason was pushing me back gently on the sofa and kept kissing me, his hand stroking my breast.

An electric shock seemed to whiz through my body, something frightening but thrilling too. I wrapped my arms around his waist as he lay on top of me, breathing hard and rubbing himself in a continuous rhythm against my body. He was thin and about the same height as me so he felt light and feathery. I took in the scent of lemon soap mixed with the sweat on his neck.

Now I was moving too—my legs spread, entangled around his.

"Celeste! Jason!"

We froze at the sound of Irma Kruikshank's voice, the squealing of a car's brakes right before impact. Jason leaped off me as if my clothes had suddenly caught fire. There was a stern lecture, cold stares at dinner, and a meeting the next morning with me, Irma Kruikshank, and the social worker at the Santa Clara County Social Services office. Jason was already gone by the time we got home—I never learned where he ended up. And by the following week I was living in the yellow-and-white house on Julian Street, the one with the cracked front steps and the rusting chain-link fence, owned by the foster couple who insisted on being called Mr. and Mrs. Cavanaugh.

It was a long time before I let another boy kiss me.

I gazed at the poster of the four young men called SMAP tacked on the mauve wall in my Tokyo teenage-girl room. They stared back at me, looking even more aloof and uninterested than I remembered. But in the same instant a pleasant surge of anticipation caused me to forget all about Jason Fullerton and my extradition to the Cavanaughs. It was as if I had something to look forward to and I did; today was another day I would have the chance to see Takuya. But should I have been feeling guilty about this? I did have a sort of boyfriend back home. What-was-his-name, again?

But there was still the matter of ensuring a lasting peace with Mrs. Kubota. I wasn't sure how to make it up to her, but then I came up with the idea of presenting her with a sketch I drew of the Japanese maples in front of the house. It would at least be a gesture of apology, of good faith.

I put on a big smile, like those of her gaijin scrapbook mates. Then in a cheery voice I greeted her and Takuya at the kitchen table by saying, "*Ohayo gozaimasu*," which I knew was the correct way to say "good morning," and not in reality the equivalent of "Please lather me in hot oil and massage my quivering body."

They returned the greeting and then I bowed my head, saying, "*Okaasan, sumimasen*," and apologized again to Mrs. Kubota in the only way I knew how. I caught a glance from Takuya, who, with a whiskery face, looked even sexier. "I want her to know that I didn't realize what I was saying last night. But I know it upset her and I'm sorry."

"She understand it mistake. But she was surprised." Takuya laughed. He still didn't seem to take it as seriously as I did, but I was the one who had been on the receiving end of the icy glares from his mother at the dinner table.

"I want to give you this." I handed Mrs. Kubota the drawing.

She seemed confused at first, but then her eyes turned bright. "*Maa!* You make?"

I nodded, smiling. "For you. *Dozo*."

She showed the drawing to Takuya and said something in Japanese.

"You are artist?" he asked.

"Not really."

"It is very good." He spoke to his mother. "She is very impressed," he said to me.

"It is the maple trees in the front yard," I explained to Mrs. Kubota.

"Yes! Yes!" she replied, placing the drawing carefully next to her cereal bowl. "Thank you!" She was beaming, and once more, to my relief, everything seemed to be all right.

That is, until I took my chair at the breakfast table and my eyes fixed on something that was all wrong. Missing were my usual cereal and toast. In their place sat a black lacquer box divided into compartments. Purple and pink pickles were tucked into one, a mound of white rice topped with a sprinkling of black sesame seeds in another. Alongside the box was a bowl of miso soup. But the main course, the showcase, concerned me the most: a piece of grilled fish, its silver-and-black skin glistening in the light.

Its tail was intact, but mercifully the head had been lopped off. It shared its space with a garnish of shredded white radish.

Fish for breakfast? Was this some kind of punishment for last night? Some kind of passive-aggressive behavior from my homestay mother?

The identical meal sat in front of Takuya and he seemed to only be picking at it.

"Japanese breakfast, okay?" Mrs. Kubota asked me with a smile that may or may not have been construed as slightly sinister.

"Yes," I said, trying to smile back, despite the queasiness overtaking my stomach and my sudden lack of appetite. "Do you always eat a Japanese breakfast?" I asked Takuya. "Usually your mom gives me cereal and toast."

"I never eat this," he said. "It is part of her 'welcome home' strategy. But you can ask her for cereal and toast, if you do not like this."

"No, no. It's fine. It looks delicious," I lied. The last thing I wanted was for Takuya to think of me as some stick-in-the-mud, unadventurous American who found Japanese breakfasts just short of repulsive. And I didn't want to be rude to Mrs. Kubota by refusing the meal, and risk yet another misunderstanding.

I bucked up my courage and imitated Takuya, taking a taste of fish, then alternating it with bites of radish doused with a lemony soy sauce, then a mouthful of rice. It was actually delicious, amazingly delicious. The fish skin was crispy with a salty taste that complemented the citrus flavor of the sauce. In the soup bowl little white blocks of silken tofu and scallion rings swirled in the reddish-brown broth, warming my body as the small black lacquer bowl warmed my hands.

"*Oishii*," I said to Mrs. Kubota. "Very good. *Domo arigato*."

"*Ah so?*" Mrs. Kubota said, raising her eyebrows. "You like?"

Was there a hint of disappointment in her tone? That I hadn't taken to gagging, then begging for my Kellogg's Corn Flakes? I wasn't sure, but how illuminating to discover that eating fish and pickles for breakfast now seemed more appealing than bacon and pancakes.

I considered not telling Mariko anything about the reaction to her "welcome home" phrase. I could act as if nothing had happened, which would possibly drive her crazy.

But by the time of the next class I was still not over my irritation with her and couldn't keep my mouth shut. Without even a hello, the first thing I said when I walked into the classroom was, "Why did you have me ask Takuya to marry him?"

Mariko burst out with her honking laugh. "That was pretty funny, wasn't it?"

"No, it wasn't. It was actually pretty embarrassing and it upset Mrs. Kubota."

"Tsk-tsk," Mariko said. "Why does this Kubota-san sound to me like she's always walking around acting like she's got something stuck up her butt?"

I considered this and had to admit that she had a point, though I refused to concur.

"But it must have broken the ice, didn't it?" Mariko was grinning.

"I didn't need to have any ice broken."

"So how did Takuya react?"

"He was laughing."

"See? Didn't it kind of lighten things up?"

I sighed. Mariko was sort of right, but I didn't want to give her the satisfaction of agreeing. In her own strange, perverted way, she must have thought she was helping. She obviously wasn't going to apologize. "So what I want to know is, how can I ever trust what you teach me?"

"Well, you can trust this," she said, handing me a book called *Fun with Learning Japanese*. The cover was of a long-eared, blue-and-white-striped cartoon rabbit playing with building blocks painted with Japanese characters. Instead of how to order wine and comment on male genitalia, it looked as though I'd be learning vocabulary appropriate for Japanese kindergartners. It was hard to know which was preferable.

"Take this home. We'll use this as a textbook from now on. There's nothing in here that will upset Kubota-san," Mariko said.

"How much do I owe you?"

She smiled. "It's on me." But then her smile disappeared and she started gathering her things.

Another canceled lesson? Why did I come all the way here? Her flakiness annoyed me and I didn't know why I put up with it.

She looked at her watch. "Sorry! I have to go visit my sister. She's in the hospital now."

Her sister. The guilt kicked in, and I chastised myself for my thoughts. "Take care," I said.

The next thing I knew she was out the door, nearly tripping over her high heels.

That night I was sitting at the dining-room table, practicing more kanji from *Mrs. Lady*. It was a plain fact that I had become a certified kanji addict. By now I had pages and pages in my sketchbook filled with characters. Mrs. Kubota had long since gone to bed, and at around ten thirty, Mr. Kubota returned from his garage outing.

"What the hell is it that you do every night in secret?" I wanted to ask him, but it just wasn't possible. Instead, I said good evening in Japanese and he smiled, returning the greeting. He glanced at my pages of kanji but didn't say anything, though I was sure he thought of me as a typical *hen na gaijin,* someone out of her mind.

Mr. Kubota pressed his hands together, cocked his head and held his hands against his cheek. "Sleep," he said.

"Yes, sleep." I nodded and said good night. He walked down the hall, taking his secret with him. I thought how I must ask Takuya about it the next time I saw him.

Takuya hadn't been around too much, which was a disappointment. I occasionally bumped into him, but he seemed busy reacquainting himself with friends and was out a lot of the time. It wasn't clear whether he'd gone back to work yet. Everything was vague as usual, as though I were nearsighted and had lost my glasses, trying hard to make the best with blurry images. But I figured his business was none of mine.

And my business was not much of Dirk's. Although I had pangs of guilt from time to time, all I did was write him a brief postcard (as opposed to a two-page letter to Zoe), one with a picture of the cherry trees blooming in Ueno Park, telling him how well things were going with my search, how great my job was—in other words, two big, fat lies. Things were also vague in this department; one moment I was thinking I had a boyfriend back home and the next thing I'd feel was that we'd already broken up.

I was startled but pleasantly surprised when, in the midst of my kanji practice, Takuya walked in the door. His face was a bit red and I wondered if he'd been out drinking. He looked as attractive as ever, his jeans molded perfectly to his legs. His hair was windblown, and my first reaction was to want to smooth it back into place with my hands.

He smiled. "How are you, Celeste-san?"

"I am fine, Takuya-san. How are you?"

"I am well."

We had just completed dialogue one from *Let's Learn English!*

He sat in the chair across from mine and looked at my kanji pages with great interest. "You are writing kanji?"

I'd been rather proud of my attempts but was now embarrassed; I knew my characters looked like the work of a rank beginner, an accurate description. "Yeah, but I really don't know what I'm doing."

"Can I read?"

I passed the sketchbook to him, explaining how I'd been copying kanji randomly from *Mrs. Lady*, trying to draw characters that caught my interest.

He nodded, then turned to my latest page where I'd been writing a headline over and over that I found in the magazine; each an attempt at making the shape of the characters as much like the original as possible.

"Why are you writing *this?*" he asked. His tone implied that I was teetering on the brink of insanity.

"I saw it here," I said, pointing to the large characters next to a picture of a middle-aged woman, pressing her index finger to her cheek, as if she were pondering something of great importance. "I just liked the way these kanji looked, their shape," I explained. I'd written these series of characters—**更年期障害**—about fifty times across the page.

He began to laugh.

"What is it?"

"Do you know what this says?"

"No, Takuya, of course I don't."

"Ah . . . I do not know one of the words in English." He went to the bookshelf and located a dictionary, unable to stop laughing. "I do not think you must be so interested for this."

"Well, what does it say?"

"Problems of . . . ," he said, turning the pages of the dictionary. "Um, problems of menopause."

"*What?*"

"This magazine for women the age of my mother, you know." He cracked up again.

"Oh, God. I can't believe it." Once more the topic had come up.

"But you are writing other kanji too. And they look nice."

"Really? You aren't just saying that?"

"Yes, I am saying it."

"I mean, you are telling the truth?"

He looked baffled. "You are artist. You draw the kanji like a picture. It very interesting. The shape and style looks good. But you need something"—he returned to the bookshelf, taking a few moments to look—"I am remembering that." He pulled a thick red book from the shelf. "This is kanji dictionary. In English. I think one of my mother's homestay people forget to take."

The book was thick and heavy, probably a thousand pages long, and definitely not the kind of extra weight you'd want to pack in your suitcase.

"You can find out what the kanji means. But I can also tell you if you ask," he said.

"I've noticed that some of the kanji have the same parts. Is this right?"

He thought for a moment. "That is true."

"Like this one and this one," I said, pointing to 花 and 英. They have the same symbol on top."

"Yes, you are right. Let me show you."

Takuya began to tell me about the three Japanese writing systems. There were *hiragana* and *katakana,* which were phonetic. *Katakana* was the type I used to write my name because it was considered a foreign word. *Hiragana,* he explained, was used for certain words that didn't have kanji, and sometimes for the ends of verbs; he apologized that he couldn't describe it well in English. But the main writing system was kanji and you had to know about three thousand characters and all of their combinations to consider yourself literate in Japanese.

To look up a particular kanji, he said, you first had to figure out its *bushu,* or "radical," which was the main part of the character. Usually it was on the left side, the top, or the bottom. But the kanji could fool you, and what you thought was the radical really wasn't.

For 花 and 英, the part on top was the "grass" radical, the symbol they both had in common. I guessed if you looked at it in a certain way it resembled a couple of blades of grass.

Once you found the radical you had to count the number of strokes it took to write, then look it up on the radical chart in the dictionary. The grass radical was three strokes and I found the section for it. Then Takuya explained that for 花 I had to count the strokes that made up the rest of the character, which added up to four. It was important to count the number of strokes accurately; if you counted three or five, you wouldn't be able to find it.

I found the character 花 was *hana,* which meant "flower," under the four-stroke section of the grass radical. I was also able to find the other character 英, *ei,* under the five-strokes section. It translated to "English."

To have the code cracked, so to speak, was exhilarating. "That's not too bad," I said. "I thought it would be much more difficult."

"Unfortunately, it not always so easy," he said. "This just tip of the ice cube."

Now it was my turn to laugh. "I think you mean tip of the iceberg."

He pouted. "You never understand my joke."

"Ah! Sorry. Thanks for all your help."

"It is not problem. Good night."

I watched him walk down the hall, taking in his slim hips, his confident steps. And I realized I'd forgotten—forgotten all about asking him where his father disappeared to every night.

A little while later as I passed Takuya's room down the hallway on the way to my room, I heard a voice. I stopped and realized it was his, coming from behind his closed door. I knew I shouldn't, but I leaned in close anyway. He seemed to be talking on the phone, sounding urgent, emotional, a tone I'd never heard out of him. It could have even been some kind of argument. Who would he be calling at such a late hour? The sound was muffled so I couldn't understand exactly what was being said, but I could tell one thing: he was speaking in English.

11

PEGGY SUE

"CELESTE-SAN! COME, COME!"

The urgency in both Mrs. Kubota's voice and her knocking on my bedroom door led me to think, what had I done now? It was around ten o'clock in the morning and I had just emerged from the shower and was starting to get dressed.

I threw on my sweater and opened the door.

"Come! My friends!" she said.

"Your friends?"

"Waiting."

I told her I'd be right there, once I finished drying my hair, but I was without a clue as to what she was talking about. I couldn't recall her mentioning any visit I was supposed to be a part of. I hurried as best I could, trying to make myself presentable. As I walked down the hall, I heard the sound of women's voices coming from the living room. Once there, I saw Mrs. Kubota perched on the La-Z-Boy and two ladies around her age sitting on the sofa. They all stopped talking and stared at me, as if a celebrity or perhaps a kangaroo had arrived.

"Celeste-san!" Mrs. Kubota exclaimed, the pride obvious in her voice, the tone reserved for when she was talking about her son's employment with Sunny Shokuhin. "Homestay daughter!"

One of the ladies was decked out in a bright floral jacket, a little more garish than usual for a fiftyish Japanese woman, at least from my observations. She sat in a stiff, upright posture and cleared her throat. "I . . . am . . . Yasuda," she said slowly, seemingly in great pain. She cocked her head, frowning, as if speaking in English gave her a migraine. Mrs. Kubota and the other lady giggled.

"Yasuda-san?" I said. "*Hajimemashite. Celeste desu.*"

"*Ah!*" Mrs. Yasuda and her cohort both gushed.

The other woman did the old point-to-the nose gesture. "I . . . am . . . Nozaki." She wore a more subdued wheat-colored linen jacket and a light orange scarf, a serious attempt at Parisian flair.

I then introduced myself to Mrs. Nozaki. This, understandably, elicited more excitement.

Standing there like a dope, I had turned into the shy, gangly adolescent daughter, ill at ease at being introduced to Mom's friends. So what was it that I was supposed to do next?

"Celeste-san," Mrs. Kubota said. "We hear '*Nozomi no Hoshi.*' "

"What?"

"Your singing! Japanese!"

Mrs. Nozaki and Mrs. Yasuda both clapped primly, more with their fingertips than their palms, the way I would have expected well-mannered, middle-aged Japanese ladies to applaud.

Mrs. Kubota sprang forth from the La-Z-Boy and went to the audio system to press a button. Instantly the opening chords to "*Nozomi no Hoshi*" filled the room.

So I was expected to sing, brought out for a recital for the neighbors. But this let-me-show-off-my-gaijin scenario felt awkward, and more than a little embarrassing. I thought hard for an excuse not to comply. A sore throat? Temporary insanity? But I melted when I saw the hopeful look on Mrs. Kubota's face, thinking of the fond remembrance of her enthusiasm at Hysteric Echo. How could I let down *Okaasan*? I put aside any trepidation, any reluctance.

"Wait!" I said. "I need to get the words." Singing in English was all well and good, but in Japanese it was easy to forget or botch up the lyrics somehow. I'd hate to have mispronounced any words in front of native speakers, singing with emotion "be my one true liver" instead of "be my one true lover." Once in my room I grabbed my *romaji* cheat sheet and managed to return to the living room right before the verse began. As I started to sing, I realized I was singing to a karaoke track; Mrs. Kubota had apparently bought this special CD for the occasion.

My voice sounded a lot smaller without the aid of a microphone. But the times when I could glance up from my lyric sheet I saw that each of the three women exhibited the same look of awe on her face, as if in the presence of a great opera diva instead of San Jose's own Celeste Duncan, riding the crest of fame after her mildly successful Hysteric Echo karaoke box engagement.

During the instrumental they broke into hearty, prolonged applause. Mrs. Nozaki, her eyes gaping, put her hand over her heart as if to calm herself, while Mrs. Yasuda swooned as though she would soon be in need of smelling salts.

When I approached the finish, I tried to give the last note the most flourish that I could. I had never seen anyone look as proud as Mrs. Kubota when her lady friends cheered. It might have been her living room, but to her it was Carnegie Hall or Tokyo Dome. My heart pounded and I gave a short bow. It seemed so silly, this fawning over a *hen na gaijin* performing a song in Japanese, and part of me wanted to run out the front door. But I had to admit that there was also a feeling of accomplishment, not to mention the pleasure of the warm glow of affection I felt for *Okaasan* as I took in her smiling face.

There was also something else. I hadn't noticed it until now, but on the mantel above the fireplace was my picture of the maples in the front yard. She'd had it framed.

The letter from Dirk was short, to the point, and absent of any highly charged emotional language, such as, I am missing you so much! or Please come home! You know I can't live without you. But why should I have expected this when my brief missive had also been devoid of such passion? He said he was happy for me that things were going so well with my job and my search for Hiromi Taniguchi (both self-propagated falsehoods), and it was great that I was enjoying myself in Japan. Oh, and one more thing, he said. It's funny, really, but somehow he had reached a major turning point; he was now able to play his music in public. He'd begun an ongoing solo gig at the Clipper Lounge in Sunnyvale, playing his original songs as instrumentals. It wasn't the Blue Note, it wasn't Birdland, but he'd finally made the plunge and couldn't have been more excited about it.

He had made this plunge without me. Had I really been the one holding him back with my "tad off" singing? It looked that way.

Well, Dirk, guess what? Things have been pretty exciting in regard to my musical career too. I have recently made my debut at the world-renowned Hysteric Echo karaoke box, which was so successful that it was followed by a command performance in the Kubota Living Room in Asahidai for an audience that numbered well into the threes.

"Do you want to come?" Takuya asked me.

He was in the living room talking to his father right before the older man was off to make his garage pilgrimage.

"You mean to the *garage?*" Would I finally be let in on this family secret?

Takuya smiled. "Come on."

"Your mother wouldn't tell me what your dad does there."

"She is not crazy for it."

I followed Takuya and Mr. Kubota out the front door and into the crisp night air. We walked only a block down the street to a gray building with two metal doors sitting side by side. Mr. Kubota unlocked the one on the left with a key and lifted it open, then pushed it up toward the ceiling. Even though it was dark I could tell the room was jammed with shadowy, oversized objects that went back pretty deep. Mr. Kubota turned on the light.

Inside were large sculptures made of wire and lights. Was he an artist? He shut off the main light but turned on more switches, causing the figures to illuminate in a huge display. I was nine years old all over again, thrilled by Dorothy Hamill's Happy Holidays, the Ice Capades show Barbara took me to after winning free tickets on the radio from KLIV. White lights sparkled, multicolored ones blinked on and off as I now made out the shapes of the figures: snowmen, sleighs, reindeer, and various Santa Clauses.

"My Christmas," Mr. Kubota said shyly but with pride.

"He makes these," Takuya explained. "And decorates the outside of our house every year. He uses"—he stopped himself and asked his father a question in Japanese—"he uses 90,000 lights."

"Wow."

"It has become famous. Each year thousands of people come to look at our house. Even police have to come to hold the crowds. It gets more big every year."

"You're kidding."

"I never saw anything this fancy when I was in Seattle. It very unusual in Japan." He laughed and patted his father on the shoulder, saying something to him. "He getting ready for this December."

"Kind of early," I said.

"He always wants to do better every year. It is lot of work."

"I guess so." I gave Mr. Kubota a smile, relieved at the innocence of his hobby. "*Totemo kirei*," I said, telling him how pretty it was.

"Thank you!" Mr. Kubota looked very pleased.

Takuya said that we should leave and let his father get to his work. I figured we'd go back to the house, but Takuya kept walking in the opposite direction down the quiet residential street. I was only too happy to follow him, wondering where we'd end up. Outside was quiet, with only the sounds of crickets alternating their chirping with the chorale of croaking frogs.

"I never would have guessed that's what your father was doing in a million years," I said.

"Yeah, it is weird. My mother does not like he is spending so much money. Now people ask him to help with their decorations. He is famous. *Kurismasu-san* they call him. Mr. Christmas. He has been on television." Takuya shook his head. "My family—crazy."

"I didn't think you celebrated Christmas in Japan."

"We do not. It is not holiday. But many stores have decorations and Christmas trees."

"What made him start doing it?"

"He did it for my sister Rika when she was small," Takuya said. "First he decorated a Christmas tree with lights. Then the next year he put up lights on all the trees and bushes in front. And after that he started with the big decorations. Like drug addict."

I pictured Mr. Kubota nervously waiting to meet his pusher on a dark Tokyo street to score a can of artificial snow.

"But Rika was his first child so he want to please her."

His first child? Was this what Takuya meant to say? He shoved his hands in his pockets, and when he sighed, I could see the cloud of his breath.

We hadn't walked too long when I recognized the shopping district. A few of the *kissaten* were still open. Takuya pointed to one called Peggy Sue. "Shall we go?"

Peggy Sue was decorated like an old-fashioned American ice-cream parlor with a soda fountain counter and a black-and-white checkerboard linoleum floor. The waitresses wore their hair tied up in bouncy ponytails and donned gingham aprons on top of their starched white dresses. I was no longer in Tokyo but in Milwaukee, on a date with Richie Cunningham at Arnold's, waiting for the Fonz to make his entrance.

We sat in one of the pink vinyl booths and ordered strawberry sundaes. "Are you much liking Tokyo?" Takuya asked.

"Yes," I said. "But I didn't expect to see so many non-Japanese things."

"What do you mean?"

"Like this *kissaten*. It doesn't look like Japan. And I went to a place with Mariko called Venezia-Lando that was a replica of Venice. And Yukiko took me to a *kissaten* that was supposed to be Greenwich Village."

"Japan. A crazy place."

"And the way foreigners—gaijin—are treated. How lucky I am that your mother wants to keep learning English so badly and will let me stay at her house."

"She love learning English, but she does not learn much."

"You know what she did?" I explained about the impromptu, rare concert appearance by Celeste Duncan singing "*Nozomi no Hoshi*" for an exclusive living-room audience.

Takuya at first looked as though he hadn't heard right. "My mother do that?"

"I was pretty much taken by surprise."

His grimace found its way to laughter. "I am sorry she so out of mind," he said. "But maybe someday I will hear you sing."

"I don't know about that."

"My mother—so much a nut."

"Maybe a little. And she loves to watch this TV show called *Hen na Gaijin* that kind of makes fun of foreigners."

His face seemed to register some recognition as to what I was talking about.

"Your mom told me that it was one your favorites."

He looked puzzled. "She did?"

"Well, I think she did. She said, 'Takuya—he like!' But it's true that we often have communication breakdowns."

He folded his arms across his chest. "I have heard of it, but I have never seen it."

I went on to tell him various anecdotes about the terrible things gaijin were put through on the show and a long laundry list of what I couldn't stand about the unbearable host. "That Sakura Sasaki is one of the most obnoxious women on Japanese television."

"Sounds like one of those very bad Japanese shows" was his comment after a sigh and a long pause. "There are many. I do not like most of Japanese TV."

I excused myself to go the rest room. Washing my hands, I looked in the mirror. What was his impression of me? Did he find me at all attractive? Did he realize I was five years older than him? I took out the blue handkerchief dotted with smiling-faced tomatoes from my pocket to dry my hands. Mrs. Kubota had given it to me; keeping a handkerchief handy was mandatory since it was rare to find paper towels in public rest rooms in Japan.

When I returned to our booth, I remembered what Takuya had said about his sister on our walk to Peggy Sue. I was still curious, wondering if he'd made a mistake. "Did you say that Rika is your father's first child?"

"Yes," Takuya said. "He is not my father. He is stepfather."

I recalled thinking that Takuya did not look like his father when I first saw the family portrait in the living room, and his tall stature confirmed it.

"My original father died of stomach cancer when I was seven," he continued. "And my mother married my stepfather a few years later. They were high school classmates and my stepfather never marry. Then they have Rika."

"I see."

"That is why there is such a big age difference for Rika and me. It unusual for Japanese brother and sister being almost ten years apart. Rika got teased a lot for that at school."

"It must have been hard for you to lose your dad so young."

"Yes. I still think of him sometime. My name before was Takuya Ishida, but my stepfather adopted me. Now Takuya Kubota."

"I lost my mom, too. When I was ten."

"Really?" Takuya's eyes widened.

After I told him the story about my nonexistent father, the hot air balloon accident, and the foster families, he seemed even more astonished. I wondered if he thought that this was a description of a typical American childhood.

"That must have been very sad to you," he said. "Your mother dying; not really have father. Like what is it? Orphan?"

"Kind of." I never liked the word *orphan*. It conjured up depressing images of Oliver Twist asking for more gruel, street urchins begging for spare change, little matchstick girls sitting on street corners in the snow. But it was an accurate term.

"Did you try and find your father?"

"Well, actually I'm trying to find him now." I showed him the photo of the man and explained how perhaps Hiromi Taniguchi might know something about him.

He gazed at the picture. "I think he look like you."

"Really?"

"The shape of his eyes remind me of your eyes," he said, gazing at mine for so long that I felt myself blushing. "Maybe you will finally unlock a secret door. No wonder why you are so anxious to find your relative."

"Well, she's not a real blood relative," I said. "But she's all I've got for now." I stared at the swirls of red sauce and white ice cream in the parfait glass. I thought of what little information I had on Hiromi Taniguchi, only a photograph and an old home movie. I thought of Mariko's haystack in a needle. I didn't mean to cast a gloom over the sunny Peggy Sue *kissaten*, but it seemed I had. We were silent as we finished our sundaes.

Walking back home, I looked up at the clear black sky. "Ah! I see the first star."

Takuya stopped and looked up with me. "It is *kira-kira*."

"*Kira-kira?*"

"Means twinkling," he said, smiling. "Star bright, a star light. I am seeing the star tonight." He laughed. "I know it is wrong," he added, looking embarrassed.

"Where did you learn that?"

"My English teacher in elementary school taught us. She was from Kansas. It American nursery rhyme, right?"

"Yes."

"How do you say?"

"Star light, star bright. First star I see tonight. Wish I may, wish I might, have the wish I wish tonight."

He looked at my face. "I guess we must wish for you finding Taniguchi-san and your father."

"Thank you, Takuya-san."

I stared at him, thinking that if I were a different person, more perhaps like Mariko, I wouldn't give it another thought and would simply lean over and plant a kiss on his lips. Instead, I gazed at the sky once more. "Yes. That is my wish."

Once we were back at the house Takuya asked if I minded if he looked at the things I brought of Aunt Mitch's.

"Are you sure you want to? I don't want to bother you with all my stuff. I know you must be busy trying to get settled. You must have a lot on your mind." I had said all of this but didn't mean it; I was excited that he'd inquired.

"It is interesting for me," he said.

At the dining-room table I showed him the photo album, the picture of me in a kimono, the photograph of Aunt Mitch and Hiromi, and the picture of my mother. We watched the DVD.

He picked up the hair ornament, holding it carefully in his palm. "That is the comb you are wearing in the picture when you are child."

"You're right," I said, surprised that he noticed.

"Nice you got it back."

I didn't bring Aunt Mitch's ashes to the table but told him about how I received them in the blue urn.

"So you want to bring ashes to Hiromi Taniguchi-san too," he said thoughtfully. "Everything about this is so important."

"And then there's this," I said, handing him the wooden box with the geisha painted on it. "I almost didn't bring it since there's nothing in it. Is it some kind of special box?"

Takuya opened it. "I do not know if it special. But if it is with these things, it must have a kind of meaning for Taniguchi family." He picked up the documents. "Do you want me to read these to you?"

"That would be great."

He read the description of the belongings and how they should be returned if at all possible to Aunt Mitch's sister Hiromi Taniguchi, which was exactly what Zoe had told me.

"'Her last known place of residence is . . . the Higashi Arakawa area in the town of Maruyama,'" he read.

"Maruyama?"

"Yes."

"But Zoe said that it was in a town called Kuyama. That the family had a tofu store there."

"Yes, it says about the tofu shop. But name of town is Maruyama."

"Are you sure?"

"Not a doubt."

I was speechless.

"I think it is easy for some people to make such a mistake," he said. "The kanji for *maru* can be read in mistake as *ku*—just one small stroke difference. Let me show you." He wrote both kanji on a piece of paper: 九山 and 丸山. "This is Kuyama and this is Maruyama."

He was right; it was understandable how someone could make such an error.

"Maybe for Zoe, her reading of kanji is out of practice," Takuya said.

She's not a professional translator. Dirk's words echoed in my head. *Shut up.* "But it's strange. Your mother found Kuyama on the map. In Hokkaido. And Mariko even got me all the details of how to travel there." A sinking feeling came over me that perhaps Mariko had tricked me again, devising an elaborate plot to send me off to a place that didn't exist, having me ride on imaginary trains where the next stop was the Twilight Zone.

"Did my mother or Mariko read these documents?"

"No. I was the one who told them it was called Kuyama," I said. "Your mother looked it up in the atlas over here." I nearly leaped out of my chair and went to the bookshelf in the living room, Takuya following. I perused the many volumes with kanji titles. "Which one is it?"

Takuya was quick to find the book and brought it back to the table. He studied the map. "Ah, this is where she found Kuyama, right?" He pointed to a spot in Hokkaido.

I peered at the area he indicated, which looked vaguely familiar. "Uh-huh."

"But if I look on the chart for Maruyama"—he ran his index finger down the page—"I find it right . . . here. Near Yamaguchi. Right before Kyushu."

His finger moved in the opposite direction from Hokkaido, toward the south, almost at the end of the page.

"And," he said, turning some pages, "just to make sure . . . yes, I see there is an area in Maruyama called Higashi Arakawa."

I was stunned. What if I'd gone all the way on that trip to Kuyama? What a waste of time that would have been, though in some respects, I thought, this whole thing could be a waste of time.

"Takuya-san, thank you so much. That would have been a disaster if I'd gone to Kuyama."

I turned when I heard Mr. Kubota walk in and say something to Takuya.

I noticed once more how there was no physical resemblance between the two, how Takuya was at least a foot taller. But they still looked like father and son because that was what they were. I thought of the resemblance I might or might not have with the man in the home movie. But weren't there cases of people resembling only one of their biological parents?

Mr. Kubota went to bed and I was ready to do the same. I saw Takuya pick up the phone. Another late-night telephone call. I was dying to know who he was talking to, but it was inappropriate to hang around and be nosey. His voice was low and his back was to me, but I could hear again that he was speaking in English. I had no excuse to eavesdrop any further and made my way to my room.

As I got ready for bed, I thought how I'd never felt so attracted to someone as I did to Takuya. He was so warm, seemingly interested in everything I had to say. But I supposed it could just be his manner, how he'd act with anyone. It could be that this was the Japanese way, and that it would be considered rude to not act pleasantly engaged with another person and rude as well to not applaud your ass off when a gaijin made an attempt at singing a Japanese song.

It was quite possible that Takuya was only being polite to one more *hen na gaijin* his crazed mother had invited to stay in their house. Nothing more than that.

12

GOLDEN WEEK

"NEXT WEEK IS THE GOLDEN WEEK," TAKUYA SAID TO ME AS WE ATE ANOTHER Japanese breakfast at the kitchen table while Mrs. Kubota picked at her toast and eggs.

"Golden Week?" It sounded like an oldies promotion on All Hits of the '80's and '90's, 96.9 Pure Power FM, San Jose, South Bay, 24/7.

"Yes, it is when many holidays come together and many people in Japan take time off for going traveling."

It still wasn't clear whether Takuya was officially back at work. "Are you going somewhere?" I asked him. "For Golden Week?"

His face seemed to turn slightly red. "If you would like," he said slowly. "I am wondering if you . . ." His voice trailed off, and he said nothing further.

"If I would what?"

"If you would be liking me to bring you to Maruyama."

"*Really?*" I didn't want to appear too anxious or overjoyed, but I was and it was probably obvious.

Mrs. Kubota smiled, though I could tell that she had no idea what we were talking about.

"Yes. I could translate for you. We could go to the city office and look at the records, if they have such a place; maybe ask people in the neighborhood. It is long time ago, but maybe tofu shop is still there. It seem like it is kind of small town. But it is far. We have to stay over maybe two nights." He looked at my face, concerned.

"So . . ."

"If it make you uncomfortable, then . . ."

"No. Not at all." I hoped it didn't sound too enthusiastic. Yes, I thought, I would be quite happy to spend a few nights with you, though Dirk's disapproving face made an appearance in my head.

"I think friends can travel well, right?" he said, smiling, seeming relieved.

This sounded downright charming. I nodded, feeling my grin increasing to jack-o'-lantern proportions.

"And maybe we will find Taniguchi-san. You can bring your aunt Michiko's ashes. It would be so important for relatives to have this. And you can ask about the man who can be your father."

My heart beat fast. This was finally all coming together.

"I can perform research and find out what trains we have to ride."

"I am so grateful for this," I said. "Thank you so much, Takuya-san."

Mrs. Kubota began speaking rapidly to Takuya, and I gobbled down my grilled fish in excitement as I listened to the flurry of words I could not comprehend. When Takuya answered and the conversation continued, I could tell by the expression on Mrs. Kubota's face and her subdued tone that she was not pleased. Were they talking about this trip to Maruyama or a completely different topic? The words flew out of my ears with no hope in understanding anything other than yes, no, and is that so? They didn't seem to be arguing, but I could deduce that it wasn't the most lighthearted conversation. Takuya occasionally sighed and frowned while Mrs. Kubota's expression could only be described as concerned, as if something was stuck up her butt, as Mariko had so delicately put it.

The talking stopped with an abruptness, and then Mrs. Kubota began clearing the table as if she were perturbed, scooping up my chopsticks and removing my breakfast box before I'd had a chance to finish. This behavior was completely out of character. How I would have loved to polish off those final bites of pickles and rice! But I was not about to say anything.

Takuya gave me a conspiratorial but sheepish look, indicating with a tilt of his head that we should leave the room.

"Is something wrong?" I asked in a low voice once we were in the living room.

"She does not like I will take you to Maruyama."

My heart fell. It was another failing grade on the test, and the guilt set in. It was bad enough that I'd been allowed to live in this house rent-free simply because I was a gaijin, but I'd been feeling a real bond with Mrs. Kubota and I certainly didn't want to displease her. Yet I could never shake the feeling that the relationship was tenuous, and I didn't want another trip to the social worker only to find myself dumped from my current home.

"Why not?"

"She invite someone to come here that she want me to see. On the Golden Week."

I couldn't understand the big deal. "Can't it be rescheduled? For when you come back?" Who could this person be?

He sighed. "It not so easy."

"Takuya-san, I really appreciate how you want to help me, but I don't want to get you in trouble with your mother and I don't want her to be mad at me either."

"She not mad at you." He smiled. "Just me." He laughed gently. "Like always."

He was being vague, and I wanted so many more details, but it was not my place to pry. "Maybe we should go another time. Or maybe I can get Mariko to take me. Her English is good, even though she is crazy." I had little enthusiasm for this alternate plan but felt compelled to suggest it.

He laughed. "Yes. I think she is crazy." His face turned serious. "I am not child to my mother. I can do my way. So let us go."

"Are you sure you don't have to be busy with work?"

"This is holiday time. I will go back for my work afterward."

It had been obvious that Mrs. Kubota was pretty clingy with Takuya, at least in what I'd witnessed so far. But maybe this was understandable since he was away for so long. And her daughter Rika was also far from home. She must have missed them terribly—it was no wonder she reached out to gaijin. I didn't want to get in the middle of this, but I, not surprisingly, found myself gravitating toward Takuya's side of things, yet at the same time feeling uneasy at doing so.

"Are you sure she's not mad at me? For making you take this trip?"

He shook his head an adamant no, but I figured he wasn't quite telling the truth, so as to spare my feelings.

"If you want to we should go," he said. "It important, right?"

I looked for a moment at the framed picture on the mantel, the one I drew of the maple trees. I knew deep down that I couldn't give up this opportunity for a trip that meant so much to me, and I hoped that Mrs. Kubota wouldn't want me to give it up either.

"Yes," I said. "Let's go."

My recent English lessons with Takuya's mother had consisted of what Mrs. Kubota called "free conversation," where we talked about any subject. These were not usually successful, as her English was so limited. Even though I had tried to introduce new words and phrases to her, she rarely wrote them down and usually forgot them by the next day. These conversations never progressed very far, and there was a constant need for me to plumb my brain for new topics.

"Next week Golden Week" is what Mrs. Kubota said at the lesson the day Takuya promised to take me to Maruyama.

I gulped. This was the last thing I wanted to talk about with her, but now it appeared unavoidable. "Yes," I said. I was in no mood to discuss the upcoming trip. How could I steer this in a different direction? "What are the holidays in Golden Week?" I finally offered.

"Holidays?"

"Special days. In Golden Week."

"Ah!" Mrs. Kubota looked up something in her dictionary, then seemed to understand. She wrote on a piece of paper in a pained and careful manner, as if she'd be graded on her penmanship. When she finished, she pointed to the *romaji* she had written and read aloud, "Golden Week: *Midori no Hi,* Green Day. *Kenpo Kinenbi,* Constitution Day. *Kokumin no Kyujitsu,* Between Day. *Kodomo no Hi,* Children's Day. This holidays of Golden Week."

"Thank you, *Okaasan,* for explaining the Golden Week holidays."

When Mrs. Kubota looked at me, it was with her face hardened in a way I'd never seen before. "This Golden Week. You go Maruyama. With Takuya."

This topic refused to go away. "Yes. Have you ever been to Maruyama?"

It was unlikely that anyone in Tokyo would bother to travel to such a little no-name town, but I said this to keep the subject neutral.

"No. I not go. Long travel. Many hours."

"Yes, it must be far."

"Far," Mrs. Kubota said, nodding. "Very far."

"It's near Yamaguchi. I think that's supposed to be a nice place."

"Nice place. Yes."

Mrs. Kubota conceded a smile, but instead of her solid sunny one this was more cracked around the edges. There was a long, uncomfortable silence. Then she came out with something I never could have predicted. "You like Takuya?"

My neck throbbed. What did she mean by *that?* Even though it seemed she had finally gotten it through her head that I wasn't serious when I asked Takuya for his hand in marriage, did she still fear that I was after her son? Was my crush *that* evident? Had I been looking at Takuya during those Japanese breakfasts with big cow eyes, my tongue hanging out like that little dog's on the cover of *Mrs. Lady?* Frankly, I'd been blissfully unaware of how I must have looked, which now struck me as foolish. Did I sigh when he came into the room? Had Mrs. Kubota caught me daydreaming among the furry pillows on Rika's bed?

It was easy to let down my guard and feel naturally at ease with Takuya, with his good English and good charm, but maybe I should have been more careful. Everyone had probably noticed it except Takuya himself, unless this was the reason why he had suddenly volunteered to take me to Maruyama. But I doubted that.

"Takuya is a nice person," I squeaked.

"Takuya busy."

What was she getting at with all of this? I could only nod, stumped as to what to say next.

"He homestay brother," Mrs. Kubota went on, enunciating the word *brother* as clearly as she could, though it still came out like *burah-zaah.* "Celeste-san, homestay *sister.*"

Watching another installment of *Hen na Gaijin* was even more painful than usual. I knew it was silly, but every time Mrs. Kubota laughed, it felt like she was also laughing at me, as someone unworthy of any serious attention or kindness from her son.

This time a Caucasian American woman, dressed in an ill-fitting kimono, was holding a fan, attempting to dance while singing a traditional Japanese song. Even to me she looked rather ridiculous, but I didn't want to be too critical. I'd gotten away with looking cute as a six-year-old in a kimono but wouldn't have been caught dead in one now on television or otherwise. Like this woman on *Hen na Gaijin,* I didn't quite have the ideal body type for it.

There was a panel of three judges, with Sakura Sasaki playing the role of the evilest judge. As usual, I couldn't make out what they were saying, but it was easy to understand that the judges, and especially Sakura, were putting the woman through serious paces, making her repeat parts of the song numerous times as the audience first reacted in shock, then finally laughed uncontrollably, because inevitably the woman always managed to mess it up.

"Oh . . . my . . . God!" Sakura exclaimed to more laughter. I winced when a picture flashed on the screen of a kimono-clad cartoon hippopotamus, batting her long eyelashes. Then the camera returned to a rear shot of the woman, displaying an unflattering view of her bouncing backside, swinging to the music.

Then it was back to Sakura, who took it upon herself to get up on the stage next to the woman, whose name I finally understood was Margaret-san, or rather Ma-ga-re-to-san, to instruct her on the proper movements that went along with the music and the correct way to hold and turn the fan. The contrast between the two was striking. Margaret-san was about the same height and weight as me. And, like me, she could have stood to lose ten pounds or so, but certainly was an average size for an American, and not a hippopotamus by any stretch of the imagination. But next to the petite, perfectly formed pixie Sakura, Margaret-san looked like a human Godzilla, as if she could lumber down the street, pluck Tokyo Tower from its foundation, and throw it into the Pacific Ocean with little difficulty.

It was a fact that no one had put a gun to Margaret-san's head and told her she must compromise her integrity by making an appearance on Japanese television as a sorry gaijin or else suffer the consequences. Mariko had told me that some of the foreigners appearing on the show went on to fairly lucrative entertainment careers as *tarento*—probably some with their faces immortalized in Mrs. Kubota's super-gaijin scrapbook at that very moment.

But even though I was aware of all this, I couldn't help but see myself as that poor woman on the television screen, while Mrs. Kubota giggled and remarked, "So funny. So strange."

I realized that Mariko had never mentioned whether she would be holding class during Golden Week. It was a good excuse to call and tell her I couldn't come anyway because the purpose of my sojourn to Japan had finally come to fruition, with Takuya offering to take me to look for Hiromi Taniguchi.

"*You're going on a trip with him?*" The high-pitched excitement running through her voice was as if she had discovered a winning lottery ticket hidden at the bottom of her purse. "Over Golden Week?"

"Calm down," I said, though I was enjoying her enthusiasm. "Yes, but I'm not sure—"

"Not sure what?"

I figured I might as well confess to her that I was falling for Takuya but didn't know if the feeling was mutual or if it was even practical to pursue such a thing due to the following: that I still felt an irrational loyalty to Dirk, that Takuya and I lived in the same house, that he was my homestay brother, and most of all, that Mrs. Kubota seemed so displeased and was against us going on this trip together.

"*What?* He might be the fucking love of your life." Mariko was incredulous. "You told me this boyfriend—what's his name? *Dirt?*—is old news."

"*Dirk.*"

"And who cares what that goddamned uptight witch thinks."

Witch. That was what my mother had called Aunt Mitch. I bristled at Mariko's harsh words aimed at a woman who let me call her *Okaasan*. "Well, I *am* living in her house. And she has been very generous. And, no, I'm not at the love-of-my-life stage."

"Not *yet*." Mariko paused for effect. "But maybe *he* is."

"Uh, I don't think so."

"It's not like you have a whole lot of time to waste, being in your thirties." She clucked. "Haven't you wasted enough time with Dork?"

"*Dirk.*"

"Anyway, Takuya's probably smitten with a capital Smit!"

"You are too funny."

"He invited you on an overnight trip, a trip that may take several nights, right? You'll probably stay in the same room and . . ." Mariko seemed to be living the experience.

"We haven't even really talked about that part of it. He said that he wanted to make sure I didn't feel uncomfortable spending a few nights away, but nothing specific about accommodations."

"What did you say?"

"That I was okay with it."

"That's my girl. Sounds pretty obvious to me what he has in mind."

"I'm not so sure. I think he could just be being nice, a good friend. We talked and we found out that we both lost parents at a young age."

"Ah! Dude, you *bonded.*"

"Uh-huh. And, anyway, he knows I don't have any other relatives and he knows how important this is to me. And I need someone to travel with who speaks Japanese. So I think he maybe just wants to help."

"Oh, come on. This guy must also know a hot gaijin chick when he sees one."

"Mariko-san!" I couldn't help but laugh.

"We must celebrate!" Mariko said.

"Celebrate?"

"I'll take you to this place. A very special place in Shibuya. Meet me tonight. Seven o'clock. At Hachikō."

"At *where?*"

Mariko explained that Hachiko was the name of a dog enshrined as a statue at Shibuya Station. "It's a famous meeting place. Everyone meets there. Take the Hachikō exit out of the station. I'll be there waiting."

13

FORTUNE SUSHI

IT WAS NOT DIFFICULT TO FIND HACHIKŌ THE DOG STATUE AT SHIBUYA Station, but I saw no sign of Mariko. It seemed true that the statue was a popular meeting place; people milled about waiting, talking, and texting into phones, or chatting face-to-face. Teenage girls screeched with joy at spotting their friends, snapping pictures with their cell phones. As in Shinjuku, huge TV screens plastered upon tall buildings, and rainbows of neon signs overwhelmed me. A constant musical din from the boutiques and bars gave me audio overload, and I became dizzy from tracking the perpetual crowds crossing Shibuya's wide boulevards at precise intervals when the signals changed. Not one person walked against the light.

I checked my watch; Mariko was nearly fifteen minutes late, but soon enough she came running toward me from the opposite direction, clad in her familiar black leather jacket, high heels, and tight jeans.

"Sorry, sorry," she said.

"So who is this Hachikō?" I asked.

"*What?*"

It was hard to hear over the noise of the crowd.

"What is the significance of this dog?" I pointed toward the bronze statue.

Mariko told me the story of the Akita dog named Hachikō who lived during the 1920s and greeted his master every day without fail at Shibuya Station when he came home from work. And the dog continued to return to the station daily to wait, even after the owner died, and did so for a dozen more years.

"Japanese like that kind of loyalty," Mariko said. "So they built a statue. I heard that one reason the dog kept coming back was because the shopkeepers would feed him." She laughed. "Let's go."

"Where are we going exactly?"

"You'll see."

We crossed the street, joining the crowds traveling up one of the intersecting sidewalks lined with department stores, pachinko parlors, *kissaten*, and restaurants.

The streets became increasingly hilly, and soon we reached a quieter, more residential area where the people thinned out. It was so still that the neighborhood felt undercover, secretive. The buildings, though, were far from subdued, looking as if they'd been pinched from Tokyo Disneyland. Sleeping Beauty's castle complete with a drawbridge stood next to a Cape Cod cottage with pale blue shingles and shuttered windows surrounded by a white picket fence. Another was in the shape of a Dutch windmill sitting on a meticulously landscaped lawn with flower boxes brimming with red tulips, and pairs of wooden shoes lined up at the entryway. I knew enough *katakana* by now that I could read at least part of the signs on these places: they appeared to be *hoteru*—hotels.

"This area is good to know," Mariko said. "These are love hotels."

"What exactly is a love hotel?"

She explained that with the cramped space and little privacy so rampant in Japan, it was often easier for people to rendezvous in love hotels. Even married couples living with parents might seek one out. "So when you and Takuya-san get back from your trip and need a place to go fuck your brains out, you can come here."

"God, Mariko!" The next thing she'd probably tell me was that she possessed a frequent visitor discount card for one of these places, which she'd be happy to loan me.

"Well, you shouldn't sleep together in his mother's house. Even *I* would think that would be tacky."

"Oh, you would?" Was I really having this conversation?

We made a left onto another peaceful street with only a smattering of low-key bars and restaurants.

"Ah! There it is," she said.

The place appeared to be a restaurant, but I couldn't understand the kanji on the blue sign. Inside was a small, cramped sushi bar with a few tables. I'd already eaten dinner, but I would never turn down sushi.

As usual, an entrance by a gaijin elicited some long stares.

We took the last two empty seats at the counter. "This is Uranai Sushi," Mariko said. "Fortune Sushi."

"Fortune Sushi?"

"They will tell your sushi fortune."

"My sushi fortune? Why do I need a sushi fortune?"

"To find out what's in store for you and Takuya on this trip," she said, as if it was obvious. "This place is very unique. I saw it on television, on this show called *Bikkuri Tokyo*."

"*Bikkuri Tokyo?*"

"'Surprise Tokyo.' This place is very popular."

There were three sushi chefs holding court behind the counter, all women. I knew that it was rare to see a female sushi chef, but these women looked more like men, with short, slick-backed hair and sideburns. They wore blue-and-white-checkered bandanas tied around their heads and bright white chef's coats.

"They don't usually have women sushi chefs, right?" I said.

"No, it's very unusual. Japanese think women have warm hands that will ruin the fish. Or that their perfume and makeup will compromise the flavor." Mariko shook her head. "Typical Japanese male bullshit."

Above the counter I could see eight-by-ten framed photographs that seemed to be of celebrities, like those you'd find in an old-school Hollywood restaurant or a Broadway deli. Some were even autographed. Yet the strange thing was that most of the people in the photos were women who resembled the sushi chefs—women with short hair wearing elaborate theatrical makeup, but appearing to try and look like men. There were also a few pictures of overly feminine women dressed in Western-style period dresses with bustles and elaborate wigs.

"What are those pictures?"

"Takarazuka," Mariko said.

"What?"

Mariko was already talking in Japanese to one of the chefs who was setting out warm, moist hand towels. I wiped my hands as the two continued talking.

Mariko turned to me. "Takarazuka is an all-women theater troupe that's very famous in Japan. All the parts in their shows are played by women; that's why some are dressed like men. Those pictures are of the famous Takarazuka performers." She pointed to the wall behind them. "See that poster?"

The picture was of two Japanese women, one in a black pin-striped suit portraying Rhett Butler and the other as Scarlett O'Hara in her green gown made from curtains. They gazed soulfully into each other's eyes, the burning of Atlanta depicted in the background.

"*Gone with the Wind?*"

"A musical version. That's their latest production." Mariko wiped her hands with her towel and folded it neatly on the counter. "The owner of this place is apparently a Takarazuka freak and wanted to give them a tribute, but it is mainly for sushi fortune-telling. Weird, huh?"

That was an understatement.

"That's why it got on TV," Mariko continued. "Aren't I always telling you what a crazy fucking place Japan is?"

Yes, she was. I looked around at the customers, all of them women, trying not to stare. "Is this some kind of lesbian hangout?" I asked in a low voice. Many of the clients also seemed to be in drag, imitating the sushi chefs who were imitating the theater performers. Mariko and I were conspicuous by our relatively mundane appearances.

"Could be," Mariko said. "But if you're looking for lesbians, I can take you to some really hard-core places in Shinjuku."

As usual, Mariko spoke with the voice of authority; perhaps penises were not her only area of expertise. I was too overwhelmed by Uranai Sushi at that point to press further. "So how am I going to get my fortune told?"

"You'll see."

The sushi chef with whom Mariko had been conversing smiled and brought out a bowl of edamame. With her feminine male look she reminded me of one of the SMAP poster boys tacked on Rika's bedroom wall.

"This is Jun," Mariko said to me. "She'll be doing your consultation."

"*Hajimemashite. Celeste desu.*"

"Good Japanese," Jun said. "Sorry. No English!" She crossed her two index fingers into the form of an X and blushed; one more Japanese who seemed to feel that she was disappointing a gaijin if she couldn't speak her language, but who would praise even the most elementary Japanese coming out of the mouth of a foreigner.

Mariko gave me a serious look. "Okay. I have told her your situation with Takuya-san, his mother, and your search for your relative. Now this is what you're supposed to do." She handed me a plastic card displaying different types of sushi. "From this card, pick out your seven favorite sushi. They don't have to be different, they could even all be the same. But the important thing is that you should choose the sushi you would eat if you never had the chance to eat sushi again in your life. You must pick the sushi that is most important to you."

I liked sushi but had never considered its importance. I had to think about it for a moment. After careful consideration I selected three *hamachi*, two *tako*, one *maguro*, and one *saba*.

Jun listened carefully to my order, then said, "*Hai!*"

"Now she will make the sushi," Mariko said.

"Will I be able to eat it?"

Mariko laughed. "Yes."

"Are you going to have your fortune told?"

"No. But I've ordered some maki rolls to eat. And some sake."

With that, a waitress wearing a man's suit and tie brought us a bottle of sake and two cups. Mariko poured from the bottle into my cup, and after her prompting, I returned the favor. We clinked our cups together and said, "*Kampai!*"

Jun was as nimble as any male sushi chef I'd encountered and soon finished making the seven pieces of sushi I specified, presenting them on a small, polished, blond wood platter with generous amounts of wasabi and ginger on the side. The sushi looked irresistible; the two helpings of macaroni gratin I had for dinner with Mrs. Kubota became a distant memory. But I didn't know the protocol and whether it would be all right to indulge before receiving my fortune.

Jun smiled at me and said, "*Dozo,*" indicating that I could go ahead and eat. Then she began a long explanation to Mariko who was nodding, again with a serious expression, two surgeons discussing their plans for the patient on the operating table.

The sushi was fresher and more delicious than any I'd ever encountered back home; the nigiri deluxe special at Sumo Sushi in Willow Glen was out of its league by comparison. The *tako* had just the right amount of chewy texture without resorting to a piece of purple-and-white shoe leather, and eating the *hamachi* was like partaking a succulent morsel of newly whipped butter.

Jun stopped talking to Mariko, and Mariko gulped down her sake. I poured her another cup.

I smiled at Jun, then looked to Mariko, "So what did she say?"

"Well, first of all . . ." Mariko paused, and her eyes bore into mine as if she was about to give me information of high importance.

"Yes?"

"You are an abalone person."

An abalone person. My first reaction was to laugh, but Jun's and Mariko's grave looks implied that this was not advisable. It was difficult, but I managed to keep a straight face. "So what does that mean exactly, an abalone person?"

"Apparently there are four categories, depending on the combinations of sushi that someone chooses: abalone, sea anemone, dolphin, and whale."

At least I had not been categorized as a whale.

"And abalone people this year have opportunities for love, but many obstacles will come in their path."

This was not exactly news.

Jun gave me an earnest look, seeming to hope that I was understanding everything correctly. I smiled and nodded to reassure her.

"Abalone people tend to be impatient. You must be very patient in regard to your love life. It may be slow moving, but it will come along," Mariko went on. "And as far as the search for your relative, you must also be patient. You may think things will turn out one way, but you could have a surprise. The result may be positive but not exactly in the way you expected."

"Okay . . ."

"You must be flexible. *Flexibility* is the key word here."

"I see," I said, downing the last piece of *hamachi*.

"I asked Jun what type would be a good match with abalone people. She said it would be best if Takuya-san was a dolphin person. She said you could bring him in for a consultation if you like."

I wanted to laugh again. Somehow I couldn't picture bringing Takuya to this place and asking him to choose sushi from a woman chef who looked like a man in order to determine if he was a dolphin person.

Mariko must have ordered more sake because the woman in the business suit was back with another bottle. By now I was light-headed, my cheeks warm. Even though the sake caused a stinging in my nose at first, I was getting used to it and barely noticed it now. We managed another enthusiastic "*Kampai!*" and drank up.

"*Domo arigato,* Jun-san," I said, holding my cup up toward her, bowing my head.

Jun grinned and held up her own cup, which Mariko filled with sake. Jun then said something to Mariko.

"She says she has a good feeling about you and Takuya-san. So he might very well be a dolphin person," Mariko said.

Mariko ordered more sushi rolls, and I couldn't stop eating them. Moments later I heard dramatic music playing and turned to see a woman dressed in a white blouse drowning in ruffles, a black waistcoat, and powdered wig—a Japanese Thomas Jefferson. She stepped up onto a tiny stage tucked in the corner near the rest rooms. Her singing voice was low, but it wasn't as though she was trying to imitate the vocals of a man. The song sounded like a cross between *enka*, like "*Nozomi no Hoshi,*" and a Broadway show tune.

"Oh!" Mariko exclaimed. "I forgot to tell you."

Her eyes were wide and a little red. I could only imagine how red my eyes were. "What?"

"Did you see *Hen na Gaijin* the other night?"

"The one with Margareto-san?"

"Yeah," Mariko said.

It was not easy to forget the American Godzilla woman clad in the unflattering kimono, her Japanese singing and dancing skills picked apart by Sakura Sasaki.

"Did you understand the part about *Sakura no Gaijin Star Tanjo?*"

"*Sakura no Gaijin* what?"

"Sakura Sasaki is putting on a special TV show called *Sakura's Gaijin Star Is Born*. It's a karaoke contest for gaijin to sing songs in Japanese."

"Yeah?"

"So I sent in your name and phone number."

"What?"

"I entered your name in the contest. They should be contacting you in a few weeks."

"You did *what?*"

"Well, you know how to sing that Maki Kanda song, '*Nozomi no Hoshi*.' You said that Kubota-san couldn't stop raving about how well you sing it."

"Yes, but why would I want to go on television and sing it? Especially with that awful woman?" It was official: Mariko had lost her mind.

"What I was thinking is that on these types of shows, the contestants always have some heartbreaking or interesting story to tell so the judges will select them as the winner. And you can talk about looking for your aunt's sister, your long-lost relative, and how she may know who your father is. You can show her picture on national television. Who knows? Maybe your relative will see the show. Or someone who knows her. These things get huge audiences."

I couldn't speak. From the corner of my eye I could see Thomas Jefferson spreading her arms wide, her eyes closed, in the throes of the climax of her song.

"You know, your relative could have moved away a long time ago. It's possible you might not find her on this trip with Takuya-san, not that you shouldn't go"—Mariko grinned and raised her eyebrows—"for *other* reasons."

I didn't want to admit it, but publicizing the search for Hiromi Taniguchi on national television actually sounded like a good idea. And part of me thought of how blown away Dirk would be to know I'd sung on TV. Clipper Lounge in Sunnyvale? Do you realize that I was on *Sakura's Gaijin Star Is Born?* But when I came back to my senses, the thought of this only brought on an intense nervousness: the possibility of making a fool of myself, of having an encounter with this horrible Sakura woman, of looking even remotely like Margareto-san, could be too much to bear. I hoped it wouldn't be necessary.

"I'm sure we'll find Hiromi in Maruyama or find someone who knows where she is," I said, trying to convince Mariko and myself at the same time. "But thank you, Mariko-san, for thinking about me."

"Well, the TV show can be a backup plan, right?" Mariko looked pleased with herself, and then was off to the rest room.

I waved my hand in front of my face; it was now almost unbearably stuffy and hot in Uranai Sushi. I was tipsy, my head a balloon ready to pop from both the heat and the sake, and also from the idea of singing on television under the critical eye of Sakura Sasaki. I yearned to cool off in the night air; it was time to leave.

Like everything here, a sushi fortune was going be expensive, along with the bottles of sake and extra sushi. I couldn't afford it but felt obligated to treat Mariko; she'd been trying hard to be helpful. I called out to Jun to ask for the check.

"*Kanojo kudasai,*" I said.

Jun smiled warmly but looked puzzled. "Eh?"

"*Kanojo kudasai.*" I smiled back, hoping she had understood this time.

Jun pointed to her nose, then to one of the other sushi chefs. "*Kanojo?*" she asked.

What was she doing? What was the confusion? I couldn't explain it further and didn't know what else to say. I'd learned this phrase for "Check, please" and used it before; everyone understood without a problem.

Just then Mariko returned and Jun said something to her. Mariko let out one of her honking laughs, which was so boisterous and obnoxious that everyone turned around to look.

"Were you asking for the check?" Mariko asked, choking on her laughter.

"Yes," I said impatiently. "*Kanojo kudasai.*"

She continued to crack up. "No. You say, '*Okanjo kudasai*' for 'Check, please.' You were asking, 'Her, please.' *Kanojo* means her or she." Mariko glanced at Jun, still laughing. "Though they were probably flattered by the nice proposition." She jabbed me in the ribs.

My face turned prickly as I cursed the Japanese language under my breath. "*Sumimasen*," I apologized, looking at Jun, "for my horrible Japanese."

Jun gave me a warm smile and finally brought the check, which was way over my budget. I was grateful when Mariko said we should split the bill, but still worried about my dwindling cash reserves and the upcoming trip.

Once outside, I breathed in the brisk air, which seemed to clear my head as we made our way back to Shibuya Station. I tried not to think about being dubbed an abalone person or *Sakura's Gaijin Star Is Born*, and instead looked up toward the sky, at the twinkling stars. *Kira-kira* was the phrase Takuya used to describe them—I thought I was remembering it correctly. The memory of his attempt at reciting "Star Light, Star Bright" made me smile. So many things about him made me smile.

When we reached the station and were getting ready to say good-bye, I asked Mariko how her sister was.

Her lively expression disappeared, and her face fell. I immediately regretted saying anything, but it was too late—I'd only wanted to show my concern.

She sighed. "You know, she has leukemia."

"No, I didn't know."

"She's still in the hospital." She looked down. "And it is not looking good."

I took Mariko's hand and patted it. "I'm so sorry, Mariko-san."

Randy Granger. I could never forget the shock when my elementary school classmate died of leukemia at the age of nine. We'd all brought bouquets of daisies to place on his empty desk.

Mariko gazed into my face. "She's too young to be so sick. You know, she's the same age as you."

The pain in Mariko's face was in contrast to her dependable exuberance. I hated hearing about a person who could die at such a young age—it reminded me of Barbara.

Mariko's gaze hit the ground. "I can't believe that I may not have my little sister around anymore."

"I hope she can pull through," I said, one of those useless phrases that come out automatically when in reality nothing you could say could possibly be of any help. I squeezed her shoulder. Shibuya's brilliant lights, the hum of the crowds, the relentlessly cheery music—all were at odds with such a somber mood, accentuating the unfairness. I opted for changing the subject. "Thanks for bringing me to Uranai Sushi. A fun place!"

Mariko seemed relieved and allowed a smile. "Yes! You got a good fortune. Abalone person!"

I laughed and it felt good.

"You must tell me every detail when you get back from your Golden Week trip. Don't you forget!"

"I won't."

She put her hand close to her cheek and waved like a little girl. "I need to go this way. Good luck and good night!"

I waved back and watched her stride through the crowd, her long hair bouncing in rhythm with her confident stiletto-heeled gait as she passed by the bronze statue of the loyal dog named Hachikō.

14

A SECRET

THE MORNING TAKUYA AND I LEFT THE HOUSE FOR OUR GOLDEN WEEK JOURNEY, Mrs. Kubota loaded us with rice balls, red-green Fuji apples, and boxes of Pocky chocolate sticks. Her disapproval of the trip did not prevent her from feeding us.

"*Ki o tsukete,*" she said, telling us to be careful, a mother sending her children off to their first day of school. The worry and discontent on her face were evident, her sigh audible.

She spoke further to Takuya, but I couldn't understand. He nodded, saying, "*Hai, hai.*"

I started to give Mrs. Kubota a cheery smile but then thought better of it; it wouldn't be advisable to look too enthusiastic about a trip with her son, even though enthusiastic couldn't even begin to describe my feelings about the situation. I was finally on my way to accomplishing my goal and with this wonderful man to boot; it couldn't get much better than this.

We made it out of the house, and after two train rides, we arrived at the station where we were to take the *shinkansen,* or bullet train, to Yamaguchi. The ride would take about five hours, then a bus and another train, which would eventually get us to the Higashi Arakawa area, which included the village of Maruyama.

The bullet train was long, sleek, and silver, like a rocket ship on a track that would reach liftoff and take to the sky. The lines stretched far and the train was completely full with travelers standing in the aisles, clutching shopping bags and overnight suitcases. Takuya explained that the wall-to-wall passengers were due to Golden Week and New Year's being the two times of year in Japan when traveling was heaviest. Thankfully we were able to sit down because he'd snagged the last two seats when he made our reservation.

Once the *shinkansen* whooshed out of Tokyo and its suburbs, the scenery changed from dull-gray buildings and telephone wires to rice paddies, tall trees, and velvet-green mountains. I had always noticed the mountains in San Jose—when the sun hit them a certain way, they seemed to shine. But when I would mention to Barbara how pretty the mountains were, she'd sniff and say they looked dry and brown. I couldn't understand this: they looked golden to me.

I had brought my sketch pad, and the bullet train ride was so smooth that it was easy to be inspired by the scenery I took in from the window. Takuya had given me the window seat.

"When did you learn to draw?" he asked.

"I've been drawing forever, since I was little," I said. "And I took every art class I could in high school and at community college."

"Your pictures—so nice."

"Thanks, but I'm strictly an amateur. Do you have a hobby? Christmas lights like your father?"

He laughed. "No, I am not that crazy. I like to listen to American jazz music like Bill Evans and Oscar Peterson. Piano players."

God, he was another Dirk. A perfectionist pianist. "Do you play piano?"

"I took piano lessons when I was child and I try to play a little jazz, but I am horrible."

I was relieved to hear him say he was no good. "Well, I'd still like to hear you play sometime." I imagined a scene in a film, sitting next to him on a piano bench, our shoulders glued together as I followed his fingers that caressed the keys. He would stop playing, mid-glissando, so overwhelmed with passion that he couldn't help but take me in his arms and kiss me. Not that this ever happened with Dirk, whose butt remained planted on his piano stool.

"Thank you. But there is funny thing. When I was in Seattle, I meet this American who is taking lessons for *shodō*."

"*Shodō?*"

"Ah, calligraphy. Painting kanji with brush, you know?"

In the time I'd been practicing kanji, I had never considered using anything but a pen or pencil, though I recalled seeing kanji calligraphy mounted and framed as paintings.

"I was never interested in that when I am in Japan and we must learn in the school. I do not like it then. But I went to classes with my friend in Seattle and I enjoyed."

"Can you show me?" I held up one of my colored pencils. Maybe he would take my hand and guide it over the page, another staple of old movies. Instead, he removed the pencil from my hand and into his.

"Well, you are supposed to do with brush, but"—he held the pad—"here is my name Kubota, regular way I write." He wrote the kanji: 久保田.

"But in *shodo* there are three different styles," he went on. "There is *kaisho*, square style."

These characters looked as if they were printed in a magazine like the ones I'd been copying.

"Then there is a *gyosho* style."

This time he drew the kanji in a looser, faster way that wasn't as discernible.

"And this *sosho* style, very, ah—how would you say?"

"Cursive?"

"Yes, I think so."

It reminded me of the artistic writing on the documents that came in the box of Aunt Mitch's personal effects. Zoe had complained how it wasn't easy to decipher; no wonder she was mistaken on her reading of Maruyama.

"Ku-bo-ta," I said, pointing to each character. "What do the kanji mean for your name?"

"Mmm. It just name, not word. But each kanji mean . . . well, *ku* is kind of long time. *Bo* mean, ah, how do you say? Keep? Hold? And *ta* is easy—that means rice field."

"So you are long time kept in the rice field."

"Yes. Too long working in rice field of the Sunny Shokuhin."

I laughed, then took the sketch pad back from him. "Can I try?"

Takuya's arm now rested against mine as he leaned over to watch my attempts at copying the three styles of his name.

"That is not bad, Celeste-san. Do you like to try writing kanji with brush? You are artist so I think you can do."

"Yes, I would."

"I can give you my *shodo* set when we get home. I will show you how to make ink and use brush."

"Thank you, Takuya. I would like that very much." I wrote my name in Japanese. "You said my name is in *katakana*, right?"

"Yes. You remember. You write good," Takuya said. "Did Mariko-san teach you that?"

I told him that I suddenly remembered how to write it when I was with Zoe.

"So you remember from six years old?" he said thoughtfully. "It must be so important to you."

It surprised me when my throat tightened and I realized I was coming close to tears. Riding the train to the place where I hoped to meet Hiromi Taniguchi and ask her about the man in the home movie, sitting next to Takuya who was being so complimentary and kind, and wondering what was going to come next was all too much. But it would have been embarrassing to go all to pieces on Takuya—that would be what one of those overly emotional gaijin might do, the type Sakura Sasaki liked to make fun of. Instead, I composed myself and turned toward him.

"Yes. It is very important to me."

My butt ached and my legs were stiff from sitting so long in the bullet train, and once we reached Yamaguchi, there was still the bus ride and one more train to endure before we would get to Higashi Arakawa. The rickety bus belched periodically, wheezing with exhaust fumes at regular intervals. It chugged up a narrow mountain road bordered by a canyon of dark green trees, their trunks looking as slender as pencils from far away. Unlike our trip on the crowded bullet train, we were now among only a smattering of passengers, our destination far from being a tourist site.

"Lots of nature here. Looks a little like Puget Sound," Takuya said. "I must travel many times for Sunny Shokuhin, but I have never been in this area before."

In another hour we were waiting for the train at the smallest, most desolate station I'd ever seen. It was possible that the train might never come, perhaps having stopped running years ago for lack of use. It finally did arrive, though it consisted of only one car that meandered along a river at one-tenth of the speed of the bullet train. Houses and civilization were few and far between, the views calm, serene.

We arrived at Higashi Arakawa around dinnertime. The area was rural, though Takuya mentioned it had been a feudal center hundreds of years ago. From the train station you could see the ruins of a castle in the distance, a stone platform and a wide moat filled with lotuses, shrubs, and trees.

Takuya perused the neatly placed brochures tacked on a bulletin board. "There is an inn close to here," he said. "They have bicycles there so we can go to Maruyama tomorrow. I think the best way to go around is by riding bicycle."

I was not much of a bicyclist, probably because I never had my own bike growing up, but I was willing and possibly able.

Takuya used his cell phone to call the inn, which was called Nakaya Ryokan.

"There is only one room. But there are two futons," he said. "Is that okay?"

I nodded, holding my breath. Dirk's face flashed in my brain and I was quick to block it out. I wondered why Takuya didn't call ahead of time for a reservation, especially during crowded Golden Week, but perhaps in such a little town it wasn't necessary. I had also wondered what kind of accommodations he would arrange. The floozy, nonguilty part of me would have been quite willing if he were to take advantage of the situation, but it seemed that would be out of character for him. And the good girl, guilty part of me said she would refuse any advances. But although we got along well and were comfortable with each other, Takuya gave no indication of any kind of romantic interest. He was so affable that it was reasonable to think he'd act this way with just about anyone—his younger sister, his grandmother.

"It about ten-minute walk from here. They will serve us dinner at the inn."

Higashi Arakawa was a complete contrast from Asahidai where the Kubotas lived. The few buildings were old and wooden, much older than anything in San Jose. Finally, though, this scene was what I'd expected Japan to look like as opposed to Venezia-Lando and Peggy Sue.

I wanted to find the Taniguchi tofu shop, but Takuya said its location wasn't clear in Aunt Mitch's documents, or if it even still existed. He told me he'd ask people at the inn and see where the city records office was to inquire about Hiromi Taniguchi. It seemed that there was no more than a population of several hundred. The downtown, if it could be called that, had only a few stores: a fish market, a rice shop, and a magazine stand selling soft drinks and snacks, which also displayed signs of my noodle-slurping penguin friend. There were no tourist trinket shops, no pachinko parlors, no television screens attached to tall buildings.

Still, this was the area where Aunt Mitch and Hiromi Taniguchi apparently grew up, and maybe it hadn't changed much since those days. The feelings aroused in me were excited, hopeful.

Nakaya Ryokan was a traditional Japanese inn, a dark brown wooden building with a blue-tiled roof and a sliding shoji door at the entrance framed by a miniature maple tree. Picturesque, like a scene out of the past. I half expected a samurai and his concubine to step out.

The elderly, slow-moving woman at the desk didn't blink twice at the gaijin who had come to call. She leisurely served us tea before showing us to our room. It was small, with a tatami mat floor, its grassy fragrance filling the air. A low table surrounded by cushions sat near the window, displaying a calming view of the mountains that I could still make out even though it was becoming dark. A closet with sliding doors held the futons that would be put out by the staff, but first we'd be served dinner in our room.

"It is okay?" Takuya asked.

"Yes. It's beautiful."

My body was gritty, and perspiration coated my back. I went to the narrow bathroom to freshen up. There was no shower or tub, only a sink and a pair of green toilet slippers. I made a mental note not to forget to take them off before exiting the bathroom.

You couldn't miss the white porcelain trough built into the floor and it took me a moment to realize that this contraption was the toilet. I'd never seen anything like it. Though I'd heard rumors about unusual toilets in Japan, every one I'd run in to had been the typical kind. I sighed, in no mood to have to figure something out. How was I expected to use this? You wouldn't sit on it; it seemed you'd have to somehow squat over it.

I wasn't much of a squatter, but there was no choice and no time to waste. How nice it would have been to have a penis at a time like this. I pictured Mariko laughing at me, or a lurking hidden camera courtesy of *Hen na Gaijin*. I straddled the trough and began to pull down my pants, dipping my butt, attempting a reasonable facsimile of a squat. *God, will I end up peeing on my pants?* Maybe I needed to take them off. But was it really necessary to get half-naked just to urinate? Thankfully I came to the realization that once I positioned myself in precisely the right way, I wouldn't get my pants wet as long as I was able to hold the proper squatting position.

There was only so much time that I was able to balance, and when my knees began to wobble, I grabbed onto the piping in front of the toilet, hanging on tight. Please, don't make me have to call out to Takuya, I thought. It would be way too embarrassing to have to beg him for help because I'd fallen into the toilet.

When I finished, I slowly rose into a standing position, my knees shaking. I had done it. I flushed with a feeling of great accomplishment.

After emerging from the bathroom chamber of horrors I asked Takuya where a shower or bathtub was.

"It is down hall. Public bath. One for women, one for men. We can go later tonight."

I heard his words, but his appearance distracted me. Takuya had changed into a white-and-blue cotton robe the inn had provided, which was called a *yukata*, a sort of casual robe-kimono. It fit him well—very well—and I could see his shiny, smooth chest peeking out. His thick hair was a bit bird-nesty and a slight five-o'-clock shadow had emerged, but the long trip did not seem to have tired him. His eyes were bright and he smiled, handing me the other *yukata*.

"You can wear this, if you like," he said. "We do that when we eat dinner. Relaxing."

It did sound relaxing. I returned to the bathroom, took off my shirt and pants and put on the *yukata* over my underwear. I thought of Margaret-san's kimono on *Hen na Gaijin* as I looked in the mirror, but fortunately it didn't resemble that. Once I tied around my waist the dark blue sash with the white stripe down the middle, I looked as though I was staying at a tony, Asian-themed spa in Los Gatos.

After a knock on the door, in came two middle-aged ladies dressed in kimonos, carrying trays overflowing with food. There'd been no menu and no ordering; I didn't know what to expect. The meal reminded me of Mrs. Kubota's Japanese breakfasts, but much more elaborate and including many more dishes.

Each dish offered its own artistic presentation, a kind of food poem, a culinary painting with just the right balance of colors and textures. The dishes and bowls did not match, the opposite of a set of fine English china, but somehow they harmonized together whether they be lacquer, wood, bamboo, or ceramic. Despite the many plates, the food portions were small, delicate.

"This is *kaiseki* meal," Takuya said. "Everything they make is in season. I have not had something like this for so long time."

He was enthusiastic to describe the different dishes to me after the women servers explained them to him. There was a fish-flavored *somen* noodle with boiled quail eggs and seaweed served in a small, gray, rough-hewn ceramic bowl. Next to that was a small black lacquer bowl of *suimono* (clear broth), a green leaf, and a delicate pink fish cake floating on top like an edible lily pad. A platter of raw fish included tuna and yellowtail, and another dish was of tofu fritters, shiitake mushrooms, snap peas, eggplant, and river eel in a light fish broth. There were also slices of steamed duck and *ayu* (sweetfish). My favorite *oshinko* pickles were displayed in a simple white dish, piled on top of one another like a pirate's treasure of precious coins, along with bowls of fluffy rice.

The flavors were all different but flowed together. I'd never eaten a meal this delectable, prepared with such care and attention to every detail—details I never even knew existed. Even the sake we shared offered a body-warming, mild, slightly sweet taste that I couldn't get enough of, and it was obviously in a different class from the one that stung my nose at Uranai Sushi. I didn't stop eating until I'd consumed every morsel, every grain of rice, on each one of my plates.

Lounging around on the floor in robes, gorging on exotic foods, getting that merry feeling just short of full-on drunkenness, all with an extremely attractive man added up to one of the most romantic experiences I had ever had. Except there didn't seem to be any romance. Takuya was his charming, easygoing self and became even more charming and easygoing the more sake he drank, but there was no hint of flirtation. To my disappointment, a romantic undercurrent appeared to be nonexistent.

"I hope your mom isn't still mad about us going away," I said.

Takuya let out a big sigh and stretched his body. "I do not want to think about my mother." His smile was weary.

"Sorry."

"Do not apologize. It okay." He paused. "She always disappointed."

"Disappointed?"

"She wants things certain way. You know?"

I didn't know, but I let him continue.

"And she may be disappointed. Again."

"Why?"

"Many reason." He downed the last drops of sake from his cup, his face now slightly crimson. "Do you know something?"

"What?"

His eyes were big. "I have one secret."

I felt my stomach flip-flop. "Secret?"

"Can you hold one?"

I'll hold anything you want, honey—that's what Mariko would have said. "Hold one?"

He stuck out his tongue. "How do you say? Can you hold a secret?"

"Oh, do you mean, can I *keep* a secret?"

He nodded vigorously. "Yes, that is it." He gave an exaggerated frown. "I can never completely learn English." He sighed again and went silent.

So are you going to tell me your goddamned secret? I tried to be patient, tried hard not to be an abalone person. Did this have to do with the mysterious visitor Mrs. Kubota wanted him to meet over Golden Week? Or the person he talked to in English on the phone late at night? Had he secretly married an American woman in Seattle and hadn't yet broken the news? Or had he secretly married an American *man* in Seattle and hadn't yet broken the news? I'd really been drinking too much.

"I am wanting, I am wanting . . ."

I am wanting to make love to you, Celeste-san, but my mother . . .

"I am wanting to quit the Sunny Shokuhin."

I could hear the sound of women giggling from outside the hall. I suppressed a sigh. "Really?"

"And if I quit, my mother be very disappointed."

"Oh, I see." Even I was well aware of Mrs. Kubota's pride in her son being an employee of the world-famous Sunny Shokuhin. "So it's true that you've been working in the rice field too long," I said. "What do you want to do instead?"

"I am not sure," he said. "I would like my own business, away from big company. But I do not know exactly. I would like to have a shop to sell old American jazz records and CDs, maybe other American things. But I know that is not good idea for making money."

"What is your college degree in?"

"Business and marketing."

"I know it's difficult, but you should do what you want to do, not what your mother wants you to do."

"Yes, you are right. But in Japan it can be different."

He grabbed a yellow pickle with his chopsticks; even the crunching sound as he chewed delighted my inebriated ears.

"I think you understand that a little bit maybe now," he said.

"Do you want to go back to the United States?"

"I do not know. I do not fit right in Seattle, you know? But now I am thinking I do not fit right in Tokyo." He pouted, but then his lips were quick to turn upward into a smile. "It is problem, right?"

There was a knock on the door and the women came in to clear the dishes. I made sure to tell them in Japanese how delicious everything was. One of them returned and spread out the two futons on the tatami floor. They were separate, the equivalent of twin beds, about six feet apart.

Takuya said he wanted to take a bath before going to sleep. He showed me the women's bath, and I was relieved that I was the only one there; I didn't want anyone staring at my *hen na gaijin* body. I'd learned by now that bathing in Japan meant you had to soap and rinse yourself first before getting into the steaming hot water to soak, in what here looked like a miniature swimming pool. I was fast turning into a boiled lobster as a result of the scalding water temperature, so I didn't stay long. Takuya had not returned by the time I got back to the room. I brushed my teeth and slid into my futon. The effects of the sake made even a hard floor feel comfortable to sleep on; I sunk into it like a soft, cushiony mattress.

I wanted to wait up for Takuya, hoping we'd talk more about his plan to quit Sunny Shokuhin, and I still clung to the hope that he might suddenly push his futon right up against mine. But the combination of the sake, my full belly, and the too-hot bath lulled me instantly to sleep. I woke up, though, when I heard him come in and go in the bathroom. He had kept the lights off so as not to disturb me. Then I heard him get into his futon. "Good night," he said.

"*Oyasumi nasai,*" I answered, then waited, holding my breath, wondering if he'd make his move. I imagined his lips on my neck, his hand reaching to untie the sash of my *yukata,* then pulling it apart in a frenzy. I'd do the same to him and then we'd both be naked, rolling around on that tatami floor doing unspeakable things that I would be able to describe later only to Mariko, who'd be on the edge of her seat, her mouth wide-open, and then would say breathlessly, "You take it," as she handed over her love hotel frequent-user discount card.

I heard Takuya's labored breathing and was still hopeful, but it turned out to be the breathing of slumber, not passion. I let out a sigh, rolling over on my side.

It seemed to be a lost cause.

15

THE PUZZLE BOX

I WOKE UP THE NEXT MORNING FEELING RESTED AND FRESH DESPITE MY SAKE-imbibing and my first night of sleeping on a tatami floor. And I also awakened with a feeling of hope. Today could be the day that I would find Hiromi Taniguchi. It was possible that by tonight we'd be having dinner with her to celebrate our reunion. She'd be grateful for the return of the comb and Aunt Mitch's ashes, and thrilled with the photo album. She'd tell us stories about Aunt Mitch and explain why they lost touch. I would call her Aunt Hiromi. I would have a relative. And, most of all, she might well be able to tell me who the man was cradling me in the movie. His name. If he was living with my mother. If she was told that I was his daughter.

Takuya and I got ready and had a quick breakfast of thick toast and coffee at a café next to the inn. Then we walked to the small city records office in Higashi Arakawa, which was only a few blocks away. But once we arrived, we discovered that the building was shuttered.

"Ah!" Takuya said. "I am sorry, Celeste-san. It must be closed because of the Golden Week. I should have thought of that before."

It was disappointing and I hoped it wasn't a bad omen signaling worse things to come. But Takuya told me of his other idea. We could visit the local temple in Maruyama since temple priests usually knew everyone in town and would be privy to all sorts of information, more than what could be found on the terse forms at any records office.

We returned to the Nakaya Ryokan to pick up some bicycles. Takuya said it would take only about twenty minutes to get to Maruyama by bike. I had little experience with bicycling, and when I first tried to maneuver the one Takuya offered me, I found the handlebars almost stuck. He gave me the other bicycle, which was a little easier to ride, though both of the bikes were old and rusted-out, with scraped paint and fraying, lumpy seats.

Takuya got directions for the temple, which was called Taisan-ji, and was told that the name of the priest was Oda-sensei. I brought along Aunt Mitch's photo album and everything else except the urn, which I'd left at the inn. Why I was bringing all these things, I didn't know; my excitement was turning me irrational.

Takuya had more fun riding his bike than I did mine, sometimes performing what I considered rather daredevil maneuvers—standing upright in mid-ride, speeding, then circling back toward me, grinning at his pokey riding companion, and teasing her to hurry up. I remained stiff and cautious, gripping the handlebars till my palms became raw as I bump-bump-bumped over the gravelly road. I was grateful for the nearly total lack of traffic; at least I didn't have to worry about dodging cars.

Taisan-ji was nestled in the mountains, and it was easier to walk the bikes up the hill than ride. The quiet was palpable except for the rustling of the leaves and the occasional cawing of a crow. I noticed the variety of trees—pine, spruce, bamboo, maple.

A young man with dark hair streaked banana-yellow and cut in a pop-star shag was sweeping the grounds of the temple and told us we could find Oda-sensei inside. But first Takuya showed me how to wash my hands using a long wooden ladle lying on the edge of a roof-covered well. This was for cleansing ourselves before entering the temple.

Taisan-ji didn't look too different from the shrine I visited in Asahidai with Mrs. Kubota, where we prayed for Takuya's "safe airplane" and for me to find Hiromi Taniguchi. I wondered if *Okaasan* was praying for the success of this trip.

We walked up the steps past the altar and Takuya knocked, then opened the door saying, "*Gomen kudasai*," which meant "Excuse me, may I come in?"

"*Hai!*" came the chipper reply. Oda-sensei looked around Takuya's father's age. He was nearly bald, but his eyebrows were a thick dark black, and a prominent mole protruded from his right cheek. He stared at me, apparently not expecting to see a *hen na gaijin*. I was surprised to see him wearing a blue parka and pressed jeans instead of a religious robe, though a bracelet made of brown beads, a purple tassel hanging from it, clasped his wrist.

Takuya began to speak and Oda-sensei acted friendly and engaged. We slipped out of our shoes and into slippers, and the priest led us to a tatami living room where we sat at a table while he made tea. I introduced myself in Japanese, but that was about all I could do.

Takuya showed Oda-sensei the photo album, and I put the comb, the envelope with the documents, and the geisha box on the table. As Takuya and the priest conversed, the older man kept nodding and saying, "A*h, so desu ka?*" which meant "Is that so?" I wished I could understand what Takuya was saying, but I trusted he was representing my story well and in the way I would have wanted to tell it. I would not have felt as confident if I was with Mariko, who would have been flirting with the priest by now.

Oda-sensei seemed to take a genuine interest in the photo album and pointed to the picture of me as a six-year-old. He looked at me and smiled. "You," he said. I tried not to get too hopeful that he had any information about Hiromi Taniguchi, but his enthusiasm suggested that perhaps he did.

Their conversation was lively, both of them exchanging nods, smiling. It seemed that things were moving along. Oda-sensei pointed to a few of the photos in the album, and sometimes paused to think, as if pulling at memories. I had a good feeling about this. We were finally getting somewhere.

But when Takuya turned to me, it was hard to believe what he said next.

"He say no Taniguchi family lives here now. He does not know any detail."

There was a big twinge in my chest. My disappointment must have shown on my face because Oda-sensei said in English, "I am sorry."

"But he says we should talk to his mother," Takuya said, with a hopefulness in his eyes that I appreciated. "She is eighty-two years old. She live in Maruyama her whole life. Maybe she know Taniguchi family a long time ago. Maybe she know where they moved. We go see her now."

At least there was another possibility. Throughout our visit I'd noticed Oda-sensei looking at the geisha box and occasionally running his fingers over it. I pointed to it. "Takuya, can you ask him if he knows anything about this? If it has some kind of significance?"

Takuya looked doubtful but asked Oda-sensei. The priest's face brightened.

"He say this is a *himitsu-bako*," Takuya said. "A secret box, puzzle box."

"Puzzle box?" I said.

"It is puzzling," Takuya said.

I didn't know if this was one of his jokes or a mistake in English.

"I have heard of this type of box," he went on. "But I have never saw one."

Oda-sensei held the box. After a few quick finger movements worthy of a magician, another part that had been hidden suddenly opened—a secret compartment. The priest took out a small red book and I saw that it was a passport. Takuya and I must have looked like a couple of enthralled kids because Oda-sensei laughed as our jaws dropped.

"Kenji Iwasaki," the priest said slowly, reading the name on the passport. He handed it to Takuya.

"It is old Japanese passport from 1973," Takuya said. "I do not know why it is hidden in the puzzle box. Do you know him?"

I looked at the picture of the sober-looking young man who looked to be no older than twenty. Somehow he did look a little famliar. "I'm not sure," I said. "I wonder if he's a relative of Aunt Mitch's." As soon as I said this, I was possessed to open the photo album. I pointed to the picture of my mother, Aunt Mitch, and Uncle Melvin standing with a young Japanese man. "Do you think this is the same person?"

Takuya studied it carefully. "Ah," he said. "I think it is so. But you do not know who he is?"

I shook my head, wondering why on earth his passport was hidden away in the geisha box.

We finished our tea and thanked Oda-sensei. On the way out I could see that the young man who had been sweeping was now sitting behind a counter at an open window in a small building next to the altar.

"We can buy *omamori* from the temple," Takuya said.

"*Omamori?*"

"It is temple's good luck charm. Maybe we get lucky."

Takuya bought two from the young man and gave one to me. The *omamori* was a small rectangle of cloth that came to a point at the top, in the shape of a little roof, and had a short white cord attached to it. The color scheme reminded me of the pattern on the kimono I was wearing in the photograph; light pinkish orange and gold. Takuya explained that the kanji on the good luck charm were the characters for Taisan-ji.

"Where is Oda-sensei's mother?" I asked.

"He said she is back here. In the trees. She is collecting leaves."

"Collecting leaves?"

"Yes. We go."

We made our way into the dense grove, which was cool and lush. I imagined Mrs. Oda gathering leaves to press them in a scrapbook, then sitting in her rocker to gaze at them. It sounded like a sad hobby for a lonely old lady.

"Oda-san!" Takuya shouted.

I joined in. "Oda-san!"

We saw no sign of anyone but kept walking, calling out again.

"Do you know why she's collecting leaves?" I asked as we found ourselves deeper into the grove.

"It kind of interesting. Oda-sensei tell me that in Maruyama many old people gather different kinds of leaves. They send them to the fancy restaurants that do not want to use plastic ones. The restaurants put them as decoration on traditional Japanese dishes. Like the *kaiseki* we had last night." He called out again, "Oda-san!"

"So they make money from it?"

"Yes. He say they make a very good money, and they like to have something to do."

So much for a depressing hobby.

"Oda-san!" Now we were in unison.

"*Hai!*"

We looked at each other and smiled when we heard the reply in the distance, then the sound of leaves moving as a figure walked toward us. Emerging from the grove was a small, robust woman wearing dark blue cotton trousers and a matching jacket, and a pair of black-and-yellow Air Jordans. A droopy white cloth hat covered her head. Her nose was covered with freckles, and I seemed to have more lines on my face than she did. She carried a wooden tray divided into compartments filled with leaves.

We introduced ourselves. Unlike her son, Oda-san did not seem fazed by the sudden apparition of a gaijin turning up in the forest. She grinned at us, showing off a couple of gold teeth, her eyes shining, and spoke in a scratchy but animated voice. Her energy was apparent in her confident stride.

I could tell from the way he spoke that Takuya was enchanted by her.

"She say that out of all the ladies who gather leaves, she sell the most. She say you must be careful not to pick ones with worm holes and make sure they have classic shape."

Mrs. Oda picked up a leaf from the ground that had a big, perfect hole in the middle as if it were manufactured that way. Pointing to it, she shook her head, indicating that it was not a proper specimen. She let it fall back to the ground.

"She say the restaurants want all different kinds—gingko, maple, pine, and bamboo," Takuya said, grinning. "She seem very proud of her job."

At Mrs. Oda's request, the three of us sat at the foot of a maple tree, the old woman squatting with ease, due, I was sure, to her many years of Japanese toilet experience. I chose to sit on my bottom, my legs crossed in front of me.

Oda-san looked with great interest at Aunt Mitch's photo album, pointing to the pictures and talking with such exuberance that I got the distinct feeling that she knew the family.

Takuya was also nodding and smiling as they talked. "She knew the tofu shop when she was girl. She knew your aunt Michiko's mother, Sumi-san, and her father, Toru-san."

My heart beat fast. Mrs. Oda smiled and handed me a maple leaf she picked up from the ground that appeared handmade to restaurant specifications.

"And she knew Michiko-san who is almost same age and knew Hiromi-san from when she got born. She say that picture is of two sisters. Michiko-san went to Tokyo after the war and married an American. She is excited to see his picture, but she knows there was family problem." He paused as he listened to Oda-san speak further. "Parents do not like her having American husband," he went on. "But she does not remember details. Hiromi-san got married, but her husband died in car accident here in Maruyama. Later in 1970s she goes to Tokyo. Marries new husband. But Oda-san does not know anything more."

I thought of how it had to have been around 1976 when the home movie was taken. Had Hiromi already moved to Tokyo by then? Was she married yet? "Are either of the parents still alive?" I asked. "Is the tofu shop still here?"

"She say tofu shop close down a long time ago after Taniguchis retired. They both are passed away now." Takuya was quiet and seemed disappointed. "I am sorry, Celeste-san. She does not know where Hiromi Taniguchi is now or if she is still living."

I bowed my head toward Mrs. Oda and said, "*Domo arigato*." I looked at Takuya. "Does she know anyone else who may know some information?"

Takuya asked but shook his head. "She say she is one of most old people in Maruyama. No one else knows."

"I see." I handed him Kenji Iwasaki's passport. "What about this person? Does she know him?"

Again, the answer was that she did not.

I was disappointed but went on to say, "Please tell her how grateful we are for the information, and we are sorry to have interrupted her work." I'd learned that apology was always the best policy here.

Mrs. Oda bowed her head toward me, and when she patted my arm, I could feel my throat about to close up. I pressed the maple leaf into Aunt Mitch's scrapbook and bowed my head in return, thanking Oda-san once more.

I'd been preparing myself all along for a dead end. It *was* like looking for a goddamned haystack in a needle. This notion of my relocating to Japan, of thinking that I could find Hiromi Taniguchi, my only "relative"; this notion, which I thought could actually get me closer to a clue as to the identity of my father was based on only flimsy evidence. Dirk was right—this could be a complete waste of time. I had made no progress whatsoever. Now the only alternative seemed to be Sakura Sasaki's gaijin karaoke contest extravaganza, which consumed my body with anxiety and was too overwhelming to think about at the moment. I was too embarrassed to even mention it to Takuya. And then there was the "other reason" for the trip, as Mariko had pointed out, which had been another failure. It was obvious that a romance with my traveling companion had been a silly, adolescent, unrealistic fantasy.

"It too bad we cannot find Hiromi-san," Takuya said as we walked through the forest back toward the temple. "But you know? I can write letter to Iwasaki-san to see if he knows Hiromi-san. The man in the picture with your relatives, your mother. There is his address on the passport."

"Thanks, Takuya. But it's from 1973."

"I know. But people here do not move around too much like in United States."

He was trying to be helpful and I appreciated it, but at the moment I doubted that anything would come of such a letter. The warmth of the sun hit my neck as the light filtered through the trees. Tears filled my eyes, but I kept my head down so Takuya wouldn't see. If he knew I was crying but did not put his arms around me for comfort, I didn't think I could bear the disappointment. It was better to keep my emotions under wraps.

I walked in silence, glancing at the leaves on the ground, instinctively looking for perfect specimens for Oda-san. Once I'd composed myself, I said, "What do you say? *Shikata ga nai?*" This was a phrase I'd learned that conveyed a sense of resignation, that there was nothing that could be done about a situation.

"Ah! You know that?" Takuya sounded impressed. "That is very Japanese thing to say. *Shikata ga nai.* The longer you stay here, you become a little more Japanese."

It heartened me to hear that, but I hated that the phrase fit my situation so well. "Did you become a little bit American? By being in Seattle?"

He blushed. "I do not know. What is your thinking?"

"I think you're a delightful combination of the two."

"Nice compliment!"

He reached over and squeezed my arm for a moment, which nearly caused me to trip over my feet. It was the first time he'd touched me.

"Are you okay?" he asked.

"Yes. Okay." How embarrassing to be such a klutz, the complete opposite of smooth about the whole thing.

Takuya said that the lady at the *ryokan* told him that if we rode a bit farther on past Maruyama we would get to the beach. We decided on an impromptu picnic and bought *maki* sushi, shrimp chips, and canned drinks at a store along the way.

We easily found the beach, which was dotted with only a few visitors. Sharp stones sticking up from the sand lined the rocky shore. There was a cool breeze and the sea was mostly calm, with only small ripples of waves, while the sun played hide-and-seek with the clouds.

We sat on the sand, our bicycles spooning side by side, leaning against a large rock.

"Shall we go home tomorrow?" Takuya asked.

The question was unexpected, abrupt. I would have loved to spend more time with him, touring around, but it didn't seem appropriate. There was also the fact that I didn't have a whole lot of money and we were splitting the costs of traveling—the inn and the train tickets, which weren't cheap.

"I don't want to trouble you any further, Takuya-san," I said. "I really appreciate your taking me here."

"I have no trouble," he said. "I am having good time, even though I am sorry we do not find Taniguchi-san."

"Well, your mother said you're busy. You need to get back home."

"Mmm," he said, eating a piece of sushi.

"And she wants you to meet someone, right?" This mystery person still piqued my curiosity so I made sure to bring it up.

"Mmm," he said again, then nothing.

I wondered if I would ever get it out of him.

Takuya crumpled the wrapper that covered the packet of sushi and put it in one of the plastic bags. "Do you know who she like me to meet?" he finally said.

My back straightened. "I have no idea."

"My old girlfriend. Even though we break up before I go Seattle."

"You don't want to see her?" My tone came out more urgent than I intended.

"I do want to see her. But I should decide on that." He paused. "But my mother, she like very much if we are boyfriend and girlfriend once more."

"Oh, I see." I felt a gurgling in my stomach that I hoped he couldn't hear. "A Japanese woman?"

He nodded. "But I have other problem, too."

"What do you mean?'

"I have kind of girlfriend in Seattle. Holly."

My heart seemed to stop for a split second. So he actually had *two* women after him? I'd certainly picked the wrong guy to have a crush on. "Is that the person you talk to in English on the phone?" Gah! I didn't mean to say it out loud, but it just kind of came out.

He looked surprised, but not as surprised as I expected. Maybe he was trying to help me save face.

"I'm sorry. I mean, I wasn't eavesdropping, but . . ." Celeste, you are only making this worse.

"Maybe I am talking too loud," he said sheepishly. "We are fighting a little."

"I'm sorry," I said. "But, ah, isn't that what your mother would like? I mean, that you are dating a foreigner?"

"That is not reason I date her." His tone was short, on the cusp of sounding defensive.

"Oh, I didn't mean to imply that," I said.

"Holly is far away. I do not know." Takuya seemed lost in thought as he stared ahead at the ocean and sipped at his can of iced tea. "My mother," he finally said. "She should—how do you say? Mind her own busyness."

"It's mind your own *business*. But I guess we could say, though, that she is a busybody."

"Busybody?" Takuya seemed delighted with the word. He couldn't stop laughing. "Busybody! I am liking that one."

"It means she is sticking her nose in your business."

"Her nose! Yes! Picking her nose!"

I giggled. "No. Sticking her nose, not picking."

"I know. It is joke." He rolled his eyes.

The wind blew stronger, beginning to carry the plastic bags away. I jumped up to retrieve them, then tossed them in a trash bin. We decided it was time to head back to the inn.

Takuya was having his usual fun riding his bike like a spunky teenager. He went off fast and furious, then turned back and circled around me, telling me in a teasing voice that if I didn't hurry up I would lose the race.

"What race?"

"Human's race."

"What?"

"One more joke." He pouted. "But I failed."

He was such a cute nutcase, and I liked him so much that it was depressing. I watched as he rode away at even greater speed, his legs pumping the pedals, his back hunched over, elbows spread like wings in perfect racing position, and, most of all, displaying a great view of his butt.

I rode behind him, trying not to think about his two girlfriends, about Hiromi Taniguchi, or haystacks in needles, looking instead at the gray clouds, wondering if it was going to rain. I took in the quiet, only hearing the sound of crows in the distance. Takuya pedaled faster and faster, and I tried to keep up with him. But something had changed. Now he seemed to be going much too fast. I was about to yell out, "Be careful!" and at the same time trying to think of the Japanese phrase, *ki o tsukete,* when the bike seemed to stall, then just as quickly sent him flying into the air, until he landed hard in some shrubbery on the side of the road.

"Takuya!"

I rode as fast as I could, leaped off, and threw the bicycle to the ground once I reached him. A scrape on his chin oozed blood and scratches etched his cheek. Dark, almost black, dirt was embedded in his arm like a tattoo. He slowly tried to stand, putting his hand on my shoulder to help balance himself, but winced in pain when he put some weight on his left foot.

"What's wrong?"

"I think I bend ankle."

"Does it hurt a lot?"

He nodded, wincing again.

I looked at his foot. "It could be broken."

He groaned. "I hope not."

"Sit here," I said. "Just wait. I will go to Oda-sensei to get help."

"But I think—"

"Just wait here. Don't take a chance."

"Do you remember how to get to temple?"

"I think so. Don't worry. I'll be right back. Maybe Oda-sensei has a car and can take you to a doctor."

He frowned at the word *doctor,* but then said, "Thank you, Celeste-san. I wait."

I dragged Takuya's bike away from the middle of the road, then pedaled on my own as if I were approaching the finish line at the Tour de France. Without thinking I tore up the hill to the temple where we had leisurely walked our bikes before. Sweaty and out of breath, I got off my bicycle and looked to see if the young man was still selling *omamori* in the window. But it seemed to be closed and I didn't see him anywhere.

I thought of the pocket English-Japanese dictionary I carried in my purse. I was hoping I'd be able to communicate in a rudimentary fashion with the priest and get my urgent point across without having to stop and rifle through pages in a book. What a pain it was to have to deal with another language at a time like this.

"Oda-sensei?" I called out, banging on the door first, then opening it.

There was no answer. Had he gone out? I didn't count on not finding him. What would I do then? Go back to the grove of trees to hunt down his mother? But I was not so confident that the old lady could be of much help even if I was successful at locating her. Would I have to ride all the way back to the inn? The women there were the only other people I knew here, and their English was as nonexistent as Oda-sensei's and his mother's.

I shouted the priest's name again and stepped into the temple, trying to calm the trembling in my knees.

"*Hai!*" finally came a reply as I heard the distant flush of a toilet. My heart was full as I was able to see Oda-sensei, looking more than a little surprised, walking with urgency toward me from the hallway.

"*Tomodachi . . . Takuya-san . . . jitensha . . . jiko,*" I sputtered.

It was a broken, horribly inept way to say that my friend Takuya had been in a bicycle accident, sure to be prime for ridicule on *Hen na Gaijin*. I could always pull out my dictionary if more explanation was necessary. But it didn't seem that I would have to: Oda-sensei, his eyes clear and wide, seemed to understand.

"Eh? *Jiko?* Ack-she-dent?"

"Yes, accident," I said, grabbing his arm. "Please."

"*Koichi-kun!*" Oda-sensei yelled, and the next thing I knew I was leaving my decrepit bicycle behind and climbing into an old white, four-door Toyota, the guy with the shag at the wheel, me in the passenger seat, and Oda-sensei in the back.

Koichi shot down the gravel road at top speed, as the priest seemed to be urging him to go even faster. I held tight to the ragged strap above the window, my back rigid, as the little car sped along, bouncing and galloping like Mr. Toad's Wild Ride. The same *omamori* good luck charm Takuya had bought for me, the one that sat in my purse, dangled from the car's rearview mirror. It hadn't done a bit of good as far as finding out more about the whereabouts of Hiromi Taniguchi, but I hoped it would demonstrate its powers now. The only thing I could do was hold my breath and keep my fingers crossed that there would not be an automobile accident on the way to the scene of the bicycle accident.

16

A CONFESSION

IT WAS ANOTHER AMAZING AND DECADENT *KAISEKI* MEAL. DARK PURPLE EGGplant and fried tofu in broth, mountain vegetables, emerald-green asparagus, sea bass, winter melon, Kobe-style beef, and assorted sashimi, all accompanied by dark red miso soup and endless bowls of pearly rice. Once more there were bottles of the same smooth sake from the night before. And at the end, when it was nearly impossible to eat one more bite, we were served hot green tea in mugs and a plate of delicate *wagashi* in the shape of pink flowers—perhaps cherry blossoms. I scarfed down this traditional Japanese dessert, as scrumptious as any shoe cream, despite the fact that these pretty pastries were filled with a concoction called sweet red bean paste.

It was as heavenly as the previous night, but the atmosphere was far different. Instead of lounging around on the floor in *yukatas*, we were in our clothes, and Takuya had been outfitted with a low chair to sit on and a small stool to keep his bandaged foot elevated.

Koichi, Oda-sensei, and I had arrived intact in the little white Toyota at the scene of Takuya's bike accident. We brought him to a doctor in the next village who determined that his ankle was not fractured, only sprained. Still, he needed to use a crutch to get around and was plied with mild painkillers and instructed to keep his foot iced. The doctor cleaned up his scrapes and a bandage now stretched across his chin. I could only imagine our return home, Mrs. Kubota's eyes bugging out, as she would cry, "*What have you done to my son?*" and refusing to believe a word when it would be conveyed that it was Takuya's fault and his alone that he suffered such an accident.

We decided to start our journey home the next day but planned to stop in Yamaguchi for one night at a business hotel since Takuya was slow-moving with his crutch and didn't want to push himself. There really was no reason to rush back, he'd said.

I felt sorry for Takuya, but I was also pleased that the situation had given me a chance to be helpful to him and return his favors. I was the one now in charge of carrying our bags, assisting him in getting on and off trains and buses, changing the bandage, and making sure there was an ice pack for his ankle. I thought of Dirk and how he would have been complaining left and right, with his why-does-everything-happen-to-me attitude. But Takuya was refreshingly cheerful most of the time and couldn't stop apologizing and thanking me for my help, all despite being in pain and quite inconvenienced.

And despite all this, Takuya managed to write a letter to Kenji Iwasaki, the man whose passport we discovered in the puzzle box. We slipped it in a mailbox once we reached Yamaguchi.

We checked into the lackluster Centraza Green Hotel, a place without charm and housed in a dull beige mid-rise building, since the rates were somewhat reasonable and it wasn't too far from the train station. The accommodations were Western-style instead of a traditional *ryokan,* like the Nakaya inn. There were two twin beds and, thankfully, a regular modern toilet that allowed the luxury of sitting as opposed to squatting, plus a combination shower and tub included in the bathroom.

"Shall we go eat ramen?" Takuya suggested when it was time for dinner—the Centraza Green Hotel didn't include meals.

"You don't want to have curry rice?"

He smiled. "Right now I do not want to think about curry rice. It make me think of Sunny Shokuhin."

Kinryu Ramen was a short walk from the hotel. A small greasy spoon, or perhaps greasy chopstick place, it had a counter and only four tables. We sat at a table so Takuya could rest his crutch on one of the chairs and easily stretch his leg.

The soup was hearty, with a mound of chewy, squiggly noodles, and juicy pork slices that exploded in my mouth. I slurped my noodles as noisily as possible and downed the broth by raising the bowl to my lips, the way I'd seen all Japanese take their soup, including the cartoon penguin in Shinjuku.

A television droned with a newscast from atop a shelf next to one of those white-and-gold cat figurines beckoning customers with its upturned paw. The man who had been cooking ramen from behind the counter seemed to have a lull in his orders and began flipping through the channels until he found something he liked—*Hen na Gaijin*.

"Oh, God!" I said to Takuya. I was both excited and repulsed. "Now you have your chance to see *Hen na Gaijin*."

Takuya did not seem to share my enthusiasm, but still peered at the set, his shoulders slumped forward, a rather grim expression on his face. I figured his foot was bothering him.

Sakura Sasaki was doing her wide-eyed innocent number as usual. But this soon segued into her evil, oh-my-god-aren't-you-a-hapless-gaijin number when gaijin guest Hank-san, or rather, Hanku-san, did his best stab at an imitation of a SMAP-type boy-band pop hit.

Takuya visibly flinched when Sakura seemed to make fun of Hanku-san's performance and the audience came out with their shouts of *heyyyyyy* and laughter. Hanku-san began to argue back, albeit goodnaturedly, and soon there was a whole team of *hen na gaijin* apparently coming to his defense as they waved their arms and shouted, the camera's close-ups of their faces rendering them practically distorted and demonic, the cartoon dialogue balloons exploding on the screen. I was glad to see Takuya shake his head slowly in disapproval—he obviously shared my disdain for the show.

"Isn't it awful?" I said when a commercial came on.

He sighed. "Yes, it is terrible, but . . ."

"That Sakura is just so dreadful. Such a phony. Ugh!"

"Ah . . ."

I decided now was about as good a time as any to tell him about the contest. "You'll never believe this, but you know what Mariko did?"

He looked at me, saying nothing.

I went on to explain about *Sakura's Gaijin Star Is Born*, how Mariko had entered my name without my knowledge, and her theory about publicizing my search for Hiromi Taniguchi. I continued on, but Takuya shushed me when the show resumed.

"They are talking about that contest now." He listened, then said, "The grand prize is 300,000 yen and recording contract."

"*Really?* Why didn't Mariko mention *that?*" Three hundred thousand yen would mightily augment my savings account. But a recording contract? *Dirk, it's a funny thing, but I just signed a record deal!* And not to mention the irony that this was Barbara's dream.

"You should do it," he said. "Mariko-san is right—it is good way for to announce about Taniguchi-san."

Even though Takuya was encouraging me, I didn't discern the usual enthusiasm or excitement in his voice I had come to expect by now. I got the impression that he was urging me on because this was what he was supposed to do, not because he believed it.

"I know it's a good idea, but I don't know if I'll be able to stand being humiliated by that horrible woman."

He winced.

"Are you feeling okay? Do you want to go back to the room?"

Takuya shook his head. "It is all right." He drank from his glass of beer, then sipped at his soup bowl.

We continued to watch the show, but now in silence. Then a commercial came on for Curry Zone.

"Ah! It's your Curry Zone," I said, trying to be cheery and changing the subject.

"Sunny Shokuhin is big sponsor for JBS network," he said quietly.

I got the impression that Takuya was not in the mood for any further conversation. I kept quiet.

We had finished our ramen and I figured we were ready to go, but then Takuya ordered another beer. This was unusual for him, but I surmised that perhaps he wanted to drink more to deaden his pain. But while I drank my tea, I realized that this was the first time that I'd felt uncomfortable with him. It had been rather amazing that we'd had no disagreements during this trip; everything had gone smoothly, even in the aftermath of the bike accident. We had traveled well together and this was not the norm with the short list of other men I'd gone out with. But, I reminded myself, I was not dating Takuya; his lack of anything that could be construed as romantic feelings was testament to that. He'd been acting sulky, had told me to be quiet, and now the conversation had ground to a halt. But it was to be expected that a sprained ankle would put anyone in a cranky, unpredictable mood; I had no right to criticize him.

By now *Hen na Gaijin* was over, and the cook had changed the channel to a detective show, police officers storming the roof of a building, attempting to wrestle a gun from a young man standing precariously close to the edge, the music straining with intensity.

"I give confession," Takuya said suddenly, his face serious.

It was as if I'd been shaken awake. "What?"

"I give confession."

Okay. I get that.

He took another swig of beer. "You know Sakura Sasaki? The girl on TV?"

"Yes . . ."

He stared at me with a pained expression. "She is my ex-girlfriend."

I froze. *"Your ex-girlfriend?"*

It was too late—my voice had been so loud that the cook, the waitress, and the other customers all turned to stare.

"Do not shout." Takuya's tone was stern, irritated, the first time he had talked this way to me.

"*She's* the one your mother wanted you to meet during Golden Week?"

I'd been trying to lower my voice, make my tone sound less incredulous, but it still managed to come out shrill and bitchy. The waitress continued to stare while she wiped the counter, banging her hip on the corner in the process.

Takuya nodded.

"Why didn't you tell me?" My voice shook. I surprised myself at how mad I felt.

"Because it is embarrassing for me," he said in a low, even tone that implied I should have already known that.

It was like being punched in the gut. I wished I could take back everything I'd said.

He gulped down the remainder of his beer and motioned to the waitress for the check. "I want to go."

We didn't exchange one word on the walk back to the hotel, which took longer than it should have since Takuya had to hobble along with his crutch. I feared that this tension would cause him to hold a grudge, that he'd refuse to talk to me for the rest of the trip as a form of punishment, as Dirk had been famous for doing. Why did I overreact about Sakura? It was none of my business, and why should I have expected Takuya to fill me in on every detail about his personal life? But, to be honest, I didn't like hearing this news. Not only was I stupidly jealous, but I felt embarrassed too, almost hoodwinked that I'd been complaining about her ad nauseam and he'd never said a word. There was a pall in the hotel room now, a strained silence that was almost unbearable.

Takuya got settled on his bed, carefully stretching out his leg. He still wouldn't say anything.

I couldn't let this go on. "Takuya-san," I said.

He looked at me with his usual poker face.

"I'm really sorry that I was so loud in the restaurant."

"It okay."

There was silence once more and I didn't know what I could say further. There was a sublime sense of relief when he began speaking again.

"My mother introduce me Sakura about four years before. She is her friend's daughter. Sakura is only accounting clerk at television network back then. We dating for two years, but when I have to go Seattle, we already had been breaking up." He paused. "But my mother, she like Sakura so much and she is disappointed."

"I see." I sat on the other bed, my back against the headboard, my arms held closely to my chest. I vowed not to overreact, to be calm and let Takuya speak.

Takuya shifted his hips so that he leaned on his side against a pillow, facing me.

"My mother write me letter, give me calls, saying Sakura is suddenly big TV star on this stupid gaijin show. My mother like her even more now."

"Did you tell her you already had a new girlfriend—Holly?"

"It is not her business!"

"Okay. Okay. I was just asking." I had never seen Takuya so on edge. "So how did Sakura get her own TV show?"

"I am not sure. But it happen quickly. Sakura even take some of my mother's homestay guests and put them on *Hen na Gaijin*. My mother—so proud." He rolled his eyes with disdain.

It was the Kubota Gaijin Talent Agency, I thought, recalling Mrs. Kubota's scrapbook. But why hadn't she told Sakura about *me?* Wasn't I good enough for *Hen na Gaijin?* Or was I immediately deemed too old? Too big-boned? Lacking perkiness? I couldn't help but feel a bit insulted, despite the fact that I would have rather been chained to a squat toilet than agree to such a thing if Mrs. Kubota had even suggested it.

"So her strategy is me back with Sakura. But that should be my decision. About her. About Holly. I have a confusion." He frowned. "I am wishing I can just move my own place, but I cannot afford. But I am saving the money and I may have enough soon. It feel good to have my own apartment in Seattle."

"I guess so."

"I want to do what I want, but it hard when I see my mother each day. I know in United States sons move out of house all of the time, but in Japan it different."

"Yes, I know that. I'm sorry for getting so mad."

"I know you are surprised. Maybe I should tell you about Sakura before. But I do not want to."

"I understand."

"But I think you should go on *Hen na Gaijin* for contest," he said. "My mother say you sing so well. Maybe you will find Taniguchi-san *and* win recording contract. You say your mother was singer, right?"

"Yeah, and I've done some singing too, but mainly in the living room."

"I will help you any way is possible," he said. "For the TV show. I will even talk to Sakura if it will help you."

It was juvenile, but my head hurt at the notion of Takuya talking to Sakura. Did he really want to get back with such an obnoxious person because Seattle Holly was "far away"? I supposed the persona Sakura displayed on television was just for show business' sake, but who knew? Yet imagining the two of them together unnerved me, and the thought of any possibility of Takuya being attracted to me felt even more foolish now. How could I compete with Sakura, the epitome of Japanese cuteness?

I could always blame Mariko for egging me on, for getting my hopes up, but that wasn't the whole story. There was no way, though, that I was about to disclose any of this to Takuya.

"Thank you, Takuya-san. I really appreciate it. I will do the contest," I said. For so many reasons it had now become a challenge.

"I think it good opportunity."

We packed to prepare for the long train ride home the next day, then got ready for bed. As we lay in the dark in our respective chaste twin beds, I said, "Why do you think that your mother is so crazy for gaijin?"

"I am not sure. But I know when my father die, this is when she become interested. She watch a lot of TV. I am sure she was sad, depressed. She became big fan for gaijin. After Rika is older she start inviting gaijin to stay at house." He was silent for a moment, then went on. "I guess she feel lonely after losing my father."

I thought back to Mrs. Kubota's laughing face at the Hysteric Echo karaoke box, her proud look during my impromptu concert for Mrs. Yasuda and Mrs. Nozaki, her delight with my picture of the maple trees. It was sad to think of her being so vulnerable and to feel that I had somehow betrayed her by going off to Maruyama with her son, a trip that hadn't done any bit of good. But I did not like knowing that she couldn't wait to get Sakura back with Takuya and that maybe Takuya would even go for it.

"Some Japanese people are having strange feelings about gaijin," Takuya said. "I do not know why it is such big deal. I was gaijin when I was in Seattle, but no one cares."

"Well, in Japan someone like me sticks out more as a gaijin than you would in Seattle."

"Yes, but that is not excuse for people to look at you like you are alien from Jupiter or science experiment specimen."

"I know."

"Sakura does not think this way. Not when I was knowing her. I am sure it is just for TV show. You know, she is half. Part Japanese, part French. So she can understand this."

Couldn't he just shut up about Sakura? Was he now defending her to me or to himself?

"You are just person," he continued. "But some Japanese think in a stupid way about gaijin. Even young people, not only the old farts people. I see on TV once they are asking people in twenties about what they think of gaijin."

I'd never heard him so worked up.

"First, what is kind of question, 'What do you think of gaijin?' Why anyone even think of asking?"

"You're right."

"Anyway, one guy say he think it very weird when a gaijin can speak Japanese well. He say it *kimochi warui.* Do you know what that mean?"

"I know *warui* means bad, but . . ."

"*Kimochi* means 'feeling.' So he say he feel it kind of creepy to see gaijin fluent in Japanese. Why is that? He say they are breaking Japanese harmony. I think that is many bullshits."

"Yes, it *is* bullshit." He really did understand.

"I want a person to like me because it is me. Not because I am Japanese. So I do not have a feeling about gaijin. I feel about the *people*. If I like the person, that is good. If I do not, then that okay too. But it does not matter how they are born."

Why? I wondered. Why did he have to say just the right thing?

17

JAPANESE TINKER BELL

MRS. KUBOTA'S EYES DID NOT QUITE POP OUT IN ABOMINATION WHEN SHE saw her newly crippled son limping with the aid of a crutch. Yet she was quite surprised and set off to fussing over him, a mama bird whose baby had returned injured to the nest.

I, however, did not feel I was being blamed for Takuya's misfortune and this time was relieved instead of frustrated to not understand much of what he and his mother were saying. I was tired from the trip and needed to proceed with the important matter at hand: practicing "*Nozomi no Hoshi*" for *Sakura's Gaijin Star Is Born*. Not only did I want to use the show to announce my search for Hiromi Taniguchi, but I was also determined to win the recording contract and cash prize.

The following evening when I'd begun another session of my singing practice, I heard a knock on the door. I'd always tried to keep my voice low when I sang, still feeling a lack of confidence, even though I'd been to the karaoke box now several times with Mrs. Kubota and had given that impromptu recital for the neighbors. But Takuya had yet to hear me, and I felt the most inhibited around him.

"*Hai?*" I said, opening the door.

There stood Takuya, leaning on his crutch, holding a box with some difficulty. "This for you," he said. "Calligraphy set."

"Oh, yes!" In the midst of the bicycle accident and the revelation about Sakura, I'd forgotten.

"I show you if you like."

I took the box from him and placed it on Rika's desk. He hobbled over, carefully maneuvering himself into the straw white chair underneath the poster of an animated cat with a wide grin and striped tail morphed into the shape of a bus.

I removed the objects from the box while he explained the purpose of each. There was a soft mat called a *shitajiki* to put the paper on. We used a blank page from my sketchbook, but he said that true calligraphy paper would be much thinner. A weight in the shape of a stick, called a *bunchin,* was to hold the paper flat while you were writing. There were two brushes—one large and one smaller, and the word for brush was *fude*. He explained that it was easier to use ready-made ink from a bottle, but the proper way was to use a *sumi*, a kind of stone that you rubbed with water to produce ink.

"I think you can make a nice character if you practice well," he said.

"This looks very interesting. Thank you, Takuya."

"Maybe you can write something better than about older women's problems."

"I will try."

"How about *hoshi?* The word for star. Like in your song. I show you."

I helped him move the chair so he could sit at the desk. He poured the bottled ink on the stone, then dipped the *fude* into it. In precise strokes, taking care to paint in a specific order, he drew the character 星, lifting the brush at certain points, pausing, then continuing on.

"Sorry, I am not real calligraphy teacher," he said.

He reacted to his character with a skeptical look, but it was one I saw as both skillful and beautiful.

"You can remember because top of *hoshi* character mean sun and bottom mean giving birth. Sun gives birth to star."

"That's lovely."

"The *shodo* teacher in Seattle, he say this not just writing, it is art. So the character must be in a balance. Straight lines are strong, curving lines more gentle. Some parts thick, some thin. You also must practice putting the right amount of ink on *fude*." He added more, then drew the character again. "Teacher also say something so interesting to me. Think of calligraphy like a music. Kanji is the note on the page, calligrapher is like pianist trying to make best sound. I cannot explain well, but . . ."

"I think I know what you mean," I said, intrigued. "Can I try?"

"You have to do each stroke in right order."

"How do I know what the order is?"

"That is good question. I can show you, but maybe I find a book for you in English that will explain."

With his guidance I drew *hoshi* in the correct stroke order. Painting the kanji with a brush was so different from using a pencil. The detail you could provide, the thinness and thickness of the lines, the uplift at the end of a stroke—the possibilities seemed endless, something a person could spend a lifetime trying to perfect. The idea of creating art that depicted both beauty and practicality appealed to me.

"It look nice for first time," Takuya said.

It didn't look too bad, but I knew that part of the character was lopsided, out of proportion. "I think I need a lot of practice, but it is the kind of thing I like," I said. "Thank you, Takuya."

He smiled at me, and it seemed as though he was about to say something else, but he stayed silent. His friendliness, his being so helpful, his sensitivity, all warmed my heart but frustrated me at the same time. I guessed I would have to settle for him being a friend, a very nice friend. Another instance of *shikata ga nai,* though I was still not so sure whether a stubborn abalone person could adhere to such resignation.

"I tell my mother about the contest and she very excited," he said.

"I guess that's not a big surprise. Gaijin on TV and all."

"Yes." His face turned serious. "But I want to give you warning."

A beautiful calligraphy moment, then a warning; this kind of abrupt switch was becoming all too typical. "Warning?"

"Yes . . . ah . . . about this Sunday."

"What do you need to warn me about Sunday?"

"Sakura will be coming for tea. In afternoon."

The knots lying dormant in my stomach now twisted and tightened. Be calm, I admonished myself. You have to get used to this. "This is the original Golden Week visit?"

"Yes. My mother change schedule. I think, I think you should meet her too. Get to know before contest."

He was right, of course, but this wasn't exactly my idea of a good time. I tried to gauge his feelings from his expression. Was he excited about seeing Sakura again? Ready to get back with the evil TV queen? It was impossible to tell and I wasn't about to ask. Instead, I swallowed hard and tried to look cheerful. "Okay. Sounds good."

"And I am also thinking one more idea."

If he was going to propose an additional outing with her, perhaps a threesome for miniature golf, I was going to kill him. "What?"

"You do not have experience to sing for audience, right?"

"Just Nozaki-san and Yasuda-san."

He gave an exaggerated frown, shifting in the chair, adjusting his leg. "You should be singing for real audience. Not friends of my mother. Strangers."

"I guess so."

"When you are ready, I take you to karaoke bar where you sing to people."

I flinched inside, terrified at the thought of actually singing in front of an audience bigger than three people in a living room. I thought of Dirk's living room, the site of many a fight about my voice.

"You look scary."

Well, thanks. I thought better of correcting him. "I guess I am, a little."

"But you will be singing on television for many millions of people. For finding Taniguchi-san."

"You don't have to remind me."

"Karaoke bar is good practice. And then I hear your singing too."

After he'd gone to bed, I found an excuse to linger around the hall to see if there was another late-night phone call to Seattle Holly. There wasn't.

It could only be compared to the preparation for an audience with the pope, a sitting with the Queen of England. It was impossible to decide what would be the right thing to wear, though my wardrobe choices were meager. I'd considered buying a new outfit for the occasion but concluded that would be giving this thing way too much importance. And I needed to save money for whatever I'd end up wearing for the contest. Finding something that would fit me in the land of petite willow women would present a challenge, a challenge I didn't want to contemplate right now. In the end I made do with my plain black pants and underwhelming white blouse for teatime with Sakura Sasaki.

This particular Sunday, which I had taken to calling Sakura Sunday, Mrs. Kubota was in the best of moods—even cheerier than when Takuya's return home from Seattle was imminent. She cleaned the house spotless with an unprecedented eagerness, even for a Japanese housewife, and I could hear her humming her greatest hits from our karaoke box visits: "Yokohama Twilight-o" and "Cinderella Boogie-Woogie."

She had forsaken the "Happy Afternoon Tea" set that she used when I first came to call and instead brought out a much higher-end collection of white English china painted with delicate still-life fruit designs. Glass vases filled with flowers—yellow chrysanthemums mixed with shoots of bamboo leaves—appeared without warning throughout the house: on the coffee table, as a centerpiece in the dining room, and on either side of the outdated family portrait.

Takuya had cleverly ducked out to be with his father in the garage, saying he'd be back by two o'clock, the scheduled time for Sakura's visit. And he did show up, about ten minutes before the heralded arrival. Mrs. Kubota, Takuya, and I sat in the living room, on edge, watching the cat clock. Mr. Kubota had somehow been excused from attending. Sakura was to come by taxi and at exactly three minutes past two the doorbell rang. As the chimes played a snippet of Vivaldi's *Four Seasons*, I could feel the dread deep within my bones.

When Sakura walked in, Mrs. Kubota's face became illuminated, as bright and striking as her husband's Christmas lights. Sakura was even prettier and more petite in person, if that was possible. She wore a white crocheted minidress with white leggings and carried a small, unbearably fashionable aqua leather bag, which looked to have cost at least a month of my salary at TextTrans. Her pink strappy sandals seemed to be slightly bigger than a child's size but gave her just enough height. She removed them with aplomb, sliding effortlessly into the Chick-a-Doodle house slippers waiting for her at the entryway, which fit her like a pair of floppy clown feet. I wondered why Mrs. Kubota hadn't purchased new house slippers for the occasion but figured she must have neglected this detail due to all the excitement.

I tried to be unobtrusive but watched Takuya with heightened awareness for any telltale signs of yearning or other lovey-dovey behavior toward Sakura. There was no grand hug—no indication that this woman was a former lover, although I sensed Sakura's eyes sparkling even more when they zeroed in on him. And Takuya's broad smile was a little too familiar for my taste.

When Sakura realized that he'd suffered an injury, she cooed an "Oh!" and emoted great concern and sympathy when seeming to inquire what had happened to his ankle. Was Takuya holding back because his mother was in the room? Did he want to take Sakura in his arms and make up for lost time? I wanted to know, but I didn't want to know.

Everything went smoothly along Japanese protocol lines, as far as I could understand. Mrs. Kubota introduced me to Sakura, and by now I could properly render a variety of polite greetings, none of which could be translated into a marriage proposal or lesbian proposition.

"Oh! Your Japanese is so good!" Sakura said sweetly in quite decent English.

I was at minimum a good seven inches taller than Sakura. Standing in front of her, I felt pudgy and pokeable, a female Pillsbury Dough Boy. I was pale and white compared to this compact, pink-cheeked cutie-pie, whose small but perfectly proportioned figure—pert breasts, a shapely but tiny butt—brought to mind Tinker Bell minus the wings. She even smelled good.

We sat in the living room, Sakura next to Mrs. Kubota's side on the sofa, and Takuya in the La-Z-Boy, his leg resting on the matching ottoman. I sat stiffly on one of the chairs brought in from the dining room that now, as I fidgeted in it, seemed suddenly too small for me.

As Mrs. Kubota served the tea, I noticed the wide selection of pastries on a large platter, much more of a variety than the lonely shoe creams I was offered on my maiden visit. Takuya was leaning toward the table, trying to grab one of the desserts, when Sakura jumped up, placed a sliver of cheesecake topped with a purplish-blue syrup on a plate, added a fork, and handed it to him, saying *"Dozo,"* before I'd even realized what had transpired. Score one for the Kewpie doll. I'd been too distracted trying to decide between the thick, dark brownie topped with whipped cream and the slice of strawberry shortcake.

Takuya thanked Sakura and began munching happily. She chose the smallest offering, a pink square cookie frosted with a yellow ribbon designed to look like a birthday present. She put it on her plate and let it sit without taking a bite, engaging in what seemed like small talk with Mrs. Kubota, her voice rising and falling in intensity like the Vivaldi doorbell chimes.

At first, I thought that it would be wise to follow suit and choose a more modest pastry, but I was too damned mesmerized by that brownie. As Mrs. Kubota and Sakura chatted, their heads bobbing, their smiles bright, I tried to be covert, taking one of the plates in one hand and reaching for the brownie with the other. But as I was about to place it on the dish and plop back in my chair, the brownie slipped from my fingertips and toppled over, falling on the carpet, whipped-cream-side down.

Mortified, I sputtered, "*Sumimasen!*" But before I could do anything about it, Sakura had already produced a pink Hello Kitty handkerchief from her purse and was now on her knees, dabbing at the whipped cream and crumb mess on the carpet. This brownie had to be the most crumbly one ever made, with seemingly thousands of crumbs covering the floor. As I looked on helplessly, I could see that Mrs. Kubota had already been to the kitchen and back and was now equipped with a cloth and a bottle of cleaning spray, which bathed the room in a lemon-lime fragrance. The two women cooperated urgently and in harmony in tidying up the mess, as if it had been well rehearsed.

"It okay! It okay!" Mrs. Kubota kept saying in response to my feeble attempts at apology, as I finally got down on my knees and tried to assist in picking up the now nonexistent crumbs. I saw Takuya only from the corner of my eye, looking amused; I purposely did not catch his glance.

After the cleanup portion of the program had finished, I sat like a stone in my chair, gazing at the sweets but deeming it too risky to go for another.

As the conversation moved along, Mrs. Kubota was smiling so much that there seemed a high probability that her mouth would be rendered disabled by the end of the afternoon. When Takuya joined in, he began to translate into English for me from time to time, explaining that Sakura was inquiring about his stay in Seattle and what he was planning to do at Sunny Shokuhin now that he had returned to Tokyo. Sakura also looked at me now and then, her chipmunk eyes blinking, and said a word or two in English.

"You are from California?" she asked, sipping from her teacup.

"Yes. San Jose."

She thought for a moment. "'Do you know way to San Jose?'" she sang, giggling.

"That's right. Yes, I do." I grinned but stopped when it felt somehow that my teeth had grown too big for my mouth. "I enjoy your TV show."

"Thank you!"

By the time Mrs. Kubota seemed to be motioning at me to allow Takuya and Sakura some time alone together, the subject of *Sakura's Gaijin Star Is Born* still had not come up, at least as far as I could tell. I looked at Takuya for a comforting glance or a raise of his eyebrows, but neither was forthcoming.

Then Takuya said in English, "We need to talk a little."

"Yes, please!" Sakura said, cocking her head, a robin intent on searching out her worm. "Thank you very much!"

Mrs. Kubota was already on her way to the kitchen. I excused myself and followed her. I apologized again about the problematic brownie.

"Daijōbu," she said. "It okay." Mrs. Kubota grinned. "So nice, Sakura-san, *ne?*"

"Yes, very nice," I replied, trying to give her my best pleasant gaijin smile as I helped put away the breakfast dishes that had been left out to dry. Was it too much to hope that Takuya was only talking to Sakura about the karaoke contest and not madly kissing her?

"So nice for Takuya!"

Mrs. Kubota was beaming. Did she notice the cloud covering my face? Stop being a busybody, *Okaasan.*

She poured iced tea for the two of us. "Soon," she said as she sat at the kitchen table. "I see you sing—TV!"

"I hope so," I said. "Then I can show Hiromi Taniguchi's picture and tell the story."

"Yes! It so nice thing. She must watch," she said. "And your singing so beautiful. You win grand prize."

"I don't know about that," I said, happy that someone had some confidence in me. But was I hearing her right? Mrs. Kubota's sentence structure sounded more cohesive than usual, as if her English had improved overnight.

Finally, Sakura entered the kitchen, and I could tell she was saying that she had to get going by her use of the phrase that literally meant she was sorry that she was about to be rude. She thanked Mrs. Kubota for inviting her, giggled, and bowed her head. She turned to me. "And Takuya-san say you like to be on my karaoke contest. I am so glad!"

"Please don't humiliate me," I murmured, not intending to say it out loud.

"Eh?" she said, wide-eyed. She didn't understand.

I smiled. "Thank you so much. I am looking forward to it. *Domo arigato!*"

We walked back to the living room where Takuya was now standing. Everyone said their good-byes and thank yous again, along with much bowing and cheerful apologizing: Mrs. Kubota for not having done enough and having to reschedule the date, Sakura for having taken too much advantage of her kindness and putting her to so much trouble. I knew by now that this was the type of banter you engaged in if you were Japanese—it was in the DNA.

Takuya accompanied Sakura outside, and I didn't know if this was now a date or what. It was ridiculous, but my heart sank. I didn't know why I had to feel so jealous of his interest in this woman, but I was heartened when he returned a few minutes later.

"She is excited to have you on the contest," he said to me.

"Yes, she told me. Thank you, Takuya."

"I will get the entry form tomorrow from her."

"You'll see her tomorrow?"

"The TV network is not too far from Sunny Shokuhin office. I go back to work tomorrow."

"I see. Thanks." Would they go ahead and have lunch too? A lunch that would lead to dinner, which would facilitate their getting back together? Had they just split temporarily for geographical reasons? I pictured Sakura in a buckskin skirt and red cowgirl boots, lasso in hand, roping Takuya in for another go-round.

Mrs. Kubota, her mouth still in an upturned position, burbled on to her son. I couldn't understand a word, but for all I knew she could have been saying, "I know a good jeweler who can help you pick out the engagement ring." I garnered no clue from Takuya's tone of voice or the look on his face. And Mrs. Kubota remained in permanent smile mode, as if she was confident that the two were on their way to resuming their relationship, and she'd help the process along in any way she could.

Now I realized there was a change in Takuya, though I couldn't pinpoint it. Yet I knew something was different. Then it hit me: he was standing upright, his posture straight, instead of leaning on his crutch.

"You're not using your crutch?" I asked.

"Actually, my foot feels good now," he said, scratching his head in wonder.

I sighed. First Mrs. Kubota's improved English, now Takuya's foot; was it that the great Sakura possessed magical healing powers as well?

"So the contest is not until July twenty-first," Takuya said. "You can practice well. Then I take you karaoke bar. Maybe in two weeks?"

"Are you sure you have the time?"

"I make the free time because I want to." His smile was endearing, warm.

Was it a different smile from the ones he'd been flashing at Sakura all afternoon? I just wasn't sure.

18

CLUB MAI

"SAKURA SASAKI IS HIS FUCKING EX-GIRLFRIEND?"

Mariko was almost shouting in the classroom.

"Not so loud," I said with a grimace. "But, yes, she is."

"I can't fucking believe it." Mariko was beyond flabbergasted and at an unusual loss for words. And when I relayed the fact that I had actually met this creature in her perfect flesh, all she could say was "*Wow.*"

Then I told her that I had found out that Takuya also had a girlfriend in Seattle, but Mariko just sniffed when she heard this. "Those long-distance things never work. Out of mind, out of sight."

I wondered if she was right. I decided to change the subject. "Can you help me translate the lyrics to '*Nozomi no Hoshi*'? So I know exactly what I'm singing? I have a rough idea, but there's a lot I don't understand."

"Tell me everything about what's going to happen with this contest."

"Well, what I know is that July twenty-first is the first round. They will have fifteen contestants. Then they'll choose five to come back the following week to compete for the grand prize," I said. "You didn't tell me anything about a recording contract and 300,000 yen."

Mariko frowned. "Well, you came here to find your aunt's sister. I thought that was the most important—not these other details. But, yes, maybe you'll turn into some gaijin *enka* rock star or something."

"I'm going to go for it."

"Good for you! Go for the gold. The whole—what do you say?" Mariko looked thoughtful. "The whole taco?"

"*What?*"

She clapped her hands. "Wait! No! It's the whole goddamned enchilada!"

"That's right."

"*Gambatte kudasai.*"

"Huh?"

"Japanese like to say *gambatte kudasai.* Do your best," Mariko explained. "That's one of their favorite phrases. Not 'good luck' like you'd say in America, but *do your best*. It's all very Japanese. Work hard, you know? Don't depend on luck. And when someone says that to you, you have to say '*Gambarimasu*'—yes, I'll do my best. It's like the law here."

"*Gambarimasu.*"

"Good!"

"Takuya said he'd take me to a karaoke bar so I can practice singing in front of an audience."

"Ah! Very nice. You better practice hard. Give him the performance of your life. Make yourself so irresistible that he'll have to grab you once you leave the stage."

I explained to her about the unromantic trip to Maruyama. "I told you, Mariko, it's a lost cause. I think he really sees me as his homestay sister."

"You can't have that kind of attitude. He's an idiot if he can't see what you mean to him. He doesn't *have* to take you to the karaoke bar, you know."

"Maybe he's just being a nice Japanese boy."

"I don't think so. Anyway, do you want him to go back to that little creep?"

"No."

"And there's old Mrs. Something-Up-Her-Butt pushing for it, right?"

"Takuya doesn't like his mother interfering."

"Don't underestimate the power of those two women. You've got to fight back. You've got to win him over."

Mariko's cell phone rang and her face went ashen, as if she dreaded that this could be news about her sister. I held my breath right along with her but was relieved to see her smile. Then she began chattering on in English about a grocery list.

"The husband," she said, sighing after hanging up. "Always so clueless." She looked at me. "Even more important, though, is what the hell are you going to wear?"

"Wear?"

"For the goddamned contest."

I sure as hell didn't know what I was going to wear for the goddamned contest.

"And you have to have *two* outfits—one for the first show and another for when you're one of the five finalists," she went on.

"But how am I going to buy anything when all the clothes here are size negative zero for all these thin, tiny Japanese women?"

"I know the perfect place in Roppongi."

"You do?" What was it—a secret store for the nonexistent plus-size Japanese woman?

"Leave it to me. Let's go now."

"But I don't have much money on me at the moment." I didn't have much money period.

"I can front you. Don't worry."

On the subway ride Mariko explained that "*Nozomi no Hoshi*" was a song about two fairy-tale lovers reminiscent of those celebrated in the Tanabata or Star Festival, held in July every year in Japan. The legend talked about the Weaver Princess and the Cattle Herder who fell in love but were separated by the Milky Way. Only once a year on the seventh day of the seventh month did they have the chance to meet. The custom was to tie a piece of paper with your wish to a wishing tree during the Star Festival.

"Takuya's mother and Sakura are your Milky Way," she said. "Preventing Takuya from crossing over."

"Oh, you think so?"

"Maybe you can wish for Takuya to meet you across that Milky Way. Anyway, ask him to take you to one of the festivals in July. It is before your contest. Maybe your wish will come true."

I was greedy with wishes. To find Hiromi Taniguchi, to find out about the man in the home movie, and to have Takuya reciprocate my feelings. Also, to master *"Nozomi no Hoshi"* and show up Dirk by winning the recording contract plus the grand prize money, as well as being able to survive appearing on television, Sakura Sasaki and all.

Mariko explained that Roppongi was an area where many gaijin lived and socialized, with stores that catered to expatriates. She pointed to a market with a window display of items targeted at the homesick American that could be had at a price: chili con carne, Bud Light, Oreos, authentic beef jerky. I harbored no nostalgia for any of these, finding all Japanese food—even fish for breakfast—supremely delicious. I didn't care if I never encountered another frozen-pizza pocket.

I feared that the dress shop would be called Big Mama's, but instead the name was the respectable Jill's Couture. A middle-aged British woman owned it—the eponymous Jill—and her husband worked at the same university as Mariko's.

"This is Celeste. She's a singer and will be appearing on television and needs two different outfits," Mariko said.

I was about to protest, about to say that I couldn't quite truly call myself a singer, but I stopped myself. No, I thought, you *are* a singer.

Jill was polite and professional and steered me toward a rack of dresses that appeared to be in my size. There was a little bit of everything, from conservative suits to slinky numbers with bright sequins and feather boas, the latter for expressing one's inner drag queen or call girl, I surmised. I wondered just how much a dress here would set me back—I couldn't find any price tags.

"How do I know how much they are?" I said in a low voice, trying to be discreet.

"They're all priced wholesale. They shouldn't be more than 5,000 or 6,000 yen each," Mariko replied.

She flipped through the rack on the other side and in five minutes had six dresses picked out, while I'd yet to choose even one.

"Try these on," she commanded. "I'll sit over here and you can model them for me."

Once I was in the closet-sized fitting room, the first dress I tried would not budge over my hips no matter how much I maneuvered it—so much for that. A blue one with a high neck and three-quarter sleeves worked better. It wasn't the type I would have selected for myself, but it fit, a fact which put it at the top of the list. And it didn't look *too* bad. I went to show Mariko.

She stuck out her tongue in response. "Yuck! Makes you look like an office lady going to her retirement party. Next!"

A purple dress hit right above the knee, and its plunging neckline rendered my breasts as two double-scoops of ice cream. The perfect outfit for soliciting outside a love hotel, this was also not the style I would have picked for myself. I wasn't surprised, though, when Mariko approved and told me to put it in the "maybe" pile.

"But doesn't it make my boobs look too big?" I asked.

"And you're telling me that is a negative?"

About an hour and a dozen or so dresses later, I had chosen two: the purple double-scoop one and a black one with form-fitting sleeves that belled at the wrist. It was the most conservative, the one that felt the most comfortable looks-wise, though I was concerned that it was a little too tight. The grand total was 10,000 yen, rather a steal, although it would be handy to win the contest's grand prize of 300,000 yen to make up for it.

Mariko handed me the plastic bag emblazoned with Jill's Couture after charging the dresses on her credit card.

"I know you're going to win," she said.

I practiced "*Nozomi no Hoshi*" until I had it memorized both in Japanese and in English translation. Standing in front of the mirror on the back of Rika's bedroom door, I sang to my reflection. I knew I sounded good even though I could, perhaps, have been a tad off pitch. But my nerves escalated when I thought about performing on television, imagining Sakura Sasaki standing next to me, pointing and laughing, visions of insulting dialogue balloons dancing over my head and cameras cutting away to animated hippos. Even the thought of singing in front of Takuya at the karaoke bar produced an anxiety hard to shake.

The Club Mai Karaoke Pub was in Shibuya. For the night of my karaoke performance I suggested meeting at the Hachikō statue, since Takuya would be coming from Sunny Shokuhin.

My heart fluttered when my eyes caught him standing in front of the dog statue. Takuya's tall, slim build was the type that wore anything well, from jeans to business attire. His gray suit was tailored perfectly to his body, his pale yellow tie still freshly knotted. He had come to my rescue, holding a large, black umbrella to ward off the light rain. I'd forgotten to bring one, even though Mrs. Kubota had warned me about the forecast of inclement weather. Almost overnight the temperature seemed to turn from spring's coolness to summer's heat and humidity. Now, the moment I stepped outside, it was like taking a shower with my clothes on; my blouse stuck to my skin, the sweat hanging onto the back of my knees, while my feet swam in pools of perspiration.

Takuya smiled when he saw me and raised his hand in an enthusiastic wave, the heat seeming not to faze him.

Ever since he'd returned to work at Sunny Shokuhin I rarely saw him at home; he left early and returned late at night.

"Have you eaten dinner?" he asked.

"No."

"Do you mind if we have something before the karaoke?"

I pointed to the bright yellow sign across the boulevard. "Curry Zone?"

He rolled his eyes. "Okay. Curry Zone."

The place was brightly lit, with yellow plastic tables and matching chairs, but still more decorative than a fast-food outfit. Bright pictures of scenes from India adorned the walls, and large, silver curry pots were on display tables.

The curry was a thick, golden-colored stew of chicken, yellow onions, and carrots, next to a heaping mound of white rice. "I know you have second thoughts about working at Sunny Shokuhin," I said once we started eating. "But I really do love this curry rice."

"As much as you like chocolate brownie with whipped cream?"

"That was so embarrassing."

"It was more embarrassment for watching Sakura and my mother in contest trying to see who would clean up first."

"Is that what that was?"

My nervousness about my upcoming appearance at the Club Mai did not affect my appetite. Takuya smiled, noticing my empty plate. "You really enjoy the curry."

"Yes. I'm afraid that I'm always a member of the clean plate club."

"Clean plate club? That is funny." He left some cash on the table. "Shall we go karaoke bar now?"

My body stiffened at his words. "I guess so."

"You look like you are going to the jail."

"Does it show that much?"

"Be strong. You will do good."

The Club Mai Karaoke Pub was several blocks away from Curry Zone. I huddled under the umbrella with Takuya, an excuse to take his arm, which was both comforting and exciting. I imagined us as lovers, intent on renting a room at one of the Tokyo Disneyland love hotels in the quiet hills I remembered from my visit to Uranai Sushi with Mariko, and which weren't too far away from where we were.

Out of nowhere, a powerful wind nearly snatched control of the umbrella from Takuya. It turned inside out, and the rain now poured down in buckets, drenching us. "It still kind of early," he said, steering me into the entryway of a department store. "Maybe we can go in here until rain stops."

He helped me find the rest room and I went to freshen up, though there wasn't much I could do to repair my sewer-rat look. When I was done, I found him sitting on a bench that was part of an elaborate display. Paper streamers in bold hues of blue, yellow, orange, pink, and green hung from the ceiling. Around the bench were bamboo trees with smaller streamers hanging from them. People gathered around a table where young women wearing Madeline hats and pink suits seemed to be selling the colorful pieces of paper.

"What are these for?" I asked, pointing to the streamers. "A big sale?"

"No, it is for *Tanabata*. Star Festival. They celebrate for it in July and August." He thought for a moment. "Are you knowing that your song, '*Nozomi no Hoshi*,' is kind of about Star Festival story?"

I sat next to him. "Mariko explained a little about that to me, but . . ."

"I will explain for you even though I do not remember each details," he said. He looked like a little boy excited to tell a story he'd learned at school. "How do you say it? Once a time . . . ?"

"Once upon a time."

"Yes! Once upon a time there was a cow-herding prince named Hikoboshi, and a princess named Orihime, who is a weaver."

I nodded.

"They live in outer space."

"Outer space?"

"It is just story. Do you not want to hear?" His voice was teasing.

"Yes, go on."

"Thank you." He collected his thoughts and told me pretty much the same tale as Mariko. "The two lovers can only meet one time a year and that is, I think, seventh day of seventh month—July seventh," he went on. "And some people say if that day is raining or cloudy, they cannot meet."

"Isn't today July seventh?"

Takuya looked at his watch. "Yes, it is!" He laughed. "Too bad the weather is horrible. They do not meet."

I looked at the bamboo trees adorned with the colorful streamers. I could see they were marked with writing.

"Are those wishing trees?" I remembered Mariko saying something about writing a wish on a piece of paper and tying it to a tree.

Takuya beamed. "You know so well. Shall we do the wish?" He bought two pieces of paper from one of the young women, then pulled a pen from his pocket. I wanted to write my wish in Japanese, but it wasn't possible without a dictionary and a few hours to kill, so I made do with English. After Takuya scribbled his, we tied them to one of the trees blooming with the little papers.

"What did you wish for?" he asked.

"Are you sure that I can tell you?"

He looked hurt. "What?"

"Sometimes when you make a wish you're not supposed to tell anyone because then it won't come true."

"Really? I never hear that rule."

"Well, it's not exactly a rule, but . . ."

"Everyone can read the wish on the paper."

He had a point, though I couldn't read his.

"So you do not want to say your wish?" he asked, giving a little pout.

"No. I'll tell you. I couldn't write all this down, but I wish that Hiromi Taniguchi will see me sing on television and hear my story about me searching for her. And that we will meet and have a reunion and she will tell me about the man in the home movie."

Takuya smiled. "Yes. That is nice, good wish."

"What did you wish for?" I almost didn't ask him. Had he wished for a reunion with Seattle Holly? A rekindled romance with Sakura? How I wished I could read his writing. If I'd had another streamer, I would wish for his falling for me.

"I think there is rule that say I cannot tell you."

"I think there is a rule that says you *have* to tell me."

He gave a sinister laugh. "If I tell you, then I will have to kill you."

I smiled. "Where did you learn that?"

"I do not remember. But my wish is for you to having success performance at Club Mai Karaoke Pub."

The rain seemed to have let up so we left the department store and made our way onto a narrow backstreet choking with people and lined with tiny bars and clubs, indicated by their illuminated red paper lanterns. Takuya led me down a teetering staircase that turned into a dark underground passageway. I held tight onto his arm until my eyes adjusted to the subdued light, and saw that we were now entering a surprisingly large room. Scattered with lacquered wood tables and chairs, a chrome bar stretched across the back.

We got settled at one of the few open tables. The lack of air-conditioning was apparent right away and I was coming close to melting. Takuya went to get some drinks, and I took out my handkerchief to wipe the sweat from my forehead and the back of my neck.

On a stage at the front of the room, a young man in a business suit sang a Japanese rock song. His friends and colleagues were cheering him on despite his being wildly off-key. But his enthusiasm was sincere, especially when he got down on one knee for the finale and sang his heart out into the microphone, banging his fist on the floor in time to the musical beat. I thought of how appalled Dirk would be. But no one booed or acted rude, as would be the case on *Hen na Gaijin,* though it was true that he was Japanese and so was everyone in the club except me. The audience rewarded him with polite applause, and he walked off the stage in triumph, pumping his fist, a boxer who had just scored a knockout. As at Hysteric Echo, there was a video screen, although about twice as large. It was attached to the wall behind the singer who read the lyrics on a TV monitor in the front.

I nearly wept for joy at the sight of Takuya bringing two frosty draft beers. "I signed you up," he said. "There are two people ahead of you."

I gulped down almost half the beer, then pressed the glass against my forehead.

Takuya laughed. "Are you okay?"

"It's just so hot."

He nodded, finally taking off his jacket. "Tokyo summer."

Next up on the stage were two women, dressed in identical outfits of white blouses, dark blue vests, and matching skirts—the office lady look. They sang a folk song in quiet but sweet voices, even doing passable harmony work. Again, they received polite applause, to which one of the women reacted by giggling and fanning her red face with her hand.

I wiped my face with my still-damp handkerchief and tried to smooth my not-quite-dry hair with my fingers. I knew I must still look like I just stepped out of the sauna but did not feel like confirming this via a trip to the bathroom. It was, as they said, *shikata ga nai.* I would be up after the next singer, an older man who sang an *enka* song in a voice more gasp than musical. I couldn't stop crossing and uncrossing my legs, which were slippery from perspiration. If you feel this way at a karaoke bar, I thought, singing in front of forty people at most, how are you going to manage performing on TV in front of millions?

There was no more time for conjecture. Over the loudspeaker poured forth the opening chords to "*Nozomi no Hoshi.*" It was time.

Takuya gently pushed my arm, "That's you! *Gambatte kudasai!*"

"*Gambarimasu,*" I murmured, remembering the word Mariko had taught me. My sweaty body seemed to tremble in rhythm with the music as I walked up to the stage and took the microphone. I thought of singing for Mrs. Kubota and the neighbors, of the female Thomas Jefferson at Uranai Sushi, of my mother onstage with her band at Alum Rock Park. I thought of rehearsing in Dirk's living room and him stopping me midway through a song.

I stood on the stage, and before I even sang a note, an enormous roar erupted from the audience. It had to be the power of a gaijin. Were their expectations ridiculously high or low? My ears filled with their whistling and yelling, and the introduction to the song seemed to take forever. Spontaneously I decided to bow in a manner as to imitate Maki Kanda, and this elicited an even stronger reaction.

Although I had the words memorized, when the lyrics appeared on the TV monitor, I made sure to look at them. I wanted to avoid any mistakes. When I began to sing, I tried hard to pretend that I was only in Rika's room instead of in front of an audience of Japanese people who seemed to be hanging on to my every word.

But next, something strange occurred. The crowd that had been so effusive in its initial reaction had become dead silent. Even the bartender had stopped what he was doing to watch. While I sang the lyrics about not wanting to be separated any longer from my lover by the Milky Way, I stole a glance at Takuya. His face seemed frozen in surprise, as if he were watching a spectacle he couldn't quite believe.

I sang on, unsure what to think of this strange reaction. Had I veered out of tune? Was I singing the wrong words? Did I look, well, just plain *weird?* I didn't know. It occurred to me that this could have been a more realistic audience than Mrs. Yasuda and Mrs. Nozaki, whose over-the-top reactions may have been the result of wanting to be polite to their friend, Mrs. Kubota. And if Dirk were in the audience, what would he be thinking?

The chorus was about to end, and in a moment there would be the instrumental break. This was when people were supposed to clap and the singer could take a breather until the reprise of another verse and chorus. Would people even applaud? I held the note, making sure to give it the vibrato that Maki Kanda did on the recording. Up until now my body had felt warm and clammy throughout the whole performance, but now I could feel chills creeping up my back. At this point it was moot to keep obsessing about what the audience was thinking. I had done my best, and it felt good to do my best. Maybe this was how Barbara felt when she sang; maybe this was why it had been her passion.

The instrumental break began, and then I heard it. The applause was deafening, like the screams of people aboard a roller coaster plunging toward its deepest dip. I looked over at Takuya who was clapping so hard his hands must have stung. Everyone else in the club kept applauding along with him.

The rest of the song was a blur. I finished somehow, amid shouts of "Encore! Encore!" I made my way back to my chair, exhausted, and once again the moisture was beading up behind the collar of my shirt, trickling all the way down to the back of my knees.

Takuya still looked dazed, as if he were in the middle of a dream.

"I do not believe," he said when I sat down. He held on to my arm. "My mother say you are so good and I hear a little bit when you practice in Rika's room, but I never think . . ."

His reaction was far beyond my expectation. "Thank you, Takuya."

He stared into my face. "How do you sing in Japanese with such a passion?"

"I don't know," I said. "This music just moves me, I guess. I'm not sure why."

One of the office ladies who'd sung before me came over to our table. "You sing beautiful," she said in English. "Better than a Japanese." She pushed a piece of paper and a pen in my direction. "May I have autograph?"

Dirk, someone asked for my *autograph*. I looked over at Takuya who appeared as surprised as I was. "Thank you," I said, signing my name.

The woman grinned. *"Domo arigato!"*

"Wow!" Takuya said. "Autograph!"

He continued to hold on to my arm, and I wondered if he even realized what he was doing.

"It is not doubt that you will win contest," he said.

When he excused himself to go to the rest room, the bartender brought two drinks to the table. "Singing very nice," he said, giving me a thumbs-up. "On za house. *Dozo*."

"Domo arigato." With a response like this, I thought, perhaps *I would* win *Sakura's Gaijin Star Is Born*.

"Did you buy more drinks?" Takuya asked when he returned.

I explained to him that they were on the house.

"You make such good impression."

When we finished, Takuya said he wanted to take me to one of his favorite coffee places, which wasn't too far from the Club Mai.

Once we were outside, the rain had turned into a warm drizzle. Steam rose in white puffs from the street, and the crowds had yet to dissipate.

We soon reached a small *kissaten* called Eighty-Eight. I sneezed twice in succession, my nose catching the chill of its air conditioner, but I welcomed the relief. Shelves were piled with the sleeves of dusty old records, as if we had stumbled into a jazz piano lover's attic. A real piano sat in the corner.

"Eighty-Eight been here forever," Takuya said. "I do not like to go chain place for coffee. This one brews with special beans and special drip water filter. They play only piano jazz music. It is more expensive, but I do not care." He sounded excited to share this with me. "This better coffee than Seattle."

I could see that the piano music that played was coming from an old record player. A man probably in his sixties standing behind the counter waved to Takuya as though he were a regular customer. Behind him were rows of jars filled with different types of coffee beans. Tiny candles flickered in empty coffee jars on the counter.

Takuya ordered two coffees, and we sat at the only empty table in the back, next to a big black-and-white poster of a jazz trio in concert, which looked like vintage 1960.

"When you say you want your own business, is this the kind of place you'd like to have?" I asked him.

He leaned back in his chair, his smile enveloping his face. "Ah, in a dream it would be nice. But I know it not practical idea. It is hard to make living with place like this now. Too many coffee chain shops make them go out of business." He sipped his coffee. "This one of last real *jazu-kissa*," he said. "Jazz music *kissaten*."

It was the perfect place to feel cozy, I thought, to dry off from a night rain, with a man who seemed to have been captivated by my singing, who couldn't stop holding my arm at the karaoke bar. I hung on to the memory.

"Thank you for taking me to the Club Mai," I said. "I have never sung in front of so many people before. I never thought that I would."

"Why? You have such nice voice."

"I used to sing with my friend Dirk back home in San Jose, but we never played in front of anyone." I explained to him about Dirk's complaints and how he often criticized me. "Hearing that over and over makes you lose your confidence."

He shook his head. "I think Dark is crazy."

"Dirk."

"Why did you listen to him?"

It was a good question. "Well, he was my boyfriend too. It was complicated."

"I see." Takuya looked thoughtful and we both didn't say anything for several moments. Then he finally said, "You sing like you have Japanese soul. And no American accent. *Enka* is hard to sing, even for a Japanese person. How you do it?"

It seemed that he couldn't stop asking that question. "I have no idea. Maybe I was Japanese in a past life."

"Past life?"

"You know. Reincarnation."

"Did someone tell you that?"

"No." I laughed. "But what other explanation could there be?"

I noticed the lightness in his face, how his expression had changed. Was it my imagination? He couldn't stop watching me, as if he'd had a realization, as if he were viewing me in a different way.

On the ride home, we sat closely on the train in silence. Takuya's head rested slightly against mine due to the pull of the train, its stops and starts nudging us together. Once we reached Asahidai the rain had cleared, the umbrella was no longer necessary, and there was no need to take his arm. The air remained warm but now smelled fresh and dewy instead of harsh and metallic. We didn't speak during the walk home either. Yet it wasn't an uncomfortable quiet—it was the feeling of not having to say a word because nothing needed to be said. Everything was understood, or at least this was how I chose to interpret it.

When we reached the front door, I could see that the lights were on in the living room, which was unusual since it was late—almost eleven thirty.

Takuya didn't open the door right away. The entryway was dark, but I could still make out that face, that perfect face. He stood in front of me, close, as if he was about to say something. Was he leaning in closer? He seemed to be. I took a breath.

"Celeste-san," he said.

"Yes?"

"I could not believe how beautiful is your singing. I—"

An intense brightness interrupted him. Nearly blinded, I instinctively tried to shield my eyes. The light next to the front door had suddenly come on with such force that it illuminated the two of us like a searchlight.

"Okaeri nasai!"

Startled, Takuya turned away from me.

The door was now open wide and there stood Mrs. Kubota, her worried face bathed with light, welcoming us home.

19

AT THIRTY-THREE

AT FIRST IT SEEMED THAT I HAD MY DIRECTIONS MIXED UP. THE BUILDING IN Shinagawa appeared to be an ordinary office complex or perhaps a small group of apartments. But when I craned my neck to scan the highest part for a possible sign, I could make out an unusual sculpture attached to the front wall—large jade-green birds, their wings spread in flight, ready to take off and soar to the sky.

Three middle-aged women, each dressed in black, entered the automatic sliding glass entrance door. This had to be the right place. I smoothed my own black jacket and matching skirt with my hands, an outfit that seemed so out of place on this scorching day, the sun beating down with full force.

Mariko had called me late the other night. At first I didn't recognize her voice. It was too quiet, too soft. She told me her sister had passed away and it would mean a lot if I would attend the memorial service. Her request surprised me; wouldn't only very close friends and family be invited? But I supposed her invitation meant how close Mariko must have felt to me, and I realized how grateful I was for her friendship. Though sometimes her behavior had been hard to understand, her help appearing misguided, she always seemed to have had the best intentions. And the more I thought about it, much of her unpredictability had probably been due to all the stress she'd been undergoing in dealing with her sister's illness. I didn't hesitate, saying that of course I would attend.

On the first floor of the building were three separate banquet rooms, each decorated with elaborate altars and each seeming to be holding separate funerals. I asked one of the attendants which was for Megumi Wada, and he pointed to the room on the far left.

This was not only my first Japanese funeral but my first funeral ever. My mother had been cremated and there'd been no ceremony. I entered the room and gazed at the altar, which took up a whole wall, brimming with pink and white lilies, and bowls filled with apples, melons, and tangerines.

Then I saw a face.

Heart-shaped, with bright brown eyes—the resemblance to Mariko was overwhelming. It was the face of her sister, in a photograph, framed in black. Megumi's smile was cheerful, robust, young; so at odds with the somber occasion that it hurt my eyes to look at her. Bouquets of bright purple orchids and more pink lilies burst from vases surrounding her picture, a valiant attempt at giving comfort, though unsuccessful. Signs with kanji painted in perfect calligraphy, all in balance, some expressing movement, others expressing stillness, hung on the walls. I thought of the childish attempts that filled my sketch pad at home.

And in the very front of the room, an open casket; I shuddered at the sight. I didn't want to look, but it seemed from observing the other mourners that paying respect in this way was natural and expected. I walked past, stopping for only a brief moment to take in Megumi's face; her cheeks rouged, her eyes closed peacefully, her lips painted pink and shaped into a serene smile. My chest seemed to sink to the floor. It was all that I could stand. I had to turn away.

A group of about fifty chairs were placed in rows in the middle of the room, with more set up on the side. They were already filling up fast, and since I had yet to locate Mariko, I decided to find a place to sit. As I was about to take a seat, I heard someone call my name.

I turned around to see a woman in a modest black dress and black flats, a delicate string of pearls circling her neck. It was Mariko, but it wasn't Mariko. At least not the one I knew, with the snazzy leather jacket and yellow spiked heels. Instead of bouncy and free, her long hair was woven into a tight bun, constricted. She looked old, drawn, as if her usual high spirits had been siphoned out of her. By her side stood a Caucasian man wearing wire-rim glasses, who looked to be in his fifties, his thin hair in blond-gray wisps. He gave off a distinguished, reserved air, apt for a college professor: he had to be Frederick Harris, her husband.

"Thank you so much for coming," Mariko said.

I took her hands in mine. "I am so sorry." I bowed my head.

She gave me a nod and I tried hard to hold back my tears when I noticed the corners of her mouth quivering. Her husband introduced himself and also thanked me for taking the time to attend. Mariko told me where I could sit, then hurried off to greet another guest.

A few of the attendees were gaijin, perhaps from Frederick's university. They probably spoke English, but I didn't feel like talking to anyone. There were also a number of Japanese people who looked my age, who must have been Megumi's friends. I continued to stare at her photograph, at that face that was much too young.

The ceremony began with several people giving speeches. I could understand only a bit here and there, my brain having turned into a colander when it came to retaining Japanese, with most of the words escaping through the holes. But I could tell that my comprehension skills had improved since the day I'd arrived at the Kubota house. A decent amount of the language now jumped out at me, words that I could understand.

Still, it was easy for my mind to meander, wandering through a maze of dark thoughts. Thirty-three. Megumi's age, my mother's age when she died, my age. It was too powerful for it to be only a coincidence, something lacking any sense or meaning. The melody of "*Nozomi no Hoshi*" drifted in and out of my head. My body ached from sitting still for such a long time, from being in a room consumed with so much grief.

There were more speeches. An attractive, vibrant woman, perhaps Megumi's friend or former classmate, broke down, unable to continue talking, as if it were unfathomable to her to be at a funeral for someone in her early thirties. I gazed at Mariko sitting to the side in the front, constantly dabbing her eyes with a handkerchief.

When the speeches were over and relatives had burned incense at the altar, I understood that now was the time for the guests to go up to the receiving line to pay their respects to the family.

"It was an honor to be invited," I said to Mariko. "*Domo arigato.*" I bowed my head.

"I so appreciate your coming," she said. She looked deep into my face. "Celeste-san, I want you to know that right now, about the only thing I have to look forward to, to get my mind off all of this, is your singing contest."

My contest? I was taken aback by her words. I did not expect a topic as trivial as Sakura's gaijin karaoke show to be brought up at such an occasion.

"So I want you to do your best. For yourself." She took my hand. "And for me."

Her eyes were watery and there was a pulsing in my throat. "Of course, Mariko."

"*Gambatte kudasai.*"

"*Gambarimasu.*"

Shaken and shaky, I rode the train home, experiencing the usual staring contest with the passengers. My eyes burned and I knew they had to be red. I also understood how upset I must have looked, and dressed as I was, head to toe in black on a stifling summer day, it had to be obvious to my railway audience that I was either returning from or heading to a funeral. I needed to calm myself, to shut it all out. I closed my eyes and kept them closed right up until I heard the announcement, "*Asahidai. Asahidai de gozaimasu.*"

I imagined arriving home and seeing Mrs. Kubota in the kitchen. There would already be a plate of fruit or rice crackers on the table, or if I was lucky and she had been to the bakery, some shoe creams. She'd fix a pot of tea and I would try to tell her my thoughts and concerns that consumed me while at Megumi Wada's funeral. With her warm eyes and the broken English that never seemed to quite get fixed, she would still be able to comfort me.

But when I arrived home, the house was empty, silent. I went to my room. Sitting at my desk, I thumbed through the dictionary to look up how to write *gambarimasu.* I took my brush, dipped it in the dark black ink, and began to draw. Began to write. Draw. Write. Draw. Write.

がんばります

がんばります

がんばります

Gambarimasu.
Gambarimasu.
Gambarimasu.

I filled page after page. I couldn't stop and continued even when my tears began falling, even when they began mixing with the ink, blurring the strokes, the characters melting into gray blotches on the paper.

Still, their meaning was clear.

20

A STAR IS BORN

THE FUTURISTIC, ALL-GLASS BUILDING STRETCHED OVER ONE FULL BLOCK OF the trendy, sophisticated neighborhood of Aoyama, appearing to have been dropped into Tokyo courtesy of an alien spaceship.

This sleek, intimidating place was the home of the Japan Broadcasting System, known more commonly as JBS, and once I entered its wide doors glistening in the sunlight, it was impossible to escape the watchful eyes of Sakura Sasaki. A banner billowed on high, plastered with her gigantic picture, strung up on the wall behind the lobby reception desk. Her eyes were wide in surprise, her smile mischievous. With her right hand she made a V sign. Huge roman letters and Japanese writing as well proclaimed *Sakura's Gaijin Star Is Born!* Along with the banner were smaller signs showing the JBS logo, an animated yellow flower with a cheerful face, a winking right eye, its mouth turned upward into a grin. It was supposed to be cute, but there was something not quite right about it, perhaps something even a little frightening. The JBS employees, scurrying about like worker ants, wore name tags with the same flower logo on their chests, next to buttons with Sakura's face. It could only be called the Sakura Sasaki cult.

Mrs. Kubota and Takuya had seen me off in a taxi for the rehearsal, promising to be at the show, which was at seven o'clock the same evening, along with Mr. Kubota and Mariko and her husband.

I had decided to bring the slightly tight black dress, not wanting to worry about popping out of the purple double-scoop one.

I wondered if anyone else would be singing an *enka* song. On *Hen na Gaijin* people sang mostly pop hits or traditional Japanese songs that everyone in Japan learned as children. A gaijin singing *enka* seemed to be an unusual spectacle. I planned to use this to my advantage and sing the hell out of "*Nozomi no Hoshi.*" And I now had a full determination to be strong enough to withstand any barbs and humiliation from Sakura.

"First you will have interview," the receptionist said, directing me to a small office down the hall.

The barren room contained only a simple metal desk and two matching chairs on either side, so different in atmosphere from the slick lobby. A clock set about ten minutes fast hung slightly off-kilter on the wall. A few moments later a young Japanese woman arrived. She was in her twenties. The color of her short, spiky hair resembled that of a maraschino cherry. She sat in the chair behind the desk.

"How do you do," she said, extending her hand. "I am Umeko Imai. I am producer for *Sakura's Gaijin Star Is Born.*"

I introduced myself and Umeko opened a binder, her finger trailing down the page. "Ah. Here you are. You are singing '*Nozomi no Hoshi*'? An *enka* song."

"Yes," I said. "By Maki Kanda."

"Very nice. But *enka* so difficult. Good luck to you!"

"*Gambarimasu.*"

"Oh! Your Japanese very nice." She turned the pages in the binder. "And are you married?"

I'd already answered several personal information questions on the application form; didn't she know that I was single?

"No."

"How old you are?"

I sighed. "Thirty-three."

She made a stabbing mark with her pen, perhaps already checking the "loser" box.

"Now you understand that you will have short interview before you sing on the program, *ne?*"

"Yes."

"And it good idea to have interesting story to tell. Judges like that. But it must be short. Please tell me your story now."

I was confident about the interest level of my story. I explained about Aunt Mitch and how I was looking for Hiromi Taniguchi to return some family heirlooms and give her Aunt Mitch's ashes. And how I hoped to ask her about information about my father. I showed Umeko the family photos, which Takuya had helped me get blown up so they would show better on television. The story seemed to please the producer.

"Very nice. So you are wishing that Taniguchi-san or someone who knows her will be watching television tonight."

"Yes. That is my hope."

"And you are singing a song about wishing on a star. '*Nozomi no Hoshi.*' Very good. Very good." Umeko seemed to approve and wrote something in her notebook. "I want to take you now to preparation room where other contestants are waiting. I will explain about show there." She stood up and bowed. "Thank you."

In the preparation room there were about ten gaijin sitting at a large conference table, reminding me of the room at TextTrans where they held company meetings. Most of the contestants seemed to be in their twenties, which was no big surprise, but there was one woman who, to my relief, seemed to actually be older than me, perhaps Mariko's age.

The chair on my right was empty, but on my left sat a woman with bright auburn hair and striking blue eyes, almost the color of the canal water at Venezia-Lando, a hue so unnatural that I figured she must have been wearing contact lenses. She had a round face, a flawless complexion, and looked no older than Kylie, the TextTrans receptionist. She turned to me and said, "What song are *you* singing?" The question sounded more like a demand, and she was not smiling.

" '*Nozomi no Hoshi,*' " I said, wondering the reason for such abruptness.

The blue eyes stared. "By Maki Kanda?"

I nodded.

"But *I'm* doing a Maki Kanda song—'*Tabibito.*' Isn't there a rule that two people can't be doing the same singer's song?"

"Not that I'm aware of." The rules for this contest were basically gaijin plus singing-in-Japanese equaled qualified contestant, as far as I knew.

The woman folded her arms against her chest, giving off a loud sigh, then swung her right foot back and forth, turning her head toward the front of the room. Her obnoxious behavior stumped me.

As a few more gaijin trickled in, Umeko returned to the room. Miss Blue Eyes waved her arm vigorously, as if trying to show the teacher she was the student with the correct answer. Once she got Umeko's attention she began to rattle off in flawless Japanese.

I could understand enough to know that she was voicing her concern about whether two people were allowed to perform two songs from the same singer.

Umeko translated the question into English and said, "It is no problem." The obnoxious woman continued to sulk while Umeko smiled and addressed the entire group. "Welcome to the first annual *Sakura's Gaijin Star Is Born* karaoke contest!" She clapped vigorously and with a nod urged on everyone else, resulting in tepid, hesitant applause from the group of nervous gaijin. "First, we will give you your performance numbers. Then we want you to sit in numerical order."

As she called out the names and numbers, I did not hear mine until, "Emiko Trenton, number fourteen; Celeste Duncan, number fifteen."

Dead last. I'd have to wait through fourteen people before I'd perform. And the red-haired freak with the too-blue eyes was still sitting next to me because she was number fourteen. She turned toward me. *"To-ren-ton Emiko to moshimasu ga. Yoroshiku onegai shimasu."* For some reason she now felt that she could introduce herself but was compelled to do so in Japanese.

Her name was *Emiko?* She didn't look Japanese at all, and I couldn't fathom why she had to speak in Japanese to a fellow English-speaking gaijin. Was she trying to psych-out her competition? I also couldn't understand why I'd been given the bad fortune to have such a weirdo scheduled right before me, and one who was to perform a Maki Kanda song as well.

"I'm Celeste Duncan," I said, making a point to speak in English.

"Se-re-su-to-san."

This was really too much. "Yes. And your name is Emiko?"

She nodded.

"Are you Japanese?"

She thrust out her ample chest and now deigned to speak in English. "No. Emiko is my adopted name. My real name is Emily, but I've become so Japanese living here that I decided to take a Japanese name."

"Oh, I see."

"So you're doing *enka*." She sniffed. "Everyone is always so surprised when they find out *I* sing *enka* since it's so hard."

"Oh, really?"

"But learning *enka* songs has never been difficult for me. I don't know what the big deal is. I guess I just have a natural affinity for the music." She tilted her chin, her face giving off a faux-sincere expression, as if she were practicing the right pose to strike for the paparazzi. "And my photographic memory helps with learning all the kanji."

"How nice for you."

Thankfully, Emiko was forced to shut up as Umeko continued her spiel. "Let me now explain the schedule for our program, which will be a live broadcast."

The lights dimmed and a screen lowered from the ceiling. It was a PowerPoint presentation and a slide appeared for each point Umeko made. I might as well have been back at TextTrans in a human resources meeting about the new health benefits plan.

"After an introduction by Sakura-san, you will march through audience together in a line and then come on stage and sit in chairs." The slide showed a caricature of Sakura Sasaki holding a microphone, an enormous but still cute head on top of a tiny body.

The next slide was a drawing of a Caucasian man with a tremendous nose, his finger firmly placed inside his left nostril.

"You will be onstage for the entire two-hour concert so you must always look alert and cheerful," Umeko continued. "Remember not to pick your nose—the camera could be on you."

There were twitters from the audience. I never expected that I would have to be onstage the entire time.

"When your name and number is called, you will stand next to Sakura-san and tell her your story of what brought you to Japan and why you have chosen your song. Chiharu-san, our translator, will be by your side if there is any language problem, as Sakura-san will speak in both English and Japanese."

A young woman sitting next to Umeko stood up and bowed. "Good luck to all of you."

"Sakura-san is the host of show," Umeko said. "There will be four judges who will give a critique after your performance, and Chiharu-san can help translation for that too."

The next slide was a drawing of the judges. Three were Japanese; two young women and an older man, but the fourth was a Caucasian man who looked familiar.

"The judges will score each person and the points will be added up at the end of the program to determine five finalists who will come back next week. If your name is called as one of the five finalists, please come and stand by Sakura-san."

The final slide showed a curly-haired woman with big eyes clutching a bouquet of flowers, shedding tears of joy.

"First, we will run through the show. I will be standing in for Sakura-san since we want her spontaneous reaction to the stories and performances."

I could only imagine what Sakura would say about my story and performance. Would she be wearing the same persona as on *Hen na Gaijin*, a persona completely hidden when she took tea during the great brownie catastrophe at the Kubotas'? Or were they really sincere about finding a gaijin singing star? Would she be doing me a favor by acting civil because she wanted to impress Takuya? I was clueless and uncomfortable that I wouldn't find out Sakura's reaction and what she had in her bag of tricks until the live show.

We were next led into a big studio for the rehearsal, which is where the live performance would take place. I was not looking forward to having to sit through fourteen contestants before I would sing, though I would be certain to know my competition well, since I'd hear everyone's stories and songs by the time my turn arrived. I gazed at the hundreds of empty seats and imagined Takuya out there watching me.

We were all told to sit in numerical order on the stage. One by one Umeko called us to be interviewed and to sing our songs to a prerecorded track. The other entrants were required to sway and clap to the music and look otherwise engaged and smiling. It was exhausting and draining, like giving a performance for each song, especially in nervous anticipation of being the last to sing.

A couple of the contestants could sing fairly well, but most mangled the Japanese language with their atrocious pronunciation, something that would surely get a rise out of Sakura. It was then that I let myself get excited—I thought I had a good chance to take the prize. But I had yet to hear Emiko Trenton.

Emiko walked confidently to the center of the stage wearing a blue jersey dress, which matched her eyes and appeared to have been plastered on after coating her curvaceous body with a glue stick. Everyone else had worn street clothes for the rehearsal, but this dress looked stunning enough to be the one she planned to wear for the performance. She bantered in Japanese with Umeko acting as Sakura. Much of the conversation was incomprehensible to me, but I understood there was some connection to Emiko traveling the world and her selection of Maki Kanda's song, "*Tabibito,*" which meant "traveler." I was familiar with the song; it was on the Maki Kanda album Mrs. Kubota bought me.

I held my breath as Emiko opened her mouth to sing but was relieved once she was into a few bars. She could carry a tune, but she sang "*Tabibito*" more in the style of a pop song than *enka,* without careful attention to the vibrato technique used. She also didn't seem to take care in her pronunciation—saying her *r*'s too strongly instead of employing that in-between *d* and *l* sound, and pronouncing the syllable *fu* in the word *futari* more like *hu*—points that I had spent so much time trying to get just right. How shocking—Celeste the perfectionist. I guessed I was turning into Dirk. And although it was clear that Emiko should know the meaning of the words, it was as if she was singing them by rote—almost phonetically. For some reason, while she could speak Japanese well, she did not sound so good when she sang it. And her accent was nothing to brag about, at least in my opinion. She was certainly attractive and had me beat in the age department, but I knew I was the better singer. Perhaps all these years singing in the living room had helped, along with my genes.

Now it was my turn. Despite my confidence, I still had to try hard to ignore my nerves and the growling in my stomach I hoped was audible only to me. I spoke with Umeko about my wish to find Hiromi Taniguchi so I could bring her sister's ashes and their mother's family heirloom comb and ask her if she knew about my father. I showed the pictures of Aunt Mitch and Uncle Melvin, the picture of Michiko and Hiromi in their youth, the photo with Barbara in it, and the one of me in the kimono. Umeko acted animated, as if she was hearing the story for the first time; I couldn't imagine what Sakura would say. How did she plan to insult me?

When it was time to sing *"Nozomi no Hoshi"* I gave it my all. I concentrated on the memory of singing at the Club Mai, the enthusiastic audience reaction, and all the complimentary things Takuya had said to me. As I held the last note, I felt I'd given the best performance I was capable of and only hoped that I would be able to perform it as well on the live show in front of Sakura, a studio audience, and millions of TV viewers.

Afterward several of the other contestants came up and gave me compliments. Emiko stayed away. It was more than clear that some kind of rivalry was afoot from her end.

"You're going to win," Jenny, a portly woman in her forties who sang Mrs. Kubota's favorite, "Cinderella Boogie-Woogie," whispered to me.

"Thanks for your vote of confidence."

Umeko explained that there would be a special guest performing after me, and then the five finalists would be announced. Now there was to be a dinner break and after that the contestants were to get into their performance clothes. The live show was set to begin in two hours.

Jenny and I sat together in the studio cafeteria where we received box dinners. She explained that she'd been living in Japan for the past two years with her American husband, a scholar doing research on tea ceremony for an Ivy League university. She found Japanese difficult and had never quite gotten the hang of it but discovered that learning songs was a good way to work on improving her ability.

Emiko was sitting on the far side of the room eating with one of the younger male contestants who seemed to be mesmerized by her face, hanging on to her every word.

"I wonder who the special guest is going to be," I said to Jenny as I plucked an oversized piece of shrimp tempura with my chopsticks.

"I heard it's Sunshine Poppy."

"Sunshine Poppy?"

"You don't know them? They do that Kirin beer commercial. And what else?" She thought for a moment. "Oh, yeah. And that lip balm ad. They're all over the place. A group of six girls."

"I was afraid it might be Maki Kanda. I'd be so embarrassed to sing that song in front of her."

"Gosh, you shouldn't be embarrassed. You're really good! I knew the guest wouldn't be Ayako Yamato, the singer of my song. They'd have to haul her out of retirement." Jenny laughed. She poked around at her food with her chopsticks. "I'm so nervous I can't eat a bite. Go ahead if you want some of my tempura."

I was ravenous, unable to resist her offer, and grabbed the two pieces of shrimp and several morsels of carrot and sweet potato. I ate nonstop between gulps of green tea.

"What made you decide to enter this contest?" I asked Jenny.

"My husband always makes fun of me when I talk back to Sakura on the TV when I watch *Hen na Gaijin.* She really infuriates me. So he bet me 10,000 yen that I didn't have the nerve to go on the singing contest and face her in person. So I won the bet!"

"Good for you," I said, now on my fourth piece of shrimp tempura. "But I'm nervous about being up there with her. She can be pretty mean-spirited."

"Yeah, but it's *supposed* to be all in fun, I guess, though she always gets under my skin."

"It's like she's out to embarrass people." I wasn't about to tell Jenny that I had actually met the little imp and that I knew her hopefully ex-boyfriend.

"I guess it's good for ratings. But at least she's not one of the judges."

When we finished dinner, we joined the rest of the women in the dressing area, which was one big communal room with only three mirrors. Clothes and shoes and bags of makeup were strewn over chairs, spilling onto the floor. The stuffy smell of perfume mingling with hair spray and deodorant was thick in the air.

I glanced over at Emiko, surrounded by three Japanese women who seemed to be her handlers, carefully wrapping an elaborate silver kimono around her body and cinching it together with a green obi. She looked good—nothing like the pitiful Margareto-san who'd appeared to have been stuffed into a silk potato sack. It was obvious that Emiko wanted to make a big splash, and even on her voluptuous figure the kimono suited her. Maybe her Japanese name was apt.

I could have used a few assistants myself because the black dress I'd brought, which had been a bit tight to begin with back at Jill's Couture, felt even snugger as I attempted to twist it around my hips and waist, wriggling my arms into the sleeves, praying that the seams wouldn't rip. What had I been thinking? Had it really been necessary to eat enough tempura to feed an entire stable of sumo wrestlers? I grabbed for the zipper in the back, finding that it wouldn't budge more than halfway up.

Jenny, primping next to me, was putting on her finishing touches of makeup, having already donned her no-nonsense, practical, and flattering gray suit, accented with an orchid corsage.

"Jenny, do you think you could help zip me up?"

"Sure."

As she pulled on the zipper, I felt the dress binding in the back.

"Ooh, it's a little snug," she said, her voice as tight as the dress.

"I knew I shouldn't have bought this," I said. "It was really too small."

"Wait, just a minute. I . . . think . . . I've . . . got . . . it . . ."

I heard a ripping noise. "What happened?"

"Celeste, I'm sorry! The zipper split!"

I was ready to sink to the floor in a puddle. "Shit!"

"Now, hold on. Hold on." She grabbed her purse and began digging inside. "I *think* I have some safety pins somewhere in here."

I didn't know what I was going to do if I couldn't wear that dress. Even if there were extra clothes lying around somewhere in the TV studio, the chance that something would fit was nil. Would they make me put on Margareto-san's leftover kimono? I shuddered.

"Voilà!" Jenny said, pulling out a baggie filled with safety pins.

How grateful I was for her preparedness and quick thinking.

"Don't worry. It's not that bad," she said as I felt her fingers traveling speedily along my back, as she closed up the dress with the pins. "It's looking fine."

"Thank you so much for doing this."

"Almost done," she said. She patted my back. "It's barely noticeable."

"Thank you. Thank you. I'd bow down and kiss your feet, but I don't want my dress to rip further."

Jenny laughed and looked at her watch. "Well, it's just about time," she said. "Are you ready to go face Sakura Sasaki?"

"Ready as I'll ever be."

21

GAMBARIMASU

WHEN THE TIME CAME FOR THE SHOW, THE FIFTEEN OF US GATHERED BEHIND A door that would open into the studio audience. As instructed, we marched down the aisle in numerical order and single file while an announcer gushed in English, "Sakura's Gaijin Star Is Born!" A fanfare of music played, a cross between a high school drum and bugle corps and a 1940s big band. The audience clapped in rhythm, everyone in perfect synch. Out of the corner of my eye I could see Takuya, Mr. and Mrs. Kubota, and Mariko and her husband Frederick sitting in the fourth row. My nerves increased further, and it didn't help to have to keep in mind that the only thing holding my dress together was a trail of safety pins.

Once we reached the stage, we sat in our designated seats like obedient elementary school students at an assembly. The announcer introduced the judges, and I now realized why the one pictured on the slide show looked so familiar: it was Trevor Templeton, one of the gaijin *tarento* in Mrs. Kubota's scrapbook, her favorite. I wasn't sure what thrilled Mrs. Kubota more—seeing Trevor Templeton, sitting in the fourth row of Sakura Sasaki's TV show, or having her homestay daughter sing a Japanese song on television.

Then with greater flourish, as if clarions were proclaiming the announcement of the monarch, Sakura burst on the scene, a comet hurtling toward Earth, dressed in a shiny pink skirt that ended at midthigh, a matching top, and knee-high black boots with spiked heels, her hair cut shorter than when I last saw her. More adorable than Hello Kitty and cuter than Strawberry Shortcake, she gave a big grin and a quick bow in response to the heartfelt applause.

"Welcome to the first annual *Sakura's Gaijin Star Is Born* contest-o!" she said in English, then switched over to Japanese.

The program started immediately with the first contestant. The lights beating down on the stage were much too hot, the sweat oozing down my back mixing with the safety pins. I tried hard to clap, smile, and sway along with each number. The show went by in a blur and in a consistent format, with Sakura chatting with the contestants about their stories, then commenting on their performances, managing to give a zinger to each one. Afterward she turned to the judges who mainly seemed to scratch their heads in wonder or give lukewarm, noncommittal compliments about the singers having done their best.

A young woman named Farrah, wearing the stiffest, most stuck-out petticoat dress I had ever witnessed, came out eager to please but looked shaky.

"Are you nervous?" Sakura asked.

Farrah smiled. "A little."

"I hear that in English when people are scared, they say they are a chicken."

Farrah kept smiling. "Yeah. That's right, I guess."

"Are you chicken to sing on *Sakura's Gaijin Star Is Born?*"

The young woman giggled and shrugged. "I dunno." She jumped, then screamed when she found herself bombarded by a flock of live poultry, simultaneously flapping their wings and pecking at her feet.

What type of prank was in store for me? I wondered, attempting to clap and smile while Farrah sang a drippy pop song called "Love Right on the Yesterday," and while the birds continued to scurry around the stage like, well, chickens with their heads cut off.

Next up was Jenny. When she finished singing "Cinderella Boogie-Woogie," Sakura presented her with an enormous glass slipper. She stared at Jenny's feet, then gave her a concerned look. "What is your *shoe* size?"

she said in English, sliding her tiny foot next to Jenny's for comparison. Before Jenny could answer, she continued, "I am not so sure the prince can even fit this on such big foot."

"My feet may be big," Jenny retorted, "but it's all the better to be able to step on you and squash you like a bug."

"*Oh . . . my . . . God!*" Sakura said as the audience applauded.

It was easy to imagine the dialogue balloons bursting over their heads.

By the time Emiko Trenton was up, I felt drenched in perspiration.

Her perfect-sounding Japanese still wasn't good enough for Sakura. "You are more Japanese than Japanese!" she said, tugging at Emiko's obi. "So *strange!*"

"Would you prefer I converse only in English?" Emiko sounded irritated. She didn't get it.

"Eh?" Sakura didn't answer but instead turned Emiko so that she was in profile, her eyes wide as she stared at her large breasts, which managed to stick out like torpedoes even though they were covered by layers of kimono. "Wah! How you get your boobs in that?" A dialogue balloon must have translated into Japanese because the audience went into hysterics. Sakura brushed her hands over her much smaller breasts and said her "Give me a break!" signature line in Japanese, then looked at the audience with a pained expression that seemed to say, "I can't compete with *those*."

Emiko's face reddened and her forced smile made it obvious that she wasn't appreciating the humor.

She sang "*Tabibito*" and it sounded much the same as it did at rehearsal. The judges gave their unenthusiastic assessments. It was difficult to figure who they'd deem a finalist, as all of their comments had been lackluster at best. "Very nice Japanese," Trevor Templeton offered in English.

It was now my turn at bat. Making my way over to Sakura was a much longer walk than it appeared. I looked into those bright, twinkling eyes brimming with mischief. Would she notice the precarious state of my dress and make a comment about how it would have been better to have chosen a much bigger size? Would she be sure to mention the fact that I was *thirty-three* and *unmarried?* And what would Dirk's complaint be once I started singing? I stopped these thoughts and took a deep breath. I would get through this. I was ready for whatever Sakura would sling at me.

But it was soon apparent that something was off. As I told the story of being called by the Sheltering Oaks Convalescent Home about Aunt Mitch, about how this woman took care of me while my mother was out on gigs; as the picture of me at six years old in a kimono was shown on camera, as well as the one of Hiromi and Aunt Mitch; the photo of Barbara as a young and pretty hippie girl; Aunt Mitch's wedding pictures, the picture of the man in the home movie who could be my father, a person Hiromi had met; as I conveyed the information about the tofu shop in Maruyama—every detail I could give in hopes that Hiromi Taniguchi was watching television at that very moment, Sakura offered not one insulting remark. Instead, she nodded sincerely and even seemed moved by my story. There were no jokes, no jabs, no pranks.

"We hope Hiromi Taniguchi-san is watching TV right now!" Sakura said, looking directly into the camera. "So Celeste-san can return Michiko-san's ashes and family belongings to her. So she can find out about her *father!*" She turned to me. "She can be like real auntie to you—Hiromi-*obasan!*"

"Yes, I hope so." I expected to get ruffled over a snide remark from Sakura and prepared myself to stay strong; I did not plan on getting choked up. I was at the brink, verging on tears, but stopped myself as I thought of Takuya, his parents, and Mariko watching me.

With a sincere expression, Sakura pleaded to the camera: "If you are watching, Taniguchi-san, please call the phone number on the screen so you can meet Celeste-san!" I could hear applause. Then Sakura turned to me. "And you are now wishing on the star for this, singing '*Nozomi no Hoshi.*' " Sakura spread her arm out wide motioning toward me to take my place at the center of the stage. "*Gambatte,* Celeste-san!"

The audience reaction continued to intensify as I hit my mark. What had happened back there? Was Sakura being nice for the sake of Takuya? Was this some kind of bizarre strategy? I glanced at the ceiling for a quick moment, making sure there wasn't a big bucket readied to turn over, bringing forth a downpour of green slime during the middle of my performance. I didn't see one. Was it possible that Sakura was actually pulling for me to win?

There was no more time to think about any of this: I had to get down to business. My first reaction was to hold my breath to keep my dress from splitting, but that probably wasn't the best thing to do right before you were going to sing. The introduction played and instead of Maki Kanda coming to mind, it was Barbara Duncan. She was onstage at Alum Rock Park, her band behind her, one of the few times I'd seen my mother perform, since her gigs were usually late at night. "*Nozomi no Hoshi*" couldn't have been more different than the songs in her repertoire, but wasn't it really all the same when you got down to it? It was all about the emotion behind the singing, feeling the song in whatever it meant to you, in whatever language. It was about Megumi Wada. It was about Hiromi Taniguchi. It was about breaking free of Dirk and his criticism.

I took those feelings and pushed every word of the song, closing my eyes, stretching my arm out toward the audience at just the right moment, my palm facing upward. I breathed deep from inside my belly and belted out the last powerful note. I could hear the clapping and cheers of the audience—even a shrill whistle that I was certain came from Mariko—before the song even ended. I had done my best, had done my *gambarimasu*. I bowed, trying hard to hold back the shaking in my knees.

Instead of readying for a cheap joke, Sakura seemed dumbfounded. She staggered, pretending to come close to collapse, and put her hand on her chest. "*Jozu! Taihen jozu!*" she exclaimed, exhorting how skillful she thought the performance was. By now it was clear: I was the only contestant Sakura did not make fun of.

The judges seemed equally impressed, Trevor Templeton saying that when he closed his eyes, he thought he was hearing a real Japanese *enka* singer.

The audience was still buzzing with excitement. I nearly collapsed onto my seat on the side of the stage, many of the contestants whispering compliments, Emiko Trenton conspicuous by her silence. This was soon interrupted by a blast of giddy synthesizer music and the explosive entrance of Sunshine Poppy. They took over the stage, six junior versions of Sakura who could not have been any older than fourteen, dressed in yellow satin hot pants and bright white blouses with Peter Pan collars, clomping about in platform tennis shoes in a color that could only be described as sparkling chartreuse. Backup dancers dressed as honeybees performed elaborate but clumsy moves as the girls endlessly sang the phrase *fu-ra-wah, pa-wah*—"flower power"—which I correctly identified as the title of the song.

Once Sunshine Poppy finished their number, we were made to wait as

Sakura ad-libbed with a gaijin comedian who called himself Nesbitt Natto, his last name taken from the Japanese word for fermented soy beans, a food disdained by many gaijin. His main talent seemed to be speaking Japanese with a Texas accent and the ability to burp on cue. He taught Sakura how to belch and she did it perfectly—twice.

Finally, the five finalists were to be announced, in no particular order.

My heart was pounding much too hard, and I exchanged hopeful glances with Jenny who mouthed "You" to me, while Emiko Trenton sat up with a rigid posture, a look of dire concern overtaking her pink complexion.

Number five was a curly-haired girl named Candy, who had barely sung on key, but without a doubt qualified in the cute department, thereby most likely ranking a full page in Mrs. Kubota's gaijin scrapbook. Number four was Farrah, the chicken girl. Jenny was number three and was so surprised when she heard her name called that she tripped when she crossed the stage to go stand next to Sakura, a move that almost looked planned when Sakura once more commented on Jenny's size twelve feet. When Emiko Trenton was announced as number two she almost knocked me over as she rushed to the center of the stage as fast as a tight kimono would let her run. One more name to go. I closed my eyes. After the audience reaction, the judges' comments, and the plaintive sincerity from Sakura, I felt it had to be me.

"Our last finalist is . . ." Sakura said, reading from the card. "Roger Berger-san!"

Roger Berger? Some guy Sakura called Hamburger-san, who displayed even less talent than Nesbitt Natto?

I was more than stunned; I was in shock. What went wrong? I knew I should be grateful that at least I was able to broadcast Aunt Mitch's story over the airwaves, and I was. After all, that was one of the main reasons for this whole endeavor. Perhaps Hiromi Taniguchi was calling JBS at that very moment, not only to contact me but to protest that I wasn't chosen as one of the five finalists. But I'd wanted to win the recording contract and the cash as well, and those chances were gone. Was it all Sakura's doing? Was the ultimate trick her sincerity paired with a punch in the gut by not having the best singer with the most compelling story be one of the finalists? The ultimate humiliation, it seemed, was being shut out.

After all the preparation, all the trepidation, the show was over and there was nothing more that could be done. It was another one of those *shikata ga nai* situations.

Jenny rushed over to my side. "There is no way I should be up here. I can't believe they passed you over."

Several other contestants voiced the same sentiments to me. I thanked them and went over to congratulate all the finalists, even smug Emiko, who now admitted that I had sung "nicely." I wished her good luck, refusing to be a poor sport about any of this, though I was certain from my teary eyes and burning cheeks that my displeasure was obvious to anyone. The five finalists were ushered away to receive information about the following week's show, and I keenly felt the loss of not being part of that group.

All of us losers, meanwhile, filed backstage, where our belongings were already neatly placed on tables for us to pick up, then to exit into the lobby. It was as if they couldn't get rid of us fast enough. Once in the lobby, Umeko passed out stuffed toys of the JBS smiling flower mascot to each of us as consolation prizes, while a female assistant pinned Sakura's face buttons to our chests.

"You did very good," Umeko said to each contestant. "Better luck next time!"

There was no way that I was joining the Sakura cult by wearing her face on my body. I pulled off the button, pricking my finger in the process. I tossed it onto a table scattered with posters of Sakura standing next to a full-sized version of the JBS mascot, an unfortunate soul dressed as a grinning yellow flower with an oversized head.

I saw Takuya, Mr. and Mrs. Kubota, Mariko and Frederick before they saw me, their long faces apparent. I had let them down and felt awful about it, but I wiped my eyes and tried to put on a brave face.

"It's a fucking travesty!" Mariko said way too loudly once I reached them. Her husband shook his head slowly, a perturbed smile on his face.

"Thank you, Mariko," I said, my voice quiet.

"There's no way that any of them are better than you, not even that pig-in-a-kimono with the red hair," she ranted.

"You were great," Takuya said. "Even better than at the Club Mai."

I wished hard for a hug or squeeze of the hand from him, but I knew that wouldn't happen.

Mrs. Kubota's forehead wrinkled, looking as though she had received some very bad news. She placed her hands gently on my shoulders. "Not good!" she said. "Not good! Why? Why no Celeste-san?"

"It so beautiful singing," Mr. Kubota said to me. "I sorry." He handed me a shopping bag.

The last thing I expected was a gift from shy, quiet Mr. Kubota. Even though I lived in his house, we rarely saw each other, and when we did, we could not communicate. I opened the bag and was touched to find one of his Christmas stars. As I held it in my hand, it sparkled in the light. "It's beautiful. Thank you so much." My eyes were starting to well up once more.

"He thought you were going to be one of the winners so he want to give you prize," Takuya explained. Then he bent his head toward my ear. "My mother very mad with Sakura."

The Sakura bubble had burst. That was one positive thing, but what did Takuya think about her now?

"Celeste, you were excellent," Frederick said in a calm voice. "But I hope you won't feel too bad."

"Thank you, Frederick."

"You know, you have to take these things with a grain of salt," he went on. "I think you need to understand that sometimes Japanese feel uncomfortable when a foreigner is too good at something they feel belongs to them."

I wondered if this was the case. I'd been receiving nothing but praise and admiration for my Japanese singing so far. "So you think they didn't like it because I'm *too* good?"

"I'm afraid you could construe it that way. It's a real disconnect for some of them—the white face, the perfect Japanese, singing *enka,* something more traditional, instead of a Western-influenced pop song. That might have had a lot to do with why you didn't place."

"But Emiko Trenton sang an *enka* song," I said.

"Not with half your grace and emotion, your authenticity," Frederick replied. "She sang hers as you would expect a foreigner to, going through the motions. On the other hand, you put your heart and soul into it."

"He's right," Mariko said, sighing. "So fucking crazy. They don't know what the hell they're doing. And I still don't trust that Sakura."

Mariko said something in Japanese to Mrs. Kubota who seemed to concur, nodding and saying, "*So desu ne!*" The hatred of Sakura had now brought Mariko and Mrs. Something-Up-Her-Butt into a shared commonality.

Once we were outside, Takuya, Mr. and Mrs. Kubota, and I said goodbye to Frederick and Mariko who were to make their way to the subway station. Takuya hailed a cab. It was one more disappointment when he sat in front with the driver and I had to squeeze in between Mr. and Mrs. Kubota in the backseat.

"Maybe Taniguchi-san is on the phone right now to JBS, and they will call when we get home," Takuya said.

"I'm not going to count on it," I said.

When we arrived home, Takuya and Mr. Kubota said good night, but Mrs. Kubota stayed up to fix green tea for me. We sat in the kitchen. The phone remained silent.

"Very sorry," Mrs. Kubota said, stroking my shoulder.

"I appreciate everything you've done for me," I told her, starting to cry without warning.

How ridiculous to shed so many tears over such a silly contest. But that was not the only thing I was crying about. It was the culmination of many things, and a feeling of what do I do now? If I had been honest with myself, I'd have to admit that the search for Hiromi Taniguchi was coming to a fruitless end. And Takuya seemed out of reach as well. What was there to keep me in Japan further? And what was I doing with my life? There had been other people who did not make it past thirty-three—it seemed frivolous to keep wasting my time. Feeling Mrs. Kubota's concern and hearing her soothing voice only made me more despondent.

"No crying," Mrs. Kubota said, her brown eyes warm. "It is *daijobu*."

She was telling me that everything would be all right, and as usual she was a comfort, but I didn't know if I could believe her words.

22

IT'S HARD TO BE A MAN

OVER THE NEXT FEW DAYS NO PHONE CALL CAME FROM JBS SAYING THAT Hiromi Taniguchi or anyone who knew her had called. I was running out of money. I contacted Zoe, who by now had returned to work, and she told me our boss had said that I could have my job back anytime. I was grateful, but it was also depressing. Returning to San Jose to the same life I had before would be like admitting defeat. Dirk was right—wasn't I always a tad "off"?

The other bad news was that we received the letter Takuya had sent to Kenji Iwasaki, the man whose passport we found in the geisha box. It was returned unopened, with, "No such person here. Return to sender," stamped on the front.

The only small bright spot was an unexpected phone call from Yukiko, my old Milky Way Text colleague. In her halting English she told me that my singing was so beautiful that it made her cry, and she expressed her outrage that I was not chosen as one of the finalists.

"I've been thinking that I might as well go home, back to San Jose," I told Mariko at our next lesson, a few days after the contest.

"Are you *insane?*"

"It looks like everything has come to a halt. I'm low on money. I can get my old job back if I want it."

"What if you get a job here? Maybe Frederick knows about something."

"That's nice of you to offer, but it's so expensive to live in Japan, and I'd have to find someone who'd sponsor me for a work visa. It isn't easy. And I can't keep living at the Kubotas forever, staying in their daughter's room."

"But you belong here," Mariko said. "The way you sang that song—it's as though you were born to sing it. Maybe a talent scout saw you on TV and is ready to call and offer you a big contract."

"Then I guess I better hurry home and wait by the phone all day."

She frowned. "And then there's that other important thing."

"What?"

"*Duh!*" she said. "Takuya-san!"

"What about him?"

"What *about* him? He's your perfect match. You're a wild and crazy woman for him, right? Sexy, sweet, has a good job—if you don't hurry up, *I'll* grab him."

"I don't think Frederick would appreciate that."

"Huh! It'll keep the husband on his toes."

"Takuya has never expressed any interest in me other than brotherly. There's Holly in Seattle, and I don't know what's going on with him and Sakura. He's got a full plate. He's not interested in me."

"Well, as for Sakura, that little bitch didn't invite you to be back on her program—I'm sure he's mad as hell at her."

"Well, maybe he is or maybe he isn't, but nothing has changed between us."

"I watched him when you were singing that night. He couldn't stop looking at you," Mariko said, excited. "If I'd been as naked as a bluebird sitting next to him, he wouldn't have noticed. And I saw his expression when you came out after the show. He felt so badly for you." Her eyes fixed on mine. "I know how much he cares."

With so much weighing on me I found that I couldn't sleep that night. Normally I would have started practicing kanji to get my mind off things, but I was not even up for that. Feeling sorry for myself and doing something passive—sitting like a lump, for example—was more appealing. I located a bag of shrimp chips in the kitchen, turned on the television, then sprawled on the couch, making sure the volume was low so as not to disturb Mr. and Mrs. Kubota's sleep. It was already eleven forty-five. Takuya had yet to come home, which was not unusual.

I watched a Japanese comedy movie on TV that looked to be from the 1970s. The main character was a bumbling middle-aged peddler who traveled throughout Japan, and whose name I gleaned was Tora-san. His poor excuse for a fashion statement was a shabby old sport coat and a kind of blanket cinching his waist that looked like an errant cousin to a kimono's obi. Tora-san shuffled along in a pair of worn-down straw sandals, a ne'er-do-well type, causing problems and amusing misunderstandings, but he was also a man who seemed to have a heart of gold. This was the general idea I could make out from the dribs and drabs of Japanese I could comprehend.

I watched, shoveling shrimp chips into my mouth, until I emptied the bag. My next thought was to search the refrigerator for another snack, perhaps one of those "health" drinks Mrs. Kubota stocked for her husband, which seemed to consist of brown sugar water infused with vitamins and megadoses of caffeine.

I looked at the clock when I heard the door open. It was twelve thirty and Takuya had finally arrived home.

"Ah!" he said, looking surprised to see me. "You are awake late."

I was quick to lurch my body into a sitting position, attempting to wipe shrimp chip residue from the corners of my mouth, and tried to alter my slug appearance into something more acceptable, though I had a hunch it wasn't working.

"I can't sleep," I said, noticing for the thousandth time his good looks, his sweet manner. Mariko was right. How could this have slipped my mind?

"Are you worried about not winning contest? Not finding Taniguchi-san?"

I shrugged. "I don't know." I decided to change the subject. "How was your day?"

"Okay."

He took off his jacket and sat across from me in the La-Z-Boy. I sighed to myself, noticing how he did not sit next to me, seeming to keep his distance.

Takuya glanced at the television and smiled. "You are watching Tora-san. Old movie. Can you understand?"

"A little bit here and there. He's a funny guy."

"They make many Tora-san movies," Takuya said. "Each one is called *Otoko wa Tsurai yo*."

"What does that mean?"

"Ah . . . 'it is hard to be a man.'"

"Is it?"

"What?"

"Is it hard to be a man?"

He laughed a knowing laugh. "Sometimes." He yawned and stretched his long legs, then fixed his gaze on the television.

"I'm thinking of going back home." I didn't plan on bringing it up and surprised myself by saying it so abruptly.

Takuya looked at me as if he didn't hear me properly. "Go back home?"

An electronic ringing sound startled him, his cell phone.

"Go ahead," I said.

"I am sorry."

He answered the phone as he got up to go in the kitchen. I couldn't hear much, but I knew he was speaking in English. It had to be Seattle Holly.

It must be nice to have two women after you, I thought. Three, if you counted me, though I'd pretty much given up on that, and it was hard to know if he'd ever even noticed my interest. But it was no wonder. Takuya was a lovely guy, and Celeste Duncan was obviously not the only one who thought so.

I turned down the volume on the TV a few notches, hoping to catch a little more of what he was saying, but he was talking so low that I couldn't hear a thing.

About five minutes later, he returned, but this time he sat next to me on the couch. I tried to discern the expression on his face, a clue as to how he felt about the call, but I saw nothing.

"I am sorry again," he said. "You say you are wanting to go home?"

"Yeah. Back to San Jose. I can get my old job back."

"But what about Taniguchi-san? What about asking her about your father?"

I heard the concern in his voice. "Doesn't look like anything's going to happen with that." I sighed. "I can't live here forever. Your parents have been nice to let me stay, but . . ."

He looked puzzled, as if he were having difficulty comprehending the concept. We were both silent, the room filled only with the exuberant but low-volume sound of Sunshine Poppy's Kirin beer commercial: *fu-ra-wah, pa-wah!*

Takuya broke the quiet. "You want this job very badly?"

"I don't know. But I need to start getting my life together, and I'm not sure what there is for me here in Japan."

"You do not like it here?"

"I like it here a lot, but . . ."

He frowned, then rubbed his eyes, looking stressed, worried.

"Is something wrong?" I asked.

He sighed. "So many things, I . . ." He leaned back against the sofa. "I speak to Holly. In Seattle."

"Uh-huh."

"I am telling her I am not wanting to keep our relationship. I feel bad, but it does not work. And I think that maybe I become her boyfriend just for pleasing my mother."

"What do you mean?"

He looked embarrassed. "Because she is American. Gaijin." He shook his head. "What do you say? My mother did number on me."

I laughed. "Sorry, I don't mean to laugh, but you said it right. I just didn't expect you to know such a phrase."

"Do not worry. But I also know Holly like me only because I am Japanese."

"She does?"

He explained that Seattle Holly studied calligraphy and tea ceremony and would constantly ask him for translation help. She also had demanded assistance in trying to get a scholarship so she could come to Japan to study. Her begging him for contacts and research overwhelmed him. "I want to help her," he said. "But it feel a little funny. Strange. It is too much."

"Do you mean that you feel used?"

His eyes widened and he looked grateful. "Yes! You understand!" He stared straight ahead. "Used." He turned toward me. "It is not always sincere."

I turned off the television with the remote.

"But I know you are sincere person," he said to me.

I felt myself blushing, my chest turning warm.

"So you are giving up about Taniguchi-san?"

"What more can I do?"

"I do not think you should go home."

I heard the sound of footsteps from the hall and turned to see that Mrs. Kubota was now in the living room in her robe, giving off her usual puzzled, concerned look. She and Takuya exchanged words.

I didn't want any trouble from Mrs. Busybody. "Maybe I should just go to bed," I said.

Takuya rolled his eyes at me and sighed.

I rose from the sofa and smiled at Mrs. Kubota. *"Oyasumi nasai,"* I said to her, wishing her good night.

The morning, as usual, brought with it miso soup, rice, fish, pickles, and tea for breakfast, and I wouldn't have had it any other way. How sad it would be, I thought, to not have this anymore. Trying to fix my own Japanese breakfast in my apartment in San Jose just wouldn't be the same.

Takuya had already gone to work, and Mrs. Kubota talked about the weather, how it would only be getting hotter as August approached. I didn't know what she'd thought about seeing Takuya and me deep in conversation on the sofa the night before, but she had managed to interrupt it, just like when we were lingering at the front door after our night at the Club Mai.

I was clearing my dishes from the table when the sound of the phone ringing gave me a start. It's JBS, I thought, telling me they've heard from Hiromi Taniguchi. I still seemed to have some hope, no matter how irrational, of something that might keep me in Japan. It had now been five days since the contest and there had been no word from them.

Mrs. Kubota's eyebrows raised slightly when she handed me the phone. But it wasn't a call from the network; it was from Takuya.

"How are you?" he asked.

I knew he hadn't called just to ask how I was, but I couldn't imagine what he wanted. He had never called me before. "I'm fine. We've just finished breakfast, your mom and I."

"That nice." He paused. "I call to tell you something."

Yes, Takuya. I guess you have to tell me something. "What?"

"I just talked to Sakura."

It was ridiculous, but it still irked me to hear him say her name. And why was he still talking to her? Did they have some unfinished business? And why on earth was he calling to tell me about it? I tried to sound casual, blasé. "Oh, yeah?"

"It kind of strange."

Strange? Why was it not surprising that something to do with Sakura might be strange? "What do you mean?"

"She tell me there was mistake in judges' scoring for the singing contest."

"Mistake?"

"You are supposed to be finalist. She want you to be on show this Monday."

"What?"

"I know it weird, but I think it is also a good news."

"So that means someone else was kicked out?"

"Kick out?"

"Someone else was dropped. Eliminated."

"No. They will instead have six finalists," he said. "So there is still chance you win the contest."

Such an odd development seemed too weird to be a coincidence. Takuya must have arranged this because he feels sorry for me, I thought. He had been concerned when I told him that I'd given up on finding Hiromi-san and was thinking of going home.

"Takuya, it's very nice of you to call her and ask if I can be on the show again, but it's not necessary."

There was silence, then, "I do not call her. She call *me*."

"Really?" I didn't believe him. "You can tell me, Takuya. I appreciate your pulling some strings about this, but . . ."

"Pulling string?"

"Making an arrangement with Sakura."

"Celeste-san, I do not do that. Sakura's call is out from the blue."

He sounded his usual sincere self, as if he was telling the truth. And when I thought about it further, it seemed uncharacteristic of him to lie. "But it's just so weird," I said. "Is it that they've heard from Hiromi Taniguchi?"

"I am sorry, Celeste-san, but she say they have not. But maybe Taniguchi-san will watch next week. The show is this Monday."

I could hear the heaviness in his voice; I felt it too. Would she be watching the show this time? Did she miss it the other night?

"Let me talk to my mother so I can explain for her," Takuya said. "I know she is so curious."

He was right about that. She'd been trying to be nonchalant, but I could tell she'd been hanging on to my every incomprehensible English word. I handed the phone to her but did not wait for her reaction. Instead, I headed directly to my room to start my practice of "*Nozomi no Hoshi*." I'd sung it the best I could on the original show and it didn't do a bit of good, but I needed to do something or else I would drive myself crazy.

It seemed that there was still a chance.

23

WISHING ON A KIRA-KIRA STAR

"WHAT ARE YOU DOING HERE?"

It was Jenny saying this in a friendly but surprised voice as she gave me a hug when I showed up at the conference room at JBS on Monday for the rehearsal of the *Sakura's Gaijin Star Is Born* finale.

"They said there was some kind of mistake with the judges' scoring," I said.

"You better believe there was some kind of mistake. That was ridiculous that you weren't chosen. God knows why they're bringing me back on for more abuse."

When Emiko Trenton walked in, her shocked face said it all, as if she'd attended my funeral the previous week only to find that I'd risen from the dead. My first thought was to torture her, to make her ask me what the deal was, but I wasn't that vindictive. Instead, I said, "They called me to come back. Some kind of error with the scoring."

Her eyes whirled. Apparently there was still something wrong. "Does that mean one of us is out?"

"Maybe so," Jenny said, giving me a wink.

"It's possible," I said.

"They can't have two finalists both doing songs by Maki Kanda! They can't kick me off the show. There's no way I'll let them do that to me. It's just so *unfair!*" She stamped her foot and slunk off to sulk in the corner.

When Umeko the producer came in, Emiko complained to her in Japanese.

"Do not worry," Umeko said in English. "There are six finalists now. No one is leaving." She turned toward me. "Welcome back, Celeste-san!"

The rehearsal went smoothly as before, but much faster since there were only six singers. I tried to keep my appetite modest at the dinner break. My purple dress did not rip, my cleavage stayed intact.

During the live show, there was joking banter but no pranks. And the now three judges were different from those on the previous show. And this time we were allowed to wait backstage instead of in front of the cameras the whole time. Nesbitt Natto made a return appearance. It was hard to believe, but this already multitalented gaijin had yet another amazing ability: sculpting animals out of party balloons portrayed in various sexual positions. The special musical guest was a young pop singer named Kazuki Kitano, who had the girls in the audience screaming, and seemed to be giving the SMAP boys on the poster in my bedroom a run for their money.

Before I sang "*Nozomi no Hoshi*," Sakura explained that there had been a scoring mistake and welcomed me back. Then I briefly retold my story, though this time she did not implore Hiromi Taniguchi to call the number shown on the screen. It was disappointing—had they given up on this too?

Yet when I sang this time, I had even more confidence. Again, I had done my *gambarimasu;* I wouldn't have known how to sing the song any better.

The program flew by, seemingly much too quickly. When the time arrived to announce the two runners-up and the winner, it seemed there would need to be much more going on afterward to fill out the remainder of the show. The six of us stood in line on the stage next to Sakura, like nervous pageant contestants. I could almost feel the Miss San Jose banner strapped across my chest.

"The third-place winner of *Sakura's Gaijin Star Is Born* is . . ." Sakura said, reading off a card, then pausing for effect. "Emiko Trenton-san!"

If Emiko was upset with her third-place finish, she didn't show it. She was off like a racehorse out of the starting gate to the center of the stage and accepted her bouquet of flowers and trophy with a huge, grateful grin, tears staining that lovely complexion.

"The second-place winner of *Sakura's Gaijin Star Is Born* is . . . Roger Berger-san!"

It was still a mystery to me why Hamburger-san was always ranked so highly. Was he sleeping with Sakura? If he could come in second, perhaps the equally inept Candy or Farrah would end up taking the number one spot. Or maybe Jenny would be the dark horse, since she was so good at standing her own with Sakura.

Now it was down to the four of us: Jenny, Candy, Farrah, and me. We held hands, Farrah grasping mine so tightly it was as if I was holding her up from near collapse.

The lights dimmed and the three spotlights circling around us made me dizzy. A rumbling of drums became louder and faster with each roll.

"The winner . . . of the grand prize of *Sakura's Gaijin Star Is Born* . . . of the 300,000 yen and recording contract with JBS Music is . . . Celeste Duncan-san!"

It took a few seconds for me to realize that Sakura had said my name. Chiharu the translator led me over to the center of the stage as the roar of the audience's applause filled the auditorium. My head spun and I was finding it difficult to walk; her steady hand on my elbow was a lifesaver.

An old man wearing glasses, walking with a stoop, handed me a huge trophy and two of the biggest flower bouquets I'd ever seen. "He is the president of JBS Television," Chiharu explained.

The man shook my hand with a firm grip that seemed to belie his frail-looking body. "Congratulations!" he said in English.

"Domo arigato." I bowed my head as two assistants hurried over and took the flowers and trophy away from me for safekeeping.

Another older man came out to the stage and handed me two large envelopes, each covered with a gold seal and tied with a stiff red ribbon. He too shook my hand.

"That is president of JBS Music," Chiharu explained. "He is giving you 300,000 yen prize and recording contract."

"Dirk!" I said under my breath. *"I have a recording contract!"*

"What?" Chiharu asked, puzzled.

"Nothing."

The music for *"Nozomi no Hoshi"* started up, and it had been explained before that the winner would sing an abridged version of the song while the other finalists gathered around. My voice was shaking when I sang this time, and tears began to fall as I thought of Barbara. Was Hiromi Taniguchi watching me at this moment? I could only hope.

The audience cheered, I waved, and the show seemed to come to a close. I was relieved to have it over, thinking of sharing my success with Takuya, with *Okaasan*, with Mariko.

"Thank you, thank you, Celeste Duncan-san, winner of *Sakura's Gaijin Star Is Born*," Sakura said, as the other contestants filed off the stage. She then began talking excitedly in Japanese, and I got the impression that something else was about to happen, though I couldn't imagine what. This was when my happiness gave way to dread. Were we now about to enter the prank portion of the show? As Sakura talked on, two young men carried out a large, blue velvet chair, bordered in gold, to the middle of the stage. It could only be described as a throne.

"Sit here, please," Chiharu instructed me.

This was either a gesture of great respect in dubbing me queen of all gaijin, who could sing a song in Japanese, or a practical joke whereby the chair would collapse once my butt hit the cushion. Thankfully, I sat down without incident.

"There be surprise for you," Chiharu said.

Surprise? I did not like the sound of this. The whole evening had transpired without any mischief. I had won the contest, everything seeming to be over and done. What more could there be to the show? Was Sakura now readying for the kill? And, more important, would she take it all back?

The sight of a large video screen floating down from the ceiling startled me. What looked like a documentary film began to play, Chiharu keeping me apprised with her running commentary in English. The old pictures of Aunt Mitch, Hiromi, and Barbara appeared on the screen, while an extra-schmaltzy arrangement of "Do You Know the Way to San Jose?" played in the background, in an odd combination of sixties rock guitars and disco synthesizers. A male announcer with a deep voice narrated in an overly dramatic fashion, explaining about my quest to find Hiromi Taniguchi, to connect with this relative I'd never known, to ask her about my father, and to bring Aunt Mitch's ashes home.

Then a clip showed of me singing "*Nozomi no Hoshi*" on the previous week's show. I thought back to my Japanese television debut at the Milky Way Text incident, the first and last time I'd seen myself on TV. I had to admit that I looked a bit improved here, but I still didn't like watching myself. Each flaw was magnified way beyond my comfort level. Was my face that big, my waist that thick? Still, I forced myself to keep watching, deeming it would look too weird if I turned my head away.

The documentary came to a close, turning into a live hookup with a young woman reporter holding a microphone, standing in front of a house.

"Hello, Ogawa-san," said Sakura, who sat on the arm of my throne on the opposite side of where Chiharu was standing, and so close that I could smell her gardenia perfume. "Can you hear me?" Sakura spoke in Japanese, and I continued to receive translations in my ear.

The woman pressed her earpiece with her index finger. "Yes!" I could hear the excitement in her voice. "Hello, Sakura-san. This is Ayano Ogawa reporting from Sendai. Celeste-san, congratulations!"

"Thank you," I said. What did this have to do with me and what was this reporter doing in Sendai? My heart pounded when I realized what must have happened. *They had finally tracked down Hiromi Taniguchi.*

"Maybe those in the audience are wondering how an American woman can sing such a truly Japanese song as '*Nozomi no Hoshi*' so exquisitely and with the emotion and fervor of a Japanese," the reporter gushed.

"Yes, that is true," Sakura said, her face looking thoughtful and serious, as if she were contemplating the complex problems of the world instead of my ability to sing in Japanese. "Why *is* Celeste-san *so* good at singing in Japanese?"

A hush came over the proceedings. Then Ayano said with great seriousness, "I have a picture here." She paused, looking into the camera, with a look of grave import. "From *1973*." She recited the date as if the year was a pivotal one in the history of Japanese-singing gaijin.

The camera fixed on the photograph of Barbara with Aunt Mitch and Uncle Melvin and the Japanese man.

"On the right is Barbara Duncan-san, Celeste-san's late mother. And on the left is Kenji Iwasaki-san, whom we are going to meet *right now*."

I have your passport, I said to myself, staring intently at the screen. It was in the geisha box.

Ayano rang the doorbell.

"*Hai!*" came a voice over the small speaker next to the door.

Ayano talked in the direction of the speaker. "Iwasaki-san, it's Ayano Ogawa from JBS. May I come in?"

On cue the door was opened by a man who looked to be in his mid-fifties but who still retained some of the youthful appearance in the photograph. "Yes, please come in. I apologize for my home being so narrow . . ."

They sat together on a small sofa in a room filled with ceramics, paintings on the walls, and shelves full of books. The camera focused on Kenji, his right eye twitching slightly, seeming uncomfortable in front of a camera.

"Celeste-san, congratulations! I would have liked to be there and meet you, but I have been ill," he said to me in good English. "But I watched you on television. You have a beautiful voice. It gave me chills."

"Thank you."

"And when I saw you last week on *Sakura's Gaijin Star Is Born* and heard your name, Celeste Duncan—"

"Iwasaki-san sent JBS this same photograph," Ayano said, almost panting, "and told us he is Celeste-san's father!"

Father?

"I hope, Celeste-san, that you can come and visit me and we can get acquainted."

But what about the man in the home movie? All I could do was nod in a stupor, wondering when I would actually awaken from all of this because it really seemed that I was in a dream.

"Celeste-san did not know her father when she was growing up," Ayano explained. "Iwasaki-san fell in love with Barbara Duncan-san when he was a college student in San Jose, staying with Celeste's aunt Michiko and uncle Melvin. But he suddenly had to return to Japan and they lost touch."

"I am sorry, Celeste-san, that I was unable to contact you. Please forgive me."

My body froze. I tried to speak, but it was as if my mouth had gone lopsided from a dentist's shot of Novocain. I nodded dumbly at the video screen, a rather surreal experience, as if Kenji Iwasaki was sitting right across from me.

"I have to say that this is wonderful news, isn't it, Celeste-san?" Sakura said.

I tried filtering this new information through my brain. So Kenji had been one of my mother's boyfriends? Why did he think he was my father? What about the man showering me with kisses in the video? Kenji was nowhere to be seen there. And how could he think I was his daughter when I didn't look one iota Japanese? No one had ever said I looked *haafu*. This was all much too crazy, but I wasn't about to hash it out in front of an audience of millions.

"Yes, it is wonderful news. I hope to visit Iwasaki-san soon in Sendai," I managed to say, my voice turning into a robotic monotone.

"I look forward to that," Kenji said.

"And so does JBS," Ayano-san put in.

"Yes," Sakura said. She batted her eyes and was almost shouting. "We'll be taking you, Celeste-san, to Sendai to meet your father on my special program, *Celeste-san: Wishing on a Kira-Kira Star!*" She looked at me and proclaimed, "Celeste-san, your wish came more than true!"

On cue a sappy tune on a piano began to play, and when the strings came in, the title of the show was displayed, already arranged in a logo, embossed over a picture of me singing "*Nozomi no Hoshi*." A large animated star twinkled in the corner above my head, the picture placed in such a way that it looked as though I was gazing at it with deep longing. It was *Oprah* crossed with an afterschool special.

My anger bubbled. Another television show? This was way too personal to have to take place on TV. The whole idea was beyond bizarre, not to mention that it looked extremely cheesy. And what made Kenji so certain that I was his daughter? Barbara had never said a word about a Japanese boyfriend, but she also was never specific about anything in regard to my paternity. But if this was true, why didn't she tell me? Did Kenji know Hiromi Taniguchi? Did he know the man in the home movie? A man I thought more likely to be my father than a Japanese person?

Of course I wanted to ask him all this and more; the questions, the connections, overloaded my brain. But however overwhelmed I was with this turn of events, I was certain that I had no desire to deal with this as the star of a reality show of questionable taste. But for the moment, while

I was still on camera, I tried to be calm and just nodded and smiled. "I look forward to it."

Sakura bid good-bye to Kenji Iwasaki and the reporter. Then Kazuki Kitano, the special guest pop singer, was brought out once more, along with the other contestants. We all clapped and swayed behind him. At the end of the song he grabbed both Sakura's and my hands, raising them high above our heads, saying in English how in the end music would save the world. Confetti rained from the ceiling, and I could feel pieces sticking to my sweaty face. I attempted to brush them off as the audience stood on its feet cheering and applauding until the show finally came to a close.

Backstage, Umeko hurried to my side.

"Celeste-san, congratulations! So exciting! We get in touch soon about TV show, *ne?*"

I nodded, still in a daze, as photographers took my picture and contestants and others shouted congratulations. Chiharu gathered my flowers and trophies and followed me to the lobby.

The first person I saw was Takuya. I knew it was him, but I almost did not recognize him. He was waving at me, his fingers spread wide, bursting forth with an uncontainable enthusiasm. His joyful look said more than just "congratulations on a job well done." There was pride but also something else. I could see it in his eyes and in the confident way he was now walking toward me; a man with a purpose. As I approached him, he came closer and we fell into an urgent embrace. This was not the platonic hug of a homestay brother for his homestay sister, one that said, "Nice going!" He held me tighter and with more feeling than I had ever been held before. Folded into the warmth of his arms, I felt loved. I held on, as if in a dream, not caring that it was certain that everyone was staring and that this clinch was going on much too long to be considered appropriate under the circumstances.

Releasing each other just a bit, we kissed, something that felt so natural and inevitable that there was no question.

"Congratulations," he said. "I am proud of you."

We embraced once more. When it was over, I could see the contrast of expressions; Mariko's beyond pleased, her face saying "I told you so"; while

Mrs. Kubota's seemed to be expressing the Japanese equivalent of "*Oh, my God.*"

But *Okaasan* was quick to regain her composure and patted my shoulder. "*Omedeto! Omedeto!*" she congratulated me, as Chiharu handed off my winnings, collected in a big basket, to Takuya.

"Is that really your *father?*" Mariko exclaimed. "I thought he was the other guy!"

"I don't know. I don't know," I said. "But I'm going to meet him and hear his story. I have a million questions for him."

"But that little witch! Tricking you like that. And that soppy show they want to do. It's the fucking tackiest thing I've ever heard of. It's tacky even for *Japanese* TV! No wonder they called you back over a 'scoring mistake.' "

I couldn't agree more with her, but it was hard to think straight.

"But congratulations on everything, Celeste! Didn't I say you were born to sing that song?" Mariko gave me a big hug, then whispered in my ear, "And didn't I tell you how much he cares?"

24

ROMANTIC JOURNEY

THE NIGHT I WON THE CONTEST IT WAS IMPOSSIBLE TO SLEEP. I WAS WOUND UP, thinking about everything I wanted to ask Kenji Iwasaki, wondering what he would tell me. I did not want to wait until JBS contacted me about this ridiculous reality show to find out. After all, this was *my* information and I was the one who should be privy to it. The more I thought about it, I realized that what Mariko had said was true; it was probably not until Kenji Iwasaki contacted the program that Sakura and her producers discovered a "scoring mistake" from the judges. They knew what a good story it would be for ratings and the opportunity it would make for another potentially blockbuster show that would have me meeting my "father."

I still couldn't get over that he said he was my father. And I also couldn't stop thinking about the recent development with Takuya. I continually replayed our kiss and embrace in my head. On the way home from the contest we'd sat in the back of the taxi holding hands. I glowed at the memory. Then to think about the cash prize, the recording contract—it was all too much.

I finally got to sleep around four thirty, and it wasn't until eleven that I woke up. No one was home, but Mrs. Kubota had left out my Japanese breakfast on the table and a pot of miso soup on the stove. As I sipped green tea, I made a decision: I would go to the JBS studios and tell Sakura myself that I didn't want any part of *Celeste-san: Wishing on a Kira-Kira*

Star. And I would demand that she give me Kenji Iwasaki's contact information.

I showered and dressed, then took out my train map and figured out the easiest way to get to Aoyama since I'd been there before only by taxi. It would take a couple of trains and a subway, but I was confident I could find it.

On the way, I wondered if the stares coming at me were from my being on television the previous night or just the regular gaijin sightings. It was hard to know, but no one asked for my autograph or called out "Celeste-san!"

I realized that I must have taken the wrong exit out of the subway station because I couldn't locate the JBS Studio building anywhere, and it wasn't like the glass megacomplex was easy to miss. Back in the station and out the other exit, it loomed large right smack in front of me.

When I entered the lobby, I was again assaulted by a Sakura Sasaki banner, but next to it was something completely unexpected, something that stopped me in my tracks and put a sour taste in my mouth. Another banner, just as big, said in English and Japanese: *Celeste-san: Wishing on a Kira-kira Star* next to that sappy *Days of Our Lives* picture of me gazing dramatically at the cartoon star. My confidence slipped and now I wanted to retreat. Maybe I'd just suck it up and go through with it. How bad could it be? Probably pretty bad. Actually, *quite* bad. I was still too angry about how they'd tricked me, messed with my emotions, and were still playing with something that was so important and personal.

Despite my huge face taking up a huge part of her lobby, the receptionist did not seem to recognize me. When I asked to see Sakura Sasaki, all she could say was, "*Eh?*" and stare with her mouth open, as if I'd asked her to take her clothes off. I decided on another tactic, asking if I might see Umeko Imai, the producer.

This seemed more manageable to the receptionist, and she told me to take a seat. In less than five minutes I spotted Umeko's cherry-sunburst hair and friendly smile. I wondered how long that smile would last once she heard my request. She led me to the same small office where she had interviewed me before the first show.

"Thank you for coming in," she said. "But, you know, it was not necessary. We were going to contact you soon about the show."

"Thanks for seeing me," I said in a cheerful voice. "I wanted to talk to Sakura-san, but maybe you can help me."

"Help you?"

"Yes. I would like to have the contact information for Kenji Iwasaki."

She flinched and looked at me as if she hadn't heard right. "But we will bring you to him on the show. We will be making arrangement for you to meet him at his house."

"I know. But it is important to me to have this information now."

She was still smiling, but her voice became short. "Maybe you do not understand, Celeste-san, but we want the program to show the real reunion between you. If you talk to him before that, it does not work well."

I, of course, understood this all perfectly and this was my precise objection, but I thought it better not to explain this, figuring that I should try to be calm, reasonable. "I'm sorry, Umeko-san, but do you think it is at all possible that I could speak directly to Sakura-san?"

"She is probably very busy and I do not know—"

"Just for a moment, please? I want to make this show as good as it can be too, but I just would like to talk to her and also thank her for everything she has done." I sounded so sugary, so Sakura-esque, that I surprised myself.

Umeko frowned, her forehead wrinkling. It was obvious she was perturbed at this development. "One moment," she said and left the room, shutting the door.

As the minutes ticked by, I wondered if Sakura would even show up. What would I do then? But after waiting nearly a quarter of an hour, the door opened and in she strode, Umeko following behind like an obedient puppy.

"Celeste-san!" she squealed. Even dressed casually in tight black pants tucked into a pair of shiny peach-colored boots, and a too-adorable white-lace peasant top, she was in a league of her own, Umeko fading into the wallpaper. "Thank you for coming all the way."

Umeko took her seat behind the desk, but Sakura remained standing over me, seeming to be in a kind of power play. I felt surrounded.

"What can I do for you?" she asked.

"Sakura-san, I appreciate everything you've done for me," I said, trying to sound as grateful as possible. "But I do not feel comfortable going on a television show in order to meet Kenji Iwasaki. I'm sorry, but I would like to meet him in private; not in front of any cameras. I'm sure you can understand my feelings."

Sakura's bright eyes showed her surprise, but not in the same way as on her ubiquitous JBS banner. "Yes, but Celeste-san. We take care of everything for you. I think you will enjoy very much."

"Maybe you don't understand," I said, attempting a firm, even tone. "I want his contact information *now*. And I want this to be private."

Sakura and Umeko exchanged pained glances. "*Chotto*, it is a bit out of ordinary," Umeko said. "We have already set this up—"

"Yes, but without my permission. Is this why you asked me back? Because he contacted you—not because of a scoring mistake with the judges? Did Hiromi Taniguchi contact you too? Have you been lying to me? And did you lie to Takuya-san too?" I was on a roll and heard my voice coming out confident, not at all shaky.

Sakura seemed to bristle at the mention of Takuya's name, but she said nothing, her doll-face now tinged gray, her arms folded across her chest.

"Iwasaki-san says he know Taniguchi-san and can contact her," Umeko said.

She's alive. I would finally get to meet Hiromi Taniguchi. This happy news was almost too much to handle, but I stood my ground. "Then all the more reason for you to give me his information. *Now*."

"Be reasonable, Celeste-san," Sakura said, her child voice turning businesswoman deep, as if she was negotiating an important deal. "This has already been set up and will benefit both of us and JBS too."

"I don't care about who this is benefiting," I said.

"If you can remember, Celeste-san, JBS just gave you recording contract and 300,000 yen."

"But that should have nothing to do with this," I said. "JBS will have opportunities to make further money off of me." Did she have the power to take this away? This former lowly accounting clerk who happened to capture a lucky break based on her adorability factor?

Sakura's voice rose. "I know it is many times that gaijin do not understand about Japanese way of being grateful and humble."

"And maybe you do not understand about being respectful of my privacy."

An uncomfortable silence took over the room. Umeko looked at her watch while Sakura continued to glare at me, then picked up a pen from the desk and began tapping it against her palm. Would she continue to be so stubborn and never back down? Perhaps I had no power here and this had been a mistake. Desperate to think of what to say next in my defense, I remembered something Takuya had mentioned at the ramen shop in Yamaguchi. Would this work? It was a long shot, but I decided to go for it.

"You know, Takuya-san is not very happy about this either, how you told him that there was a scoring mistake, which was a lie," I said, putting on my own businesswoman tone. "He may very well talk to the people at Sunny Shokuhin about their sponsorship of *Hen na Gaijin*."

Sakura's big eyes turned into tiny slits. She sighed, then said something to Umeko in Japanese that I couldn't understand. The producer answered, "*Hai!*" and left.

"Celeste-san, it seems you are going to be uncooperative. That does not make good show," Sakura said coolly, in control. "Umeko is getting your information. You can pick up at reception desk."

"Thank you. I appreciate it."

"May I ask one thing?"

I nodded.

"Would you consider meeting Iwasaki-san first time by yourself, then be interviewed on a show for me?"

She just wouldn't give up. "No, Sakura-san. I will not."

"You did *that?*" Takuya was saying as we sat on the living-room couch after he got home from work late that night. I had explained to him about my meeting with Sakura and how she had finally relented.

"I sure did."

"Did you talk to Iwasaki-san?"

"I called and left him a message this evening. But I haven't heard back." When I got his answering machine, I was caught off guard and stumbled through my words, not expecting that I wouldn't be able to talk to him.

"I am sure he can call soon," Takuya said, taking my hand.

"Yes, I'm sure he will."

"I will like to see Sakura's face when you walked in and tell her. She must be so surprised."

He squeezed my hand. I couldn't wait any longer. I removed my hand from his and put my arms around him, leaning in to kiss him. He began responding as if a switch had been turned on, the one in his father's garage that set off the Christmas lights. Once we started, we couldn't stop. My entire body turned warm, feverish. Takuya's hands pressed my back with a firm grip, and I pulled him toward me as I leaned back, his chest now against mine, my legs underneath his. It excited me when I heard him sigh, when he buried his face on my neck, showering it with kisses. I could feel the softness of his hair under my chin, his hand stroking my thigh.

I began kissing him again, pulling at his shirt buttons, and when he clasped my breast, I was ready to forget about unbuttoning his shirt, thinking seriously of simply tearing it off. He was just slipping his arm out of his sleeve, his chest exposed, when I heard a noise, as if someone was creeping along the hallway, trying to be quiet but not managing well.

I pictured his mother bursting in, and I guessed he did too, because he immediately sat up and pulled himself together.

He sighed. "There is no privacy here," he whispered. "But there is other place . . ."

"A love hotel?"

He raised his eyebrows. "You know *that?*"

"From Mariko."

He laughed. "I see." He looked at his watch. "It is only ten o'clock. Do you—"

"Yes," I said. "Just let me pack."

"Pack? No, there is no need." He smiled. "Everything is there."

In the hills of Shibuya I picked the love hotel that looked like Sleeping Beauty's castle—Hotel Romantic Journey.

While Takuya explained to me that, yes, there were indeed people working at the hotel, it was not apparent from the small, quiet reception area. He checked in by using a computer touch screen and inserted his debit card to pay, then received a plastic card that served as the key, and a receipt with the room information. Beethoven's "*Für Elise*" echoed through the hall as we made our way to a spiral staircase that took us to the second floor.

I expected a tiny room, like at the karaoke box or maybe the inn in Maruyama, with not much more than a bed, sink, and toilet, but the room was beyond plush. A big square canopied bed was adorned with thick black chains on each side, rendering it as a kind of drawbridge. Takuya pressed a remote control and showed me how it could be raised and lowered. I ran my hand over the pink-and-white flower-patterned velvet wallpaper, then gazed up at the crystal chandelier with plastic candles, their electric flames flickering in unison. The plastic stained-glass windows were blackened from behind for privacy.

Along with the old-world touches were many modern amenities. An endless loop of porno films flashed on the built-in TV screen. Two video game machines sat in the corner, along with a karaoke system with two microphones and a directory of 1,000 songs.

I laughed. "This is so over-the-top."

"Over-the-top? You do not like it?" Takuya looked concerned.

"No, no. I love it," I said. "It has everything." I opened a small, black refrigerator to find cans of soft drinks and beer. Packages of instant ramen lay on a counter next to a microwave.

"Come in here and see," he said.

I followed him into the bathroom, which seemed the size of a studio apartment. The fake marble tub looked to fit four comfortably. A hair dryer, shaving kit, soap, shampoo, and hair rinse were lined up neatly on the counter. Two crisply pressed *yukata* robes hung on hooks, with matching pairs of blue slippers that said Hotel Romantic Journey.

"Yes, there is everything. You can even sing to me '*Nozomi no Hoshi,*' " he said, taking me in his arms, nuzzling my neck.

"I didn't come here to sing."

He laughed. "I guess that is so," he said, leading me to the drawbridge bed, where we took off each other's clothes and proceeded to make love throughout the night on the bed, the floor, in the bath, without inhibition, and without any interruption.

25

A POSSIBILITY

"PLEASE DON'T BE UPSET, TAKUYA, BUT I THINK IT WOULD BE BEST IF I WENT BY myself."

His wounded look of disappointment pained my heart, the guilt dumping on me like a sudden cloudburst. I especially didn't want to cause him any unhappiness or hurt at this point, at this perfect time. This perfect time when we were both naked, our bodies entwined, wrapped in the bright white sheets of the drawbridge bed at Hotel Romantic Journey, which, after a number of visits, had quickly become our second home. But these romantic journeys would be coming to an end soon because Takuya had found an affordable apartment in Shimokitazawa. He was going to, as he put it, "cut the strings of apron" and finally move out from his parents' home.

Before coming to the hotel this time, we had devoured bowls of *hiyashi chuka*, ramen summer salad. The mix of noodles, crunchy bean sprouts, shredded egg, and sliced cucumbers, all so refreshingly cold, offered a respite from the sultry, humid temperature that never wavered, even at night.

Now, on our continual romantic journey, I had been devouring Takuya every chance I could, as if I'd been starved and locked in solitary sexual confinement, unfairly punished with a too-harsh sentence. He devoured me as well, this passionate and enthusiastic lover, and I was not disappointed. My small number of sexual partners had been put to shame, and still would have even if there'd been a list as long as the San Jose telephone directory. But amid the lust and debauchery there was a closeness and affection I'd found lacking in other relationships. Sincerity and lightheartedness, sweetness mixed with seriousness.

There was only one thing; he had not said "I love you," and I'd held back from saying it too, though I felt it from the moment of our first kiss in the JBS lobby. Dirk had said it all the time, which rendered it nearly meaningless. It was a quick fix to him, something to say along with the bouquet of pink miniature roses with a spray of baby's breath on special at Safeway—discounted because the petals were just at the ready-to-fall-off stage—accompanied by the box of third-rate chocolates from the all-night drugstore. "I love you" was a convenient antidote for my anger, an apology after arguing about music or whatever. It was one thing to say "I love you" and another to demonstrate it, and it seemed Takuya had been showing it in many ways all along with the concern and care he'd been bestowing upon me.

So with all of these new emotions and the trying on of new feelings, it was difficult to tell him that I wished to go visit Kenji Iwasaki, the man who claimed to be my father, alone.

"It so important for your life," he said. "I like to be with you."

"I know," I said gently, stroking his cheek as his arms squeezed my waist. "And I want to share all of this with you. But I feel it's just something right now that I want to do on my own. And who knows if it's really true that he's my father?"

Dirk would have turned away and begun sulking, but this was not Takuya's style, something I could really appreciate.

"I understand," he said, though it appeared that he was being more of a good sport than actually understanding. "But let me help you with the bullet train ticket for Sendai. And I get you cell phone so you can call me if you want to."

I kissed him.

"It is still hard to believe that you are *haafu*, though."

"Well, I think I'm pretty whole myself," I said.

He touched my nose with his index finger. "Your singing of the song, your feeling, is so Japanese."

"But do you think that has anything to do with having Japanese blood?"

"Not at all."

"That's what Sakura seemed to be implying on her show."

"That is for them to make drama. It is silly. But if it is for truth that Iwasaki-san is your father, I hope I can meet with him sometime."

"Yes, of course." I rested my head on his shoulder.

When I'd heard back from Kenji Iwasaki, we spoke only briefly and he seemed nervous, which had made me nervous also. I told him there wasn't going to be a television show chronicling our meeting after all, and it was a relief to hear he was glad about that. It confirmed that he wasn't looking for stardom or attention.

I didn't want to begin asking him detailed questions over the phone; discussing specifics about how it was that he might be my father seemed the kind of thing that was important to talk about only face-to-face. His English was good, and I was confident I could communicate with him on my own. But even though it was all quite understandable, his style of speaking seemed to have a slightly stilted quality that caused it to be a little off, almost as if he was taking extra care to memorize his words ahead of time.

Kenji Iwasaki wasn't unfriendly, but he was reserved. This could have been just his manner, or else he could have been uncomfortable. Perhaps it was a bit of both. I couldn't blame him; I felt the same. My excitement at finally meeting him was mixed with anxiety. It was such a strange situation: How could anyone have been expected to act in a normal way about it?

As Takuya promised, he set me up with a cell phone and helped me buy a ticket for the bullet train that would take me to Sendai. The morning I was to leave, he rode with me to the station and picked out a gift package of extra-fancy *senbei* rice crackers for me to give to Kenji. The big train stations were dotted with booths and stores selling specialty foods and souvenirs because of the common custom to bring a gift when traveling a long distance for a visit.

Takuya bought a special ticket that allowed him to go through the turnstiles and see me off on the train platform. When we arrived, I could see his mother waiting.

"*Okaasan*," I said.

Takuya and I had spent the previous night at the love hotel, so it was a surprise to see Mrs. Kubota coming to see me off. To my relief, she seemed to have accepted the new relationship by basically ignoring it, appearing to have learned to mind her own "busyness."

Today she looked as if she was the one about to embark on a trip, clad in a pretty beige summer linen dress, clutching a smart straw purse. She dabbed at her forehead with a handkerchief. It was another warm day, though Takuya told me that it would be a bit cooler up north in Sendai.

"She wanted to see you off and wish you a good luck," he explained to me.

Mrs. Kubota handed me a lunch bag adorned with a portrait of the Shinjuku cartoon penguin. "Rice ball," she said. "For you are hungry."

"*Domo arigato*. Thank you for coming to see me."

I boarded the train and took my seat next to the window, then looked out to the platform to see Takuya and his mother waving. It would only take around two hours to get to Sendai, and I was to return the same evening, but the sendoff gave me the feeling that I was about to undertake a long journey. Gazing at my lover—how I enjoyed referring to Takuya that way—and his mother, with their earnest, warm smiles as the train left the station, I felt as if I belonged to a family.

And now I was on my way to find out if I had even more.

I recognized Kenji Iwasaki immediately when I scanned the people waiting on the platform as my train pulled into Sendai station. He gave me a tentative wave when I got off. Seeming older than he looked on the video screen, he appeared frail and withered, as if he'd topple over if there were even the slightest gust of wind. I remembered him mentioning that he was unable to come see me in person on *Sakura's Gaijin Star Is Born* because he had been too ill.

As I approached him, a stocky woman with a pie-shaped face walked purposely toward me, her smile brimming with an expression that said she knew me. I didn't recognize her, and it gave me a start. Had Kenji brought along Hiromi Taniguchi? Did she run ahead to meet me? I soon realized, though, that this woman looked much too young to be her.

"I sorry," she said in halting English. "Are you Celeste-san?"

"Yes."

"I see you on Sakura Sasaki TV show. You singing so nice!"

Her recognizing me was hard to believe and I could only blurt out a thank you as I noticed Kenji from the corner of my eye, carrying a bouquet of flowers. He stood a few yards behind the woman, keeping his distance; too polite to interrupt.

The woman fumbled through her purse, pulling out a crumpled notebook and a mechanical pencil. "You please sign?"

"Ah, sure." Still startled, I somehow managed to write my name in both Japanese and English. Passersby looked on with curiosity.

The woman stared at the signature as if it was an important message. She thanked me, then disappeared into the crowd.

When I reached Kenji, he was smiling. "Someone recognized?"

"Yes. Such a surprise."

"You sing so well. I am sure many people enjoyed it very much." His face turned serious as he handed me the flowers, purple and yellow irises, and gave me a formal bow. "I am so sorry that I did not look for you. Please forgive me."

"Don't apologize," I said. "Thank you. And this is for you." I handed him the bag with the box of rice crackers.

"Ah, *domo!*" he replied, looking pleased. "We can take a taxi to my home, if you do not mind. It is only for ten minutes or so."

We made small talk in the cab, Kenji asking me how long I'd been living in Tokyo and if I had enjoyed my ride on the bullet train. I was anxious, jumpy; not at all sure how to behave. According to this person, I was his daughter, but it would have felt odd to hug someone who was basically a stranger. After having it in my mind for so long that the man in the home movie was likely my father, it was difficult to conjure up a feeling of connection based on Kenji's claim. It was an awkward situation, but I hoped he wasn't sensing my uneasiness.

The driver dropped us off in front of the house. I recognized it immediately, having viewed it from my throne on the video screen on *Sakura's Gaijin Star Is Born*. And when Kenji and I ended up sitting on that same couch in front of the bookshelves where he'd been with the reporter, there was a sense of déjà vu, yet at the same time it felt like being on the set of a TV show.

He turned on a fan to cool the stuffy room, then fixed glasses of iced tea and served up the rice crackers I'd brought. He also presented me with a plate of plump, reddish-pink *wagashi.* The sight of them brought back pleasant memories of the *kaiseki* meals with Takuya at the Nakaya Inn in Maruyama. Their presence comforted me.

"Oh! I love these," I said, popping one into my mouth.

Kenji seemed amused by my enthusiasm. "They are from a famous shop. Here in Sendai." He smiled. "Please eat many."

No one ever had to tell me *that.*

I hadn't noticed when I viewed the room on the video screen, but I now saw, hanging on the wall with prominence, a framed poster of the Beatles from their early days, the four standing in front of a hedge, bundled up for the cold, wearing woolen mufflers. Another poster was of the *Sgt. Pepper's Lonely Hearts Club Band* album cover. Underneath the posters a bookcase consisting of four shelves nearly spilling over with Beatles records and books about the group in both English and Japanese—I could read *Bi—to-ru-zu* in *katakana.* To the right of the bookcase several wooden shelves displayed ceramic bowls, vases, and plates, some painted with calligraphy, others with subtle glazes of green and blue. The apple-green plate he'd selected for serving the *wagashi* was equally artistic.

"These ceramics are beautiful," I said.

"Thank you very much." He seemed to blush, which gave his face a healthier color. "This is my profession."

"Your profession?"

"I am employed as a potter. My wheels and kiln are located in the back, behind the house." He stood and reached for a black bowl from the shelf, handing it to me. "Please. I want to give this to you."

Smooth in texture, the inside was bathed in a brilliant glaze of turquoise, giving the illusion of being filled with water.

"It's gorgeous," I said. "Thank you." I carefully placed it on the coffee table. "I draw. Pictures. Just a hobby."

"Ah! I would like to see your art."

"It's nothing special, but it makes me feel good to do it. Calms me down when I have a problem."

"Yes. I understand that well. It is the same for me with the feeling of clay."

"And I have been learning Japanese calligraphy. But I am not good at all."

"You have much talent," he said.

I heard the shrill ring of a bell from outside and jumped at the sound of screeching brakes.

Kenji smiled. "Do not be alarmed. It is only the postman arriving on his bicycle."

I took another *wagashi*, washed it down with several gulps of tea, then distractedly began eating countless rice crackers. Despite the fan whirring in the background, the room was still warm. Perspiration built up on my neck and on the back of my knees. I wasn't sure what to say next. Of course I wanted to hear his story of how he knew my mother, but I also wanted to ask him about Aunt Mitch's sister.

"I came here, you know, to meet Hiromi Taniguchi and to bring my aunt Michiko's ashes to Japan," I said. My voice quavered. I did not say that I also was looking for my father, though I had mentioned it on the television show. I didn't know if he had felt bad to realize that he wasn't the person I'd been searching for, though there'd have been no way for me to know about him. At any rate, I'd debated about it and in the end decided to bring the DVD with me to show him, if it seemed like it would be the right thing to do. Perhaps he could tell me the man's identity.

Kenji nodded. "Yes. I spoke to Taniguchi-san. She is very excited to meet you. She did not view your program, but I sent her a video. She lives in Yokohama, which is not far from you in Tokyo. If my health permits, I would like to visit there with you."

So Hiromi Taniguchi had been in my own backyard this whole time. My head swam at the thought that I would soon be able to meet her. "Yes. Thank you. It would be nice to be able to go there with you." I put my hand on my chest and swallowed hard. "And, and there is so much I want to ask you. I don't know where to begin. . . ." I seemed to be turning into an inarticulate child, attempting to wrap my brain around a concept too complex to handle. "So, I . . . I guess you knew my mother, but she always said she didn't know who my father was. And I don't remember her ever telling me about you." The words tumbled out. "And I feel that I don't look half Japanese at all."

"I agree with you; you do not look like a person with Japanese blood," he said, his face serious. "But when I saw you sing on television and I heard you were Barbara's daughter, I had to contact you because I think there is much possibility." The excitement in his voice relayed that he believed this and that he wanted me to be a believer too.

He leaned forward, nervously wringing his hands. "Will you permit me to tell you the story?" He waited a beat, then cleared his throat. "My wife died two years ago. Afterward I began to suffer from stomach ulcers. They worsened. Then, about one month ago, I was admitted to the hospital for surgery."

"I'm sorry."

"Right before I was released, I saw you on the program. I was shocked to realize you were Barbara's daughter. You sang '*Nozomi no Hoshi*' so beautifully. All the memories returned of Barbara and me in San Jose."

"You saw the show when you were in the hospital?" I imagined him in a drowsy haze, not of sound mind, lying in his bed watching me sing, drawing conclusions that may not have quite added up.

He nodded.

"So that's why they came here to put you on the show instead of you coming to Tokyo?"

Kenji smiled, shaking his head. "I had no intention of appearing on television. When I called them, I simply wanted to find out how I could contact you. But they were very excited to hear from me. They arranged to have me on the program from here, as my doctor did not want me traveling."

I pictured Sakura rubbing her little munchkin hands together with glee, that such a high-concept idea—the appearance of a surprise guest who claimed to be the long-lost father of one of the show's contestants—dropped in her lap.

"So I was ill and still thinking about my wife," he said. "We never had any children, even though we desired them."

I could hear a catch in his throat, a sound that pulled at my heart.

Sighing softly, he went on. "My wife endured many health problems. It was a long and winding road—like the song." He looked into my eyes. "Forgive me, Celeste-san, but I think I was wishing for you to be my daughter." He looked down at his hands that were now pressed together, as if in prayer. "But still, I think there is a good chance that you are."

I didn't know what to say. Had Kenji been so lonely and depressed that he'd reached out to me even though the possibility of him being my biological father was so remote? Was he in such a fragile, yet understandable, psychological state that it caused him to imagine I must be his daughter?

He finally broke the silence. "I was quite sad to hear that Barbara had passed away."

"You didn't know?"

"No." His face showed his pain. "What happened to you after she died?"

I explained how I'd lived in foster homes since there had been no relatives to take me in, or at least none the authorities could track down.

"So Michiko-san, she did not know?"

"Not that I know of. How do you know Aunt Michiko?"

"That is how I met your mother. Michiko-san was my father's cousin. And so is Hiromi-san."

I couldn't speak as I tried to take this in. For a moment I wondered if I was dreaming and would wake up soon to find the scene evaporated. "My mother and I lost touch with Aunt Mitch when they moved," I finally said. "She seemed to be mad at her sometimes, but I never knew why. It seemed like an old grudge. She called her Aunt Mitch the witch."

When Kenji nodded slowly, it seemed as though he might know the reason. I shivered.

And it was when he said *"Dozo"* and reached over to pour more tea into my glass, his head turned to the side, that my hands began to tremble. I had to fold them tightly together to make the shaking stop. Because it was at that moment that I was struck by Kenji Iwasaki's profile: the thin shape of his nose, the slightly high bridge, the small nostrils. I hadn't noticed it before, the familiarity. I'd been so set on him not being my father that, frankly, I wasn't looking at him carefully, in so much detail, like I had with the man in the home movie.

Was it my imagination or now a desire to believe? Or was it true that his profile was identical to mine?

I sat spellbound as he began to tell me his story.

26

THE INCENSE GIRL

IT WAS 1973 AND I WAS EIGHTEEN YEARS OLD. MY DREAM WAS TO ENTER A student exchange program to study English. I was determined to attend such a course in England because that was where the Beatles were from. I worshipped the Beatles, and they still mean a great deal to me even today. By that time they had already broken up, but I still had hope that they would get back together, to get back to where they once belonged, to coin a phrase. But my dream of living in London or, better, Liverpool did not come true. My father said that to save money I should go to school in the San Jose area of California. His cousin Michiko, whom I had never met, lived in a town called Saratoga with her American husband. She said that she would be happy to let me stay in their extra bedroom while I attended school. Once I was accepted into an exchange program with a small, private university in nearby Santa Clara, I moved in with Michiko-san and her husband Melvin.

Melvin's niece, Barbara Duncan, lived in a cottage behind the house across the street. She was twenty and sang in her own rock band, a group I heard practicing every day in that little house. I was shy but was struck by her beauty the moment Michiko-san introduced me one night when she came over for dinner. Her thick blond hair reminded me of the mane on a Palomino, and her brown eyes were warm and friendly yet mischievous.

Her high nose was the prettiest I had ever seen, and her laugh crackled like a fire. She laughed a lot. I liked how lively and talkative she was; always cheerful, free.

Barbara said that she was a student at San Jose State College, but she never seemed to go to class. She had lots of free time and was always rehearsing with her band. On her visits to have dinner with her aunt and uncle and their naïve houseguest, she was always the high point of the evening. I appreciated how very patient she was with me and my hideous English while she made a great effort to explain about American jokes, music, and television shows.

Michiko-san referred to Barbara as "the incense girl," when speaking to me about her because she thought that she always smelled like an incense burner. She also informed me that Barbara was a hippie. Hippies were irresponsible and lazy, she said. According to her, all they did was lie around all day and take drugs. Michiko-san did not like Barbara's music either. She complained about the noise when the band would rehearse late into the night. I knew that Michiko-san felt she needed to tolerate Barbara because she was part of Melvin's family. Therefore, I did not hear her say much to him about any of this. Instead, I was the one who always seemed to be on the receiving end of her rants.

A few months after I met Barbara, the cottage where she was living was to be torn down, so she moved into an apartment in San Jose. It was then that we became close. She drove a dilapidated old blue Ford with balding tires, which I thought would break down at any moment. But Barbara could not be bothered to worry about such things. She would pick me up after school, and then we would drive to her apartment. I was a young, inexperienced boy, so fresh off the boat that I was still a little seasick. She seduced me and I was ecstatic to be seduced. I had never been so happy in my life and I was crazy with love for her. Her nickname for me was Kenji-boy. My heart swelled whenever she called me that; it made me feel that I was a little bit American.

Barbara promised that once she became a big star she would take me on her rock band tour. I dreamed about that endlessly, imagining that it was quite possible that I would meet one of the Beatles—maybe even more than one. It was hard to believe that Barbara was not already famous, that she had not been discovered. She was so good-looking, along with being a great performer. Her voice was strong, powerful, and to me she sang better than any female singer you would hear on the radio.

I felt like a child compared to all her musician friends, and I wanted to remedy that as soon as possible. I began growing my hair longer and got started on a Pancho Villa mustache, which I thought made me appear older, more experienced. Though when I thought about it later, I believe it was my innocence that Barbara fell for. I was so different from the other men she knew. At any rate, with my new facial hair, I liked to think that I looked like George Harrison on the cover of *Let It Be*. I threw out my button-down shirts and polyester slacks, and Barbara took me to the thrift shop to buy jeans and T-shirts.

The change in my appearance infuriated Michiko-san, and she suddenly began complaining even to Melvin about how she thought Barbara was a bad influence, accusing her of turning me into a hippie. Melvin was always busy working—he had left the army and taken a job in the electronics industry. He said he had no time for his wife's trivial complaints. Even though he'd been a military man, he seemed more freethinking than Michiko-san. He did not seem to be bothered by hippies or rock music. He thought it was all harmless, but Michiko-san could not tolerate it. When she spoke to me, she always used Japanese, which Melvin could not understand. I was the one to whom she expressed her true feelings.

Finally she had had enough. "You must stop seeing Barbara," she said to me one day. "Or I will tell your father."

I was surprised to hear her say this but brushed off her admonishment. I was cocky, confident that she would not tell him anything. I figured she needed to save face in front of my father and would not admit to him that I was out of control. She would only end up looking bad for not taking good enough care of me, I reasoned. Maybe she hoped that I would eventually see my wayward ways if she nagged me hard enough, if she threatened me. Then I would eventually see the light without my father having to find out about any of this.

I let Michiko's nagging go in one ear and out the other. I was selfish and inconsiderate and should have respected her wishes. But I have the excuse, I suppose, of having been foolhardy and young. It was an exciting time to be alive, to be in America, to be under Barbara's spell. And there was nothing that would have kept me from seeing her, short of being put in jail.

I do not recall why, but one day Barbara came to visit me instead of us going to her apartment. It was a bit unusual, but no one was home so I did not think about it one way or the other. I knew that Michiko-san was going to be out all day on a trip to Japantown in San Francisco with one of her lady friends.

I was playing the Beatles album *Abbey Road* at such a full blast—I remember that "I Want You (She's So Heavy)" was on—that I did not hear the banging on the door. So I was shocked to see Michiko-san barging into my room, a look of revulsion engulfing her face. Barbara and I were both sitting on the floor naked, sharing a marijuana cigarette. Barbara just smiled at Michiko-san; she was not concerned about covering herself. That was the way she was; I think she thought she could disarm anyone with her smile and good nature. And she felt being naked was a natural thing, nothing to be ashamed of. But Michiko-san was in a rage: she was having none of it.

"Go out! Go out!" she screamed at Barbara.

It took me a minute to grab my pants and throw them over my lap. I was too busy sitting there trying to figure out why her English did not sound quite right. Is it not "get out"? I wondered in my marijuana stupor.

"Okay, okay," Barbara said. She shrugged, then stood up and threw her long purple dress over her body. She grabbed her fringed bag, the one that reminded me of Davy Crockett's jacket, and said, "Later," then walked out the door.

The next thing I knew Michiko-san was on the phone to my father. My hunch had been all wrong—she relayed every excruciating detail of my misbehavior. I could hear her clearly, and winced at the sound of her angry, forceful words.

By the time she handed me the phone, my father was on a tirade, berating me, insisting I come home immediately—saying how embarrassing it was to have a member of his family have to endure such a burden of taking care of his insolent, ungrateful son. I felt like an idiot, and an unbearable sadness consumed me: my whole world was crumbling before my eyes.

Things moved fast after that. I withdrew from school and prepared to return to Japan. Michiko-san was cool and distant toward me, and Melvin seemed to be at a loss for words.

I heard nothing from Barbara for days after Michiko-san threw her out of the house. I missed her desperately and called her many times, but there was no answer. I was afraid that I would never see her again. The night before I was to leave to go back home I heard a tapping sound on my bedroom window. I looked outside and saw Barbara throwing pebbles at the glass. I snuck out the front door to meet her.

"I have to talk to you," she said. Then she stood back, looking stunned. "What happened to your *hair*?"

The local barber had shorn off my long hair and mustache at Michiko-san's insistence. Now, instead of a Beatle, I looked like a crestfallen, baby-faced salaryman.

"Let's go," Barbara said, grabbing me by the hand. She led me down the street to a small park a few blocks away, where we had spent a lot of time in the past.

"I have been trying to call you," I said. "Tomorrow, I must—"

"I'm pregnant," she interrupted.

She always got right to the point—so unlike a Japanese person—and this was no exception. This was a characteristic I liked about her, but I was not so sure if I appreciated it in this situation since her words just about knocked me off my feet.

"*What?*"

"I'm going to have a baby."

She said it without expression, flat. It was impossible to tell whether she was happy or full of dread, or somewhere in between. I started feeling dizzy and I had to lean against the trunk of a large oak tree to keep my balance.

"But it might not be yours," she said.

"Eh?"

"I, uh, I don't know whose it is."

I was so naïve, so dense that I could not understand this at first. I guess it was not hard for her to sense this because she gave me a gentle smile. "Because I've been with some others too . . ." she said. "I'm sorry."

I hated hearing that, but I could not go into a jealous fit. We never talked about our relationship; it just came about and we enjoyed it.

"But it could be yours. I mean, I've been with you the most because I love you."

I could not speak for what seemed like minutes and then was unsure how to respond. But I also had to get to the point right away. "I am going back to Japan tomorrow," I finally said.

She looked alarmed, and even though this situation was becoming more and more upsetting, it felt good to see her look of disappointment. It confirmed to me that I must have meant something to her, that her saying "I love you" was sincere.

"You're not coming back?"

I explained to her about Michiko-san calling home. "My father is so angry. Michiko-san is so angry."

Her face reddened, her eyes catching fire. She tossed her long hair with a thrust of her head. "Ugh! That witch! That fucking witch!" She folded her arms and stood there fuming.

"There is nothing we can do about it," I said quietly. I touched her hair.

She finally cooled down, then turned sweet. She put her hand on my cheek. "I'm going to miss you so much."

Then her arms encircled me and I grabbed her and held on as if I would never let her go. It was unimaginable that this would be the last time I would be with her. We walked in silence to a deserted part of the park. The next thing I knew we were making love behind the bushes. If I had been thinking rationally, I would never have done such a thing, but Barbara had a way of throwing rationality out the window.

"Don't worry about me. Don't worry about a thing," she whispered. "I'm going to have an abortion."

Another shocking declaration, and once more I could not speak.

"I've decided," she said.

"But—"

"It's okay, Kenji-boy," she said, putting her fingers over my lips. "It's okay. I love you."

And that was the last time I saw her.

27

A PHOTOGRAPH

HEARING ABOUT BARBARA'S FREE-SPIRITEDNESS DID NOT SURPRISE ME; IT WAS spot-on to the way I remembered her too. But no one could be prepared for the odd, shaky feeling in response to finding out that you very well could have been aborted. Had she actually considered it? Or was it possible that this was something she'd told Kenji so he wouldn't worry or feel any responsibility? Or perhaps she had seriously planned on it but later changed her mind.

Kenji told me that once he returned to Japan he was never in touch with Barbara again. Michiko-san did find out eventually that Barbara was pregnant and called Kenji's father to warn him that his son could be the father. But when the baby appeared to have no Japanese blood, she told him it wasn't Kenji's.

"I was glad to hear that Barbara did not have an abortion. But at the time I guess I was relieved that I did not seem to be responsible. I did not even know if the baby had been a girl or boy. Michiko-san never spoke to my father again. She apparently was always one to hold a grudge, still mad, I suppose, that I had been so difficult. And, of course, my father remained mortified over the whole incident."

Kenji explained that he then moved on with his life. He enrolled in art school and, after he started making his living as a ceramicist, married a former classmate when he was twenty-seven. He hadn't thought about

Barbara for years until he saw me on *Sakura's Gaijin Star Is Born* and was shocked to see her in a photograph with him along with pictures of Michiko-san.

By now I had consumed the entire platter of *wagashi,* the remaining rice crackers, and four large glasses of iced tea. I excused myself to go to the rest room. Looking in the mirror as I washed my hands, I stared hard at my nose, turning and looking at it in profile. Did it really resemble Kenji's? But still, I did not look as though I could be half Japanese. Why would Kenji now think after all these years that I could be? Was it his desire to have his own children and the death of his wife that made him want to believe this?

When I returned to the living room, I heard the melody to "Imagine" coming from my purse. It took me a moment to realize that this had to be my cell phone, the temporary one Takuya arranged for me at the convenience store. Unless it was a wrong number, it had to be him. I smiled at Kenji when he said, "Ah! John Lennon song!" as I answered the call.

"Celeste? How is going?"

"Fine, fine," I said, happy to hear his voice.

"So I will see you on the eight o'clock train?"

"Yes."

"I am missing you."

"Me too."

I flipped the phone shut. "My boyfriend." I enjoyed being able to say that and finally have it not mean Dirk. "A Japanese man."

Kenji smiled. "I see."

"I have something of yours," I said. I showed him the geisha puzzle box.

"Ah!" he said with great surprise.

I explained to him how this was included with Aunt Mitch's personal effects and that it took a priest in Maruyama to discover that his passport was hidden away inside. He looked absolutely incredulous.

"Why did she have this with her things after all this time?" he asked, shaking his head. He pointed to his picture in the passport. "Such a young man is so old now." He went on to explain that when he was preparing to go home to Japan, he could not find his passport anywhere. The box was a gift from one of his friends, to wish him good luck on his journey to the States. "I must have put my passport in the secret spot and forgotten all about it. I thought it would be a safe place." He shook his head. "I had to get a new passport from the Japanese consulate. Michiko-san was not pleased. I must have left the box behind in all the confusion."

"I'm so happy to be able to return it to you," I said. I took another sip of tea and prepared myself for what I wanted to say next. "There is one more thing I want to show you. Do you have a DVD player?"

He said yes and I explained to him what he was about to see and also told him that I wanted to know if he knew anything about the man with the long brown hair.

I watched Kenji's face as the short film played. He gasped at the sight of Michiko and Hiromi waving to the camera. But it was when Barbara came on that his shoulders slumped and his face both lit up and became sad at the same time. It was then that I could tell how much he'd loved my mother. His mouth opened in surprise, and he said something in Japanese that I couldn't understand. He sighed, then slowly shook his head, and when I looked at his eyes, I could see they were filling with tears. He watched in silence as the man held me, kissed me, and helped me wave my tiny hand.

We both stared at the television that now showed nothing but a bright blue screen.

I took his hand in mine and we held on tight.

And we both cried softly without saying a word.

When Takuya met me at the station, I knew I must have looked like an emotional mess, as wilted as the bouquet of irises Kenji had given me, which now drooped in submission to the heat. I saw the concern on Takuya's face. He suggested we go to a *kissaten* near the station, a quiet place where we were able to sit on a love seat in a dark corner. We didn't touch our iced coffees.

"Kenji let me have this," I said.

I handed Takuya an envelope with a photograph in it, a photograph I couldn't stop looking at the entire time I'd been on the train home. I would put it away, then pull it out again and continue to stare.

I told him about Kenji's relationship with Barbara and how Aunt Mitch became so angry with him that she called his father, which resulted in Kenji having to abruptly return to Japan.

"And we watched the DVD together," I said as I relived the moment. "And we both couldn't stop crying."

Takuya took me in his arms and tried to kiss away the tears that now fell on my cheeks.

"He said he never saw that man before. The one in the home movie. He doesn't know who he is."

"And this picture . . . ?" Takuya said. He had now opened the envelope and removed the photo, one that looked like it was taken during the early decades of the twentieth century. It was faded, tinted in shades of brown, a picture of a Japanese man who looked to be in his late thirties or early forties, standing behind a Caucasian woman sitting in a chair, who was probably no older than twenty-five. Both wore kimonos and serious expressions on their faces, the style of the day.

"Kenji says that even he doesn't think I look Japanese, but . . ."

"Who are they?" Takuya asked.

"They are his grandfather and his wife. Her name was Abigail Summerstone and she was from England."

Takuya's eyes turned wide.

"They had two sons who both married Japanese women, one of which was Kenji's father," I said. "He married a Japanese and they had a daughter who died as a baby and then had Kenji."

Takuya continued to stare intently at the picture.

"So Kenji thinks because his grandmother was white, then it's possible he could . . . he could be my father and that would explain why I don't look half Japanese."

"She is very beautiful," Takuya said. "Like you. There is resemblance."

I put my hand on his cheek. "You're so sweet," I said. "Aunt Michiko found out that my mother was pregnant and she suspected Kenji could be the father. But when I was born, she called Kenji's father and told him I wasn't Kenji's baby since it was obvious I was Caucasian. I guess everyone was relieved."

Takuya shook his head in disbelief.

I rested my head on Takuya's chest. "So Kenji wants us to get DNA tests, to see if there is proof that he is my father."

"Do you want to?"

"Yes."

Takuya pointed to a shopping bag. "What is in there?"

"Oh, I forgot," I said, taking out a wooden box. I removed the lid and showed him the elegant black bowl that Kenji had given me. "He made this. He's a potter."

"Potter?"

"A ceramicist. A person who makes ceramics."

Takuya picked up the bowl and examined it with care. "I do not know about this kind of thing, but it looks so full of art." He placed the bowl back in the box. "And he knows Hiromi Taniguchi-san, right? Does he know where she is?"

"Yes. He told me had tried to call her when he saw me on television, but the phone number was disconnected and had been from a long time ago. Then he did some research and tracked down her daughter. Her married name is Hiromi Amano and she lives in Yokohama."

"So close!" he said. "And we went all the way to Maruyama."

"But I'm so glad we went there. I had such a good time with you."

He looked in my eyes. "Yes. That is when I am knowing how special you are."

28

HEN NA GAIJIN

SAKURA'S GAIJIN STAR IS BORN BROUGHT WITH IT MY FIRST ENCOUNTER WITH Kenji Iwasaki, but there was also the recording contract. Despite my refusal to participate in *Celeste-san: Wishing on a Kira-kira Star,* a meeting had been scheduled for me at the Shinjuku office of JBS Music. To my relief, either Sakura had no power at JBS Music or else she had decided not to give me any more grief.

As I strode through the massive Shinjuku Station on my way to the west exit, I remembered my first time here, ready to pass out from the dizzying array of distractions—the kanji, the crowds, the noise. And all of these remained in full force, but now weren't much of a bother or frustration. They were all part of Tokyo, the place where I was beginning to feel at home among the thirteen million.

Once outside, I maneuvered my way past the Studio Alta building, displaying Sunshine Poppy's latest video on its massive TV screen, and down the two blocks to the JBS Music building, a more modest space in comparison to the network television studios in Aoyama.

As I rode the elevator to the fifth floor, I could only think of Dirk. After all the fights, all the doubts, my plummeting confidence, I could finally say to him: "I am on my way to a meeting to discuss my record deal!" I had purposely not written him about any of the latest developments; my fantasy was to simply send him a copy of my CD, autographed with "Best Wishes, Celeste Duncan."

I had spent many moments thinking about the type of recording I wanted to do, perhaps a remake of "*Nozomi no Hoshi.*" But the idea that appealed to me most was the possibility of an *enka* song composed specifically for me, a song about a gaijin who had traveled far away to another country only to discover her heart and family waiting there. Was it too corny? As cheap and calculated as a reality program showcasing my reunion with Kenji Iwasaki? Perhaps. But I didn't care; at least this would be my own brand of sentimentality that would be in my control.

Once at the reception area, I waited only a few moments before I was taken to Hirano-san, the producer.

He looked about thirty-five and had the appearance of a man involved in some aspect of the entertainment business. He wore rectangular, black-rimmed hipster glasses, and his hair, while shaved short on the back and sides, remained long and stringy on top. He spoke decent English. We exchanged pleasantries, and he congratulated me on winning the contract.

"Do you know that this contract is for one single recording?" he said.

I replied that I didn't know that. So much for the album I'd been assuming would be in the works. I had to admit that this was disappointing, but I rationalized that maybe it was best to start out small and go on to bigger things from there.

"So would you like to hear it?" he asked.

Hear it? I didn't know what he meant. "I beg your pardon?"

"We made a demo of your single with studio singers so you can learn."

"It's already made?" Another disappointment. This wasn't looking so good, but I was hopeful that at least it might be an *enka* song written especially for me.

"It's a duet," he said, cueing the CD player.

"A duet?"

"Yes. So you will hear a man's voice and a woman's."

"And the woman's part is mine, I guess?"

"Eh?"

My attempt at a feeble joke seemed to go over his head, or maybe he was just being polite.

Despite the tiny speakers sitting on Hirano-san's desk, the song played at a loud volume. From the very beginning, a queasiness overtook my stomach. Instead of a lush *enka* like *"Nozomi no Hoshi,"* the tune seemed to be a slightly updated version of "Cinderella Boogie-Woogie," the obnoxious song Mrs. Kubota had sung at Hysteric Echo, and the one Jenny resurrected on *Sakura's Gaijin Star Is Born*. And, like that song, many of the lyrics were in English. Although I couldn't understand everything, I could tell that it must have been called something like *Hen na Gaijin* because that was the phrase the duo sang in harmony during the chorus, if you could call it singing; it sounded more like a chant.

My heart dropped further every second that it played on. It was about the worst thing I'd ever heard. Sakura must have had her hand in this. After all, it was the name of her television show. Was it that she had no taste and deemed it a fantastic song that would be perfect for me, or had she selected it as an insult? But the worst part was Dirk and what he would think of it. There was no way I could ever send such drivel to him. The song was so dreadful that I wanted to run out of the room screaming, but instead I sat still, smiling politely at Hirano-san from time to time but mainly staring at my hands folded in my lap until it mercifully faded out.

"Pretty catchy, huh?" Hirano-san said, grinning. "We think it could go over quite well, especially if you sing it on Sakura-san's show."

I nodded, not wanting to appear rude.

"And your singing partner will be Nesbitt Natto," he said enthusiastically. "I think you know him. He was on Sakura-san's program with you both times."

How could I forget? The gaijin who could not only burp at will, transform balloons into fornicating animals, but whose Japanese boasted a Texas twang.

I had stood up to Sakura Sasaki, I thought, and Hirano-san appeared to be a more reasonable person, or at least I hoped this was the case. I figured I had nothing to lose.

"You know, it's a fun song," I said. "And I'm sure I am being highly inconsiderate to even suggest something else since I am so inexperienced in the music business." I cleared my throat. "But I was wondering if perhaps there was any chance that I could do an *enka* song?"

"Enka?" he said, surprised.

I went on to pour my heart out to him, explaining how Aunt Mitch used to sing these types of songs to me, how I'd fallen in love with "*Nozomi no Hoshi*" from the moment I first heard it, and how my rendition seemed to move so many people. I told him about my meeting with Kenji Iwasaki, how there was a chance he might be my father, and that I had also found the love of my life as well as a wonderful *okaasan* here.

"I would love to do a song with these kinds of elements," I implored him. "Something I could sing with deep emotion."

I was proud of myself for sticking up for what I wanted, though I was doubtful that such a little speech would change his mind along with the powers that be who had come up with my debut song. I wasn't sure what I would do if he refused and said take it or leave it—a humiliating duet with Nesbitt Natto or nothing.

Hirano-san didn't answer right away but looked thoughtful, as if he was at least considering my request.

"It is a bit irregular," he said. "But I understand, Celeste-san. Let me relay your suggestion and I will get back to you."

29

LOVE IS EVERYTHING

KENJI HAD ARRANGED ALL THE DETAILS FOR OUR DNA TESTS. I TOOK A MOUTH swab at a laboratory in Tokyo and he had one taken in Sendai. My specimen was then sent to his where tests were run on both. It did not take long to get the result, and he telephoned me as soon as he received it.

"Hello, my daughter, Celeste," he said.

"*What?*"

"The test is conclusive. It is 99.9 percent that I am your father. That is the best result you can receive."

I sat down hard on one of the few chairs in the room. I was at Takuya's new apartment, and it was filled with boxes and little furniture.

"*Otousan!*" I said the word for father. "The test is a match!" I said to Takuya. "He's my dad." I began to laugh and couldn't stop. "I'm so happy." Takuya lifted me from my chair and hugged me. "I am so glad to call you Dad," I said to Kenji.

"And I am happy to call you my daughter," Kenji said. "So you are going to Hiromi-san's soon."

"Yes." I wiped my cheek with my hand, as my laughter had turned to tears. "I wish you could come with us."

"There will be many more opportunities for us to meet," he said. "Right now my doctor says I must rest. There has already been so much excitement. I hope you have a marvelous time."

"I want you to be *genki*," I said. "*Gambatte kudasai.*"

"*Gambarimasu.* I think this good news will make my health improve very soon."

We talked more, and then I put Takuya on the phone. They spoke in Japanese and I could tell he was being respectful and a little bit formal. It made me proud.

"He seems like very nice guy," Takuya said after hanging up. "You are so lucky."

I gave him a hug. "I want to do something for him. To celebrate. Especially since he can't be at Hiromi-san's."

"What do you want to do?"

"He loves the Beatles," I said. "Maybe I can do calligraphy for a Beatles lyric."

"Yes, since he gives you pottery, his art, you can give him your art."

"But a Beatles song would need to be in *katakana,* for foreign words, right? I'm not sure how artistic it would look. Something in kanji would be so much better."

"Sometimes the Beatles song titles are translated into Japanese and do not use the English," Takuya said.

I thought for a moment. "How about, 'All You Need Is Love'?"

"That would be good one. Because the title for that is in Japanese. It is '*Ai Koso wa Subete*.' That mean 'Love Is Everything.'"

"Love is everything. That's perfect."

I practiced writing "*Ai Koso wa Subete*," which were the characters:

愛こそはすべて

until I could do them justice. Takuya had bought me special paper, and I was attempting to paint the final copy at his apartment on the dining-room table. After several tries and wasting five sheets with mistakes and errant ink-stain blots, I finally painted a version that I thought acceptable. I showed it to Takuya.

"I can see how much you have an improvement," he said. "In the shape, and the confidence in brush strokes."

I laughed. "You sound like a respected calligraphy sensei."

He narrowed his eyes and put his index finger under his chin, giving off a professorial look. "Well, am I not?"

"I guess so. You've taught me everything *I* know."

I grabbed at his sides and dug my fingers in to tickle him. He let out a laugh and pulled me out of my chair, pushing me on the couch, playfully pinning me down. He began returning the tickling favor. I screeched with laughter until he began to caress me and our playing turned into serious kissing, a not uncommon occurrence. But I was puzzled when he abruptly stopped participating in our make-out session and got off the sofa.

"There is one more thing you need for your calligraphy," he said, and went to the small desk in the corner of the living room, opening a drawer.

"What's that?" I asked, sitting up.

"This." He held a small wooden box. "Come here. I will show you."

I went to the dining-room table and saw that he was holding a small rectangle-shaped piece of wood and an ink pad.

"This is *hanko*," he said.

"What?"

"A hand stamp. I got this made for you."

He pressed the wood against the ink stamp, then held it down on a piece of paper. The stamped characters were in *katakana* and said Duncan:

ダン
カン

"This is what the great calligraphy artists do for signature of their work," he explained. He pointed to the corner of the sheet where I had painted the kanji title for Kenji. "You can stamp here."

"That was so thoughtful of you," I said, hugging him.

"Well, I am nice guy."

We managed to find a picture of the cover of the single recording of "*Ai Koso wa Subete*" that came out in Japan. The four Beatles held placards saying, "All You Need Is Love" in different languages. I had both the picture and the calligraphy framed together, side by side.

A few days after I sent it to Kenji, I received a letter:

My Dear Celeste,

I cannot fully express my gratitude for your thoughtful and heartwarming gift, one that I will treasure for all time. It is now hanging in my living room. Your calligraphy is beautiful and I think of you every time I look at it. It means so much to me to have you in my life as my darling daughter.

Please give my regards to Hiromi-san when you see her. And my best to Takuya-san. I hope to see you again very soon.

Love from,
Dad

I went to meet Hiromi Taniguchi with three out of the four most important people in my life: my lover, Takuya; my *okaasan*, Mrs. Kubota; and my "sister," Mariko. It could have been a trip for only Takuya and me, but I was indebted to Mrs. Kubota and Mariko for their help and encouragement on my quest to find Hiromi Taniguchi. It was fitting that they should get to meet her too.

My father had been the one to set it up. He'd spoken to Hiromi-san and received the directions from her, which he passed on to me. She lived just about forty-five minutes by train from Asahidai. As I had only those two photographs of her—one as a child and the other as a still young woman probably in her early forties—I did not know what to expect. I knew that her name was now Hiromi Amano and that her husband had died about two years ago.

The bright gold, orange, and red leaves on the trees in Hiromi-san's quiet Yokohama neighborhood, as well as the chill in the afternoon air, signaled that it was autumn. Seeing the leaves scattered on the ground, I thought of Oda-san in Maruyama, collecting her wares for Tokyo restaurants. I imagined Hiromi-san resembling a slightly younger version of her—robust and sturdy, wearing a practical jacket and trousers, able to squat on the ground with her strong legs.

When we reached the rather large Western-style house, Takuya said, "You should be the one to ring bell."

"I'm kind of nervous," I said.

It was hard to believe that I was finally about to meet Hiromi Taniguchi. It had been nearly a year since I'd received the phone call from the convalescent home that started my mission. So much had happened and so many times there seemed to have been every indication that I would never meet this woman. But that was in the past and here I was. I pressed the buzzer next to the brass doorknob.

The first thing I heard was the high-pitched barking, or rather yapping, of a dog. The door opened and the culprit—a tan, overfed Chihuahua with soulful brown eyes, donning a bright pink sweater—sprang forth and immediately began humping my leg.

"Well, somebody sure likes you," Mariko said as I tried to shake the dog off without success, as he clung to me even tighter.

Takuya was laughing at the antics of the dog, but Mrs. Kubota could only stare at the woman who cried out, "*Burando-kun!*" prying the dog off my leg. She held him to her chest, whispering a gentle scolding in his ear.

"*Gomen nasai!*" she said to us.

The woman who said "I'm sorry" was a petite elderly lady with short curly hair in a coiffure also with a canine-like quality, though more like what would be found on a poodle. The color was a pumpkin-orange, the curls tight and wiry. The powder on her face was as thick as plaster and the bright fuchsia rouge dabbed on her cheeks nearly matched the shade of her sequined tunic. Rounding out her ensemble were skinny black pants and bright green house slippers with a platform of about three inches. When I peered hard past the harsh makeup, it was somehow possible to make out the characteristics of Hiromi Taniguchi.

"Hiromi-*obasan?*" I said.

Her face broke into a friendly smile. "*Maa!* Celeste-san!"

"*Burando?*" I heard Mariko say and she took the dog as Hiromi handed him to her.

It wasn't typical for Japanese people to go around hugging each other as casually as Americans, but Hiromi Taniguchi took to this naturally. We embraced warmly, like old friends, Hiromi-san giving me three firm pats on the back. She felt to me like a fragile, brittle doll, and I took care not to squeeze her too tightly. As my head rested briefly on her neck, a pungent scent of lavender shot up my nose. I had to hold my breath for a moment to keep from sneezing.

Takuya took over and made introductions in Japanese as we entered the house. He also gave Hiromi-san a box of *wagashi* we bought at Shibuya Station. She thanked him with wide-eyed appreciation.

"The dog's name is Brando, for Marlon Brando, one of her favorite American actors," Mariko explained, the Chihuahua wildly licking her face. "You little freak, you!"

She placed Brando on the floor. He scurried around the room, barking for joy, and stayed clear of my leg. Mariko lowered her voice. "Did you see the look on Takuya's mother's face?" she snorted in a whisper.

I glared at her. "Shh!"

It had been evident that Mrs. Kubota was trying to be polite, attempting to downplay her shocked expression in response to Hiromi-san's surprising, gaudy appearance. She tried her best not to stare too much but was only partially successful.

Although Hiromi-san did look rather unusual, the house seemed tasteful—sleek and modern. The large living room was decorated with Scandinavian-style furniture in muted blond wood tones. A fire crackled in a stone fireplace in the corner; a blue pillow set in front of it seemed to be Brando's. He sat there now, panting and eyeing his visitors with friendly curiosity.

Mariko and *Okaasan* sat on the sofa, Takuya and me in chairs across from them. Hiromi-san began chatting in Japanese and brought out plates of cheese and bread and a bottle of wine. She poured glasses for all of us.

"This is great stuff," Mariko gushed, after taking a gulp from her glass. She smacked her lips, then gave off a satisfied sigh. "Hiromi-san says she has a whole goddamn wine cellar in the basement. This is a zinfandel from California."

Takuya and I clinked our glasses. The wine was a bit sharp but smooth. Even this tiny amount pleasantly went to my head.

Hiromi-san kept grinning at me as if she couldn't believe I was there. I felt the same way, even though I still could not get over how different she was from what I'd expected. I kept smiling, wishing I could say everything in my head that I wanted to.

"Tell her I've brought Aunt Mitch's ashes," I said to Takuya. "And the comb. And I want to show her the home movie."

Takuya spoke to her, but Hiromi-san began talking over him.

Everyone seemed mesmerized by what she was saying. It was frustrating not to be able to understand as everyone around me nodded, saying, "*So desu ka? Ah, honto ni?*"

Takuya noticed my frustration and translated for me. "She say she does not speak to Michiko-san since about 1977. She say they have sisters' quarrel, and she feel bad now, but Michiko-san always held the grudge," he said. "Michiko-san moved to Tokyo in 1950 from Maruyama to go work at the army base. And that is where Michiko-san meet Uncle Melvin. Her parents are against marriage to American so they get married quickly in Japan, then go California."

Hiromi-san went on, pointing to me, smiling broadly.

"She say she heard about you when your mother was pregnant," Takuya said. "The sisters write letters. And Hiromi-san hear many story about Kenji-san. Michiko-san was very angry with him. And she sent him home. She was mad at Barbara-san too, but they started talking again when she say she is pregnant. Barbara-san said she was going to have an abortion, but Michiko-san said no, that she and Melvin would help her if she had the baby."

She wasn't a witch, I thought. How could Barbara have kept calling her a witch? Had my mother loved Kenji so much that she always resented Aunt Mitch for sending him away? "And she knows that Kenji is my father, right?"

Takuya said something to Hiromi-san, and she grinned and nodded as she answered him.

"Yes," Takuya said. "Kenji-san called her and told her the news. She says she has never heard anyone so happy."

"I am happy too," I said.

I opened the shopping bag I brought and pulled out the photo album, the handwritten documents, the comb, and the urn holding Michiko-san's ashes and put them on the coffee table in front of Hiromi Taniguchi, something I had been waiting so long to do.

"Taniguchi-san, *arigato,*" Mrs. Kubota said, bowing in the direction of the urn. She looked at me and said in English, "You becomes born baby!" Then she said something to Hiromi-san.

"Finally you can give her these!" Mariko said, grabbing my arm and squeezing it. She seemed so happy it was almost as if she was having her own family reunion.

I handed Hiromi-san the papers detailing Aunt Mitch's instructions. She gripped them hard with her fingers, reading intently, nodding once more.

"Hiromi-san says when baby is born, when, Celeste, you are born, Michiko-san is thinking that Kenji-san is not your father because you do not look half Japanese," Takuya said to me in a quiet voice.

Mariko was saying something by now to Hiromi-san. "Show her the comb," Mariko said to me gently.

I opened the box, presenting it to her. It was so well preserved that it looked as though it could have been bought yesterday, but had to be at least seventy-five years old.

"*Maa!*" Hiromi-san said, holding it in her palm.

"She says she remembers this comb well," Mariko said. "Her mother's."

I opened the photo album to the page with the portrait of Hiromi-san and her sister dressed in kimonos. I pointed to her twelve-year-old self. "Hiromi-san," I said.

"Much young girl!" she said and everyone laughed. She looked at me and pointed to her nose. "Now—old!"

I smiled as she turned the pages of the album, stopping long at the pictures of Michiko-san and Melvin, and the one of me in the kimono. She made comments in Japanese, and Mariko and Mrs. Kubota chimed in.

Takuya gave me a warm smile.

I turned to Hiromi-san. "Michiko-san," I said in a solemn voice, pointing to the urn.

Hiromi-san's brightly painted face paled, her eyes turning downward. "Yes, yes," she said. She looked at me. "Thank you."

Takuya said something in Japanese, and Hiromi-san carefully took the urn in her hand. She rose from her seat and walked to the corner of the room, opposite the fireplace where a small wooden cabinet sat. She knelt in front of it.

"You can go with her," Takuya said softly to me. "To her family *butsudan*. Altar."

I knelt next to her. She lit several candles, then burned incense, rituals that reminded me of what I'd seen at Mariko's sister's funeral. The smell of cedar soon filled the room. To the right of the candles were two framed photographs, one of a man probably in his seventies—perhaps her late husband—and another of a couple that I assumed could be her parents. Hiromi placed the urn on another shelf. She tapped a small metal bowl with a brown wooden mallet. It made a deep, ringing, reverberating tone. Then she put her hands together in prayer. I did the same.

"You brought Michiko-san a long way to finally be home," Mariko said.

Hiromi-san turned to me and took both my hands in hers. "*Domo arigato,* Celeste-san," she said. "Thank you."

I couldn't help it. I began to cry.

"Goddamn it, Celeste, if you don't stop, *I'm* going to start bawling," Mariko said, wiping her eyes with her sleeve.

When I returned to my chair, Mrs. Kubota handed me a handkerchief.

Hiromi-san said something to Takuya. "She is asking if you know that she met you once when you were baby."

"The DVD," I murmured, and Takuya explained to Hiromi-san that we had part of her visit on film. Hiromi-san looked as though she could not believe it.

"*Maa!*" she said, pointing to the DVD as Takuya placed it in the player.

Showing her this film was another experience I had looked forward to, what had propelled me here, although the burning question about the man with the long brown hair had been eclipsed by Kenji. Still, this was a precious movie, the only footage I had of Barbara, of Aunt Mitch. And I was still curious what Hiromi-san could tell me. I thought back to watching it with Kenji, the emotion still raw.

Hiromi-san stared at the screen, her hand over her mouth, her fingers splayed, as the image of her with her sister came on. I had been so consumed with the man kissing me that I did not realize until now that this was probably the last time Hiromi-san saw her sister.

The screen going blank brought a hush over the room. Hiromi-san sighed and began to speak. Takuya translated for me.

"She say this is very nice visit and her only time in America. She stay for five days and they go to San Francisco, see the Golden Gate Bridge. You were living with your mother and were visiting that day to meet her."

"And the man?" I asked.

"She remembers him well because his name was Clint, like Clint Eastwood, Hiromi-san's favorite American actor except for Marlon Brando," Takuya explained.

"Dirty Harry," Hiromi-san said.

I couldn't help but smile.

"She know only that he is friend of your mother and played guitar. He play very well. Maybe he was your mother's boyfriend, but she does not know. But she know what happen to him. About two months after Hiromi-san goes home she get letter from Michiko. 'Do you remember Clint?' she asked. 'He die from the drug overdose. Only twenty-seven years old.' It was big shock for Michiko-san and for Hiromi-san too."

"I have to say thank you to Clint," I said. "For at least getting me to come to Japan to search for who you were."

"That is true," Takuya said.

Mariko spoke to Hiromi-san, then looked at me. "I told her that we need another bottle from that cellar!"

Leave it to Mariko to lift the heavy spirits of the room. Hiromi-san smiled, seeming relieved.

"It is the wine her husband, Eiji-san, collected. It was hobby for him," Takuya said.

Hiromi-san returned from her cellar with a bottle of petite syrah and freshened our glasses. As she drank, her face became nearly as bright as the rouge on her cheeks. The mood turned merry, her laugh louder.

Brando jumped on his mistress's lap, balancing on his hind legs, and began to lick her face. She giggled. "*Burando!*" Turning to us, she said, "I like! *Za Godfather! Sutreet-o Car Name Desire!*"

"*So desu ne*," agreed Mrs. Kubota.

Brando next jumped over to Mariko, planting kisses on her cheek as she screamed with laughter.

"Now he's in love with *you*," I said.

Hiromi-san grabbed the dog, pointed at his pillow, and told him to go sit. Amazingly, he obeyed.

She talked about her family. Her grown daughter named Rumiko lived near Nagano with her husband and son.

"Hiromi-san's grandson is—" Takuya said, then stopped to ask her the grandson's age.

"Eighteen!" she said in English.

Mrs. Kubota, who had been quietly sipping only thimblesful of wine brightened, looking especially impressed. She flashed her eyes at Takuya and said in English, "I like to having baby grand!"

Mariko's honking laughter caused Hiromi-san to laugh even more, and Takuya and I joined in.

"Grand*baby!*" Takuya said, shaking his head. He looked at me, rolling his eyes.

"Maybe she really wants a piano," I said.

"I am thinking that is less the trouble," he replied.

Hiromi-san didn't get the joke, even after Mariko explained it to her in Japanese. Mrs. Kubota's mistake did not seem to dampen her happy thoughts of grandchildren, and she was smiling now.

Hiromi-san went on with her story.

"Hiromi-san's husband, Eiji-san, retired about ten years ago. He was government worker. Then they open a *kissaten* in Yokohama," Takuya said. "Eiji-san died two years ago and now Hiromi-san is tired and"—he asked her a question—"and she is thinking to find new owner for *kissaten.* Her daughter wants her to move to their house where it is more like countryside. She will live with her, her husband, and grandson."

"How nice!" Mrs. Kubota exclaimed in Japanese.

"She say *kissaten* is close-by and she will show us," Takuya said.

The café was only a couple of blocks away from Hiromi-san's house in a pleasant shopping district lined with trees, smaller than the one in Asahidai.

I knew well that *kissaten* in Japan had all different kinds of décor and themes, from Café Greenwich to Peggy Sue to Eighty-Eight, the *jazukissa* that was Takuya's favorite. Hiromi-san's was named Tarot and was furnished in a modern style, with silver metal tables and matching chairs, looking slightly industrial. But on the walls were posters depicting tarot cards.

There were only a few customers and a young woman behind the counter greeted Hiromi-san respectfully.

"Your aunt Hiromi like to do the fortune-telling as hobby and she offers it to her customers," Takuya explained after speaking with Hiromi-san. "So she design this *kissaten* with theme of tarot cards."

When I heard this, her off-the-wall attire and appearance seemed to make sense.

As the young woman served us coffee and slices of strawberry short-cake, Hiromi-san walked over to a shelf lined with books and reached for a glass orb and a small box.

She placed the ball carefully on the table, as though it were a treasured, sacred object, then pulled out a retractable cord, and plugged it in the wall. Once she turned on a switch, the orb glowed a sunny yellow-orange, gray clouds swirling inside like a witch's cauldron. It seemed both crystal ball and kitschy lamp.

"Ha! A crystal ball!" Mariko said.

"And tarot cards," said Takuya as Hiromi-san presented the cards in a fan, facedown, and told me to pick one.

I didn't really believe in such things but didn't want to insult Hiromi-san, whose face showed so much enthusiasm. I only hoped she wouldn't pronounce me an abalone person. I pulled at one of the cards. She turned it over.

"Oh!" Mariko exclaimed. "The Lovers' card!"

"Eh?" Mrs. Kubota said.

Mariko looked over at Takuya's mother. "Maybe you will get your baby grand soon," she cracked.

The other customers were staring at us, the usual commotion over a gaijin, but Hiromi-san ignored this.

"Eh?" Mrs. Kubota said again, looking at Takuya for help in understanding.

"Mariko!" I said.

Mrs. Kubota and Hiromi-san were confused, but Takuya laughed, and said something in Japanese to Mariko.

"Shh! Shh!" Hiromi-san hushed everyone, trying to be serious. She held my hands in hers, then placed them over the ball, which was warm to the touch. She removed my hands and gazed into the orb, then picked up the Lovers' card and began to speak.

She explained that, yes, the card was called Lovers, but in my case it meant love that indicated maturity and growth. Love was a force that would make me decide something important, surrender to a higher power. I was about to come across something that I would fall in love with, she said. But it wouldn't be a person. It could be a career, a challenge that would put me on a new path. Trust your instincts, she said. Know that you are about to embark on an endeavor that will emerge from your soul, that may be challenging, but something that will make you a whole person and will give you a feeling of accomplishment.

I may not have had much faith in the tarot, but I couldn't help but be intrigued and pleased by her prediction.

But Mariko told me that she was disappointed. "Career? New path? So dull, so *serious*. I was hoping she was going to predict the date of your wedding with Takuya."

After dinner with Hiromi-san, she requested that I sing for her, and we were off to a karaoke box not too far from her *kissaten*. Much glitzier than Hysteric Echo, My Singing Heart was in a tall, towerlike building where we had to ride an elevator to the tenth floor to get to the entrance. The young receptionist was dressed as a maid in a black dress and white-lace apron. Her several assistants wore similar outfits, along with pink cloche hats. Each box sported a large window that looked out over the city street. Our room was huge, with three sofas and a video screen that took up one entire wall.

I never failed to get chills when I heard the introduction to "*Nozomi no Hoshi*." The song was beautiful on its own, but its personal meaning made it even more special. It was a pleasure to sing it again in a more relaxed setting, not worrying about whether I would win a contest.

Hiromi-san patted me on the arm. "Beautiful! Beautiful!" she said.

"She say she is so sorry she missed you on television. She would have called JBS right away," Takuya said.

I sang another Maki Kanda song, then handed the microphone over to Mrs. Kubota who performed her "Yokohama Twilight-o," with Mariko and me backing her up. Hiromi-san sang an old *enka* song called "*Yagiri no Watashi*," and Mariko went for a very heartfelt, serious version of "I Left My Heart in San Francisco."

"Can you find me 'All You Need Is Love'?" I asked Takuya. This karaoke box was so modern that the way you looked up songs was via a computerized directory instead of a binder of worn pages. I looked at my watch. It was almost nine o'clock. "I thought maybe we could try calling my dad. And he could sing along." I hoped it wouldn't be too late for him.

"How sweet!" Mariko said.

Takuya smiled. "That good idea." He explained to his mother and Hiromi-san, and managed to get Kenji on his cell phone.

"*Otousan!*" I didn't think I would ever stop feeling excited to be able to call him father. "I hope you weren't already asleep. We are in a karaoke box and I wish you were here."

"Ah! So nice of a surprise to hear your voice, my dear Celeste."

I told him of the meeting with Hiromi-san as Takuya cued up the song. I held the phone up and we all sang, letting him solo on the verse parts, which we could hear clearly, and us joining in on the chorus, "All you need is love, love, that is all you need."

When the song ended, we applauded and cheered, then he spoke briefly to Hiromi-san. She handed the phone back to me.

"Thank you, Celeste, for thinking of me. It is my joyous moment," Kenji said.

"I will see you soon," I said. "Good night."

"You have a nice *otousan*, Celeste," Mariko said.

I smiled at her. I have a nice sister too, I thought.

"Ah! There is one person who has not sung," Mariko said, her eyes on Takuya. "What will you sing, Takuya-san?"

I had never heard Takuya sing.

He made a face. "I am not good."

"Come on," I said, smiling.

"Takuya—nice voice," Mrs. Kubota said.

"Takuya! *Utatte kudasai!*" Mariko implored.

He perused the song list, then finally made his selection. "I know this one by pianist Dave Brubeck, but he does not sing. So I will try singing. I dedicate this for you, Celeste," he said, looking at me. The song was "The Way You Look Tonight."

Mariko pretended that she was about to keel over. "*Such* a romantic boyfriend, Celeste," she said. "How lucky you are!"

"It was in the stars," I said.

"Maybe you can help me sing," Takuya said to me.

I didn't know the song well, but I picked up the other microphone and did my best to sing along with him. He knew it better than he claimed, and his voice was pleasant, steady. I joined in, trying to put on a harmony. It wasn't the most skillful, and I'm sure we were a tad off, but our voices blended well, and our audience was hushed, enchanted, as if they could feel the love we felt for each other.

This meeting with Hiromi Taniguchi, one that I'd fantasized about for so long, had been more successful than I thought possible. After all the ups and downs of being in Japan, this was something I could relish, this feeling of family, of belonging to people who cared for me, with whom I shared a history.

After saying good-bye to Hiromi-san and riding the train from Yokohama, we arrived at Shibuya Station. Takuya's apartment was in Shimokitazawa on the Inokashira line so we said our good-byes to Mariko and Mrs. Kubota, who were taking the Toyoko train.

The night was cool, the sky clear when we walked the five blocks toward Takuya's apartment.

He stopped and gave me a kiss.

"What's that for?"

"Because I am loving you," he said.

He had said it. So simple, so natural, so right. "I love you too."

He looked up at the sky. "Star light, star bright. First star I see tonight. Wish I may, wish I might, have the wish I wish tonight."

"You said it perfectly."

"I have good teacher."

"But the sky is full of stars," I said, gazing upward. "There is no first star."

"That is okay. It mean many wishes to come true."

"Many wishes already have."

He held my hand as we walked along. "I was talking to Hiromi-san at dinner," he said, "and she was saying that I can take over her *kissaten* if I want to. Make it *jazu-kissa*. I think it may be good idea, do you?"

"You mean you would quit your job?"

"Eventually. She say the place is paid for. I think it is good chance."

I squeezed his hand. "I think it is an excellent chance. You can finally get out of Sunny Shokuhin. Have your dream business."

"I think I can take the shot."

"Gambatte kudasai."

"Gambarimasu."

Looking into his eyes, I could see they were as bright and *kira-kira* as the stars in the sky.

30

"MY HEART'S HOMETOWN"

It was almost Christmas and Mr. Kubota was blossoming like I'd never seen him before. He stood proudly outside his home decorated with his masterpieces of lighted reindeer, Santas, sleighs, and trees. He couldn't stop smiling and talked on with the throngs of passersby who congratulated him on his displays, thoughtfully answering the multitudes of questions.

Takuya had said that this year, in my honor, his father had decided to showcase the theme of stars. They dotted the roof of the house, and strings of them framed the windows and draped the trees, gently twinkling, *kira-kira.* The television crews and reporters kept coming, the crowds increasing. Takuya said his mother was going crazy.

But the Kubotas were able to get away from all the madness on Christmas Eve when they came along with Takuya, Hiromi-san, Mariko and Frederick, and my father Kenji, to the Ozawa Kaikan Hall in Shinjuku to see me perform in concert. JBS ended up going along with my idea of singing *enka,* and I had recently finished my first recording.

There was nothing that prepared you for the thrill of holding your own CD in your hands. The title was *Celeste Duncan,* written in both English and Japanese. The cover showed my face, my eyes gazing at my palm, which held the comb Aunt Michiko asked to be returned to her sister, the one I wore in the old photograph. It was tasteful—nothing like you'd see on *Hen na Gaijin*—and I didn't look half bad.

My debut song, called "*Kokoro no Furusato*," or "My Heart's Hometown," told the story of a woman without a family who had never been to Japan, but once she arrived she found her home, the place where she truly belonged. It was where she discovered the people most important to her and where she'd found her soul.

The moment I received some copies I sent one to Dirk, which I autographed. I couldn't resist adding something else, not a letter but a piece of paper where I'd written, "So what do you think of *this?*"

A week later I received a note from him. "Congratulations! You should be proud of yourself," he wrote back, minus any comments on my singing. And it was such a coincidence, he went on, because he had also just made a CD himself, though self-produced, entitled *Live from the Clipper Lounge*. He enclosed a copy for my listening pleasure.

Now, backstage at the concert hall, I waited to hear my introduction. I looked in the mirror, brushed an eyelash from my cheek, and added a little more powder to my face. I was ready.

"Ladies and gentlemen, please welcome Celeste Duncan."

I walked to the middle of the stage, which was decorated with a set of a Japanese screen painted with white cranes resting near a lake, the stars in the black sky shining bright.

Even though it was my first concert, I did not feel nervous or ill at ease. At last I was ready for this, at last I knew this was what I was meant to do. And I could also share it with Takuya. When I waved in his direction, I could see him blow me a kiss.

I bowed deeply and the audience applauded. I felt their warmth and was glad to see them. I would do my best, my *gambarimasu*. And I would give them my all because they had come all this way to listen.

They had come to hear me sing.

No visa. No money.

Nowhere to go...but up!

Midori Saito's dream of a new life in the United States is about to come true—until her fiancé dumps her! Now Midori is stranded in San Francisco. Her only hope is her new acquaintance Shinji, a successful graphic artist who makes Midori realize she will do almost anything to hang on to her dream of a new life.

"Tokunaga suffuses the book with warmth and lightness.... Just as the right dessert hits the spot, reading this delicious slice of escapism makes for a perfect afternoon."
—*San Francisco Chronicle*

St. Martin's Griffin **www.stmartins.com**